LOVE-CHAT

Olivia frowned. 'Oh, I am so inexperienced in life, my lord. I have not seen a proper whipping – only of servants for misdeeds. Not a sexual whipping as an accomplice to pleasure.' She toyed excitedly with the metal instrument.

'Whipping is not a wifely grace.' He stared at her, then sighed. 'But I am moved to make an exception: you shall whip her all you please.'

'My lord – do you mean it?' Olivia offered her lips; when he returned the favour she bit him slowly and long.

'But I warn you, my cruel young voluptuary – Iroise's pleasure is hard won. Her discipline is self-imposed, true to the keenest Tantalite tenets wherein fulfilment is a sin.'

LOVE-CHATTEL
OF TORMUNIL

Aran Ashe

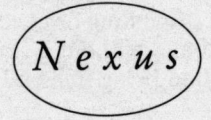

Nexus

This book is a work of fiction.
In real life, make sure you practise safe sex.

First published in 2003 by
Nexus
Thames Wharf Studios
Rainville Road
London W6 9HA

www.nexus-books.co.uk

Typeset by TW Typesetting, Plymouth, Devon

Printed and bound by
Clays Ltd, St Ives PLC

ISBN 0 352 33779 6

Contents

1

Baron's Lair

In the middle reaches of the great lake dwelt the Baron, waxing fat upon the generous favours of the initiates schooled by the Abbey across the water. Deep inside his castle, devotions were untrammelled by pious strictures. At dusk his skiff would slide across the moonlit straits, his henchmen at the oars, his hulking figure enthroned at the tiller. His bulbous greedy eyes would be fixed on the lights of the Abbey tower. Ashore, the secret doorway would be opened and the Abbess would receive him. The initiates would be nude and full of fervour, tutored in the basics but with many things still to learn, which the Baron would teach them. The Abbess would bid him taste their graces. Before dawn the chosen one would be hurried – naked – across the damp grass to the lakeside landing.

The most precious of his acquisitions was the lovely Iroise.

On that evening when Iroise was destined to be taken, the Abbess, with measured solemnity, ascended the last few steps of the tower. The Baron, huffing and grunting, lumbered after her, his men trailing behind. At the heavy black wooden door, the Abbess halted, with one hand poised on the latch, and turned to him. 'Before you consider accepting her there is something you should know.' She lifted the swaying lantern and searched his face.

'Know? Know what?'

1

The Abbess waited for the spark of hunger in those eager eyes to glow. 'Iroise is special,' she whispered reverently, pushing the door ajar.

The grim-faced nun inside the room stepped back from the bed and clasped her hands to her breast as the hulking form of the Baron filled the doorway.

A beautiful, nude, young female creature was standing on the bed. Her complexion was unblemished. Her eyes were of the purest azure blue. Her hair was of softest blonde and it fell in perfect ringlets round her cheeks. Startled, she had twisted round to look. The unrehearsed innocence of that pose rendered her bewitching.

'Sister Sutrice – as you see – our guest is now arrived to view Iroise.'

The nun bowed and retreated quietly to the corner, where she lowered her clasped hands and stared at the floor while the viewing was conducted.

'Kneel down, Iroise,' said the Abbess. 'Remember your place,' she whispered. Though the voice was gentle and encouraging, still the girl was visibly chastened. Her eyes remained cast down in frightened shyness. She knew to kneel open with her hands behind her head. The Abbess allowed her guest free play and soon Iroise was shivering.

'Her flesh is keenly responsive,' the Baron said.

'Iroise is Tantalite,' the Abbess explained. 'The Tantalite discipline is simple: pleasuring is mandatory but completion is a sin. Any master or mistress who takes her on will need to understand this. But it is Iroise herself who must carry the delicious burden of pleasure constantly and without prospect of release. We are merely the instruments through which she strives to achieve perfection. In this she knows she has some way to go. She asks only that her master endeavours to steer her flesh from the brink of sin and – should it transgress – to punish it.'

The Baron took the Abbess aside. 'You know my requirements?'

The Abbess conferred with Sister Sutrice then whispered, 'The timing is auspicious. And no male has used her since she was taken under our wing.'

The Baron nodded to his purser and the bargain was sealed in gold coin. Then the Baron said, 'I shall need collars for her wrists and ankles.'

Iroise shivered, naked at the end of the small wooden landing where the little boat was tied. The men were ominously silent, as if planning what to do. There were leather collars round her wrists and ankles – purchase points for tying her open. A cold draught of wind swept up the lake, driving the waves before it. The little boat rocked and tugged upon its moorings. One of the men was standing in the boat: he took her by the wristlet and Iroise half jumped, landing in his arms. It caused a peculiar feeling in her because she was naked and he was clothed. The boat sagged and heaved when her new master landed heavily behind her. As he tried to steady himself his large hand pressed into her naked back. The third man sprang in and helped him to the thronelike seat then untied the boat and the men began rowing.

There was no seat for Iroise. She crouched unsteadily, clutching the sides, facing her master with her head bowed. Her face was close to his booted feet. She could feel his bulging gaze burning into her nakedness as the little boat moved out into the lake and the chill crosswind gathered strength. Her knees were on the wet boards. She thought of what had happened in the tower – her kneeling on the bed while the Baron examined her, then, later, the other things once the Abbess and Sutrice had left.

The oars scuffed the cold wave-crests and the boat began pitching erratically. Iroise looked up with frightened eyes. The master's fingers immediately reached around her cheek, under her curling dangling locks of hair, conveying silent reassurance at her time of need. Her cheek and neck pressed to the warmth and steadiness of that hand, which swept round behind her head, drawing her upwards to a kiss. At the moment that his moist fleshy lips engulfed hers, the toe of his boot, nudging, gently split her nude sex open. His thick hot tongue entered her mouth. The toe was dainty, the leather smooth, and the lips between her legs were plucked completely naked but for a few downy new hairs. The boat rolled her aroused belly gently upon the urging toe, rekindling the stimulation that had begun in the tower. It made her moan. It made her body oil the toe as if it were the shiny cap of a monk's sheathed penis. It made deep dimples form on each side of the base of her spine.

A squall came. Her master turned her round and half swathed her in a blanket with her breasts bared to the squall. In the glowering dawn, fat freezing raindrops clung to her shivering teats. His hands were hot under her arms. She could feel the caressive urgency in them as the oarsmen rowed ever more keenly for the dark shape of the castle.

Iroise was lifted from the boat then hurried up the slipway, past gatemen and waiting servants, and into a large hall. Lamps were quickly lit. Her master gave directions for the fire to be stoked. Iroise was bundled upon an ample couch. The freezing raindrops still clung to her goose-pimpled breasts and she was shivering all over. 'Find her a shirt,' he instructed. There was great urgency in the Baron's gaze and keen desire upon the faces of his men. 'Spread your knees,' he then demanded of her. Iroise obediently raised them so that her master might have unhindered access. His hot hand was drawn to the place where she was most naked. She glimpsed the men's desirous faces as his fingers spread her just as his booted toe had done.

'I shall have you tattooed,' he murmured, smoothing it open, 'in here, in this lovely place – now.' His other hand closed over her mouth to stifle any protest while he gently split her softness wider and rubbed a fingertip over its moist flat shiny inner surface.

2

The Galled Leaf

Lady Olivia paused at the top of the gallery stairs overlooking the Great Hall before she tied her green satin gown. Weak daylight was beginning to colour the high windows. Her lord was below, warming by the fire. His new trinket lay half naked, splayed. The apothecary placed his bag on the table and knelt between her soft white legs. Two footmen stood ogling her. Lady Olivia swept swiftly down the stairs.

'My lord – dismiss these idle oafs,' she said loudly.

The Baron, glowering, took her aside. 'They are two of my most trusted men.'

'I don't want them watching me,' she whispered.

He frowned. Then light dawned in those stolid eyes. Turning, he nodded curtly to the two men. When they were gone, Olivia reached up, caressing his barrel chest. She stared sidelong at the girl for some time. Then she looked up at him. 'My lord?' she murmured, shyly.

'What troubles you, my precious?' He stroked her kohl-black hair.

'Remember the night I let you use me like a slave – in every way you wanted? "A slim willow-wand body with perfect breasts," you said. That night I thought my lord's strength would surely break me.'

His swollen eyes closed in rapture; his broad nostrils dilated. Olivia could feel his sex coming erect against her leg. Her fingertips slid under the gold chain around his bull neck; her face moved teasingly close to his. 'Her scent is on my lord's lips,' she whispered. Olivia licked them then sucked them voluptuously. 'Now it is on mine.'

A gentle whimper drifted across the hall. It was like the sound of curtailed pleasure rather than pain. The white thigh was jerking open in tiny movements, almost as if the girl were reacting to the deep probings of a penis against the mouth of her womb. But no penis was involved in this case. The apothecary's was surely standing high between his legs. But what the girl was responding to was the fine, precise pricking taunts of the tattoo needle against the inner surface of her open flesh.

Olivia went to her. She studied the wrists and ankles, too narrow for their leather collars which, upon so flawless a body, seemed more adornment than restraint. Olivia moved behind the couch. She ran her fingers under the soft blonde ringlets and drew them back to expose the ear lobe. It was burning. Bending, she took this burning droplet between her lips and sucked it slowly. The girl was moaning under her breath. Taking her by the wristbands, Olivia drew her arms up. She slipped her fingers through the bands and pinned her wrists together against the back of the couch. The girl's breasts were heaving against the tightened shirt. Her deliciously plucked belly was swelling out beneath it. The apothecary's fingers tested her then the needle began pricking again.

'Ooooh,' the girl gasped, her head arching back. Olivia's tongue went into her mouth. Olivia's fingertips gently unbuttoned the humid breasts and pinched the trembling nipples.

She gazed up at her husband, whose eyes were as helpless and avid as those of a starving chained whelp at a feast.

The apothecary paused to rub liquid with bare, clinical fingertips into the immaculate girl.

Olivia arose, took her lord by the arm and led him through the doorway of the small room beside the great fireplace.

'What is it?' he asked, hoarsely.

'You find her comely?' she asked, defiantly.

'You must surely know I do.'

Olivia opened her satin gown, baring to her lord and to the mirror her breasts, which were full and beautiful, her nipples dusky and tight. She had rouged them. She set herself in profile to show them off.

'Fuller than hers?' she asked.

'Oh yes.'

'Then kiss your wife, my lord,' she murmured, 'even as your excitement burgeons for the lowly girl.' She felt his hands inside her gown, clasping her slim body as hungrily as he must have clasped the girl. Lifting her off her feet, he sucked her breast wetly into his mouth, wanting to swallow it whole, drawing gasps of pleasure from her body, leaving the nipple distended, wet and unrouged.

'I have never seen you this way,' he said, passionately caressing her black locks, fervently searching her glittering eyes.

'And I have never felt such sweet agitation: it taunts inside me.' Olivia reached again to kiss his lips, pressing her breasts against him. Her fingers slid inside his gown, feeling the warmth of his generous chest, wanting her own breasts against it skin to skin. She unfastened him, kissed the dome of his paunch that was crowned by a second gold chain. Her lips teased its links. She could feel his erection through his gown, harder than she had ever felt it. The girl had caused this – with her perfect sexuality so ravishingly displayed.

'I had to kiss her,' Olivia confessed.

'What you did with her did not displease me.'

'I had to know what it was like to kiss her – like a lover.' She felt his erection harden. 'I want to kiss her love-mouth too. Did my lord kiss there – inside her little cunny?' His breathing had changed. He did not answer. But she knew her talk moved him deeply. 'Let me see your manhood. Has it too been inside her?' It sprang up when she opened his gown. She kissed the thick gold ring encircling the base of his genitals. The black hairs were already plastered down and redolent of girl. 'Did she make my lord spill?' She took the fat aromatic bulb of his penis deep into her

7

mouth and made him groan. Then she drew away and watched it pulsing. She let its wet tip smear her breasts. 'Is my lord's spill still inside her cunny? Then let me seek it – please?'

'My dear – sweet prurient creature – what demon of lust is unleashed within you?'

Her eyes were defiant; her cheeks were flushed with impure excitement. Her mind was racing. She stood up and went to the desk. Her shaking fingers extracted from the drawer a slim trumpet-shaped instrument of polished steel.

He stared at it. 'Have you been consulting with the apothecary? What potions has he laid upon you?'

'My lord has often said he wished me more voracious at the cup of lust. Then let me use this on her – please?'

Olivia went to the connecting door, opened it and peered out at the scene on the couch. 'Surely what he is doing must sting inside her?'

'Yes.'

'My lord has already whipped her?'

'It became necessary – to prevent transgression.'

Olivia frowned. 'Oh, I am so inexperienced in life, my lord. I have not seen a proper whipping – only of servants for misdeeds. Not a sexual whipping as an accomplice to pleasure.' She toyed excitedly with the metal instrument.

'Whipping is not a wifely grace.' He stared at her, then sighed. 'But I am moved to make an exception: you shall whip her all you please.'

'My lord – do you mean it?' Olivia offered her lips; when he returned the favour she bit him slowly and long.

'But I warn you, my cruel young voluptuary – Iroise's pleasure is hard won. Her discipline is self-imposed, true to the keenest Tantalite tenets wherein fulfilment is a sin.'

'Then we must return to her post-haste: for if transgression threatens she shall surely need the guiding hand of a confessor.'

Iroise's belly, softly obedient, was thrust forwards between her tucked-up feet. A few downy blonde hairs adorned its open split. The fingers of her right hand held the right lip stretched out and pinned down, like an exotic canvas upon which the tiny ink-pricks beat out their tattoo. Her clitoris was swollen as if the nearness of the minute pricking had coaxed it from its hood. Olivia's fingertips now pressed to each side of it, forcing it further out, drawing it to the attention of the apothecary's busy fingers, making Iroise murmur. The needle rubbed it, made it jump, made Iroise moan in sexual stimulation. Then it returned to plague the inner surface of the lip, implanting the tiny motes of colour into her skin.

'How sweet a gift to bear, my lord – her master's own seal inside her body, that any gallant to whom her love becomes entrusted and all those there by proxy, shall promptly discern the beneficiary.'

'If I should choose to share her favours.'

'My lord shares her even now.' Olivia went to him and found his racing pulse belied the calmness of his words. She put to his lips the fingers that had teased out Iroise's clitoris and she felt him shiver. She slipped her fingers into his gown and found him charged with fervour. The apothecary, working meticulously slowly, was wiping the inside skin of Iroise with balls of moistened wool. The action was gentle so as not to arouse her but the effect was quite the reverse. She seemed afraid to breathe. The lip being tattooed had thickened but the other lip was thin, as if all the blood had retreated from it. Olivia returned to her to pursue her masturbation in greater depth.

Every few minutes, Olivia's fingers refocused on the soft moist hood of yielding skin, trying to turn it inside out, to make the lovely, bulbous clitoris protrude for the shaft of the needle to slip across it, upwards and from side to side. Iroise's breasts, though much smaller than her lady's, had nevertheless acquired a concentrated rising roundness, with the nipples distendedly inviting sucking. More colour was being applied inside her pubic lip; Olivia gently held the top of the vulva tight for the rapid pricking to impart its sweet vibration which induced the lovesome girl to utter such soft deep-throated moans. Still Olivia's slow masturbation of this girl continued. It extended to the breasts in little finger-slaps. And it descended to the anus.

Olivia was now crouched between Iroise's legs. She could hear her lord's anguished breathing. 'Draw her knees all the way up,' she told the apothecary, who was now standing behind the couch. Very gently, very slowly, very sexually indeed, Olivia introduced the shiny flared pipe of lubricated steel into Iroise's perfect body, through the purple mouth unused to broad sexual advances yet all the more receptive for that: its insertion almost made her climax. Then, delightful, frightened muscle spasms half sucked the bedded pipe each time the harried clitoris was teased closer to the brink.

Iroise gasped out loud a man's name – 'Josef' – and Olivia suffered a delicious icy shiver that lifted the hairs at the back of her neck. She stared around, for it almost felt as though an ethereal presence was in the room. 'Curb your tongue, my sweet one. Do not call in vain for former lovers lest your master becomes displeased.' She stared at the alluring combination of fear and arousal in those deep blue eyes.

By intimate persistence the tattooing was completed and the apothecary dabbed inside Iroise's vulva one final time, then stood up and moved aside.

'Hold your cunny open for your master,' Olivia ordered. She watched the frightened delicate fingers tremblingly draw the flaccid lip to one side. 'Tighter, girl – stretch your canvas. Display your master's insignia proudly and bravely.' Inside the stretched right labium was a perfect rendition of the taloned foot of a falcon piercing a sweet red cherry. From the puncture a shiny crimson droplet of juice swelled like a droplet of blood.

The Baron crouched and ardently fingered the icon while Iroise shivered and held her breath.

'Is she yet tender, my lord?' Olivia whispered.

The apothecary warned, 'If the friction is too severe or too soon and the skin becomes abraded, then the image may smear.'

'And then my lord must needs dispense with her as tainted.'

'I have experience in such matters,' the Baron answered, curtly. But Iroise was shaking when he finally desisted

10

from touching it and he took her in his arms as she crouched open on the couch. Her shirt was agape and her young pink-tipped breasts were squashed against his barrel chest. The gold chain about his paunch pressed against her open sex. When he drew his lips away from her soft white neck there was a purple blemish. Olivia did not wait for the girl to catch her breath before she stepped forwards and slipped a hard, white comfit of compressed powder up the shiny neck of the funnel. She withdrew the funnel, leaving the stimulant locked inside. Iroise suddenly began gasping. Olivia sat her up with her feet on the floor. 'Keep your thighs wide,' she whispered, 'that your master might mark the way they shudder.' She showered the girl with breast kisses and the pink nipples came up so hard that they felt brittle enough to snap off between Olivia's gently pinching teeth. 'Lift her feet off the floor,' she told the apothecary. She wanted the girl's bottom fully bedded to the seat while the stimulant worked inside her. The lovely young vulva was open; no pressure was exerted on the clitoris, yet the climax came and in so beautiful and deep a way that there was wetness on the seat. 'She blows bubbles, almost,' Olivia crooned. How she ached to punish this young sweetly sobbing, near-naked creature.

When the apothecary had collected his bag and left, Olivia told her husband of this overpowering sexual feeling. He said it was the natural reaction to a girl who was Tantalite and had been forced to climax but Olivia knew it to be much deeper. She watched her husband explore the beautiful tattooed inside of that naked throbbing split; she watched the way its sweet wet flesh became re-aroused despite the stinging. And the feeling of desire inside Olivia, the need to punish that lovely pink-lipped vulva, was irresistible. She pleaded and pleaded. 'I want her alone.'

'Why alone, my darling?'

'I am shy of . . . certain practices.' Her cheeks flushed. 'But I wish to learn, how I wish to. She is special and beautiful: I can see why my lord has chosen her. In privacy I may test my wings.'

11

Opening her gown she put her arms around him, seducing him with her trembling breasts and the fervid hardness of her nipples.

The morning was thoroughly advanced by the time the apothecary entered the kitchen. He placed his bag beside the small stone flagon on the sideboard while he poured his customary measure of spirit into the small silver cup. He downed the drink swiftly then picked up his bag to go.

'Is my lady still with him?' The speaker was a girl – Rhislin – who called herself a valet and dressed like a man in drab, high-collared brown.

' "Him?" I take it you mean your noble lord and master, the Baron?'

Rhislin was sitting sipping broth at the corner of the table. 'I mean, is my lady still in there?'

The apothecary sighed resignedly, nodding. 'She may be some while.'

'Then have another drink. Cook cannot mind.' The apothecary found himself relaxing, warming to this singular girl despite her strange combination of quiet consideration and defiance. He sat down at the table with two cups and the flagon. He poured a measure and offered it to Rhislin.

'Never touch it . . . Poison.' The certainty of her stance and the depth of her young frown he found endearing. 'The girl – I saw her,' Rhislin said. 'She is really beautiful. Too beautiful for him. But you tattooed her?'

'Yes.'

'I've seen your tattoos. They're nice.'

'Thank you. So would you –'

'No. Never. But they're nice on girls.' Suddenly, she asked, 'Why do you let him make their bellies swell?'

'It is not I who –'

'No, but you can stop it.'

'To a point, I can, if the master is willing and takes steps.' He stared at her. Suddenly she seemed younger yet and very naive. 'Tell me, Rhislin, how much do you know of such matters? Has your lady not explained?'

12

Rhislin's cheeks turned beetroot red above her stiff collar. 'I have to go now.' She hurried from the kitchen, leaving her broth unfinished.

Beyond the yellow curtains, in the heart of her lady's bedchamber, Rhislin's heart was thumping as she went back to the nude tethered slave. Males were so different, their flesh felt so strange against her fingers; again she tried to make the fluid come out, moulding her hands like the split of a girl around it; again it would not happen, only a twitching in the flesh and a shivering in his belly. She closed her lips about his nipple and made him moan.

3

In My Lady's Bedchamber

Iroise heard the heavy iron key being turned in the lock behind her, then she heard the door being bolted. Lady Olivia drew aside the dense yellow velvet curtains and the warmth met Iroise.

'My little world,' said Olivia. 'Safe from prying eyes, unmolested by my lord.' She pushed Iroise over the threshold and buttoned the curtains.

Iroise did not advance; her frightened gaze assessed her surroundings – a lady's boudoir, softly furnished, cosy and secure, bearing tapestries of sunlit scenes. There was a welcoming hearth and a sumptuous bed; a plush rug caressed her feet. A girl, very strait-laced, dressed like a man in a stiff brown suit, was placing ironed garments in a tall chest of drawers. On the dressing table – amidst the brushes, combs and perfumes – a nude young man was crouched like a monkey. He was gagged and his wrists were fastened to one of the columns supporting the mirror. His body was half turned as if to be available to a person seated before the mirror. His sex lay twitching against the polished surface of the table.

'His name is Hefron. I shaved him today – just like you girls at the Abbey – did I not, my love?' Olivia pouted, sidling over to him. 'Though Iroise is plucked. There you see, my dear,' she said, turning back, 'I now notice these things, though I had not expected quite how hot such denudation makes the skin feel.' Her fingers enveloped the naked ball sac. 'For all of this is new to me. But with this

14

slim youth I am discovering there is life, love and lust in me far beyond the blinkered whims of an overblown Baron. Kneel down, girl!'

Olivia's resentment closed upon Iroise. She grasped her by the chin. 'Now answer truthfully in all I ask or I shall whip you till you cannot sit. Has my devious husband been inside you?'

Iroise paled and trembled. The girl in brown quietly closed the drawer and turned to watch.

'Answer!'

'Yes,' Iroise whispered.

'You let him spend inside your body?'

'No! I, I mean . . .' But in the face of a grim truth so starkly put, the tears began to well.

'I knew it!'

Even the young man seemed to be looking at Iroise accusingly. She tried to hang her head in shame. Olivia's fingertips dug into her jaw. 'You fancy yourself lady of the manor? Idle concubine to your fat lord, with your fat little baby on your knee?'

'*No! Oh, no.*'

Olivia's eyes narrowed to cruelty. 'Rhislin.' The girl in brown jumped to attention. 'Make ready the bed.'

'It is ready, mistress,' she whispered, drawing back the cover.

'Good. I am pleased there is one girl in this house upon whom I can rely.' Rhislin looked embarrassed. Olivia turned to Iroise. 'Get on the bed.'

All had been made ready, as Rhislin had said. It must have been planned. In the middle of the bed sat a small bulging satin cushion. Beside it was a long, supple birch stem. Olivia grasped the birch.

'Lie down – on your front. Get your belly on that cushion and spread. We may yet redeem you.'

She whipped Iroise's naked bottom, driving cold shivers up her back, driving her open sex against the cushion, making her buttocks burn and her bottom cramp. She wouldn't let her close her legs. 'Expel it, you little slattern, every vile grey drop.' She lashed harder and quicker until the contractions cascaded and Iroise's womb ached from the squeezing. Between her thighs the cushion became warm and sticky.

'There!'

Olivia, breathless from her cruel exertions, twisted Iroise on to her back. Triumphantly she plucked the cushion from the bed and flung it on to the fire. Enraptured, she watched the flames consume it. Only when it had burnt black and shrunken did the demon that had gripped her relinquish its hold sufficiently for her to notice Iroise's tears. She returned to the bed and sat beside her. The girl in brown had watched it all without a flicker of emotion.

'By our tears we are made winsome,' Olivia murmured, staring down at Iroise with strange calmness and composure. She touched the damp ringlets of hair, arranging them gently against the sheet. She slid her fingers under the leather wristlets. 'Your eyes are beautiful; your flesh is precious. Howsoever my lord may defile you, I shall make you whole.'

The words laid bare a taut string of emotion that had lain buried deep within Iroise. Olivia leant closer – so close now, pinning her by the wrists – with her lips parted, waiting; Iroise could smell the warmth of the lady's skin and could feel the echoes of those graceful words. Iroise reached up and softly, repeatedly kissed her mistress's lips, which remained parted but unmoving, offering themselves in neither affection nor chastisement. Iroise sank back against the cool sheets. Her lips tingled from the sensuality of that female contact – the gentle closure about her mistress's upper lip. A warm glow spread through her punished body; hot aches licked her bottom; her womb throbbed. As her mistress continued to stare at her in close enquiry, and the girl in brown just stood there, emotion filled her soul to overflowing.

'Let me dry you,' said Olivia, raising a hand and waiting. Rhislin suddenly came to life. Hefron watched her with anxious eyes as she silently took a large soft scarf, richly embroidered with crocus flowers in magenta, blue and yellow, from the slim top drawer of the dressing table beneath him. Then Rhislin did a strange thing: she briefly touched the shaved place at the root of his naked penis, which responded by raising its head from the surface of the dressing table. Though generously endowed, he seemed young and inexperienced. He watched forlornly as the girl touched his tip with her fingertip then rubbed the clear secretion between her thumb and finger. Then she picked up a hand mirror along with the scarf and came to her lady.

Olivia pressed the scarf to her lips, inhaling its scent. 'Sit up, Iroise, and spread. No, not that way – legs open but straight. And fold your arms behind your back. Take no heed of Rhislin; she likes to look. Present your body, as your nuns have surely taught you. For I cannot think they would leave you unattended in your bed.' These knowing imputations triggered capricious feelings between Iroise's legs.

She was now balanced, her breasts and belly thrust out, her arms and thighs out of the way, her sex pressed down against the sheet. Olivia put the mirror face up between Iroise's thighs and then, by feel alone, found and opened her sex, spreading its hot lips back, making Iroise shiver, making her nipples come up, making Hefron's penis come on hard. 'Your cunny feels so smooth and pliant.'

Iroise then experienced the introduction of the embroidered scarf into her body at the front, slowly distending her until it felt as if she were sitting on a penis. But Olivia's purposeful fingers continued to insert the crumpled material ever deeper into Iroise. Blue and yellow silken crocuses slid across the sheet and slipped inside the pinkness. 'Head back, don't tighten.' The pleasure–pain of stretching deepened, with the keenest pressure focused against the mouth of her womb. Iroise shuddered as the fingers kept pushing, causing her flesh to spasm.

'Look,' said Olivia, tilting Iroise's head forwards. Iroise stared down into the mirror's reflection of the place between her thighs. The scarf was fully inserted; the lips were reclosed but her cunny looked swollen, like a small bald extra belly. Olivia kept nervously stroking its taut

17

skin. 'It looks so starkly beautiful and smooth, it makes me want to whip it.' She glanced sidelong at Hefron, whose penis was twitching.

'Turn over and lie down,' she said to Iroise. 'Let Hefron look at you from behind. Spread your legs for him – casually, carefree. There – behold her, Hefron – so blonde and beautiful, with waist so narrow and cunny so bulging and bare. Small wonder that your penis yearns. Attend him, Rhislin.'

A silence ensued; Iroise held her breath. She could see nothing beyond the crumpled sheets in which her face was half buried. Her ears strained for sounds of movement from the dressing table: she heard nothing save sighs; Olivia was still on the bed. Suddenly she felt light finger pressure between her thighs, making her want to close but she knew to resist the urge. Shivery tendrils danced up her belly from where the tops of her labia were being teased open. A cold tip of metal touched her: it felt like the round head of a heavy pin; it pressed against that most intimate of places, the tiny mouth reserved for peeing. Shiver upon shiver ran up her back as the round cold head lodged and then was pushed up a little way further. Olivia rose from the bed and Iroise was left with the heavy tiny metal instrument protruding.

Olivia stared down at this beautiful girl-slave, this chattel of desire whose comeliness was now enhanced by the special treatment that she had inflicted. Paying court to a girl was a new experience endowed with many pleasures, singular and subtle. As the experience progressed late into the afternoon, Olivia's emotions churned. She had never been inside the Abbey. She looked again upon that narrow waist – too narrow almost – and the tight round buttocks now etched with purple weals. The downy, blonde hair of the armpits glistened with nervous aromatic sweat. She imagined the penitent girl lain thus upon her humble bed in that sequestered place. There would be sounds of plainchant; and the nuns, skirted, booted and bare-breasted, would attend her initiation. Instruments would be used, like the miniature steel rod Olivia had filched from the apothecary's bag; there would most surely be tying open – hence the anklets – and whipping of the unchaste places; beyond that Olivia could only surmise, but Iroise would in time be made to re-enact her escapades.

Olivia, relieving Rhislin, approached Hefron, pressed her fingers under the hot root of his erect penis, encouraging new leakage, and then opened her satin gown and stood before his crouched, perched form, her belly button just sucking the unctuous tip of his penis. She ungagged him and kissed him silently and deeply and felt the hot cap of his penis trying to bury itself in the cool well of her belly. Clear fresh seminal moisture leaked slowly from within his body. Olivia drew back, clasping the penile root and through the mirror she saw Rhislin watching the glistening droplet swell like crystal. She twisted round still holding him, drawing sustenance from his continuing arousal. She could see the steel protrusion between her slave-girl's legs, puncturing her perfect pink pouch, glinting with her breathing. In the mirror of the dressing table, she could see the profile of her own breasts, more generous than those of Iroise. She trapped the head of the penis firmly against the table top and as the glass-clear fluid issued, she painted it on her nipples until they shone. Then leaving her taut, proud breasts exposed, she returned to Iroise.

The girl had the most perfect buttock cleavage; in the bottom was the purple-brown mouth. When Olivia stroked the base of the spine, sweet pulsations gripped the purple mouth. Olivia touched it; it was as hot as the root of Hefron's penis. The protruding steel rod quivered below it. Olivia held the rod and touched the hot mouth with her thumb. She heard a stifled moan.

'You like my touching your anus?' she asked. 'Well?'

Iroise muttered inaudibly into the sheets.

'Speak clearly. Rhislin and Hefron cannot hear. You like my touching your anus?'

'Yes, mistress.' The steel rod pulsed in Olivia's fingers.

'But your lovely face is turned quite the wrong way. Turn your cheek – look at Hefron. His penis needs to know.'

The lovely blush on Iroise's cheeks deepened.

'No – open your eyes and look at him.' And the pupils were already deeply dilated.

'Now tell again, in full.'

'Mistress, I . . . I like it when you . . . touch my anus.' A shudder came. Olivia increased the pressure of her thumb. The muscle responded; gentle coercion beyond a certain threshold triggered a slow pulsation, gradually fading until the coercion came again.

Iroise gasped and begged.

'Eyes wide and look at him. See how hard he is. Lips parted . . . Beautiful . . .' The sexual gasp came again. 'Would that he could hold this little steel wand in his fingers,' Olivia whispered. She leant back and opened Iroise's buttocks that he might glimpse the gentle finger-taunting of the steel insert that accompanied the more focused pressure of her thumb.

Suddenly, Iroise's legs stiffened; she groaned; her belly writhed; her projecting steel rod oscillated in a circle.

'What is it?'

'Mistress, please,' she begged, 'don't make it come.'

'Why not?'

'Deliverance is wrongful. It is not permitted.'

'But when you were there with the apothecary did I not detect . . .?'

Iroise burst into tears.

Olivia turned to Rhislin. 'She is Tantalite – between us we must learn to deal sympathetically with that condition. I understand there is a treatment.'

The deep anal whipping caused expulsion of her minia-ture steel rod. Though Hefron had been made ready, his penis sheathed, deep penetration of the punished aperture did not have time to come about, for the messenger was at the door; the Baron was impatient. Hefron had to be hidden from view before the messenger could be admitted.

Iroise was on her back, her legs spread in submission. Her mistress, watching her face, gently withdrew the scarf, soaked and burning hot. The steel was reinserted, just a short way, so that it would be visibly protruding when she

20

walked into the ogre's arms. Then Olivia gently twirled the steel until Iroise's legs reached open, her cunny pulsed and her anklets trembled, defying her shame in the messenger's presence.

When Iroise had been taken away, Olivia tied the male on his back to the bed and wrapped the girl-warmed scarf tightly round his face. Rhislin came near to watch and to learn. The erection that had never left him bulged against the sheath. Silently and closely, Olivia birched the naked root of his penis – the only sounds were his stifled gasps and the crisp lashes – till the thick fleshy feeder tube beneath his penis swelled and jerked and swelled again, repeatedly, and the sheath ballooned with boiling semen, which burst against her fingers when she slit the sheath. Slowly, leisurely, Olivia smeared his fluid over her aroused breasts and her protruding nipples until her fingers clung together with drying stickiness.

'Mistress, will she be all right with him?' whispered Rhislin, hovering at the foot of the bed, an unfamiliar anxiousness misting her inscrutable face.

Olivia stared at her. 'Well, well. Did you hear that, Hefron? I do believe my imperturbable young valet is finally smitten.'

4

The Smoking Room

When Iroise was eventually brought into the dining hall it was night and the repast was almost finished. Only the Baron was still eating, smacking his lips and grunting. The servant refilled his glass, and he quaffed noisily, taking no notice of Iroise but continuing to banter with the three younger men seated opposite him at table. Iroise had been left at the corner of the room in a narrow bay that was part of a turret. Through the slit windows she glimpsed, far below, the moonlit edge of the lake. On the wall behind the Baron was a large tapestry carrying the same image that was now pricked into the tender inner skin of her sex: the falcon's talon clasping the ripe red cherry.

Her labium was stinging; her body glowed from the bathing and the embarrassment of having been made to perform her most intimate toilet nude in the arms of a male servant. The steel insert had dislodged. After the bathing, he had belaboured its reinsertion, repeatedly finding the tiny gape then withdrawing the instrument but fingering the area all about while Iroise lay defencelessly on the rough wooden table, her thighs wide, her desire still keenly primed after what Olivia had done.

The act of walking down the stairs with this strange cold object partly inserted engendered new sensations of depravity. The servant made her open and he repeatedly touched it; then with every step she felt its gentle weight pulling inside her as if a tiny mouth were sucking her pee-hole. At the third landing, Iroise stopped and pleaded.

He made her describe what the mistress had done and he made her use the word 'cunny'. He made her stand still while he opened its nude, firm outer lips and its hot soft inner ones to their full extent and he touched her steel insert with the tip of his tongue. Then, still holding her cunny wide open, he introduced the middle finger of his other hand slowly into her bottom, sexually, deeply, all the way and she moaned and her bottom-muscle clutched his finger and her fingertips clasped his head as if he were a lover. And her tiny insert trembled against the tip of his tongue.

That was what had happened on the stairs and now she stood in the narrow bay, her cheeks flushed, her cunny aroused, the tiny weighted pleasure probe still inserted in her pee-hole.

One of the men she remembered from the boat: his name was Tolron; he was the Baron's land agent, tall and swarthy, and not so young as the other two, who looked like brothers and might have been footmen, such was their demeanour, though they wore no uniform and the Baron treated them with great familiarity, addressing them by name. The younger of the two – Raiff – kept throwing glances towards Iroise when he thought his master was not watching; he was more handsome than his brother, Sethan.

'Gentlemen,' the Baron announced, 'you may be wondering why I have asked you to sup with me tonight?'

Iroise's heartbeat quickened. Tolron smiled and sat back in his chair. The Baron stared at the other two, who seemed anxious and uncertain.

The Baron waved to the servant. 'Recharge their glasses – though not too full – I would not wish their concentration to wane.' His gaze refocused on the brothers. 'Remind me, Sethan, of your duties here.'

'I ... I see to the horses, my lord,' he answered worriedly.

'And your silent young soulmate, what of him?'

'Raiff – he helps me.'

'And – from what I am told – no one sees to them better?'

23

'It's in the blood, my lord.'

'Oh there's more to it than blood, I'm sure.'

'Well ... Sweat and brute strength, sometimes. You have to show them who's master.'

'And use the whip?'

'But temper it with kindness.'

'And sometimes it takes the two of you?'

'Mayhaps three.'

'Then we are quorate.'

'My lord?' he frowned.

'Sethan, I dare not ply you with more wine, for you seem already dulled and much is yet expected of you both. But Tolron shall assist where needed.' The Baron waved to the nearer servant. 'Bring the girl here.' He heaved himself round in his sturdy chair.

A broad footstool was placed beside him and Iroise was lifted on to it standing. He rubbed the weals that his wife had put across her bottom. 'Turn round to face my guests, my dear.' All of her nakedness above her knees was now visible to those across the table. Iroise did not look at the three men but kept her gaze cast down while her master extolled to them her virtues. He spoke about her breasts and her plucked sex. He stroked her back in that sensitive spot where the curvature changed; he found her dimples and made her shiver. He made her edge her feet apart.

'Hold it open – show my mark, that no one may become confused.' Tremblingly she opened her cunny. She heard Raiff's gasp. 'No – hold your head up proudly.' The Baron lifted her chin. Iroise could not look them properly in the face, with their eyes so avid. But her master drew her curls away from her cheek. Then from behind, his thick wrist reached through the gap between her thighs and his thumb and finger touched the protruding insert. 'What's this?' he whispered. 'Oh, you little lewd beauty.' She shuddered. His inner wrist, so hot and smooth, pressed against the firm erect bridge of flesh between her cunny and anus, threatening to lift her bodily from the stool. Through this irresistible upwards pressure, Iroise moaned softly and her cunny gaped – its moist walls moved apart; she heard the brothers gasping simultaneously; she felt cool air inside her body. She was balanced on her toes, her belly pushed out, her breasts shaking. Her master was twirling the steel ball of the insert back and forth inside her pee-hole. It felt as if an oily thread was being drawn endlessly out through that tiny tube.

'See – her belly's distending as if she's pregnant.'

'She seems experienced, my lord,' said Tolron.

'The nuns have a way; their girls learn quickly.'

'No, I mean she seems well opened, as though – despite her shroud of shyness – she is used to men.'

'Ask her. Test her, Tolron. I pass control to you.' Iroise shuddered again as the Baron sank back into his chair, staring at the little steel instrument he had pulled like a thorn from her body. Tolron rose from his seat and walked menacingly round the table.

'Don't close, my dear,' he said. 'Did your lord instruct that you close?'

Iroise anxiously shook her head.

'Correct. He simply passed control to me.' The emotion welled within her under the harshness of his gaze. He sat casually against the edge of the table. 'Such pretty blonde hair. And such ringlets.' He stroked them mockingly. 'What heartaches have they spun? Tell me: what made you take the veil? Was it choice or conscription?'

Iroise's hunted gaze darted about the room. Then she whispered, 'We were chosen – from our village. The Perquisitor came and we were taken.'

'Relinquishing all?'

'That is the way it is ordained.'

'But relinquishing all? What of lovers?'

Her lips trembled as his words kept picking at this unhealed wound. He lifted her chin; she could not look at him, at anyone. Silent, leaden tears of unstoppable remorse issued down her cheeks, a remorse more spiteful than the cruellest whipping.

'You have a way with women, Tolron,' the Baron sighed, shaking his head. 'Girl – come here,' he said sensitively. He put his broad arms around Iroise and drew her on to his generous lap. 'Gentlemen, if you would care to adjourn to the smoking room, Iroise shall join you just as soon as she is supped and ready.'

Her master did not revile her with barbed aspersions but soothed her tears with gentleness as she clung like a baby to his ample breast. He fed her small morsels and he supported the glass while she drank. Dribbles of wine spilled on to his bared chest. Iroise sipped them from his skin. Then she settled against him, her arm slipped under his leather waistcoat, her fingertips shyly stroking his girth.

He wanted to examine once more his insignia tattooed into her skin. Iroise submissively opened the lips of her cunny for her master, unfurling the right one and staring up at him shyly. The flesh inside her was now so hot and red that the image of the cherry had darkened to purple.

The Baron then made this promise to Iroise: 'No harm shall ever come to you while you are under my protection.'

He lifted her by her haunches into the air, so she was sitting astride his powerful hands with his thumbs inside her thighs, pressing into the sensitive creases at the tops of her legs. And he sealed his promise with a kiss inside her, upon her tattooed lip then in beyond, and Iroise experienced a deep sensation of repeated falling coming between her legs each time his tongue slid into her. He held her high and open while her sexual unguent, welling from inside her, gathered in loving droplets at the feather-edges of her lips.

When the servant re-entered the room a few minutes later, Iroise's naked body was curled like a kitten's within her master's capacious lap; her glistening cunny was pouting brazenly between her tucked-up thighs; and her small teeth were clenched impishly about the tip of his foreskin, nipping it closed while the plum of his erection burgeoned against this singular restraint.

'She's ready to receive them,' sighed the Baron.

From the security of her master's arms, Iroise stared across the threshold. Tiny birds fluttered inside her belly: it was always so when she was being put to new men. Decanters of wine rested on the leather-topped table; three walls were covered in lewd engravings; the fourth had shelves of leather-bound books. The younger brother, Raiff, seated in one of the winged armchairs, was poring over an open tome. Other books lay open on the table and the floor. Upon their vellum pages, Iroise glimpsed images of nude girls, their mouths, nipples and labia tinted with vermilion. Sethan was examining the leather restraints dangling from the ceiling in front of the fire. A large mirror was angled over the fireplace. In the hearth lay a smouldering long-stemmed pipe. Each of the men wore only either an open waistcoat or a short shirt. The images on the walls and in the books had overcome the brothers' shyness.

The Baron whispered to Iroise, 'You see now why I chose them for you: it's working with the horses that does it; eventually they come to hang the same.' Then he laid her on the leather table top with her hands under her to raise and distend her belly. It made her cunny gape and she felt the little birds frantically fluttering and tumbling inside her belly. The men were watching her as if she were their prey. 'Show them how you kiss me,' her master urged.

The men drew closer, Tolron closest. Raiff laid the heavy tome on the table. Iroise glimpsed his generous penis, which was standing vigilant as she pressed her open lips against the thick gold ring encircling her master's swollen genitals. His warm paunch protectively overhung her face; his stubby fingers drew her ringlets away from her ear and neck. Iroise closed her eyes and mouthed soft kisses where the gold ring was embedded into the base of his erection.

She thought about the repeated penetrations of their first encounter, when his thrustings had pushed so deeply that his gold ring had threatened to bruise her as her body opened ever wider. His dense black pubic hair had been plastered down by Iroise's expelled juices, which had dried to lacquer upon it.

Her tongue-tip now dissolved this lacquer, freeing the individual filaments of hair, which sprang up in ticklish curls inside her lips and under her tongue.

'I cede her body to your undivided attention,' said the Baron, lifting himself away.

Tolron raised her to a sitting position with her hands still pinned behind her. Sethan brought the long-stemmed pipe, handling it carefully. They made her inhale repeatedly its unfamiliar smoke. Iroise coughed at first; her belly went queasy. They recharged the pipe with crystalline powder. Tolron, urging her wrists up her back until her breasts thrust out, told her, 'Breathe it deeply.' Its cool, sweet sluggishness filled her lungs; her nipples tingled; Raiff caressed them because they had come up. Iroise felt drowsy, distant; the flutterings in her belly felt pleasurable; her open cunny felt warm. Her skin felt highly sensitive; the warmth of Tolron's penis was against her outer thigh and it felt like a separate entity, a special creature that she wanted to take into her mouth and play with.

They lifted her yielding body off the table and hoisted her up, slipping her ankles through the leather loops of the dangling restraints. She felt the loops sliding up and up her legs, until they formed twin lovers' grips lodged at the naked tops of her thighs. As her weight was taken by the loops, the pressure in the creases reopened her cunny and maintained it thus. Her wrist-straps were secured to thongs higher up the leather ropes. Her body hung in front of the fire, its warmth caressing her naked skin. Queasiness in her belly flesh gave way to heightened predisposition. The intimate cosiness of the setting forestalled the need for urgency. In that long delicious conference of the flesh she was the cherished one – open, pliant, sensual, wanting to be loved and touched.

The men brought books and compared her to the images of the vermilion-lipped creatures. They discussed painting her labia. They examined her sex and nipples and anus, making her shiver. When she looked up into the angled mirror she could see the room and Tolron, who was behind her, and the Baron, who was watching all. His penis was fully erect for her; its ruby plum was bared, its stretched-back foreskin bore tiny nip marks from her teeth. Iroise half closed her eyes and opened her mouth and through the mirror offered herself to her master and wished that he could see her open cunny. She moaned; her belly bulged into Sethan's cupped, caressing palm as Tolron's finger entered her anus to the hilt. Raiff recharged the pipe and held it to her willing lips.

The Baron, from his vantage point, watched Iroise inhaling the potent vapours that would temporarily assuage all vestiges of inhibition. This night her Tantalite traits would be set aside and her true fervour tested. Tomorrow would come certain reproach, but he would be there to comfort her and to teach her self-forgiveness. She was the most beautiful creature he had ever purchased; she stirred desire in all who beheld her; even Olivia had been moved to a depth of passion he had never witnessed. He stared at the tiny steel instrument in his fingers and contemplated her using it on the girl. He looked at the purple crop marks on that beautiful bottom.

Then from the corner of his eye he saw Olivia's valet just beyond the open door. When he turned she hurried on down the stairs; he closed the door.

From behind him came the dull snapping sound of a short-tongued leather strap. Then he heard Tolron's voice, then the snapping sound again, then Iroise's shivering murmured replies. The Baron moved closer, with his finger to his lips, then spreading his hand in deference to indicate that Tolron should continue the interrogation.

Iroise was being smacked between the legs, at the front, while her body was still suspended in the sling. Her labia and her nipples had been inked with red; Raiff was holding the brush; Sethan was watching from an armchair by the fire; Tolron was cross-examining her about the monks in the Abbey.

'Where else?' he demanded.

'On my breasts.'

'Go on.'

'And sometimes I would try to hold them shut but it would spill into my hair.'

'They asked you to do it that way?'

'They were not supposed to undergo discernible emission.'

The Baron moved quietly away. He watched this lovesome girl in profile, her beautiful lips moving as though in prayer, then gasping as the leather snapped deep punishment between her open legs and her anklets shook. He looked at her touchable blonde ringlets now stretching down, no less lovely though made limp by streaming sweat and the warmth of the fire. It made his fingers want to curl them anew and his lips want to caress their silken smoothness.

The time was nigh. The Baron sidled silently back to the fireplace. From an enamelled box by the pipe stand on the hearth he took a small ivory-coloured lump resembling wax which he popped into his mouth and under his tongue to soften it. He waved Tolron to one side and stood before Iroise, not directly in front for he wished to see the firelight's play upon her loveliness, which was open, beautifully bare. The spanking had rendered the external skin a uniform deep warm pink; the outer lips were swollen; the inner ones, originally inked red, now looked magenta. He took the soft ivory dollop from his mouth and introduced it into the hot female pouch of Iroise's body, far up inside, deep-fingering, moulding it by touch all around the neck of her womb, sealing it off. His fingertips ventured laterally inside her, ingratiating themselves; at the front, a girl had so many intimate nooks and niches. Iroise was breathing shallowly; her nipples were up; under the deep inner upthrusts of his fingertips her clitoris protruded.

'Hand me that brush,' he instructed the younger brother in a whisper. 'Ink it first.'

'See what you're doing to him,' the Baron softly scolded Iroise. Her languid half-closed fluttering gaze seemed to stroke the young man's bulging penis. 'Hold her hood of skin back, there, above her knob. Further.' The flooded brush tip converged with her erection; electrically the ink drop touched it, drowning her clitoris. Instantly he felt her gaping sex tighten deliciously about his fingers; then her tongue thrust out; she moaned as the moist warm loving clutchings of her inner flesh continued round his fingers.

The protection had remained in place. The Baron returned to watching.

His erection would not subside, nor would those of any of his men; he could not tear his gaze away. He wished Olivia here to empathise with this lovely sexual creature now being penetrated so deeply but he himself could not leave and no servant was here to fetch her.

The Baron edged round the room, listening more than looking, listening to the liquid sounds, the grunts, Iroise's little gasps of breathless pleasure. He turned and saw her body rising in its sexual stirrups, urged up by the ardent passion of the two penises lodged within her. Her wrists were still tethered above her head, yet her fingertips were reaching out, blindly seeking to caress her lovers. He poured himself a glass of wine.

When he turned again she was being lifted down and carried to the leather-topped table. Her lovely eyelids were weighted with desire; she was beautiful, biddable, pale against the leather surface; her knees were up; the ink between her thighs was smeared by early spillage of semen. Raiff's penis was streaked pink. The men knew to withdraw but by applying the sealant the Baron had taken no chances. Her inked nipples were smudged by the urgent suckings and fingerings; Sethan's lips were reddened.

Under the renewed penetrations Iroise's body stayed open. When the first full spillage happened she needed scant coaxing to be made to drink: she gripped Raiff's purple stem as if to crush its life away; her tongue-tip danced in the spurting issue; her limp, lovely, twisted strands of soft blonde hair were wetted by the spray. Sethan's bursting penis rubbed up and down to the side of her sex; Tolron's re-entered her bottom. Her fingers clutched Sethan's balls; her nails dug in beneath them and his ejaculate spurted from the top of her leg to her nipple and armpit. Her lips opened against the underside of Raiff's penis, capturing the last trickles of drink.

Tolron held her bundled in his lap, his shaft thrusting ever deeper up her bottom. Suddenly she moaned, her eyes closed. The Baron shivered at the sight, for she was holding herself open for him – so sexually, the lip drawn to one side – so his insignia could plainly be seen.

He went to her, pressed his deliciously aching penis between her legs and tried to hold back but could not stop it; her dark dilated sensuous gaze, reaching deep within him, triggered the inexorable flow; he looked down to see her tattoo submerging in a sea of pure white.

Gently he closed her before lifting her off Tolron's penis and carrying her to the chair where he placed her sideways on his lap. He slid two fingers under her bottom, gently into the anal gape, gaining a purchase within her. 'Open your thighs,' he whispered. His buried fingertips could feel how close she was to climax. He took the tiny steel ball on its stem and pushed it through the creamy sea of spillage, pushed its semen-laved tip inside her pee-hole and slowly twirled it back and forth. Deliverance was immediate, profound and prolonged; she attempted to sit up while she was coming. He kept twirling the stem and edging it gently deeper while pressing inside her bottom with his fingers. Iroise cried out and bit and sucked his breast below the nipple. He cradled her. At length she looked up at him and – still trembling – reached to kiss his lips. Then suddenly her bottom tightened in a frightened spasm about his buried fingers.

Olivia was standing in the doorway. Her breathing was uneven; desire was in her breast.

'Dismiss the men,' she whispered.

The Baron waved them away. Olivia then approached him, her eyes burning with an ardour he had not seen. 'Tonight – now – I must come to my lord's bedchamber. My lord cannot refuse me this.'

The Baron sighed. 'No, but what of Iroise?'

After the whippings and after Olivia – having wreaked her vengeance on Iroise for having attracted the master's doting attentions – was finally sent to her own bed, Iroise's master came to her and unfastened her wrists from the twin bed pillars between which she had been tethered and lifted her from her knees. Iroise felt as though her bottom had been branded. She could not stand. Her master took her in his arms.

'It pleased me, watching Olivia whip you,' he murmured, searching Iroise's eyes. 'It pleased me. You understand?' Iroise then burst into tears. Hot aches swept across her skin. Gently, he raised her higher until he was caressing the roundness of her naked belly with his full, warm, open lips. The little birds inside her womb fluttered and dived anew; tortured emotions of warmth, pain and longing enveloped her. He carried her sobbing round the room then, drawing aside the coverlet, placed her in the middle of his great bed.

'Belly down,' he said gently. Iroise sank into the soft surface that still retained the warmth from her mistress's naked body. She pressed her cheek against the aromatic sheet. To the side of the bedhead she saw the heavy, solid carving of the bird's talon piercing a swollen cherry – the Baron's insignia – that was now tattooed between her legs, where it still throbbed and burnt in little fiery billows, an ineffaceable mark of sexual possession.

He took her hand and slipped her thumb into her mouth. He opened her thighs wide and wider yet, until she moaned and her cunny projected behind her. 'I should have Olivia back here and let her whip this too,' he whispered and Iroise gasped and shuddered and opened. She felt his fingers up inside her, searching for the buried lump of wax sealing her womb. She felt a tugging, like a bird's beak picking at her entrails. 'There,' he said. The wax came free. He pressed her belly to the bed and made her expel it. Then he guided his penis inside her cunny, deep, riding her with his penis yet not touching her elsewhere. Her hips moved; her nipples rubbed against the sheet; her bottom thrust against his belly; her knob stood proud; the glans of his penis pressed directly against her womb. Suddenly, she shuddered and bit her thumb and groaned; she felt a stabbing pleasure as if a thick needle were being pushed up the pith of her clitoris. Her climax deepened as the hot gush of semen came inside her. The Baron's broad hand pinned her bucking bottom down, and thumbed her pulsing anus very slowly.

Afterwards, he pushed a soft pad of cloth inside her sex, then bound her ankles together and kept her in his bed that night, whispering that henceforth no other man would have access. In the night, the effects of the smoke she had been made to inhale abated to a pall of remorse that darkened until it threatened to overwhelm her. Though he was an unbeliever, the Baron did not attempt to belittle the gravity of Iroise's sin. He coaxed her as a master should when her tears of desperation came – kissing her nipples, softening them with prolonged wetting, twisting and wresting them with his fingers, making the nipple flesh burn. 'Tonight, you must search your soul to disinter the mote that repeatedly enkindles transgression,' he whispered. 'Tomorrow we shall instigate a programme of systematic flagellation that shall excise that mote and bring this errant flesh into accord.'

The next day he had her fitted with a special halter that bedded deep into the split of her sex and bottom and fastened round her waist and was locked with a key. He kept the key hidden and kept Iroise a prisoner in his room. Olivia was no longer admitted.

Each night the Baron would return with one of the servants who would whip Iroise's bottom while the Baron looked on. 'It makes you soft, soulful and receptive,' the Baron would whisper to her. Then he would unlock her sex, kiss it and make her ride him till his fluid gushed against the entrance to her womb. Each ejaculation in there frightened Iroise. Yet, set against the fear of that uncurbed embrace was a depth of warmth and a primal intimacy which Iroise cherished – the broad hands cupping her punished buttocks, drawing her open belly closer, sealing it against his as his crisis came, then her body's deep gloving of his waning penis. Lady Olivia's words – about his wanting her as a concubine and bearer of his child – haunted Iroise. But her belly craved the undiluted warmth of that close embrace and did not want to break the seal. That night she dreamt that she was heavy with child and that she was taken into the stables for rutting with the men.

On the afternoon of the third day, Iroise heard the door open and she immediately turned on her back and spread her thighs to expose her leather halter for her lord to unlock. But it was not her lord. A tumbling feeling came inside her belly.

5

Keys

Standing with her ear pressed to the back of the bedroom door was the misfit girl in brown, Rhislin, listening for sounds from the corridor. Silently she bolted the door. Anxiety clutched Iroise's belly.

Rhislin looked slowly round the bedroom, absorbing its every feature. Then her dark-eyed gaze settled upon Iroise. Iroise could discern no emotion in that youthful face, set upon its stiff brown collar like a bronze upon a plinth. She lay, not moving and scarcely breathing, waiting for Rhislin to determine the path of this confrontation.

The girl went to each window in turn, staring out and down, then testing the fastenings. She began opening cupboards and drawers like a thief seeking booty. But she did not take anything until her fingers alighted upon a signet ring in the bureau. She scrutinised it. Silently, she unfastened her collar, threaded the ring on to her gold neck chain, tucked it in and refastened the collar. Then she came to the bed and searched under the pillows. Finally, she sat at Iroise's feet and said, 'Where does he keep the key?'

'But you got in without one.'

'I mean the key to your belt.'

'My belt?' Iroise whispered in dismay. 'But why?'

Rhislin glanced away as if her confidence had waned. Contradictory feelings beset Iroise as she waited for an answer. None came. So Iroise said, 'Did the mistress send you?'

Rhislin smiled askance, shaking her head.

'Then who?'

Rhislin looked at her. Iroise wanted to cover herself; she could not face the dark dilated pupils of that reckless gaze.

Finally Rhislin said, 'Have you not wondered where the other girls are?'

'What other girls?'

'The master goes to the Abbey and gets girls,' Rhislin said slowly. 'Have you not wondered where they are?'

Iroise moved up the bed and drew her knees up. She stared wide-eyed at Rhislin. 'Where are they?'

'You know why he makes you wear this belt?'

'That no other man may possess me.'

'And when he keeps on "possessing" you, what will happen?'

Iroise had put this to the back of her mind. 'It might not happen,' she whispered weakly.

'It happened with the others.'

'Then tell me – where are they?'

'Who knows? Not here. My lady will not abide them. They are sold on as pregnant slatterns once their bellies are too swelled.'

The words plunged like a freezing knife into Iroise.

Then Rhislin twisted the knife. 'Your lord's tattoo is far-famed in the brothels.'

Through the chilling numbness Iroise whispered, 'He would not cast me aside like that?'

Rhislin shook her head but would not look Iroise in the face. It seemed that now she had got the stark words out, her callousness had melted. Her fingers agitatedly smoothed the sheet under Iroise's feet. Her silence spoke volumes.

'Rhislin – what can I do?'

The fingertips stopped moving. Iroise watched them. In awed and frozen silence she watched them, in slow motion, lift from the bed and hesitate then descend and stroke her toes, sending shivers to her core. 'Come with me,' Rhislin whispered, still not looking at her.

'With you? Where?' Iroise gasped.

'Away.'

'You mean – run away?'

'Yes.'

'Where to?'

'Does it matter where?'

'Yes. Yes, it does. You cannot run with nowhere to go.'

'Just away. I will take you and keep you safe.' The words, so gently and earnestly spoken, were heart-melting. Rhislin looked at her with those soft dark eyes and Iroise felt the emotion brimming inside her. She could not speak. She reached with trembling fingers for Rhislin. The girl intercepted them and kissed their tips. Shivers ran up Iroise's arm. Tears brimmed in her eyes as she whispered, 'I cannot go. My fate is decreed. I must take my chances with my master. I am too weak and frightened to resist.'

'What if I were your master?' Rhislin offered bravely.

Iroise smiled sadly through her tears and tried to answer lightly, 'Then I must needs follow where my master led.'

But Rhislin was serious. 'Then I make this pledge: only call me master and it shall be so. And we shall fly from here – tonight, together.'

Iroise shook her head. But she had been deeply touched.

'Then kiss me?'

Iroise offered her lips. The kiss was gentle, long and sweet. Rhislin's lips were soft and warm. The stiff brown cloth of Rhislin's suit tickled Iroise's naked body. When the kiss was complete Iroise lay back shyly on the pillow.

'I brought you this,' said Rhislin, offering what looked like a pigeon's egg.

'What is it?'

'I got it from the apothecary. It melts inside a girl. He says it lasts a few days. It can spike the fluid that the male emits.' She placed it in Iroise's hand. 'You'll have to hide it until he unlocks you.'

Iroise clasped it tightly, pressing her fist to her lips to stem the tide of emotion.

'Don't cry,' Rhislin whispered, biting her lip.

'How can I ever thank you?' Iroise was choking back the tears.

'Tonight, when the moon is highest I will be waiting – don't shake your head – I will be waiting in the stables with the two finest, fastest mounts. And neither will be mine but I shall make them mine.'

'Like you would try to make me?' Iroise tried to smile.

'And we shall fly.'

That night the Baron dismissed his servant and came to Iroise as she lay face down on the bed. 'Turn over.' In the candlelight, he stared at her nude breasts and belly. He explained that he personally wanted to whip her. She shuddered gently as he slid the gilt key into her lock and twisted it slowly like a skewer until the heavy click reverberated through her belly. He unhitched the heavy leather flaps of her belt and drew them aside, to right and left and down, laying bare her humid cunny, its lips collapsed and twisted by the trapped warmth and damp of imprisonment.

He made her lie on her front with her left hand clasped round her cunny during the whipping. First, he pulled the remaining bedded thong of leather gently from her crease. The sensuous feeling came to Iroise as all between her legs was rendered fully nude after the tight hot proximity of the leather. She felt him press the leather crotch – still warm and aromatic – into the palm of her right hand then he closed her fingers round it. He made her lie like that, on her front, with one hand clasped around her cunny – 'as if you're masturbating,' he said – and the other hand stretched above her on the sheet, 'clutching the leather tongue of sweet imprisonment'. Then he whipped her to the next rung of arousal.

Her face was half buried in the rucked sheet. Her flesh swelled into her cupping hand. The Baron told her she was beautiful. He put his distended penis against her cheek, under her ear lobe, using it to lever her silken curls from her neck that he might kiss its nape. Then he whipped her again.

When he turned her on to her back, her hand was still clasping herself. 'Show me,' he murmured. Iroise felt a deep draw of submission as she exposed her intimate flesh to her master's gaze. 'So swollen . . .' he whispered. Desire was written on his face. She opened her hand and it was wet. He touched the wet and shivered. She knew to open her legs very wide. Without prompting she drew open her tattooed flap. And with the flap stretched flat, Iroise bore down between her legs and watched his face. He gasped and shivered again in pleasure. Then he whispered, 'I fear my attentions may be beginning to distend you. Yet I find it all so very beautiful in that state.' He touched the inside that was pushing out.

When his heavy paunch sank between her legs Iroise felt the purple glans go deeper than she had known. Her flesh desired this primal contact even as her conscience was beset with fretting. Her fingers slid under the pillow, seeking the smooth comfort of the little egg that lay hidden until the time would be opportune for implanting its protection. Then the boiling seminal fluid spilled against her womb.

He said he wanted to go into her bottom. 'Turn over, little temptrix.' Iroise swallowed softly and complied.

His face appeared close to hers as it lay half buried against the pillow. 'Shall I oil the way?'

'No,' she murmured bravely. Her flesh would accept the 'burning'. The burning was for Iroise a kind of deliverance; the aftersensations in so intimate a place were deep and strong. Yet still she gasped as this fiery form of deliverance came; the drying stickiness on the penis only made the friction worse; she felt as if her bottom would split and still the rubbing swollen clinging girth kept coming in. The Baron thrust until the gold ring around his genitals pressed against the seared entrance to her bottom and she was plugged completely. The fierce passion of core distension spread warmth through her vitals to her neck and cheeks. She shivered sexually as he murmured that such distension might engender a permanent gape. At his crisis the gold ring itself partly entered her body.

After he had rested, Iroise begged leave to lie with him that night without her belt, 'that my master might swiftly come inside on impulse'. She lay back shyly on the pillow and casually slipped her hand beneath it. There was no egg there – nothing there.

'Your eyes betray you.' The words froze her. The Baron held up the missing egg. 'My lady's wiles?'

'*No*,' Iroise answered, without thinking.

'We shall see. My dear wife must have a key to this room because her valet was seen leaving. My servant thought it strange. And then we find this.' He crushed the egg to powder then brushed the crumbs aside and wiped his fingers disdainfully on the sheet.

There was a knock at the door and the breathless servant entered. 'Rhislin is not to be found, my lord. Unless she is with my lady. Shall I –'

'No.'

'Tolron is searching the yard and grounds.'

'No matter. We cannot blame the valet when the breach of trust happens in this bed.' He glared at Iroise. 'But I may be prevailed upon to forgive. Leave us: I shall not require any more messages tonight.'

The Baron rose from Iroise's side and locked and bolted the door. He came back to her, lifted the leather halter from the pillow and stared at it. Then he whispered, 'Of course.' He smiled. 'The pessary could not be administered. Therefore Olivia may have a key to the door, but she does not have a key to this.' He spread its leather leaves open on the sheet. 'Get in it, little one,' he instructed Iroise.

Though her sex and bottom were now sealed, her mouth was free to make amends to her master. He used it almost brutally. Her jaw ached from keeping open, and the repeated enforced gorging on his flesh was making thick saliva that she could not control. It was running down her chin. But still he made her keep open, telling her he wanted her lovely lips touching the gold ring that clasped the root of his penis. At his crisis, Iroise's nostrils flared – 'Keep it in, keep it in,' her master gasped as she gurgled and her belly distended in a deep shudder of submission. Her reaching lips suckered up against his genital ring and he rubbed her dense drools of escaped spittle into her nipples, stretching the nipple flesh until it necked to shiny pink beads.

For Iroise there was gratification in this act of selfless giving. In becoming the servile vessel for her master's emissions she experienced a kind of release. As its delicious afterwarmth filled her body, she thought of Rhislin – the kiss, the sweet gentle kiss. She kept reliving it and then must have fallen asleep.

She woke on the crest of a dreadful nightmare. The master's hand was on her belly. The awful consequence that might stem from what he had put inside her forced beads of sweat on to her brow. She pulled away from that hand and sat crouched, clasping her knees to her breast. The Baron hadn't woken. Eerie moonlight drenched the room. Suddenly Iroise decided. And the enormity of that decision set her trembling. Not since abandoning her husband had she taken up so weighty a burden. She felt breathless yet afraid to breathe. Guilt and fear of discovery beset her though she had not even moved. She stared in terror at her master's sleeping form, expecting him to wake at any second and read the betrayal that had seeded in her mind.

She had to will her legs to move. Every slight quiver of the bed, every minute rustle of the sheet made her heart beat louder. Her damp, bare feet were sticking to the floor. Her hand was shaking when she reached the door. The turning of the key made a terrible clatter. She froze, not daring to look back as she lifted the latch. The door shifted but would not open. Panic welled. 'Please,' she mouthed silently. '*Please.*' Then she remembered the bolt. It groaned and clunked as she slid it aside. Again she froze, her forehead pressed against the door. She couldn't hear the master's breathing. When at last she turned to look, the door swung silently open against her shoulder. He was still asleep. She crept through the gap holding her breath then very slowly closed the door.

The stairs were in total darkness. Iroise gingerly felt her way down the first flight with her back to the wall. There was no sound; she pressed on. Halfway down the second flight her heart stopped; she still wore the belt; it was locked and the key lay in the bedroom. She had to go back. But she couldn't. She started shaking uncontrollably. Fear and indecision stymied prudent reason. In the urge to get away she stumbled down the rest of the stairs.

The first doorway led to the kitchens. Iroise tiptoed through, past the dying embers of the fire, and headed towards the windows and the moonlight. The outside door was ajar. She could see the moonlit yard. She hurried through but hearing a noise ahead, turned back. And suddenly she was trapped in Tolron's arms.

6

At the Smithy

'Not the one I was looking for – but you'll do.' Tolron tightened his grip so much that Iroise felt faint. He peered up at the darkened bedroom window then stared into her terrified eyes. 'Does the Baron know his protégée is abroad in nakedness at night?'

Iroise began sobbing.

'I thought not. Then this shall be our little secret. We may find some quiet quarter in the woods where I may test my lock-wrangling.' She fell to her knees, pleading with him. Suddenly she turned wide-eyed and limp; her mouth fell open. Tolron stared down at her as if she was deranged. Then the pole slammed down across his shoulders, snapped and the broken spar thudded against the back of his head. He collapsed as if his legs were cut from under him.

'You surely kept me waiting long,' said Rhislin, staring at Iroise and prodding the unconscious heap lying on the ground.

The horses were ready – two horses. Iroise stopped in her tracks. 'I cannot ride properly,' she whispered, anxiously.

'I'll lead you,' Rhislin said, simply.

Then, at the exit from the stables, Rhislin suddenly said, 'Wait!'

'What is it?' Iroise, startled, fearing imminent discovery, peered outside.

Rhislin tethered the horses and folded her arms. 'Have you forgotten?'

44

Iroise didn't understand her.

'You said that wherever your master leads, you must go; that such is the way of things for a Tormunite slave. Am I then your master?'

Iroise hesitated. She looked at Rhislin – this quiet girl in brown, so gently dark-eyed, yet so sure in what she wanted. And tonight she had abandoned all: master, mistress, duty, position. Iroise bit her lip as the emotion surged inside her when she thought of what this girl had done to save her. Then she said in a low voice, 'I know only that a Tormunite master or mistress has a duty of care and love and protection.' She looked again at Rhislin. 'And yes,' she nodded slowly, 'in one day, you – more than anyone ever – have proved you are my mistress.' She wiped her eye.

'Master,' Rhislin corrected.

'Master,' Iroise acceded in anxious, hopeful unease.

'Then swear to it.'

'There is no formal oath. It can be left unspoken.'

'But I am your master and I want it spoken. Kneel down and say after me.' She made Iroise repeat each phrase.

'I, Iroise of Servulan . . . accept Rhislin of Cotiak to be my only lord and master. Henceforth I am my master's slave . . . to be used and disposed of as my master chooses . . . according to the Tormunite rule.'

Rhislin took from the saddlebag of her mount a simple breast-halter of leather. 'I chose it for you.' She fitted it to Iroise. It had narrow straps that went under her arms and over her shoulders and buckled tightly at the back. It had rings of waxed, thin, twisted leather rope that Iroise's breasts had to be forced through, so tight was the fit. The tightness of the cinctures made her breasts more rigid. Iroise then knelt in true slave fashion, with head draped back, mouth wide open and belly thrust out. Rhislin kissed her, rubbing her palm back and forth across Iroise's shaking, cinctured teats.

Then Rhislin opened Iroise's knees. Her agitated finger-tips tested the edge of the leather belt in the crease of Iroise's thigh. The female fingertips, small and soft, made delicious feelings. Iroise leant back on her hands while Rhislin crouched and touched her.

'No key ... And how your master craves to get inside this belt and consummate the covenant. Did you get to place the protective egg?'

Iroise shook her head. 'The Baron found it and destroyed it.'

'I have more. But we need the key. I'm going back for it,' Rhislin announced curtly.

'No!'

'Where does he keep it?'

'No! It's hidden,' Iroise lied.

'Then I'll have to search. It must be in there somewhere – probably in his pocket.'

Rhislin rose to her feet with Iroise pleading round her ankles: 'No! Don't go back. Tolron will have wakened. You'll be discovered!' Tears were streaming down her face. Rhislin was disappearing. In desperation, Iroise cried after her, 'They'll punish you and send you away. And all over a stupid belt. And then I'll never see you again!' Rhislin stopped dead.

At last Iroise had found the words to convey what she truly meant. Rhislin stood for a few seconds just looking at her. 'Don't leave me, master, please?' Iroise whispered. And Rhislin came back and kissed her with a fervour deeper than before, her agitated fingers clawing at the rigid belt.

'Cut it off me,' Iroise murmured.

'No. I cannot bring myself to destroy it while it provokes such soulful passion. I'll find a way of getting it open.'

Skirting the villages, the fugitives rode through the morning, the master on her sleek black gelding, the body-slave on her small bay mare. The cloak that Rhislin had clothed Iroise with billowed out behind her. Her breasts and nipples bathed in the swift cool stream of woodland air. Each time Rhislin called a halt, Iroise dutifully clasped her hands behind her in readiness for the touching. Rhislin's palm felt hot against her skin; Rhislin's lips felt like burning circlets around her freezing nipples.

The scant provisions – a little bread, a pouch of cheese, dried apricots and weak wine – tasted like manna. Iroise sat upon her cloak in the sunlit glade and received the small morsels from her master's ministering fingers. Rhislin seemed curiously untroubled by the midday heat. She sat in her stiff woollen suit without unfastening a single button. Iroise kissed the fingertips that administered the tasty morsels; then she kissed the lips that were moistened with the spilled wine rescued from the ticklish skin of Iroise's belly. Rhislin's breath was warmly aromatic with the yeasty scent of bread. Iroise lay contentedly with her head in Rhislin's lap, with Rhislin's fingers stroking her hair and curling it round her fingers. Then Rhislin told her that she wanted to watch her pee.

She took her amongst the fronds of vegetation and cleared a circle with her feet. Iroise's cheeks glowed with embarrassment: the leather belt contained no cleft. Rhislin made her crouch and lean back on her hands, with her belly out and her knees wide open. For a long while nothing happened, though Iroise was bursting. Rhislin tore a green whippy shoot from the base of a tree and began stripping its leaves. When the shoot was naked, Rhislin knelt with it between Iroise's legs. Iroise shut her eyes as she felt the cold flexible tip of the shoot poking into the crease of her leg, searching for a gap under her leather.

'There,' Rhislin murmured. It started sliding under the tight flap of leather at the front.

'Ohh,' Iroise gasped. It slid coldly across her humid cunny, then started wriggling up and down against it. 'Ohh!' she cried out. It felt as if a little icicle were trying to worm across her pee-hole; she felt shivers of gooseflesh on her breasts; her legs started trembling. Rhislin began to pinch her rigid nipples, then suddenly all inside her belt turned warm and wet. It issued up her belly, up the crack of her bottom and into her cunny. Rhislin forced the wriggly shoot further until it emerged at the other side, then she drew it, dripping, all the way through. 'Now your scent is on my skin,' Rhislin murmured, drawing the wet stem through her closed palm, stripping away the moist softened green. She anointed Iroise's nipples with it, then nuzzled her cinctured breasts and sucked her pee-moistened nipples. Then she sucked her mouth. Iroise shivered as the short bristly hairs of her master's suit came against her naked breasts and belly.

Suddenly, Rhislin stopped kissing Iroise. She put a finger over her lips and tilted her head to listen. 'Did you hear something?'

Iroise shook her head. Rhislin stood up, craning her neck. 'I thought I heard hounds. We'd better make more distance, to be safe.'

Rhislin put her body-slave wet astride her horse. The outer wet dried swiftly in the breeze; the inner wet stayed trapped under the belt, making her sex and bottom itchy. There no more sounds to suggest pursuit. In the midafternoon, they came upon a hamlet with a smithy where Rhislin said it might be safe to seek assistance.

Rhislin was soon in confrontation with the young owner who, bared to the waist, was working over the brazier. 'But you are a smith, are you not?'

'Aye – blacksmith, not locksmith.' He put the tongs down and drank a ladle of water.

'So you cannot help her?'

He walked over to the horse, nodded deferentially to Iroise then stared at her belt. He had not smiled, yet all his actions towards her seemed kindly. He turned to Rhislin. 'Why don't you have the key?'

Rhislin answered swiftly: 'She has escaped. Only her rightful owner has it. I need to see that she bears his mark.'

'What mark?'

'Unpuzzle the lock and you'll see.'

'I am suspicious.'

'She will not harm you. I give my word.'

He smiled then he lifted Iroise gently down. As he carried her inside, Iroise sensed her master's resentment of this stranger's unassuming intimacy.

He took her through to the little stable and placed her on the flower-strewn hay then went to get his tools. Rhislin watched without speaking as Iroise lay in the sweetly scented hay and opened her thighs for him. Iroise wanted her new master supportive and near, not stony-faced. She beckoned with her eyes until Rhislin relented.

Rhislin showed no restraint in the young man's presence. 'Pursue your soundings,' she told him as she drew Iroise's arms out of the way, exposing her breasts, each individually clasped by the halter. She spread the silken strands of Iroise's hair upon the hay. Then her open lips descended, enveloping Iroise's pouted lower lip within a slow, sensuous kiss. The hay strands tickled the soles of Iroise's feet. Between her legs she felt the wormings of the angled, thin iron rods inside the lock that lay so close against her cunny; she felt the hairs on the back of the blacksmith's busy hands springing against her naked thighs; she felt his warm ample thumb press gently into her crease to steady her against the deeper probings. She murmured when Rhislin's lips closed about her nipple.

An inviting gap appeared at the back of Rhislin's tight collar as she bent over Iroise's haltered breast. Iroise's arm automatically moved from the position where Rhislin had put it and caressed Rhislin's hair as she was sucking. The hair, sandy brown, was lighter and softer than Iroise had thought. In the castle she had only seen it in the half light. Her fingertips slid a little way down into the gap at the back of the collar just to touch the fine delicate skin hairs of that lovely, sensual nape. Rhislin moved Iroise's arm back above her head. She sat up, idly stroking Iroise's exposed underarms and watching the blacksmith working. He had not stopped during Rhislin's display. He was young, strong and gentle.

The lock between her thighs clicked. The blacksmith sat back and stared at Rhislin. When she said nothing, he started putting his things into the wooden box until Rhislin leant over Iroise and tugged at the stiffly slotted flaps of leather. Iroise tried to cover her face with her hands. Rhislin drew them away. 'Look at him. Now ask him to open you.'

Iroise, her lips trembling, turned pleadingly to her master, indicating by tiny shakes of her head that she did not want to be made to say it. His kindness and gentleness made the burden of such forwardness immovable.

Silent displeasure welled in Rhislin. When the blacksmith made as if to speak she held her hand up, then said, 'Ask him.'

'Please . . . Open me,' Iroise at last whispered.

The blacksmith didn't move. Rhislin crawled back across the hay and took up a position behind Iroise's head where she stretched Iroise's arms back and held them.

Iroise looked askance at the blacksmith. His gaze moved slowly up her haltered body. Her breasts were rising and falling though she was trying not to breathe. 'Please,' she whispered again, shivering as she felt Rhislin kissing the tips of her fingers. Then the warm strong hands were between her thighs, gently prising her stiff leather fastenings open. Suddenly, she was afraid of what he would find in there, her flesh besmutted and ill-scented. She tried to hide her face. Rhislin would not let her. 'Open your eyes and look at him. Be proud for you are beautiful.'

Her moist flesh at first clung to the flaps of leather. As he drew them aside a waft of chill air came between her legs. As he pulled the belt from under her, her damp bottom sank into the clinging strands and flowerheads of hay. 'Spread wide,' Rhislin instructed. Then she said to the blacksmith, 'It seems too damp and sticky to open of its own accord. You will have to use your fingers.'

Iroise shuddered at the tender approach of those broad, hot, thick-skinned fingers, which could scarcely grasp the collapsed, sealed sexual lips, could scarcely split the paper-thin seam, yet they tried so hard to be gentle. This very gentleness when her thighs were so tautly open, heightened her arousal. She felt the lips being peeled open; she felt her clitoris slipping through its hood. 'Wider . . .' Rhislin whispered. She felt her clitoris being pushed out by the gentle stretching of the lips. She heard his gasp as the smooth inner canvas of her flesh was exposed and her tattoo was bathed in filtered daylight.

'The clawed cherry . . . She is her master's slave,' Rhislin declared. 'Leave her like that. She needs to show it off to remind her of her errant ways.' The thinned labia lay back against the hairless mount. Rhislin lifted Iroise's hand and spread its fingers. 'Kiss the tips,' she told him. 'They will consummate her gratitude if you can fashion a key.' Rhislin handed him the belt. She waited until he had left the stable.

'Deliverance,' Rhislin whispered, smiling. Held between her thumb and forefinger was one of the small eggs of powdered protective. 'No, don't touch me while I put it in you,' she murmured, kneeling beside Iroise. 'So smooth and slippy, the way . . .'

Iroise gasped and shuddered. The tight walls of her cunny were forced apart by the smooth egg of deliverance being propelled so slowly by this invasive female finger. The delicious insertion seemed to go on and on and up inside forever. Rhislin leant down and kissed her. The knuckles of the small hand pressed against her sex, which clasped the middle finger that pushed the egg against her womb. The egg began to shatter softly and to dissolve, bathing the deep interior of Iroise's cunny in coolness.

'Turn over.'

'But . . .'

'Turn over. I want to make quite certain.' The hay stems sprang inside her open cunny. 'Legs wider.'

Iroise moaned, clutching the scented hay. The feeling was so sexual and strong, of having a girl push this smooth firm egg right up her bottom. The slim finger stayed in, tapping the egg until it broke and dissolved and coldness seeped up Iroise's bowels. Rhislin kept her open-legged with the finger still sleeved while she kissed and licked her naked back. She pushed a stiff stem of hay under from behind, gently flicking and rubbing the stem against the protruding clitoris until liquid issued from Iroise's belly and the blacksmith returned.

'It's an old key I've worked to make it fit. It springs the lock most times,' he said but his interest was with the lovely blonde curly-tressed girl with her bound breasts and nude sex buried in the herbs and hay. Rhislin kept her bargain.

51

When the blacksmith turned Iroise over, he was already naked, his trembling penis curving above her. Rhislin had moved away and was testing the key in the belt. But her gaze kept returning. Iroise reached up with her mouth and kissed the underside of the silken penis just below the tip. She felt his belly-shudder coming through his penis. She could feel the warmth of his sac above her face. She pressed her fingers behind it and turned her head and the hot skin of the ball sac touched her ear lobe. Rhislin was still watching. Iroise did not take her eyes from her beautiful dark-eyed master as she did what had been commanded.

The blacksmith twisted round to examine her belly. She clutched the silken head of his penis tightly in one hand, closing the end off in her palm and squeezing, making him groan. She clasped her other hand tightly round the first hand, sealing the glans deep inside so no escape could come. As she felt his wrenching shudder, her nipples came up; with her eyes, she kept offering herself to her master. She kept imagining what it would be like if their roles were reversed – the blacksmith drawing Rhislin's thick trousers down and lying between her naked thighs, going deep into Rhislin's cunny, which Iroise had never seen nor kissed. But Iroise would be holding Rhislin and caressing her throat gently while her cunny was being delved.

The blacksmith's tongue-tip touched Iroise's tattooed cherry and she could not stop herself – her mouth reached again and sucked the place between his balls, sucked hard there, as all the hot semen flooded into the tight cocoon of her hands. He gasped and thrust but Iroise would not release that burning glans until every last dreg had issued and he had collapsed beside her. Tenderly, still looking at her master, Iroise extended her drenched sticky palms and smeared them up his belly to his breast and nipples then back to his balls until all the smearing had dried to a shiny coating. She wanted to tease him up to a second standing but Rhislin's eyes told her no. So she sprinkled broken flowerheads upon his torso and kissed his glans, then crawled on her knees to her master.

Rhislin hauled her up by the back of her breast-halter. 'The debt of work is paid,' she told the blacksmith. Then she put her hand between Iroise's legs. 'I want this in the saddle – naked.'

They rode on through narrow woodland tracks until they emerged at the edge of a large, still pool in a silent glade.

'Supper,' Rhislin whispered.

Iroise stared round the empty glade.

'There – in the water – see?' said Rhislin, dismounting.

Slinking lazily through the shallows were sturdy fish in shades of silver and gold. 'How will you catch them?' Iroise whispered.

'The same way I hooked the blacksmith.'

Rhislin's trousers were rolled to her thighs. Her legs were slim and lightly bronzed, not pale. The fine light hair was dense and made patterns like brush strokes where the water had run; the droplets on her calves glistened in the sunlight. The tepid water rose up Iroise's thighs as she knelt, nude from the waist, in the shallows. A tickling line encircled her above her belly. Her knees and toes bedded into the soft black leaf mould at the bottom.

'Lean back on your hands and spread your knees,' Rhislin said, bending over her, casting a shadow across her lap. Tiny shimmering bubbles of trapped air escaped up Iroise's belly. 'Stay still now. They will come.'

Rhislin's hand gently wafted between Iroise's legs then stopped, then teased her labia open, then wafted again, then rested perfectly still against her thigh. Tumbling feelings came in Iroise's belly. She looked up at Rhislin's bowed profile, silent, still and unblinking. The merest flicker brushed those lovely eyelashes; the lips parted in anticipation; Iroise was afraid to breathe. From the corner of her eye she saw the surface of the water shimmer. Something weighted and slippery brushed her knee then bumped and slithered along her inner thigh. Cold rubbery tickling fish-lips latched upon her wafting bait, teasing the unresisting edges of her labia, triggering shivers.

She felt Rhislin's hand move against her thigh. She looked down and shuddered sexually. Between her legs, undulating lazily, slunk Rhislin's prey, sheathed in splendent gold and silver, as thick as an arm, open-mouthed and toothless, lips protrusive, planting little biting sucks that reached ever deeper into Iroise's opened body, inducing contractions in that sexual place, causing her to gasp and bite her tongue. Suddenly, a whipping splash exploded upwards from between her legs; water charged with molten gold and silver arched through the air. The writhing creature thumped down on the grassy bank. In two strides, Rhislin had it by the tail and had smacked its head against a stone while Iroise was still kneeling in the water.

Iroise's eyes smarted from the drifting smoke of the dry-grass fire but she could not rub them. Her back was against a tree; her wrists were tethered to a branch above her head. Her arms ached pleasurably; her legs were pegged open. Her sex throbbed gently where the fish had kissed her. Inside her flesh were raised red circles which Rhislin had studied and traced and then smacked with the tips of her fingers. Then she had knelt between Iroise's legs while she scaled and disembowelled the fish and filled its belly with herbs that she had gathered. In the midst of the filling, she stopped and put her arms round Iroise's waist, drawing her close until the sinews of Iroise's arms were stretched to breaking. Rhislin kissed her lips, her exposed armpits, her stiff nipples, then kissed her lips again and pushed soft aromatic leafage into Iroise's body, violating her gently while her ankles were staked to the ground. Then she left her swollen pouch pursed around the green and put the fish, sheathed in oak leaves, into the embers of the fire.

For the first time, Rhislin removed her brown jacket and her shirt and lay down, breast-naked, between Iroise's ankles while she reached back with her fingers – on to, underneath and into Iroise's belly. Around Rhislin's neck was the gold chain and the Baron's stolen signet. Iroise watched the beautiful, naked, bronze-skinned, lovely-breasted torso and yearned to kiss its little black nipples.

The small glazed toying fingers between her legs pumped love juice from her body while the aroma of charring fish skin filled the air.

Iroise had never tasted any fish flesh so sumptuously delicious. The skin was crisped, tanned and pungent. Rhislin administered warm, moist titbits to her mouth. Between the bouts of feeding, Rhislin's fish-oiled fingertips worked between Iroise's legs, gently withdrawing each body-warmed strand of herbage; Rhislin's slickened lips closed lovingly about her nipples. Then Rhislin's nipples touched Iroise's inner thighs. She felt the pointy tongue reach in to lick her herb-scented cherry tattoo. She felt its slick caresses around her clitoris. She shuddered and moaned and gasped and begged and prayed Rhislin not to force her to completion.

'If you transgress this one little time, who is to know?'

'Please understand, I beg you,' Iroise cried in gentle anguish.

'Then what would you have me do? For I must do something.'

'In the Abbey they would whip my bottom – deep into its wicked heart.'

Rhislin required no second telling. She untethered the trembling ankles and roped them up and wide apart. She found a birch switch whose tip thrashed sweet deliverance into the velvet maw of that wicked place until it swelled so hard that even her slim finger could not be admitted, though it persevered while Iroise, now nipple to nipple against her master, moaned into her mouth.

Then Rhislin took the stolen signet ring and impressed it into the left lip of Iroise's sex – holding it tightly squeezed there for a long time, while Iroise murmured – and when the ring was finally retracted, a beautifully precise Tormunite cross was impressed into the living flesh. Finally, she took a long needlelike fish-bone and pushed it through the lovely wrinkled ridge of skin between the sex and punished anus and left this in place and sat looking at her chattel-slave and sometimes kissing the cross impressed into her labium and pulling the lovely impaled ridge and pushing a finger through the swollen ring. When the toes curled up she kissed them. She kept her in that sexual state until the sun subsided.

'What was that?' Rhislin whispered. A sound like interrupted footfalls had come through the trees. The horses shifted uneasily. Rhislin turned and picked up her knife.

'Don't leave me,' Iroise whispered.

'Shh.' Rhislin put a warning finger to her lips then slid off into the deepening gloom.

Many minutes elapsed but Rhislin did not return. Iroise listened for her but all she could hear was the rustle of leaves in the warm breeze and the soft snorting of the horses. She was afraid to call out after Rhislin. Suddenly, the horses turned nervous. A light was glimmering and dancing through the distant trees. It was getting larger, slowly nearer, and the footfalls sounded again. Iroise could not hide; she could not move. She closed her eyes in terror as the bushes shook and the heavy footfalls came steadily closer.

7

Kinsmen

'A strange sight, Kin-Dariun?' The hooded, stooped figure held the lamp aloft over Iroise's trembling, bound, naked body.

'One could scarce have prophesied a stranger one, Kin-Cague.' The second speaker was younger. He stared at Iroise with cautious fascination.

'She's not one of ours. Look, here.' The stooped figure's hand extended gently from within the ample sleeve of his coarse-woven habit. His nimble fingertips closed upon the fish-bone impalement and with one deft movement drew it out of Iroise's flesh and held it to the lamplight, where it glistened like pearl.

The younger one gasped as he took the instrument from his colleague. He drew back his hood to examine it. Iroise looked up at him. His eyes were agile and his chin was pointed. His hair was close-cropped and the colour of sand. He turned the twinkling fish-bone slowly in the light. Then he whispered in a shaking voice, 'What manner of cold-blooded master would so punish her and leave her trussed like this, Kin-Cague? What trespass can the little one possibly have perpetrated?'

Tears formed in Iroise's eyes; yet she knew not why his words had triggered them.

'Calm down, kinsman,' Kin-Cague whispered. 'Judge in haste, atone at leisure. We know nought of the situation. She seems more afeared than harmed.' He wiped her tears very gently with the pad of his thumb. Concern was in his mature gaze and when his eyes met hers, the tears ran again. 'Are you unharmed?' he whispered anxiously.

Iroise nodded, trying to control her breathing. From the distance, came the sound of barking dogs. Kin-Dariun went to the horses, steadying them and talking to them, examining their packs briefly before returning bearing the locked leather body-belt.

'A Tormunite weapon of chastity,' Kin-Cague whispered to him. 'Here, hold the lamp for me.' Then he knelt by Iroise and began gently to untie her. His skin smelt faintly spiced as if fresh from bathing. His fingers were soft for a man of his years. 'Is your master near?' he whispered, removing her wristlets and anklets, rubbing the marks bedded into her skin.

Iroise shook her head, afraid of giving Rhislin away. The sound of barking came again. Kin-Cague stood up and said loudly, 'We cannot leave her here. Help me get her on a horse. We'll take her up to the infirmary.'

In lifting her, the kinsmen were very gentle, wrapping her in a blanket from one of the saddle-packs. They themselves did not attempt to ride but led the two horses onwards through the woods. Kin-Cague, with the lamp slung over one shoulder, led Iroise's horse and Kin-Dariun followed with the spare one. It seemed that, having identified their task, they were content to execute it without questioning her further. Silently they trod round the edge of the pool then up a grassy slope to a second pool, then a third. Though she might have been able, Iroise did not seek to escape; without knowing where to go, escaping might only have taken her further from Rhislin, who must surely be hiding, perhaps waiting her chance. But looming ahead were dark high walls. Kin-Cague led the little party down into a stone-clad defile that turned towards the foot of one of the walls and came to a tunnel-like entrance whose gate was open.

Beyond the gate, a hooded agitated kinsman emerged to intercept the incoming party. He held up his lamp then drew breath sharply as Iroise's nakedness, incompletely sheltered by the blanket, was illuminated in the swaying light. 'You found her! Providence be praised. The Prior expects her directly.'

'How so, Meltaig, when we only came upon the waif by chance?'

Meltaig shrugged. 'Ours is not to question, kinsman. If she was by the fish-pools then she is the one.'

'I'll have her bathed and rested,' Kin-Cague said, lifting Iroise down. Kin-Dariun led the horses across to the stables.

'But there is urgency, kinsman,' Meltaig insisted. 'The Prior is waiting.'

'Then we are defeated and the bathing must wait.' Kin-Cague lifted aside the blanket now hiding Iroise's cheek and looked at her with kindness. 'Oh, that gaze, beset with so much trepidation. There is nothing to fear from an audience with the Prior. He is firm – with girls, none firmer. Yet he treats all with consideration and justice – though we cannot have you set before him in a blanket. Kin-Taig – have we the cloth of a mendicant that will fit her without draping on the ground?'

Kin-Cague, still carrying Iroise, followed the anxious Meltaig across the courtyard in the opposite direction to the stables and into a long, stone building. Once inside, he tried to carry her after Meltaig up the broad stone stairs. Kin-Cague was not young and though Iroise was slight of body he was soon forced to hesitate.

'I can walk. I am not harmed,' she whispered, gently.

'And you can speak, it seems at last,' he sighed, nodding approvingly, softly lowering her to her feet. As she held the blanket round herself he looked at her with warmth. 'Tell me your name?'

'Iroise.'

'A lovely name.'

She smiled then looked up the stairs where Meltaig was impatiently indicating that she should follow.

She began taking the steps slowly, checking that Kin-Cague was following. At the top, Meltaig crossed a wide stone landing and hurried through an open doorway. At the threshold Iroise hesitated and peered inside.

It was a robing room, fitted out in heavy dark polished wood. Meltaig had already selected for her a one-piece, hooded habit of pale fawn. He spread it carefully on the shiny surface of the low, flat chest of drawers and removed the aromatic leaves infolded within its creases. 'Come forward. Lift your hands,' he told her. As her blanket fell to the floor, leaving her bare breasts poking through the twin loops of their halter, he draped the habit over her head, pulling her hands through its broad sleeves and allowing the hem to fall to her ankles. He drew her hair back and tied it with a black braid before raising the hood. 'Clasp your hands thus,' he told her. 'There.' He turned her round and knelt down to fit sandals to her feet.

The scent of camphor filled her nostrils. In the mirror she could see this slight individual shrouded in fawn, the hood setting her face in shadow, the formless habit concealing her figure. Its cloth felt rough against her skin yet reassuring in the simple way it enveloped her body, providing a safe separation from her immediate surroundings.

Meltaig stood up. 'Now she must be taken to the Prior without delay.'

Kin-Cague led Iroise through the robing room and along a series of panelled corridors lit by intricately fashioned lamps. Their route crossed intersections and ascended more stairs, this time of polished wood. Occasionally, they passed kinsmen who greeted Kin-Cague by name and nodded to Iroise's shrouded figure but did not appear to find her presence worthy of remark. For this she was grateful; it helped offset some of her anxiety at having to meet the Prior. She heard singing – simple chanting, solemn yet warm – then the corridor came to an end at a large door.

'Wait here.' Kin-Cague rapped at the door and immediately entered. A long minute passed during which the chill waves of unease began breaking over Iroise's body, inside its shroud. Then the door opened and Kin-Cague beckoned with his generous eyes.

Iroise stepped across the threshold with hood drawn forwards and eyes downcast. The floor was magnificently inlaid with precisely shaped interlocking wooden blocks in richly varied stain and attractive grain, forming a large pattern of interlocking curves. She tried to keep looking at the floor. Kin-Cague guided her to a gentle halt in the middle of the room. She felt the warmth of a fire to her left and saw its reflection in the polished flooring.

'Look up, my child.' A soft deep voice resonated in her ears. She raised her eyes in the direction of the voice.

Standing before her was the man she took to be the Prior, dressed in olive-coloured cloth, white of hair and large-framed – a big man but not fat – pink-skinned and with a gaze that emanated gentle self-assurance. Then her blood froze, for seated by the fire was the Baron.

Iroise, trembling under his brutal glare, turned away and into Kin-Cague's arms. 'Steady. Do not be frightened,' Kin-Cague whispered.

'She has cause to be,' growled the Baron.

'In this house – no,' said the Prior, crossing the Baron's line of vision and placing himself by the fire. He folded his arms. 'Look at me, child.' There were tears in Iroise's eyes as he fixed her in his steady gaze. 'Speak truthfully and, if you have not transgressed, you have nothing to fear.'

But Iroise had transgressed. The tears welled until she could barely see.

'You know this noble lord who now graces our house of meditation with his presence?'

'Yes,' she whispered.

'You dwelt in his castle?'

'Yes.'

'And shared his bed?'

She nodded.

'Your flesh bears his seal?'

Desolation swept her up.

'Then he is your true master?' The Prior stared quizzically.

Iroise did not move. Then her head shook almost imperceptibly. The Baron lurched forwards, glaring. The Prior raised his hand to stay him. 'Tell us,' he encouraged Iroise.

She opened her mouth, then closed it, biting her lip. 'No,' she whispered, looking at the man who had used her so cruelly without regard to any protection. 'No. He is not my true master.'

'Liar!' cried the Baron. 'She's lying. Open her – she bears my mark!'

'My lord, calm yourself. I understand well your claim but can you not appreciate her present state of distress? We are not Tormunites here yet we have many Tormunite maids pass through this place – girls cast aside as damaged. We respect every one of their customs and beliefs. And I know through my own witnessing, that a maid reunited with her master would prostrate herself at his feet and kiss the very hand that laid punishment upon her. That is their nature and their training. We are even obliged to keep a flagellant-master to minister to this need.'

'She ran away!'

'And do you wish to return?'

'No,' Iroise whispered, shaking her head, fighting down the dread emotion.

'Tell me again.'

Her heart was bursting through her breast. 'I will never go willingly,' she whispered in scared defiance of the Baron's evil glare.

'Kin-Cague,' said the Prior, 'make arrangements for whatever beast and chattels the girl was found with, to be returned forthwith to my lord's entourage. She shall remain here, a mendicant, whilesoever she wishes.'

'But . . .' the Baron blustered.

'My lord, I myself shall be pleased to hear you out, to your contentment. Kin-Cague, remove the mendicant immediately and put her to her duties.'

With that pronouncement, the ties were cut. But Iroise carried with her the Baron's malicious parting stare. And that was not to be the worst hurt she suffered that night. When Kin-Cague was leading her down a corridor over-looking the road beyond the outer walls of the Priory, she saw far below, a group of men with horses and dogs. Iroise begged Kin-Cague to stop. Full of dread she stared down from the window. 'The Baron's men,' he whispered.

'Oh, no!' she cried, straining at the bars of the window.

'They cannot harm you. They are in their world and we are in ours. The Prior will not admit them.'

'No – you do not understand,' Iroise cried in anguish. 'Look, they have captured Rhislin!'

Kin-Cague gazed down at the girl in bondage in their midst. 'Then she was the one with you? The one who . . .?'

'Yes. You must save her. Tell the Prior. Please!'

'But he has no jurisdiction beyond these walls.'

At that point, the dogs began barking as Kin-Dariun emerged from the main gate with the two stolen horses which he delivered to the Baron's men. Then the Baron emerged and mounted his heavy horse. He took hold of the reins of Rhislin's horse and shouted a command and the company began to leave.

'Stop them! Oh, please,' Iroise begged. 'Rhislin, Rhislin!' she shouted, clinging to the bars but her voice was lost in the clatter of receding hoofbeats while Kin-Cague, mute and bemused, stood helplessly by. When the group had receded into the darkness, Iroise subsided into a sobbing heap on the floor. For many minutes, Kin-Cague tried to console her. In the end, he was forced to call for assistance. The two kinsmen collected her up in their arms and delivered her back to the Prior's study where they placed her in the very seat that the Baron had occupied.

'Leave us,' the Prior said to his men.

When the door had closed, the Prior stood opposite Iroise and waited.

'You knew they had captured Rhislin?' she sobbed accusingly.

'Yes, I knew. They all came knocking at my gates.'

'Then why did you not tell me?'

'Because you would have given yourself up from sympathy and your mistress did not want that.'

'You spoke to her?'

'I insisted on it once I heard they held a female captive. I went out beyond the walls because he wouldn't allow her in. She told me what had happened and where you were and I sent out for you but you had already been found.'

'Why could you not have hidden me from the Baron?'

'He would have plagued me. And how could I know whether your mistress was speaking the truth? The meeting was necessary to resolve the issue.' He hesitated. 'She said she would come back for you.'

Iroise's eyes widened. 'But how can she, when she is in bondage?'

'That I do not know.'

'Is it that you want to keep me here?'

'I cannot deny that your beauty is a blessing to us all. But you are free to leave should you wish to go. Should you wish to stay then there are rigours: the life of a mendicant, especially that of a girl, carries obligations – the willing sublimation of the self and the adherence to our code of obedience. And we, for our part, will respect in depth the tenets of your Tantalite training.'

Iroise looked at the Prior, whose gaze was steadfast, strong. She looked away, her heart in turmoil. Rhislin was gone. It seemed everyone that she had loved was wrenched away from her. Then she whispered, 'I wish to stay if you will have me. Rhislin – my master – has decreed it. Till she returns, I bow to you and I accept the rigours of which you speak.' Rigours would be a sweet deliverance from this torture of her soul. She sank to her knees before the Prior and murmured, 'Only tell me, my lord, what you will have me do?'

He said nothing and at first did not move. She could hear his breathing. She bowed and pressed her lips to his sandalled feet. Still he did not move. Immediately, she realised her action had been a forwardness. She sat back on her heels and could not look up as she felt her complexion reddening. The Prior stepped back in silence. A bell rang and after a few seconds a kinsman entered.

When she looked up, the Prior was seated at his writing desk, pretending to scribe. The memory flashed back to Iroise of a person she had loved and lost, through cruel misunderstanding. And if that person were here now, sitting in that writing chair, she would make amends for the ills that he had suffered.

'Escort the mendicant to her quarters. She must rest tonight. No duties,' the Prior told the kinsman. Iroise's gaze met her quiet master's and saw in them all the kindness that in her heart she knew she did not merit. How could she rest tonight? How could she know rest, alone in a soundless cell, when her emotions were in tatters?

'My lord, I beg leave to stay awhile and mend the fire, which is dying.' She bit her lip to fend back the tears.

The Prior stared at her then nodded gently. The kinsman left quietly.

Iroise knelt before the great fireplace and looked into its glowing embers, which shed a sleepy warmth upon her face and hands. She grasped the handle of the iron and with both hands began to poke the ashes through the grate, watching the charred logs gleam anew. The Prior bowed over his writing. With bare hands, Iroise placed new branchlets on the pyre and watched them smoke and crackle and release their delicious scent of burning cedar. She sat back on her heels. The licking flames lifted higher, sending flickering shadows across the room. The Prior still worked. Iroise's moving gaze fell upon the sideboard. She arose quietly, went to it and poured water from the large wooden pitcher into the wooden washbowl. She laced it with droplets of aromatic oil and distributed the fragrance through it with her fingers. She opened the drawer and found a fresh dry cloth. As she turned, holding the bowl and cloth she glimpsed the Prior looking up at her, then returning to his writing. She carried the bowl across to the writing desk and, kneeling, placed it on the floor, then soaked the cloth and wrung it. As she was reaching to take his foot from his sandal and bathe it, his hand descended and intercepted hers, grasping her wrist gently.

'My lord, let me bathe you?' she murmured weakly.

'The fire is mended,' he whispered. 'Your duty is well accomplished.' He took the cloth from her trembling fingers and captured upon it the brimming tears that trickled down her cheeks.

'Then bathe me?' she begged, her heart surging in her breast.

'You should repair to your quarters,' he whispered.

She closed her eyes as his fingertips cradled her upturned face. 'Oh, but you are beautiful,' he sighed, shaking his head.

The writing was put aside and the Prior rose quietly from his desk. He went into the next room, returning with a blanket which he spread in front of the fire. He lifted the kneeling Iroise on to the blanket then brought across the washing bowl. Gently, he drew back the hood of her mendicant's gown, exposing her tied-back hair. Then, without ceremony or affectation, he proceeded to wash her – her face and neck to her hairline, making trickles that ran down her front and her back inside her gown, sensitising the fine hairs on her skin, catching on the leather thongs of her halter. He washed her fingers and – removing her sandals – washed her toes, which peeped from under her as she leant back on her heels. She shivered softly as the moist cloth then advanced up inside the broad sleeve of her one-piece gown, bathing her underarm coolly and then her breasts, whose nipples came up to meet the trickles.

'Your breasts are cinctured,' the Prior whispered. 'Do you want me to remove the cincture?'

'Just hold me; hold them,' Iroise murmured, swooning against him. She offered up her lips, wanting him to kiss her. Her breasts inside the gown were steeped in warm humidity which made the breast-skin cling wherever his fingertips touched. He recharged the cloth and put it up her sleeve again and did her other underarm and then her underbreast. The trickles of water warmed and tickled her belly. She eased the hem of her gown above her knees and opened them. When he washed softly between them she felt as if the pleasure would come. When she shuddered and tried to stay his hand he said, 'You do not wish it?'

'My flesh is close to sinning, my lord. The craving is so sweet.'

'Then I must be slow and circumspect. Close your eyes and lean back.'

His naked thumb pressed gently down against her swollen vulva; his naked middle finger pressed up against the crease of her bottom, squeezing the delicious sexual swelling between her legs. 'Hold the sin in check, my child; stay still and resist it.' Her thighs began to tremble. He held the pressure steadily. The mouth of her bottom put little pulsing warm kisses against the joint of his middle finger, and the lips between her legs burst gently open round his thumb. Iroise swooned, so keen and near was that delicious, sinful feeling. The Prior understood her plight and waited until the feeling between her legs had sufficiently calmed before he drew away his thumb and resumed the gentle washing.

'Now dry yourself before the fire.' He lifted her arms out of the loose sleeves of the gown then drew it completely up from her belly and draped it over her shoulders. It hung down her back like a cape and she was nude at the front from knees to throat. Her nipples came up when her skin cooled as the trapped humid air billowed away. They stayed up as the fireglow warmed her. The Prior, now seated on the edge of the chair at the corner of the hearth, asked her to open her knees. Her cunny was still agape from the touching. She felt it open wider and, from shyness, she turned her gaze away. She could feel that her clitoris was engorged. The radiant warmth of the fire bathed her cheeks, breasts and inner thighs and now she could feel its kissing inside her body. Her nipples burned cherry red.

'You look sleepy – dreamy, pinkened, ringleted and beautiful. If Tantalism is embodied in that angelic countenance then your creed has much to commend it.'

A knock came at the door. Iroise became anxious. 'Stay still,' the Prior told her. 'No one shall harm you. It is only Dariun.' From the corner of her eye she glimpsed the young kinsman entering.

'Dariun, move over here, that our mendicant may see you so you do not make her fearful. Her name is Iroise.'

'So I understand, Prior. Is she all right?' Dariun knelt down and studied her anxiously. 'The quartermaster said that –'

'She has asked to stay awhile.' Then the Prior turned to Iroise. 'I had asked Dariun here to have him recount the circumstances of your discovery.'

'There is little to tell, my lord. We heard the dogs and headed that way but instead found a lovely girl. She was bound and . . .' He stared at the nude front of her body.

'And . . .?'

'There was this.' He held up the pearly fish-bone. He then explained where it had been found.

'You took it out of her flesh?'

'Kin-Cague did.'

'Then neither of you realised she was a Tantalite?'

Dariun looked uncertain. 'Kin-Cague did mention the word.'

The Prior came to Iroise, slipping his arm under her breasts from behind. 'Dariun is young and new.' The Prior's hand and wrist felt deliciously cool against her warm breast-skin. 'Lean against me. Back. You are hot. Are you hurting?'

She shook her head. She was hurting, aching, though not from the lovely tingling swathes of deep pink put across her skin by the radiant heat of the fire.

'Dariun – you've been outside in the night air. Cool her with your fingers.'

Under the Prior's guidance the nervous young kinsman's cold hands bestowed gentle gooseflesh upon Iroise's belly and breasts. The Prior watched, nodding sagely as Iroise sighed and murmured. Then he opened her between the legs and examined the Baron's mark. Dariun was aghast to discover that it was a permanent infusion into her skin. But the Prior seemed to treat it as a beautiful adornment rather than a seal of slavery. His gentle fingertip touching inside her body was delightful. 'Even the warmth of the fire cannot fully dry inside you. See, Dariun, the flesh makes its own rules, which Tormunil may illuminate but cannot rewrite.'

'My lord? I fail to understand.'

The Prior found the site of the puncture in the seam of flesh between Iroise's sex and bottom. The puncture had resealed. Iroise's chin was tucked down against her breast as she watched in timorous arousal. 'The perineum is already sexually sensitive in a girl. The Tormunites know this and work upon it to bolster their hold. Watch.' He held the point of the fish-bone against that place. Iroise's legs trembled but stayed wide open and compliant. Sweet tumblings of anticipation came; the stimulation was intense and the feeling overpowering.

Dariun gasped. Iroise moaned and her tongue thrust out. The newly reopened impalement shivered. 'Kiss her,' the Prior whispered. The young kinsman gently sucked the underside of her protruding tongue. A delicious tightness came between her legs, as if a creature were biting there and would not shed its hold. 'Smack it. Smack my open slit,' Iroise murmured lewdly into Dariun's ear. She clasped his head and tried to kiss his ear lobe but he pulled away from fear and shame. He did not understand how strongly she needed that intimate pain. She wanted to feel his cool hand smack her where she was leaking so freely that even the heat of the fire could not burn the wet away.

The Prior was watching again from his chair. 'Fear not, my child. Dariun is lost and I – for all my worldly wiles – must confess I am besotted. Before the night is through, you must surely have your way with one or other.'

'Both,' Iroise whispered.

Dariun was inexperienced – unused to dealing with a submissive – and the reference to sexual smacking had shocked him. The Prior was therefore obliged to give guidance and to take the lead. Iroise responded in loving submission to the directives being laid upon her as he moved her about his quarters. At first he kept her in her mendicant's habit, since her nudity under the cloth aroused her. When things were done to her while the ample hood of the gown was raised, her excitement seemed keener and her flesh more willing. The hood provided a sheltering separation from shame: many girls experienced pleasure more acutely this way. When at intervals he ventured inside her hood to read the expression written on her beautiful face, Iroise would be trembling and the Prior would kiss her very gently, knowing that this slow kissing under cover, however innocently phrased by himself, would stir resentment in the inexperienced kinsman and strengthen his response.

To this same end, the Prior withdrew the fish-bone insert and replaced it with a short length of unsharpened naked quill, which widened her puncture slightly. He made sure that Dariun was watching and that Iroise was bare to the armpits while it was happening. 'Watch her nipples,' the Prior said as he forced the smooth blunt insert through the axial seam of sexual flesh along her perineum. Then he made her stand.

'Bare your bottom to the fire,' the Prior whispered to her under the hood. He could not see what was happening, but he could feel the slight adjustments in her stance and hear the shuffles as the cloth was lifted. All the while, he could smell her warm female scent which had not been taken away by the washing. Under her ears she smelt delicious. He continued kissing there until suddenly she collapsed against him, open-mouthed and shivering. The Prior drew back a little to look. Dariun's cool hands, gaining confidence, had found the mendicant's red-cheeked bubble-buttocks and the trembling stump of quill that was protruding beneath them.

'Open for him,' the Prior whispered, lifting her cloth at the front. 'I can see the lips between your legs.' They were nude, depilated after the Tormunite fashion. Her belly was still red from the earlier basting by the fire. With her thighs so spread, the lips stood proud. The Prior gently twisted the cloth tighter about her middle and held it up above her navel while he toyed with these lips, which were hot and smooth on the outside, moist within. He opened them and held them spread. Murmuring, she moved on to her toes. Her knees began gently to tremble. Then he felt the delicious inner pink part of her sex thrusting out in slow rhythm as Dariun's fingers probed her responsive anus from behind.

'He does not understand in which direction to push,' the Prior whispered in her ear. Yet the very ineptitude of the thrusting was effectual. The Prior supported her limp, lovely body, so naked from the waist down, and he encouraged his young kinsman. 'Push down. Keep the rhythm steady. Be firm with her.'

Iroise moaned. The Prior felt her inner pink flesh being thrust out repeatedly between his fingers that were holding her labia wide apart. She shuddered under the curious inside-out penetrations that her sex was undergoing from behind. Her knees gave way when he tried to smack her between the legs – tried to smack the pushed-out part with the flat of his hand – and she collapsed on to them while still impaled on Dariun's fingers. Gently, Dariun withdrew his hand and touched her naked narrow back and her burnished buttocks and, emboldened, he tugged upon the quivering little stump of quill that pierced her perineum.

The Prior turned her round while she was kneeling and exposed her open belly and her cinctured breasts anew to the warmth of the fire. The delicious bulge of pink inner flesh that had come out between her legs was still partially visible. He bent down and finger-smacked it back inside her.

'Kiss her,' he told Dariun. The young kinsman now needed no second telling. He took her upper body in his arms and slipped his hand under the cincture between her breasts. The firmer pressure made her gasp; the hood of her gown fell back; her beautiful blonde ringlets glistened. While Dariun kissed, the Prior gently smacked her lovely body to excitement, up between her legs until she moaned into Dariun's mouth and begged her tormentors to desist.

'Look, kinsman,' the Prior said. 'See how soft is the flesh in this place.' Her labia would not stand unassisted, her clitoris had retreated, and the narrow pierced ridge of skin connecting her sex and anus was wrinkled and moved like paste when the quill was twisted.

Desire for the Tantalite girl burned blatantly in Dariun's eyes. The girl knew it and felt it. It was time for the Prior to dismiss him.

Dariun did not challenge the dismissal; Iroise did, with her baleful gaze, which followed the young kinsman to the door, then remained fixed there, watching like a puppy awaiting the resumption of sibling games.

'Go to the bedchamber,' the Prior whispered to her, 'and make ready.'

Iroise lay prostrate on the bed. The Prior approached quietly. He peeled the mendicant's habit completely off her body, leaving her face down, clad only in her breast-harness and the black ribbon loosely tied to her beautiful hair. He bade her open her thighs to expose her quill. Then he inserted a crooked finger into the front and pressed up against the back wall. The wrinkled velvet ring pulsed visibly. He pressed again and the velvet bulged. 'Let it open.' She moaned as the muscle yielded and the inner pinkness erupted. 'Close it tightly now – tighter!' He felt the lovely circular muscle gripping his fingertip, gloved lovingly by the soft protruding inner wall of girl-flesh. 'Hold it tight. Keep squeezing.' Droplets of sweat formed like quicksilver in the hollow at the base of her spine. He ran a hand beneath to search out her buried clitoris and in that delicious time of searching her climax came and seemed to go on until his fingertip hurt.

Iroise could not control the tears that followed this infraction. It was not proper to continue with her in that state. The Prior put her to the flagellant-master and, when she was finally brought back, her little quill insert was bent and twisted and there were red lines in the flesh all about it and her labia were unnaturally swollen, fiery against the backs of his fingers. Though her face was tear-streaked, she had borne the pain bravely, the flagellant-master told him. Gently, the Prior removed the damaged insert and, with finger pressure, worked atonement into the punctured skin. He tried to adhere to the Tantalite practices she was used to.

'Let her sleep by the embers of the fire. But tie her open. Let her search her soul and contemplate the inner cause of these transgressions.'

He himself could not sleep. He worked an hour or two at his books – he found a treatise on the Tantalic rites and ways – then he put them all aside and sat in his chair by the dying fire just watching her beautiful sleeping form. Finally, he knelt beside her and again squeezed the punctured skin between his fingers. It was cool; the punished lips between her legs were cool, dry and ductile, because she had been asleep and was open. One could not tire of touching them in the last glimmerings of the fire. He examined her tattoo, carefully stroked its raised skin, traced the image of the cherry. Then he released the ties from her ankles. When he picked her up, the blanket slid off her breasts. Her nipples were warm but her labia were still cool. He carried her to his bed and laid her open-thighed upon it. She watched him choose a sheath. When he went inside her belly, her labia clung, dry and cool, to the base of his shaft but, deep inside, her slippery heat burned like molten metal through the thin skin of the sheath. At his climax, she drew her thighs together round him to make his expulsion keenly complete. As he withdrew, she reached to kiss him. When she sank back on to the pillow, her jaw went slack and she plunged into deep, peaceful sleep.

He found himself covering her beautiful fragile body and relinquishing his bed. He went back to his writing but left a lamp burning in the bedroom, so that he could return to look at her at intervals and gladden his spirit.

8

Confessional

The first loaves of the day having been despatched, Kin-Erwyn curbed the bakehouse fire, raking its coals to a slow burn. Once the new sacks of flour had been brought and the cistern was recharged with fresh spring water, he dismissed the junior kinsman and fell to crushing coarse salt with a pestle. So engrossed did he become in this simple task, that he did not hear the mendicant enter. She must have been standing there some while before her nervous shuffling broke his reverie.

'Yes, my child?' he reproved her gently. 'Are you come to assist? You are not apparelled in baker's whites.'

'Sir, please excuse me. The Prior instructed that I enquire here for my confessor.'

'Then you must be Iroise?'

She nodded shyly.

'I saw you in the walled garden yesterday.'

Her breathing quickened and she lowered her gaze. Kin-Erwyn lifted back her mendicant's hood, raised her chin and gently brushed aside her dangling curtain of blonde curls, still damp from the bathing. Her cheeks were burning.

'There is no shame in female pleasure.'

'For me there is,' she whispered, soulfully.

'But she was lovely and wanted it?'

'Yes.'

'And you did?'

'Yes, but . . .'

'You are Tantalite?'

She bit her lip and nodded.

'The Prior has explained. But there is more to it all than just a label. You follow these strictures for a deeper purpose?'

She stared wide-eyed at him as if waiting for him to reveal this purpose. He shook his head. 'You must tell me.'

'Tell what?'

'Anything. Everything. What you will – and I will listen.' He cleared a space for her to sit upon the kneading table near to the oven. In keeping with tradition he bared her body as precursor to her baring her soul. He folded the mendicant's habit neatly. Then he cut her halter where it bridged her breasts. The action came so swiftly that it made her gasp. Her breasts shuddered and swung apart; the leather strap across her shoulders loosened. He cut that too, so the separated parts of her harness dangled from each breast.

'Who fitted you with it?' he asked, setting down the knife.

'My master.' Her breathing was unsteady.

'Then my mutilation of this symbol of your bondage might be considered an affront to him?'

'Is that why you have done it?' Her defiant words proved her loyalty was intact.

'No,' he said simply.

'Then why?'

'Because the tightness is too great for prolonged imprisonment of such tender organs.' He could not use the knife on the breast-cinctures themselves, which were too deeply bedded. Her breasts must have swelled following the application of their bonds. 'Lean forwards.' Her breasts dangled and swung while he pulled the two fragments of harness free as gently as he could. She shivered though the fire was near. There were deep grooves around the base of each breast where the thongs had bitten in. Her nipples brushed the back of his wrist; they were not hard but the flesh felt full. She did not attempt to sit up. Because her frame was so slight he could see every bump of her naked spine. He dipped his fingertips into the jug of milk and touched her dangling nipples. 'Did he tie your breasts to make them bigger?'

'My master is a girl.'

Kin-Erwyn did not allow his surprise to stay the fondling of her beautiful nipples, which in their fullness had stayed soft and warmly pliant.

'Tell me about the girl in the walled garden yesterday.'

'She befriended me. Her name is Saronam. She is a refugee like me.'

'She is comely – with beautiful breasts, which you were caressing.'

A soft shiver moved through Iroise's body. He continued to touch her nipples with milk-wetted fingers. 'Do you not think her breasts comely?'

Iroise nodded, her head still bowed. Then she whispered, 'She spoke about an instrument – a wheel – that girls are slung upon. Last night I dreamt about it – that I was on it.'

'The Wheel is for the deep submissives.'

'I know,' she whispered, looking up at him with eyes haunted by longing. She sank back upon the table, her breathing coming ever swifter and shallower as she bravely spread her thighs.

The flagellant-master had been there and she wanted to prove it to her confessor. She shuddered as the kinsman's milk-soaked fingers touched the punished tissues. 'He dealt discipline to you well.' Kin-Erwyn had sometimes witnessed such things being done, where the flagellant-master would lie the girl down – much as Iroise was lain now – and use a special yoke to keep her knees trussed up and very open for the whipping. But there were also coloured marks inside her sex. He gently cleaved it, revealing a precise tattoo of a bird's claw puncturing a ripe berry. 'Was this what you would have wished that Saronam was kissing?' He tapped it gently with a fingertip. The talk of the girl magnified the effect of these genital caresses.

'You did not kiss her, other than on her lips?'

'No.'

'But you wanted to?'

'Yes.'

'But you were afraid to initiate deeper advances?'

'Yes.'

'Then you shall create for her an offering.'

He lifted Iroise to a sitting position. The milk had dried upon her nipples. Her soft blonde hair hung down round her shoulders which were now dusted white by flour from the table. Her lovely body was illuminated between the glow from the oven and the daylight seeping through the narrow window. 'Was your master the first female to commune with your body?' She shook her head but the words had made her tremble with excitement. 'Tell me,' he said, stroking her inner ankle.

'In the Abbey it was encouraged.'

'Did you resist?'

She shook her head. 'The novices were made to punish each other with clysters and whips. Whatever was done to me, I never resisted.' She closed her eyes. 'It was beautiful – the burning pain and then the gentle kissing.' She looked up, eyes languorous with arousal at the memories.

'Open your legs – properly.' Kin-Erwyn placed a small bowl of cornflour beside her. Cornflour, finely milled and silky to the touch, was superior to wheatflour for this purpose. He began gently to anoint the erogenous places until the skin was smoothly slippery. The perfect inner flaps of her sex stayed open and her bright berry tattoo was sheathed in a sleek misty coating. There was a piercing through her perineum which he had not noticed until it sealed itself with the white powder. The fine creases in her swollen labia were filled to smooth flat snowy lines. Her anus made a dusky silken funnel, delightful to the touch. 'What if Saronam were to go in here with a clyster?'

The reaction was immediate: Iroise collapsed backwards, shuddering. Her coated labia were still standing open. They widened as Kin-Erwyn pressed his thumb against the tight, sensitive muscle in the funnel beneath. Her thighs were nude of pubic curls: how sweet the flagellant's pleasure in staking his whip-strokes upon that unspoiled surface.

The large wooden basin of dough, proving in front of the oven, was ready to be kneaded. He lifted Iroise down. 'I have a task for you,' he said, looping a thin full-length white apron over her neck. He sprinkled fresh flour on the table then heaved the large basin up on to it. 'Dust your hands with flour.' He tilted the basin. 'Now lever out the dough.' Her nostrils dilated, embracing the yeasty scent. Her delicate hands responded to the living mass of warmth, scooping gently yet efficiently, sensitive to the need to keep the warm mass whole. When it collapsed upside down on the table she sprinkled flour upon its damp, bubbly underside without his having to instruct her then, with minimal guidance, fell to kneading. Though her hands were not large enough, still she tried. The kinsman warmed to this lovely girl. He wondered how she had fallen into the grasp of the Tormunites but he knew he must not phrase the question with such blatant bias.

'Did you learn your bread-making skills in the Abbey?'

Wistfully, she shook her head. 'I used to bake bread for my former husband and tend his home.'

'Was it not your home too?'

'No.'

Kin-Erwyn waited. Iroise stopped kneading, then said, 'I was given young into marriage. My husband was set in his ways; he did not want me for myself but for what I could provide. He showed no warmth nor tenderness yet wanted to make me with child. I ran away and found work at an inn. I was lonely and unhappy but afraid to go back. Eventually, my husband found me but nothing had changed: there was no love nor human kindness in his words nor in his eyes; his only concern was that I had shamed him. He tried to take me away there and then but the Warden intervened.'

'The Warden?' Kin-Erwyn frowned.

'The Warden was our light and our protector. No one had ever done this for me – spoken up and taken my part. The next night he took me to watch one of their rituals. There was no coercion and I only watched. But it excited me – witnessing the bodily reaction in the girls, which I had not known could happen. The Warden told me about the Tormunite rules – the selfless giving of love, the receipt of pleasure, and the principle of protection. He told me too of the punishment – how that would be used to test me – but I was not frightened: the other rules burned too brightly in my mind. I submitted to his protection. He whipped me that night and then brought on my pleasure – in full, and it was beautiful. He told me that as part of my training I would be put with other men but that no harm would come to me while I was under his protection. Then I was chosen along with others to be taken to the Abbey.'

'But what of your Tantalite ways?'

'There was a girl – beautiful and dark-eyed – who stopped off with her Tormunite master at the inn. I was chambermaid and glimpsed some of the things that were done to her. Men came to her master's room and sometimes there were ladies who arrived in spotless carriages. The faces of these ladies were never disdainful; they were always keen, desirous. The girl's countenance radiated a contentment I had not seen. One night I was told to bring fresh towels to the room. She was standing nude by the fire and though she was dark-haired, all the curls that should have been between her thighs were missing. Her flesh was beautifully naked and her master was pinning her arms behind her back and the lady was touching the deep place that was naked, exciting it to the point where the girl was swooning. Then her master said, "Stop. Go gently. Let it ebb a little then we may continue."'

Iroise stopped. She repeated in a whisper the last sentence she had quoted. Then she begged Kin-Erwyn, 'Touch me.'

He put his hand between her legs from behind, and her labia felt beautifully silky, swollen, and her clitoral knob protruded like a shiny, polished node of marble, which he caressed while Iroise continued, falteringly, her legs deliciously atremble: 'Then the other man with them carried the girl to the bed and the lady followed. I made excuses to keep coming back to the room. The girl's treatment continued through the night.

'Afterwards, I ran to the Warden to ask him why the girl was being done in this way and why so many people craved involvement and he explained that she was Tantalite: she had taken a deep oath to pursue submissive pleasure but to eschew deliverance, and that even within the discipline of the Tormunite community, such creatures were special. Their arousal never went away. I told him I wanted to be special.'

'You are special,' Kin-Erwyn whispered, gently tapping her lovely shiny knob.

Iroise shivered. She seemed frightened to move. Carefully he eased his hand away and her body seemed to go limp. 'See –' she almost sobbed '– I try and try to keep my vows, but always I succumb.'

'But if pleasure should flow, what harm ensues? Some avow that virtue is embodied in pleasures of the flesh and that the crisis of pleasure is but the natural culmination of the process of giving.'

Iroise shook her head. 'But what of strength of will? The Warden was right: my constant failings are because I am so weak-willed. Even after the flagellant, when I was with the Prior, it happened then.' She turned pleadingly to Kin-Erwyn. 'You are my confessor. Help me.'

Kin-Erwyn walked quietly to the door of the bakehouse and shouted, 'Have Saronam brought directly!' He came back to the trembling Iroise, who was shaking her head. 'Yes,' he said firmly. 'And when she gets here, I want you ready.'

Iroise's trembles deepened; her breathing was more unsteady. He did not need to explain further what he would have Saronam do. Anticipation is a sweet thing. He knew how deeply moved she was by the thought of female love – exemplified by the gentle incident between the two girls in the garden and, more profoundly, by Iroise's tale of the deeper explorations committed by the lady upon the dark-eyed Tantalite submissive.

'Continue working the dough,' he whispered. 'Saronam will want to see these muscles in motion.' He took gentle hold of the beautiful flange of flesh that fed from her armpit to her breast and shook it. Her skin turned to gooseflesh. She bowed forwards; her apron sank in a billow, exposing her breasts, which shuddered independently. He dipped his fingertips in cornflour and, from behind, took precise hold upon those slippery projecting labia and worked the silky powder under the hood of skin at their conjunction, pushing more powder under until the hood swelled and tightened to a little pregnant knot that pressed against her sexual pip. Then, he pinched the front of her apron to a narrow band between her shivering exposed breasts.

When the door opened quietly she was on her toes. 'Stay thus,' he whispered, holding the slippery nodule sleeved inside its hood.

Saronam, bright-eyed, keen and daring, was clad in a moleskin gown fastened by three fat buttons down the middle. 'Come, help me with Iroise,' Kin-Erwyn called to her. Saronam moved with graceful alacrity. She bore none of Iroise's reservation. 'Touch here,' he directed. Her fingers were lithe; her hair was black; her breasts, generously replete, swayed unconstrictedly under her moleskin gown. Kin-Erwyn retreated.

Her nimble fingers found the pregnant pip of caked cornflour crammed under the hood of skin and worried it cautiously till Iroise was at the point of moaning. 'Kin-Erwyn, smack her buttocks gently,' Saronam said, knowingly. She laid her fingertips, silken with cornflour, against the small of Iroise's back, and stroked there through the smacking. Then, she exposed the flour-filled piercing. 'Smack upwards, here,' she whispered. 'Smack until the flesh goes numb.'

Iroise's trembling breasts dipped into the rising dough upon the table. Her sex gaped open from the smacking. Saronam's busy fingers worked slippery cornflour up into the living cavity until her whole hand, save the thumb, was deep inside. The thumb tapped steadily into the smooth funnel of the anus. Saronam was staring innocently at the kinsman all the while. Her thumb kept tapping out an audible pulse then it stopped abruptly. 'She wants to come – I can feel it at the mouth of her womb.'

'How so?'

'Like something is in there and is trying to push.'

'Then wait until it stops.'

Saronam stared sidelong for a few seconds then whispered, 'It's stopped.'

Kin-Erwyn approached Iroise. He trailed his fingertips slowly down her spine. 'Wait!' said Saronam, then, 'Go on.' He slid his hand under the buttock to tease the tautly crimped fleshy ridge of perineum and the lovely feather-edge of lip that was so stretched round Saronam's buried hand. He put his other hand under from the front. 'Slower,' Saronam warned.

'Tap the entrance to her bottom again with your thumb.'

Saronam's thumb began snapping down, accurately and firmly as if driven by a spring. Iroise turned her face to the side and began to gasp. Kin-Erwyn bowed and gently kissed her lips, which were softly warm yet laced with potent desire. The tapping had again stopped. He touched the belly very gently, found the pregnant pip – it was now dangling, so soft and malleable had the female foreskin become. Saronam's hand slid slowly out. 'She's ready now,' she said.

'Then fill her,' he whispered. And he felt the dangling pip between his fingers trying to retract.

This ritual of the 'Proving' was bestowed with special import when performed by another girl, especially a girl as beautiful as Saronam. Her slim, lithe form belied the fullness of her breasts. She left Iroise bent over the edge of the table while she languidly removed her moleskin gown. The flesh between her legs was freshly shaven, leaving a sensual purple shadow punctuated by cherry-red lips. When she turned around, her waist seemed disproportionately narrow as if she had been routinely corseted to emphasise the outswell of her buttocks. From behind, her naked sex was visible even while she was standing straight, and its separation from the mouth of her bottom was narrower than the finger-spacings of a glove.

Such thoughts – of gloving one's fingers separately into a girl – inveigled the kinsman's mind as he watched the filling. The repeated insertions of the soft, warm, pliable substance into the submissive, whetted Saronam's desire for more earnest things. The apron was taken off Iroise and she was stood upright. Sticky strings of yeasty dough adorned her breasts and belly.

The kinsman knew that the vessel of love between a girl's legs was capacious. Accommodation occurred by its changing shape. The very stretching of the inner walls was pivotal to arousal – the pressure on the womb and vulva and the sexual passage in behind, which in some girls was more erogenous. He wondered if these feelings in the girls were akin to being bloated with child. In advanced pregnancy, the vulva protruded; sensitivity was acute and the climaxes often came more swiftly. He knew this much from dealing with Chloe, who had come into their community too late, having been used by her master and his friends without any manner of protection.

Saronam had now placed Iroise in front of the oven – the inner stretching had induced shivering, though Iroise was not cold. Her hands clasped one of the high horizontal warming bars; her feet pointed outwards. Kin-Erwyn moved across to the chimney corner to achieve a vision of her lovely nude front. She was leaning forwards; the glimmer from the oven illuminated her sweet, round breasts; the pouch of her sex was beautifully nudely split and so swollen that she could not have closed her legs even had Saronam been willing to let her try. And the thinly sheathed genital pip was still there, protruding desirously, begging to be kissed or bitten.

'Let me test the progress of the proving,' Kin-Erwyn whispered.

From the front, he slid his cupped hand under. His middle finger extended softly along the velvet ridge of pierced skin and into the cleft of her buttocks. The ring-muscle was displaced back: it bulged from the cleft like a seed pod about to burst. Kin-Erwyn gently burst it with his middle finger. He felt the delicious humid warmth inside Iroise's body; he felt Saronam's enquiring finger join his inside Iroise. 'Her pouch is so swollen that her back passage is almost closed,' Saronam murmured, her finger advancing to the knuckle. Iroise moaned. Saronam's open lips moved gently up the side of Iroise's naked torso to her underarms, then round to clasp her nipple. The sheathed clitoral pip slipped under the massaging of the kinsman's thumb. It felt curiously hard yet weakly attached to her body. Her ring-muscle had softened. Saronam's finger retreated to ream the part of the rim that the kinsman was not gripping. She was now kneeling at Iroise's side, studying the dangling pip while she performed the slow reaming, her generous breasts bestriding Iroise's trembling knee. 'She's nearly coming. Keep still.'

Iroise's lovely body stiffened. 'Ohh,' she shuddered. A delicious pressure came against the length of the kinsman's finger inside her. Beads of sweat formed on the underside of her breasts and in the small of her back.

The climax had been fended off. Tiny musclelike ridges now disturbed the smoothness of the hood of skin attached to her pip. Saronam gently licked them individually with her tongue-tip to stimulate new arousal. Kin-Erwyn sucked the nipples, which had retained the malleable softness he admired.

The proving dough had begun to be extruded. The inner warmth of Iroise's body was the catalyst. The kinsman kept her standing as long as possible, with Saronam continuing the stimulation, then he lifted her and laid her belly-down on the warm, oiled tray. Slow masturbation continued through delivery, which took many minutes, with stops whenever climax threatened. Speed was anathema to precision. Gentle fingertip pressure might be applied to the small of her back, with gentle squeezing of an exposed nipple, soft kissing of her lovely mouth, and cornflour gently drizzled down to make the muscle of her anus satin-slippery to the coaxings of a finger. Kin-Erwyn periodically advanced her belly along the tray with gentle lifts. When nearly all was yielded, Saronam's fingers slid up the bottom to complete expulsion from behind. Then, Kin-Erwyn turned Iroise on to her back.

The lips of her sex were softly warm. When he put his fingers inside there was nothing in there: the swollen dough had parted perfectly cleanly. 'Wait,' said Saronam. 'Hold her open.'

Iroise lay there, blonde hair tousled, one leg nearly straight, the other bent, open, the flesh between her legs gently stretched to make a sexual gape. Saronam crooked two fingers upwards inside and rubbed slowly. 'Let it come,' she crooned. 'Let it trickle.' The beckoning fingers continued to move. Iroise murmured and her jaw fell slack. The kinsman felt the walls of her sex tightening even as he held them open. 'There.' Silent, oily, colourless gushes wetted Saronam's fingers, which flicked the oily fluid over the bloated roll of extruded dough then went inside for more. The beckoning action triggered new wetting until the length of dough was glazed with female sprinkles.

With swift incisions of a wooden pallet, Kin-Erwyn subdivided the length then slid the tray into the oven. Before Saronam had washed and dressed Iroise, the rolls were baked. 'Your offering is ready. The timing is providential; the Prior entertains guests who may wish to meet you.'

9

A Reacquaintance with Submission

Beyond the walled garden was a pool with a wooden boardwalk to a low-roofed villa projecting over the water's edge. Iroise, attired again in the garb of a mendicant and nervously carrying her cloth-covered tray, followed Saronam, who was carrying a small flagon of mead.

By the time Iroise reached the door of the villa, Saronam had already entered. Inside was a broad, well-lit room overlooking the reedy pool. The floor was waxed and the sparse furnishings were upholstered in leather. There were three men in the room. But Iroise saw only one. He faced away, staring out across the reedy scene. Yet the severe dark form of the tutor-monk Dom Enken could never be mistaken. Her grip on the tray went limp.

The Prior's gaze showed he knew something was amiss. Before he could speak, Dom Enken turned and stared at Iroise. Her hooded gown momentarily confused him; his eyebrows furrowed. He glanced at the Prior then strode over to her with all the strength of purpose she remembered of him. With fingertip stealth that made her shiver, he slid back the hood of her gown. Then he shook his head and sighed, 'Iroise. Such curls of blonde – how could there be another like you?'

'You tutored her?' the Prior asked.

'Not nearly enough. There was – how shall I put it? – unfinished commerce between us.' He stared down into her frightened eyes. 'A beautiful creature held aloft in a silver cage; a plaything of an iron mistress. But surely you remember – in the garden, on our journey to your nunnery – the night before your cage was sprung?'

She shuddered, as if he had stripped her naked.

He placed the tips of his fingers under her chin. 'Iroise – you do remember? How, with myself and others, you cuckolded your own lover – and then threw him to the wolves?'

The words pierced her exactly as he had intended. Iroise stood there shaking. Saronam was wide-eyed. The Prior seemed at a loss for words. It was left to the third man – who had not spoken and whom Iroise had seen and knew was younger but had not fully noticed – to intercede on her behalf.

'Lord Prior, I fear the wolves are with us yet: can the brother not see the girl is quaking. If he persists, the dedication shall be marred and I for one would never wish that.'

'Nor I,' the Prior answered. 'Saronam, help your sister regain her composure.'

But Iroise, tearful and distressed, shook her head. 'Every word is the truth. How I wish it were not.' She thanked the gentle young interloper with her eyes. Then she fell to her knees before the tutor-monk and, head bowed, offered up her tray.

'Our host takes precedence,' Dom Enken whispered in stern tutor fashion. His sharp glances silenced intervention by the others. Iroise shuffled on her knees across the shiny floor to the Prior.

From the inner pocket of his robe Dom Enken slid a crop. 'Hold your offertory high,' he ordered. She felt the hem of her habit being lifted; she saw concern and arousal in the Prior's eyes; she glimpsed the gentle interloper's gaze upon her naked bottom. The tutor-crop whipped across it three times. 'Hold the offertory high,' Dom Enken reminded her sternly, then said to Saronam, 'Is there a rope or cord I can tie her habit up with?'

Meanwhile, the Prior drew the cloth from the upraised tray, releasing the warm yeasty fragrance, which – with eyes briefly closed – he savoured. The gentle one had sat on the arm of a chair, never taking his gaze from Iroise's extending nudity, which had reached her back and belly as the lifted gown was tied tightly under her breasts.

Saronam distributed small loving cups of mead, which the two older men tasted in small appreciative sips. The younger one, intent upon Iroise's plight, quaffed in innocence until the Prior explained, 'The subtle undertaste is Saronam's. Of our girls, she is the most distinctive.' The young man stopped in mid-sup. Saronam's eyes swept shyly away and a blush beset her cheeks. The young man's eyes refocused on her generous breasts outlined through her moleskin gown.

The Prior took a proffered bread and kissed its smoothly glazed surface. He broke it gently. Dom Enken whipped the crop twice more across Iroise's bottom. 'Arms high,' he whispered. All eyes were back upon her.

The Prior pulled morsels of warm soft innards from the ruptured bread and, closing his lips about them, rolled them on his tongue and swallowed reverently. 'The scented salt is in the crust but all the softness is within. And it is perfect.' He nodded with gentle approbation then sipped from the cup of Saronam's mead. 'The commingling of female essences is exquisite. Connal.' He deferred to the watching young man, who suddenly seemed overawed.

Dom Enken gathered Iroise bodily, his strong arms about her where her tucked-up gown abruptly terminated under her breasts, and he lifted her in a kneeling position across the floor to young Connal's feet. Her upraised tray of ritual offerings almost spilled. Dom Enken whipped her naked bottom again. Cold shivers ran up Iroise's deeply hollowed spine.

'No more, good brother,' Connal whispered.

'My young lord does not understand.'

'Maybe not. So I wish for a desistance while my understanding develops.' He turned round on the arm of his chair and faced Iroise. As she held her tray aloft for the young master, the muscles of her arms were burning as keenly as her bottom. Tears dribbled down her cheeks.

Dom Enken fell back, sheathing his crop, and stood by the window observing her.

'Accept her offering,' the Prior prompted. Connal hesitated. Then he took the complete tray from her shaking arms and put it on the chair. He took aching wrists and arms and rubbed them gently. Then he kissed her fingertips one by one.

Dom Enken shook his head in feigned despair and turned to Saronam. He held out his drained loving cup. When she started to recharge it he grasped her wrist – not gently, as Connal had done with Iroise – and forced it up and back until her moleskin gown had cleaved open at the neck. He freed the top button and the fullness of her breast protruded through the gap. He took the flagon from her fingers and from behind brutally dragged the gown down from her shoulders, baring both breasts and upper arms and pinning her elbows to her body. The swiftness of the act left Saronam breathless; the nudity of the rising goosefleshed breasts was shocking. They shook as the tutor-monk wrenched the crumpled moleskin more tightly down her arms.

'Don't spill her flagon,' the Prior warned, his countenance inscrutable. 'There are others who might care to sample.'

'I swear it is her distillate that drives me.'

'You need no coercion, brother. But the young master is new, I take it?' The Prior went over to where Iroise lay crouched at Connal's feet, her hands in his, her belly and bottom still bare. 'Her offering is growing cold, my friend. Surely you will take it? Iroise?'

With shining eyes she looked at Connal; with trembling fingertips she lifted up the smallest bread. Then with precarious boldness, reaching high – her breasts, moving under her gown, brushing against his thigh – she put the bread to his lips. He kissed it. She shuddered as she knelt there, bottom-naked, bottom-striped and burning, belly shivering, a tiny missing touch away from his shiny booted foot. The stinging in her bottom triggered delicious cunny-quakes. She wanted his soft hand pressing deep into the

89

hollow of her naked back, drawing her yearning split gently tight against the polished leather while Dom Enken lashed her bottom from behind.

'This room has no proper corners.' The tutor-monk started dragging aside furniture. Saronam, still bare to her waist and with arms restrained, was thrust by the elbows into the tightest corner. He made her stand on tiptoes. Then he drew her breasts by the nipples up the facing walls and forced her body tightly into the gap. 'Stay there,' he ordered.

Iroise trembled, for she had seen this punishment being enacted before, on a fateful night long ago when her own master had whipped her with his leather belt and then had given her away. It made her cling to Connal for protection. 'What is it?' he whispered with aroused concern. Iroise shook her head and kissed his sleeve. But Connal was becoming intrigued by the effect that these practices were having upon Iroise. He removed the tray from the seat and settled down with Iroise slumped sideways between his knees. Taking up the bread that he had kissed, he fed small pieces of it between her lips and while she ate he held her gently by the throat and kissed her. The Prior brought Saronam's mead and Connal put the lip of the flagon to Iroise's mouth and Iroise took tiny, sexual sips of Saronam's honeyed musky issue while Dom Enken lifted high the hem of Saronam's moleskin gown and started whipping her.

'Her breasts stay up, as if she's holding them,' Connal said.

'It's because the whipping keeps her against the wall,' the Prior explained.

'They look so buoyant and keenly whetted,' Connal whispered. He put his hand down Iroise's gown and found her nipples that were keenly whetted too as she watched Saronam's lovely bottom moving. She wondered if the same fragrant moisture that laced her lips was being distilled anew by the tutor-monk's whipping. Her wrist brushed between Connal's legs and found hardness and hotness. He tugged her gown ever higher under her breasts, making her breathing deeper and more strained. He touched her nude bottom and belly. 'Show me where you made your bread,' he whispered avidly.

The Prior looked on as the young master bent her back across one knee. She kept her legs half open and all the pressures of the doughing were still visible as a soft-lipped dark pink oval gape.

'She's hairless,' Connal whispered. 'Beautiful – pink and clean – in every finger-tempting rib of flesh and lovely crease. I had not known there could be so much texture in this delectable place.'

The Prior sighed and nodded. 'Nature surely rendered it for kissing.'

Iroise's belly shivered as the next shiny cob of bread was lifted and pressed against her split. Her young master's fingers were trembling with aroused excitement. Every tiny, tickling touch stirred rippling beads of pleasure. The tip of his dangling little finger pressed against her anus and made her moan. The nose of the cob, which had partly opened her, gently pulled away. 'You can see inside her. Oh.' She felt it nosing back; this time, the smooth, rounded top was pressed between her lips and held. 'Close your thighs,' he urged. And when she did, the pressure felt so strange, so focused, as if she were sitting with her cunny clasping the shiny top of his boot. He lowered her to her knees once more.

Dom Enken was keeping Saronam on tiptoes with the thin stem of the crop arched into the crease of her buttocks. While her bare breasts pressed upwards into the corner of the wall, he was interrogating her. Then he said, 'Prior, she informs me that you have a girl with breasts that are fuller yet.'

'Chloe – but she is pregnant.'

Iroise shuddered. Connal briefly closed his knees about her midriff, under her breasts. Then he gently turned her head and kissed her, slipping his hand down her belly, barely touching the skin. His trembling fingertips slid into the nude join of her legs, found her sheathed clitoris and knew what it did. Her legs closed tighter about the shiny hard cob. He asked her, had she kissed Chloe? He drew

91

back her sheath and her clitoris came out, moist and naked, pressing against the shiny crust of the cob in tiny, uneven pulses which she could not control and which made her whimper into her young master's mouth.

The Prior and Dom Enken were already discussing the arrangements for the two visitors' meeting with Chloe. Dom Enken wanted to know how advanced her pregnancy was and what restrictions her condition might impose for tutor play and pleasure. 'One danger is of course already averted,' Iroise heard the Prior answer.

Connal was examining Iroise's punished bottom. 'You enjoyed it when Dom Enken used the crop?'

'My bottom hurt and burnt. It burns, still,' she whispered, meekly. She closed her eyes and shivered while Connal touched its cheeks. In her mind she was reliving the night of the flagellant: the delicious lashing that had come between her legs while she lay trussed open on his table; the stinging fire upon the outside, throbbing pleasure deep within; and afterwards, where the Prior had touched her flesh so gently, a soft sweet tingling ache. Connal's fingertips traced the new marks across her buttocks and dallied in the crease. He made her erection come that way – like she guessed it might come for a man. She heard his breathing deepen with arousal as he encountered the hot, small crater of flesh pushed back and deepened by the pressure of the cob against her open split. Her head sank sideways; her lips pressed against his burning erection trapped against his belly. She ran her teeth down its underside through the cloth, flattening the fleshy veinlike tube that carries semen to the tip. Connal gasped and lifted her up in a bundle, with her knees tucked up and her thighs together and the cob still trapped between them. He exposed her breasts by thrusting the crumpled mendicant's gown up to her armpits then he sucked her nipples while Dom Enken turned Saronam around and held her swollen breasts high and asked the Prior if Chloe's breasts had reached the stage of yielding milk.

'My kinsmen have not sought to obtain it.'

'Then my visit may prove timely.'

Connal continued to stimulate Iroise's breasts. The pressure of the bunched-up cloth above them made them change shape, necking, their weight gathered at the ends. He opened her thighs and the cob adhered to her moist inner flesh. 'It's half inside you.' He tried to stretch her labia more open until she moaned and attempted to stop him. Then he lifted her and started eating her bread. Her legs dangled over his shoulders; her arms flopped, doll-like, backwards to the floor; her manipulated, weighted breasts overhung her cloth until her nipples nearly touched her ear lobes. Dom Enken paused from what he was doing to Saronam in order to watch. The pressure spreading Iroise's split suddenly weakened; she felt her stretched labia curl inwards and collapse. The last wisps of white and fragments of crust trickled over her belly and breasts as Connal sucked her cunny. Then he lowered her body gently and stared at her tattoo. He did not ask how she had gotten it, but each time that softened lip collapsed, he reopened it. His fingertips kept straying over its inside surface, causing shivers. He asked her if it hurt. She shook her head. He asked her if anyone had whipped it and she told him about the flagellant-master. She felt his erect penis come stiffer beneath her. She wanted to touch it, to bite it properly, in its soft underside, when it was naked. He took Saronam's little flagon and made Iroise spread her legs. 'Wide. Wide,' he whispered. 'Wide as if two tethers are pulling.' Her cunny opened. Small drips of Saronam's liquor plummeted all the way down inside her, in little heavy thumps against her womb. He closed her flesh again, infolding one lip – pushing it inside – then stretching the other across, slipping his palm inside her crotch, pressing down gently but firmly, holding her thus until her own slight stickiness sealed her. The feeling – the hand, firm and warm, bridging the sensitive tops of her inner thighs, fitting tightly between them – was deeply sexual. And the warm breath of Saronam's mead was seeping inside her.

'I need to take her to bed,' Connal said.

'It is only afternoon,' Dom Enken answered, grudgingly.

'What say you?' Connal whispered to Iroise.

He kissed her slowly, while his hand was still between her thighs. And he kept it there while he drew the mendicant's gown completely off her.

'Kin-Cague will see you to a comfortable room,' the Prior said. Then he glanced through the window, beyond which two figures were moving swiftly closer over the boardwalk.

The door opened and the flagellant-master entered, ushering before him a pretty girl, breathing quickly as if she had not been able to keep up with his pace or as if he had forced her to run. The girl's hair was short and straight and copper-coloured, her face small and pixielike, her limbs lithe, her belly heavily pregnant. Her elbows were pinned behind her, which thrust her gravid breasts outwards. They looked hard, and they shuddered when she stumbled as he thrust her further into the room. The surrounds of her nipples were large and black.

'Dom Enken,' said the Prior, 'I feel that your questions about Chloe are about to be answered.'

Connal wanted to keep Iroise naked but Kin-Cague, intercepting them soon after the entrance to the Priory proper, insisted that, in the corridors and public spaces, her nakedness be covered. 'Even when we brought her in, a homeless waif, we wrapped her in a blanket,' he whispered, wistfully. His words pierced her with guilt. She looked at him forlornly and tried to hide her nakedness behind her young master, who stared defiantly at the dignified kinsman. Iroise, wanting no bitterness between them, tugged at her young master's coat. Connal cast her habit casually about her shoulders, hiding nothing. Kin-Cague was affronted. Iroise knew not what to do. She tried to put on the gown until her young master froze her with a cruel stare. 'Get upstairs!' he hissed. She glanced one soulful glance of supplication at Kin-Cague. Connal took it as a further betrayal. He ripped the gown away and left her shivering, starkly naked. 'Shall I have to tell you yet again!' The cord, stripped from the gown, lashed diagonally across her body. 'Go!'

Kin-Cague did not intervene. Iroise started running up the stairs, blindly, knowing only that she was naked and reviled and that all the gentleness that had gone before accrued to nothing. Through her tears she glimpsed Dariun's face – Dariun, the young kinsman who had comforted her on that first night. He was startled and concerned – he shouted after her – but Iroise kept running, running, finally bursting through a door that might have been the one Kin-Cague had mentioned to her master.

There was a bed and she flung herself upon it, burying her face in the pillow and awaiting retribution, which came swiftly. Her wrists were tied up to the corners of the bed; her breasts hung down; her legs were wrenched open.

From beyond the door, Kin-Dariun paled at the sound of the lashing, which did not stop, despite her pleas for mercy. He ran downstairs and sought assistance from the senior kinsman. 'Hurry!' he cried. When at last Kin-Cague had reached the door the only emanating sounds were murmurs of instruction and subdued sobs of pleasure.

Kin-Cague shook his head. 'We cannot intervene when a conjunction is in progress. However uncouth, he is a guest – an influential one, at that – and Iroise was willing.'

'No.' Dariun's countenance was deeply furrowed with concern.

'Dariun. Desire is a strange mistress to a young girl. I have seen this many times and know that it is not for us to try to obstruct the tide of a pleasure that we may not understand, however much we may dread its flow. Go about your duties, kinsman. I will keep watch. But I cannot interfere.'

Kin-Cague had long to wait, but he waited. When the lashing restarted he was grateful that Dariun was out of earshot: the kinsman was young and impulsive. Kin-Cague tried not to close his eyes for it was then that he could picture her most. She was the most beautiful creature he had ever beheld. In the woods, his heart had soared when he had seen her. And on the stairs just now he had watched her, lithely, beautifully running. His confrontation with the truculent young male was as much Kin-Cague's own doing – the shock, the surge of jealous lust at seeing her naked and aroused because her man was so urgent in his need to take her to bed.

Footsteps sounded within the room. Kin-Cague retreated into the shadow of an alcove. The young male emerged, dishevelled, still putting on his jacket. He glanced up and down the corridor and then disappeared in the direction of the stairs.

Kin-Cague crept into the bedroom. The scent of her body hung like musky nectar in the air; he could hear her strained breathing; she was blindfold. Her naked body hung face down on the bed, tethered at the wrists and arching downwards in a curve as if draped like a chain. Her legs were tethered open, her ankles fastened to the bottom corners of the bed. Marks of a belt cauterised her bottom and thighs. The muscle of her anus had been forced.

Kin-Cague moved swiftly to the bed. When he pulled her blindfold down, her silken blonde locks brushed his fingers and her eyes blinked tightly shut.

'Refasten it, please.' Standing at the door was Dom Enken. Bundled in his arms, her wrists draped languorously around his neck, was the pregnant, naked Chloe.

10

Examining Chloe

'Kinsman, take her from me,' Dom Enken said, 'and I shall see to Iroise.' Chloe was sluggishly unwilling to let go of the tutor-monk's neck. She was like a kitten clinging to her master.

'What drug have you given her?' Kin-Cague asked, suspiciously. Chloe came to him more readily when she realised she would still be held. Her cheeks were flushed.

'Nothing that will harm.' Already Dom Enken was with Iroise, testing the reinstatement of her blindfold.

Kin-Cague, still distrustful of the Tormunite intruder, put the back of his hand to Chloe's forehead, under her fringe of copper hair. 'Are you all right?' he whispered. Chloe nodded, but her dilated gaze stared bewilderedly about the bedroom. It was not certain she had even noticed Iroise. Kin-Cague carried her to the armchair and sat with her in his arms.

Though her belly was so bloated, her body was yet slight, as girls in that state sometimes go, when all the resources of sustenance become focused into womb and breasts. Her nipples had recently been stimulated or used in some way: oily wetness was distributed about them in the velvet blackness of the surround but these smears were not the simple vagaries of leakage. The nipples appeared stretched and necked, bearing generous bulbs like rose hips but softer.

'What did he give you?' Kin-Cague whispered against her soft warm ear lobe. The soft clean fragrance of her copper hair was like a breath of youthful spring.

'He put something between my legs,' Chloe murmured. 'What was it?'

'I don't know. It disappeared. It was like a wafer but it melted into me. Afterwards, it felt nice.'

Her sex was beautifully naked, after the Tormunite fashion. The inner lips were well extended and half open though the outer lips were tight. Her baby was carried high and to the front. Her umbilicus protruded and the dark centre-line had developed down her belly, like a suture. Elsewhere her skin bore a delicate translucency; her breasts were indulgently distended. She was comely in body and warm and welcoming of heart. It was hard to imagine why her former master would so wantonly have allowed his men to put her into this state of swelling – an indiscretion proscribed even by Tormunite mores.

Both girls were beautiful: it seemed the Tormunites singled out the most precious beauties and the most generous, loving hearts for their reckless depredations. Chloe snuggled to his chest, her wide eyes watching the blindfold Iroise. Chloe's breasts rose and fell gently with her breathing. Kin-Cague asked her if Dom Enken had used a breast pump on her nipples.

'How did you know?' she murmured, still intent on Iroise.

'I just wondered.' He took her left nipple very gently between his fingers. It felt so beautiful and soft yet fat and when he pressed – squeezing its narrow neck and pulling – there was a delicious hardness underneath, a core of flesh or gland that felt charged as if to bursting point. Chloe murmured and opened her lips and beautiful liquid like melted butter issued on to his fingers. Under his gown, his flesh was coming hard; control was weakening, yet to have so sweet and sensual a girl within his lap and so relaxed in body, with nipple leaking into his fingers, was an experience that defied control. 'I can feel it swelling,' Chloe murmured nonchalantly, snuggling closer, putting her bursting belly nearer to his penis. He put his finger along her dark centre-line.

'Why is her bottom open?' she whispered.

'It is what a man does to a girl, sometimes.'

'You did it to her?'

'No. The visiting young master did.'

'Why does it stay open?'

'If the penetration is prolonged and keen, the girl's muscle may temporarily weaken.'

'She cannot get with child that way?'

'No.'

'Why does Dom Enken touch and then stop?'

'Iroise is Tantalite.' Kin-Cague then explained. Chloe listened with great interest. Each time Iroise began to moan as the pleasure became too intense and near, Chloe held her breath. Kin-Cague put his hand between her legs and stroked his thumb gently against the place where the inner lips met, measuring the stroking against her breathing.

'Her bottom is closing – look,' said Chloe.

'The continued stimulation overwhelms the pleasure centres; when you touch one place, the other knows and responds.'

'In compassion?' Chloe whispered.

He nodded and kissed her very gently on the lips. She responded by holding his fingers closer to her belly. His penis ached. Again he took to toying with her nipple, using his free hand; his fingertips simulated the pulling and squeezing action of a baby's lips, though more slowly and softly. She slid her thumb into her mouth. Melted butter began to be issued again between his fingers. The soft rose hip of nipple flesh turned slippery. He milked a little more keenly. The substance of her breast seemed to gather and tremble. She stopped sucking but her thumb stayed in her mouth. Then her lovely eyes defocused, flickered, and he felt something like a stumbling heartbeat inside the warm soft flesh between her legs, which tightened deliciously round his fingers until that swollen shiny belly looked as if it would split. The slippery rose hip in his fingers turned hard and very wet; he put his lips there and kissed it and the milk of her despoiled innocence tasted delicious. She shuddered as her rose hip squirted into his mouth, warm and watery and weakly sweet.

'Oh, you are beautiful: how could your master ever have abandoned one so beautiful as you?' She buried her face against his breast and wrapped her arms around him and her breast milk seeped through his gown.

Dom Enken had unfastened Iroise's arms. He had placed a pillow under her breasts but had kept her ankles fastened open. She was still blindfold. He was questioning her in a low drone, sometimes sitting on the bed beside her, sometimes dragging her body a little further up the bed to keep the tension in her legs and the roundness in her buttocks. There was mention of a lady. Sometimes, Dom Enken's fingers would slide under Iroise's belly from the side – testing her erection – and her buttocks would rise and tighten and she would begin moaning.

Gradually, Chloe's inquisitiveness forced her to turn her face to watch. Kin-Cague stroked her fragrant hair. Her back was lovely, naked, delicately curved, enticing to the fingers. Her belly lay, a warm fat weight, against his swollen penis, separated from it only by the thickness of his gown.

'What is he doing to her?' Chloe whispered, enthralled.

Dom Enken had made Iroise open again in the stretched place that had nearly closed. He was holding a broad silk ceremonial sash. Iroise's arms were gripping the pillow and her back was deeply hollowed. The monk began inserting the sash into the gape of her bottom. Her toes tightened up. Chloe began to squirm.

'I think he means to clean her of her master's issue,' Kin-Cague whispered. But the manner of execution was far more profound than was necessary for ablution. From what little could be overheard of the questions and whispered answers, it seemed to represent a re-enactment of some incident from her past.

Chloe strained to listen. 'Who's Olivia?' she whispered. Kin-Cague shook his head. Chloe's eyes almost popped as the sash pushed deeper. She leant forwards, inviting Kin-Cague to touch her in the lovely cleft of her buttocks, which in Chloe was nearly black – whether through pregnancy, he did not know – and the mouth of her bottom was shinily smooth and pouting. The sash in

Iroise's bottom started twisting, curling up in fat, slack knots as it was being pushed inside. Kin-Cague rubbed Chloe's pouting exposed rim in a circle until she caught her breath. Then her thumb went into her mouth and she settled on her side against him, to feel, watch and listen.

The sash was long. Dom Enken continued silently with the exorcism. He stared pointedly at Chloe, making her shiver and hide her face. Yet she encouraged Kin-Cague's fingers to continue touching. He started patting the pleasure centre of the pouting rim.

The penetration of Iroise was complete. The distension of her bottom had made her open at the front.

Three swift erratic pulses shook the mouth of Chloe's bottom. The kinsman sat her up, so his thumb went inside, a little way. He curled the thumb over to the front, and now her body was hooked upon it and she could go nowhere, even should someone try to lift her. He told her so and she began breathing quickly: the thought and actuality of sexual pinioning aroused her. He smacked her partly open sex while she was pinioned by her bottom, and the intimate shock of this molestation awakened feelings that must have lain dormant but, once empowered, were intemperate. He tried to retreat from the encounter but Chloe pursued him. Her hand slid under his gown and took hold of his burning penis with a self-assurance he had not expected. She laid it bare against her naked belly; he thought he felt movement inside her.

The coiled sash came out of Iroise, its spirals glistening with Connal's copious issue. Dom Enken brought it across. Chloe grasped it lewdly in her fingers, her belly bulging down between her knees, her inverted umbilicus touching the tip of Kin-Cague's erection like a teat.

Dom Enken spoke directly to Chloe. 'I want you to be present when Iroise is taken down to the vaults.' Chloe sat there, licking the silvery trails from her fingers, not understanding the full weight of his words, but looking proud when he knotted the moist sash over her shoulder and between her breasts. Then he stood behind her, pinning her arms back and lifting them until her heavy breasts rolled wide apart and her back hollowed deeply. Her belly pressed shinily hard against the underside of the kinsman's naked penis. Up and back, Dom Enken continued to draw her arms until she gasped and the blades of her shoulders separated, stretching the skin like erupting wings. Her breasts bobbed with every little jerk that shuddered through her; her nipples tightened like threatened, soft-bodied sea creatures. Kin-Cague grasped them softly in each hand; milk issued down his arms.

Dom Enken drew Chloe backwards then slipped between her legs a resinous yellow translucent wafer, pressing it against the moist female opening until the wafer collapsed and infolded. Then he lifted her upright and Kin-Cague set her body gently sideways so her legs overhung the soft arm of the chair. Between her thighs he could see the protruding edges of the folded wafer. She was already trembling with the anticipation of what it would do. Kin-Cague put a fingertip there. 'No,' she protested. 'Ohh.' He was pressing the edge of the wafer very gently and her fingertips reached out, not to stop him, but to touch his face and chin, as a blind person would. 'Oooh.' Her head sank back and she was coming in little shudders transmitted through the wafer's edge to his fingers. The skin of her bursting breasts looked so stretched and thinned that the veins made a web of delicate blue lines under their surface. He tapped the edge of her wafer until it collapsed: the part inside her had already dissolved into the sensitive inner flesh. In his fingertips, he could feel nothing but the faintest tingle and now the protruding selvage of wafer which had come free from the luscious lips which had completely softened and almost felt semi-liquid. 'Hold me,' Chloe murmured, sinking against him, kissing his neck. She wriggled down his body and sought his naked penis again, clasping it in her fist. Her breathing steadied and her eyes refocused upon Iroise. Her thumbnail pressed into the underside of his penis.

'What is the tutor doing?' she asked.

'He's putting in a ring.' It was a large, polished steel ring, about the size of a man's palm and as thick as a stout bootlace.

'Will he put a ring in me?'

'Iroise already has a piercing.' But Kin-Cague had not answered in full because he did not know what practices the tutor-monk might use on pregnant girls. So he reached beneath and nipped the very place – the perineum – between his fingers, holding it until she gasped. Then he slid the fine twiglike selvage of remaining wafer all the way through her little circular anal pout and followed it with the first joint of his thumb which bent forwards and, once again, gently pinioned her bottom. When Chloe's second climax had been delivered, Iroise was already standing on the bed and Dom Enken was preparing her for going. He resecured her blindfold, tied her wrists behind her, then lifted her down and led her stumbling to the door. Before he left he nodded to the kinsman.

'Am I going too?' Chloe whispered nervously, as Kin-Cague lowered her gently to her knees.

'Dom Enken said you would be needed.' He unknotted the damp sash from her body. When he began to bind it round her eyes she acceded, holding her head up bravely. 'Are you afraid?' he asked.

Her fringe of straight hair shook. 'But stay with me, Kin-Cague.' Blindly, she reached for his hands, then kissed his fingers. He could not bring himself to tell her that whatever befell would be beyond his paltry jurisdiction. So he leant forwards and, taking her beautiful elfin face in his hands, planted light kisses all over it.

Iroise, driven onwards by Dom Enken, padded barefoot and blindfold along the corridor, her hands fastened behind her, her bottom stretched and burning, the cold steel ring weighing down between her legs. He did not guide her properly. On the stairs she was terrified of tripping. She managed to edge herself to the inner side and tried to press herself against the wall; her breast, knee and forehead kept grazing the stone. 'Don't dislodge your blindfold,' Dom Enken warned, severely. Then the wall suddenly changed to balustrade and there was no contact possible above her middle. Her legs were jelly, her footsteps insecure. She started to sob. The sobbing echoed.

'Get on. Don't try my patience.' Every time she took a step down, the sloping balustrade receded further. She heard loud voices approaching from below then footsteps clattering up the stairs. She stumbled, cried out and banged her knees. And, suddenly, there was no support and she was toppling over the edge.

At the very last instant, a strong hand clenched the tether between her wrists. The top of the balustrade smacked against her belly. Her steel ring clattered against the edge. Her wobbling breasts and reeling head overhung the dreadful drop. Her toes clawed the shiny floor of the landing for grip. She heard gasps of excitement.

'The ring's standing up. Oh God. Will you look at it. Sweet fuck that she is,' a voice resonated.

'Who is she?' another asked.

'Mine! Get up, girl, get your belly on there, now! Help me with her.' Hands clasped her thighs, hauling them open, hauling her higher. She shuddered as her toes left the floor and the cold steel of the pushed-up ring, thrust ever backwards by the edge of the balustrade, pulled against the piercing and pressed into the furrow of her buttocks. 'Get it up against her bottom, hard against the mouth.' She gasped when it touched there. 'Now get your hand under, lad – get hold of her clit.'

'It's sticking out. Sweet fuck. Oh, God. And it's moving. Look, her legs. The little bitch is in heat.'

'Get her cheeks open.' A hand pressed the ring against her anus. 'I need a cloth – a bandanna – something. Quick!'

Her blindfold was dragged off; the tiled floor far below her swayed giddily. Men in unkempt uniform were rushing across it. Iroise moaned and shuddered: the fingertips were still tormenting her knob. Then, she felt the ends of the bandanna being pushed inside her, round the rim of the steel ring, pushing ever tighter, one side then the other, dry cloth against her insides, ring against the mouth of her bottom, thumb-thrusts making her want to come.

'Clench it! Clench it!' The strong hand started slapping her buttocks until the muscle tightened hard.

'Stand her up. No. Round this way. On her knees. Oh, yes.'

It stood straight up like a sun-bronzed pillar. Her lips were forced against it just above the swollen sac. Meaty maleness steeped in the scent of unwashed girls assailed her nostrils.

'Your men are early, Captain,' Dom Enken smiled grotesquely.

The great hand encompassed the back of her skull just as if it were an egg being squeezed to the point of cracking. The leather boot-tip toed her cunny open. The toe was too wide to go inside her. The shiny tip persisted cruelly. Iroise shuddered; her arms were still fastened behind her. Her lips kept sucking until the toe-tip thrust her backwards on to the floor. Her steel ring stood erect between her legs, pulling on the tie pushed up her bottom. 'Lie down,' her ravager ordered. 'Legs straight.' She shivered. The ring stood stiffer; the lips of her open cunny collapsed around it, the cheeks of her bottom settled against the cold tiles and the pulling in her bottom worsened. The giant hand reached down and grasped her steel ring that was fastened through her flesh.

'Oh no, no,' she begged.

'Then open properly,' the Captain demanded, pitilessly. 'White thighs. Gurian, whip them.'

Dom Enken offered his crop. While it was being done, the Captain stared about him. 'Not a bad billet, brother?'

'I take it your company is not of our persuasion?' Dom Enken replied.

'If your persuasion is of gold, then, yes,' the Captain laughed.

'There is the matter of the Prior.'

'The Prior is already under close arrest, as my lady has dictated.' The Captain stared down at the sobbing Iroise. 'Enough, Gurian.' He intercepted the hand that was whipping. Then he crouched between her punished thighs. 'She cannot sit with this ring in place?'

'That is partly the intention.'

'And what's the rest?'

'To put her to the Wheel,' Dom Enken sighed.

'For breaking?' The Captain curled his fingers round her steel ring. She began to close her trembling thighs until he shook his head threateningly.

'In a manner of speaking, yes,' Dom Enken answered.

The Captain waved the crop slowly above her cunny. Shivering, Iroise closed her eyes and spread until her cunny, bisected by the pushed-up ring, gaped in lewd submission.

'Servulan's mark – so the Baron has already been here. Let me greet him,' the Captain said coldly, whipping inside her genital flaps to each side of the standing ring.

Chloe was bundled in Kin-Cague's arms. The door to the woods was blocked by a soldier in a ragged jacket. Kin-Cague turned back in desperation. But the game was up: kinsmen were already being herded into the yard. The girls were being separated. Any feeble protests were beaten down. The Prior was manhandled into the open by two soldiers.

Suddenly, in the distance, the main gates were flung wide. A carriage clattered through the arches and came to a halt almost in front of Kin-Cague. The door, emblazoned with the Cross of Tormunil, was opened and a lady in a pale grey hooded gown alighted, refusing assistance from her footgirl. She bore a short, straight, red cane with gold ferrules. Her gaze fixed upon Kin-Cague and the naked Chloe, then took in the gathering crowd of dazed onlookers, as a liveried horseman began reading a proclamation.

In the brief delivery of its threats – 'wardship', 'annexation', 'transfer of control'– and its charges – 'indoctrination', 'immurement', 'despoilment of nubility' – the kinsmen's tiny empire crumbled to a greater will. 'Behold your new Prioress,' the horseman declared.

The Prior turned ashen. Kinsmen edged away from him. No one would look at him but Kin-Cague. The pale lady stepped between them, turned her back on the Prior and faced Kin-Cague, still bearing Chloe in his arms.

'Kinsman, perhaps you should set the girl down. You seem a mite breathless,' she said. 'I trust this does not reflect your contribution to her pot-bellied state.' Then she pointed the red cane at Chloe's swollen belly and raised her voice, 'If anyone should doubt that intervention was sorely needed, then the answer lies here. Within your hallowed walls of "pre-Tormunite values", the most basic tenet of female usage has been violated, flagrantly and beyond redemption.'

'But . . .'

'Silence! I want them all examined – every girl – before the others get here, lest the taint has spread. Any hopeless cases shall be brought to me.'

11

The Prioress

'My lady,' the footgirl announced, 'the postulants who
arrived in the night are rested and ready. Dom Enken is
with them.'

'Good. Our audience with the errant Prior – cancel it.
Let him simmer.'

'Ma'am. He was asking again about his writing desk.'

'He can have it. And his diaries – rows of tosh.'

The Prioress flung the louvred doors wide. 'Laxness and
lubricity. We need a breath of air here. My girls will bring
it.'

'The gardens are pretty,' the footgirl whispered.

The Prioress withered her with an icy gaze. 'You think
so?'

The girl nodded uneasily.

'Then I shall hold you responsible if anything in my
garden is amiss. Now get out.'

'Ma'am.' The girl retreated, chastened.

In the chapter house, which was more airy and refreshing,
the Prioress, able at last to relax, removed the rings from
her narrow fingers one by one, starting with the little
finger, working round to the forefinger, the left hand then
the right, taking care not to damage her manicure –
pausing only when a soft murmur escaped a girl's lips –
and placing the rings in their individually sculpted receptacles beside the porringer of warm aromatic oil on the
alabaster pedestal table. Then she dipped her fingertips

into the bowl as she looked around the circle of unspoilt, untasted, youthful, anxious, softly feminine beauties – the flower of her new demesne. Muted sounds of punishment drifted down the stairway, bestowing the sweet gift of fear upon those soft-eyed countenances. One girl – the chosen one – was standing below the Tormunite icon newly hanging from the pillar that was to become her pillar.

The tutor-monk, Dom Enken, sat next to the girl. She had eyebrows denser and blacker than any other girl in the room. Her eyelids were languid, the lashes soft, the eyes closed. Her breathing had that unsteady yet hypnotic slightness which at any second – without warning, like the direction of a dream – might change and shatter, as when the chasm suddenly opens out below the dreamer and the dreamer abruptly drops. It was as if every face understood the imminence of this chasm, as if every girl were balanced there.

The standing girl with black hair suddenly lifted herself very slightly – one heel left the floor – and her hand descended, the fingers arched, lightly pressing on Dom Enken's shoulder. Her head bowed as if she were swooning, mouth aspirating gently, 'Nnnmmh . . . Nnhh,' then even less distinctly, making small, soft, pleading sounds. The stirrings of sexuality in a girl were quite delicious. The monk caressed her and instructed her gently, then her heel pressed back to the floor and her body gradually straightened. Then his fingers slid out moistly from the right leg of her knickers.

He began to unfasten them.

The Prioress took her hand from the bowl and dried it on the towel. The girl beside her was visibly shaking. 'What is it, my dear?' the Prioress whispered, moving aside the pedestal table. The girl began to cry silently. Perhaps she was fractious from her journey. The Prioress moved across to the bench where she was sitting then lifted her delicate chin.

What is it about tears? Is it the tears themselves – the tangible yield of expressed liquid – or is it the sweet signal of submission of the will? Or is it – shining through the fear

– the arousal that even tears cannot dispel? The Prioress's thumbs swept down the tear marks on the soft young cheeks. Her fingers unhitched the middle two buttons of the blouse, exposing all the intimation that she needed: the flawless smoothness of those breasts was crowned by tumid tips of puckered velvet that responded to the fleshy pads of testing fingers, to the soft scratches of manicured nails. The Prioress allowed the velvet tips to trace warm soft lines along the coolness of her inner arm. When the dark girl's crisis was again impending, she helped her own initiate up from the bench and drew her knickers down – as a Prioress sometimes must – and gently stroked her inner thigh. And she could feel it there, all the arousal, in the tight, trembling surface of virgin skin. So she slipped her fingers into the bowl of oil and let them soften while the girl stood next to her, shakingly waiting.

The dark girl had been allowed to sit. Her clitoris was being nipped to coax it out and she was moaning.

The Prioress then asked the girl standing beside her to raise her skirt at the back. 'All the way,' she whispered. The tears began flowing. 'Now make a hollow with your back, as deep as you can.' And it was deep indeed, that girlish hollow. 'Now lift your skirt up at the front,' she whispered and, naked from the breasts down, the girl really understood how to hold that hollow. Her belly arched down to the level of her bottom, her sex projected back between her legs – almost as if she had already paid the price of sin and was pregnant. But her cherry was still unbroken.

The Prioress's fingers emerged from the oil and brushed the protruding pubic lips – they were already pendent, not hard, but weighted and were warmer than the oil. The testing fingers were curious about the girlish anus: how elastic it might be; how deep a pleasure the girl might suffer; the extent to which she would disguise or display it; the effect upon her climax and upon her tears. As the oil was being rubbed into her labia, her anal ring moved gently; it was a perfect spiral, swirling tighter, then pulsing, but with no clear pattern, however smoothly the Prioress rubbed her.

The dark-haired girl lay on her back on a small bench placed at right angles to her pillar. Dom Enken was tying her cuffed ankles to waist-high rings on each side of the pillar. Her blouse was open, rucked up her back and her breasts were fully exposed.

The Prioress asked her initiate to remove her skirt completely. Then she made her sit knickerless. The lovely girl sat forwards on the bench. When asked to sit back, she glanced down, afraid she might stain the leather. 'A cunny must acclimatise to contact with its new surrounds,' the Prioress whispered. She therefore made her sit astride the bench, making her spread her knees out sideways, '. . . as far as they will go,' she said. They went far indeed: her pubes stood out from her belly. When the Prioress touched the lips, they opened. She could see the delightful clitoris trembling. Very carefully she lifted across the bowl of oil.

'Put your hands behind you on the bench. And lean on them.' The open pubic lips made a small enclosure with the seat. Against this, into it, the Prioress poured the oil to make a pool on the upholstery. 'Sit forwards – gently.' She watched the lovely clitoris pulsing – drinking oil, it almost seemed – then the lips spreading open and the oil being expressed. Then she took the blouse off her, leaving her the only one of the group who was completely naked. Her arousal was all the more telling. She shuddered gently when made to stand. Her labia, soft and thickened, were dripping oil on to the seat. She began to cry when the monk approached her.

But he was very gentle, making her turn to face him before applying the remainder of the oil. She stood between her two instructors, supported on their oiled hands, crying softly, legs open, sagging gently, breasts full, as if in need of milking, and her anus, now sleeved around the Prioress's probing finger, so hot and sucking and tight.

When her legs buckled, Dom Enken lowered her to her knees. He suggested that she be restrained. Once she was fastened in a kneeling posture with her hands secured behind her and breasts and sex exposed, he wiped away the oil and applied instead a tincture, using a little brush, painting it around her nipples, her labia and her anus. She began again to cry, murmuring that the pleasure hurt her. The monk took a silver ball the size of a walnut on a rod from the alabaster table and placed a drop of the tincture on the tip, then slipped it into her anus. The ball slipped swiftly, though the anus was already swelling. While she was still gasping with the shock of silvered coldness and penetrative anal pleasure, he began to twist the rod, slowly, very gently, always in the same direction. The girl began to moan and pull away; eventually the rod slipped from his fingers; he caught it and drew it slowly from her bottom and her climax started. He slid it in again and twisted it in the same direction and the climax was sustained. Within a short time he had re-aroused her. 'Leave her ball inside her,' the Prioress whispered.

She went across to the dark girl, whose ankles were above her head and cuffed to each side of the pillar. Her lovely bottom was in the air. Had they been alone, the Prioress would have disrobed to the stockings and lain between those trussed-up thighs, arching above her, splitting those luscious love-lips and seeking friction, clit to clit.

The cream was on a warming plate in two silver jugs. 'Look at me,' the Prioress whispered. Her palm pressed against the base of the spine, her thumb stroked softly in the furrow and came to rest against the velvet sump. The thumb began pumping it like a heartbeat. 'Lovely little back door – shall you open to my soft entreaties?' As she lifted up the jug of cream, the breasts shuddered beautifully; the little door burst open and the thumb slid gently to the knuckle. The fine stream of warm cream from the jug was directed exactly against her clitoris. It billowed under the hood. Her hips writhed slowly; her clitoris poked like a drowning worm. She began gasping; the muscle tightened delectably round the thumb, then tried to relax but failed. The stream of warm cream kept running, escaping down her belly, round her breasts, soaking her rucked-up blouse. When the first jug was empty, the Prioress took up the second, lifting it higher. The stream of liquid cream was warmer, finer. The girl was visibly coming. She was trying to escape the pleasure. Dom Enken returned and moved the bench a little further away from the column, so her legs were stretched and her bottom lifted higher. Her vulva pulsed, her anus squeezed the thumb; her breasts shook gently; the cream was running down her back. Her head slid over the edge of the bench as her hips lifted to meet the torturing stream. 'Draw the bench further out,' the Prioress urged. The girl was now supported only by her shoulders. She wriggled and gasped. When her breasts moved over the edge, the tutor-monk crouched and caught them, kneaded their slippiness, sucked their cream away as she shuddered upside down and the climax rent her body. The thumb kept urging her from inside; the cream was running down her skin, her hair was in Dom Enken's lap; her wanton lips pressing to the hot red tip of his exposed penis. His hands clasped her head in place. His voice whispered urgent encouragement as the red bulb of his penis spurted hot buttermilk upwards to her throat.

The Prioress collected from the monk the labial and body rings, then ascended stairs to the suite where the delinquents were being retrained.

In the first room, she went to the chair where the pregnant girl, Chloe, was curled up, nude, watching. She slid her fingers through Chloe's straight short copper hair. Chloe's small mouth fell submissively open – a little red maw of delicious provocation. The Prioress felt an urge to put her fingers in – to penetrate that maw, to widen and abuse it, to punish it for the deep insertions that had come between Chloe's legs to make her belly so clumsily bloated.

'You have sinned, my child – if not through intent then through complicity.' Chloe's breathing deepened. Her black-brown, fatted nipples brushed the velvet arm of the chair. The Prioress fought the urge to trap them under the heel of her hand and squeeze them into the velvet. 'You try to hide your thoroughfare of shame. Henceforth you shall not. Spread your legs and show it.' Chloe lifted her trembling thigh. 'Wider. Over the arm of the chair.' Her bursting belly shifted; her puffy-lipped vulva stood vulnerably revealed.

The Prioress turned, head to one side, as the punishment progressed, the smacks echoing from the pale blue walls and polished black marble floor. Shuddering, naked, the girl Saronam slumped across the immense four-poster bed. 'She is being punished for her narcissistic flaunting of her breasts,' the Prioress told Chloe. And while she questioned Chloe intimately about her former master and that fateful week – how many men he had put her to without protection, how they had treated her, what they had done, whether there had been commingling of their issue, how many times Chloe had come – she toyed with her between the legs, spreading the gape wider, gently trying to turn it inside out, slapping it with her fingers. Chloe, huddled deep in the bowl of her chair, her sweet cunny terrified yet deeply aroused and wantonly submissive, watched Saronam's punishment.

'Take her arms,' said the Captain to his aides. 'Hold her.' Saronam's large breasts rolled outwards, her nipples were already overfull from the prolonged masturbation and her clitoris protruded wetly. The Prioress watched the belt being unbuckled, heard it sliding from the Captain's leather-clad waist. 'Legs wide. Tongue out,' the Captain instructed.

Broad flashes of leather struck the insides of Saronam's thighs, smack upon burning smack, to left and right. She was holding her breath, with lips squeezed tightly round her thrust-out tongue, and her nipples stiffened up to points so tight they must be stinging. The Captain's eyes were dark with lust. Saronam's thighs were bright red, her nipples dark brown and wrinkled. When the first lash struck her slit, her breath burst out round her tongue and she twisted so her breasts squeezed against the bed. She was forced on to her back again with her arms pinned more tightly.

'Bend her knees,' the Captain said. He stood back. 'Further up. Wider. Get her cunt in the air.' The hand bearing the belt was lifted high.

The Prioress heard Chloe's murmur. She took her leg and gently pushed it further back along the arm of the chair, so her gaping sexual maw protruded. She clasped the nearer nipple, choking its little nipple-neck, pulling it like a fat berry. The leather smacked down between Saronam's legs. And very softly and sweetly, Chloe murmured again. Her thighs were restless against the velvet. Her clitoris protruded like a tiny cock. The Prioress directed the girl's own fingers to this place and made her hold it while the lashing of Saronam's cunt was completed. And the Prioress discovered that she did not have to touch Chloe other than by the gentle choking of her pinioned nipple, and that she could simply watch over this nude, lewd, pregnant creature whose ungainly body was twisted, whose bulbous breasts writhed gently, whose fingers were between her legs, just cosseting her moist bright bead of passion.

'Look how near she is,' the Prioress whispered. The spanking had stopped and Saronam was moaning, her belly slowly squirming, the small bronze mouth of her bottom pulsing below the weeping junction of the reddened pubic lips. She was coming – so slowly, so sweetly – as girls sometimes can, nothing touching her between the legs, and nothing caressing her but the air. 'Pin her knees apart,' the Prioress called. The clitoris seemed to reach out, then the climax came intensely because her knees were held so open. Saronam gasped through clenched teeth. Her nipples looked as if bones had been thrust up inside them. The small round mouth of her bottom jerked and squeezed.

'My lady Prioress,' said the Captain, 'the penitent awaits your pleasure.'

The Prioress approached the bed. 'Give her to your aides,' she whispered, nodding softly. 'But she must wear this.' She placed the heavy metal ring on the bed. It was a finger-thick torc with silver ball-shaped terminations at its open jaws, which could be tightened by turning a sleeve.

'Would my lady care to do the fitting?'

There was something profoundly satisfying about the execution of this simple task: the cold thick roundness of the steel against her fingers; the two accesses, reddened and distended by spanking; the insertion itself, done very gently, the ball-jaws pushed through the soft warm openings; the way Saronam's body was already responding, deliciously, as the ring was tightened, not too tightly, but firmly enough that it would not become dislodged. When the deed was done she was nude with every sexual part aroused, her one adornment this thick steel ring between her legs, sealing off the two critical accesses, yet leaving all else – lips, breasts, nipples, labia, clitoris, even the anal ring so invitingly pouted round the steel – available to be played with by the aides, freely to be kissed or licked, or enslimed with copious semen.

As the Captain turned Saronam on to her belly, the circlet of partly buried glinting metal shifted between her tight round buttocks and the inner mouth that gorged upon it momentarily swelled.

The Prioress stood awhile at the door, just watching the aides' first approach then, sighing, went out on to the wide crescentic balcony and leant on the balustrade to survey the scene below. The dark-haired one was still splayed about her pillar. A smacking was in progress: one of the other girls, hunched over the tutor-monk's knee, was being simultaneously spanked and masturbated, her knickers round her knees. Weighting her knickers down was a kitchen pestle, unglazed at the wide end, tapering at the grip. The Prioress watched Dom Enken lift it up and use it: its rough weighted bluntness worried that virgin anal muscle gently open and twirled inside. When the muscle had sufficiently softened, the instrument was drawn out and inverted. The shiny bulbous tip slid under. The tremors proved that it had found the little girlish pip of resistance at the junction of those virgin lips; the moans became specific. Then when the blunt end of the pestle was being reintroduced into her bottom, she gasped, tightened and began to squirm. The tip of the bedded pestle danced with the contractions from inside her. Dom Enken started spanking and thrust a hand beneath. The climax was beautiful – protracted, virginal yet deep. The monk continued gently to claw her cunny until the climax came again, then he stood her upright, with her knickers round her ankles and the pestle up her bottom and her labia puffed up and clothed in bright red stripy grazes from the clawing.

The Prioress turned away and continued her journey to the opposite room.

The girl – Iroise – had been fastened naked, on tiptoes, her wrists above her head, and her buttocks to the wall. Connal was sitting on a stool watching her. The young kinsman, Dariun, was kneeling on the floor, tied to the leg of the table. The Prioress had taken him under her wing: she believed that Dariun, of all the kinsmen, had the most potential for change. It had soon become apparent that he bore a torch for this sweet submissive.

The Prioress went to her. 'Blindfold her,' she instructed Connal. She went to the dressing table, picked up a rough wooden comb then crept back. Gently, she scratched it upwards underneath the girl's breasts then slowly down inside her legs. The steel ring through her piercing clattered against the comb. This ring was finer than the one in Saronam and it went through the prominent seam of skin underneath the girl's naked vulva. The Prioress stood aside that Dariun might see. His blue, blue eyes were glazed with desire. The Prioress might have kissed him, had Connal not been present. But Connal – empowered to touch while Dariun could but watch – was truly needed. On the floor between Iroise's ankles was a twisted bandanna, damp and streamlined as though drawn out of her body against tight resistance.

The Prioress took a gold scarab pin from her gown. 'Move your knees apart – only your knees,' she instructed Iroise. And when Iroise did it, she appeared the very embodiment of submission: blindfold, naked, hands bound and pressed together above her head, feet on tiptoes, everything between her legs trembling, open, the ring swinging slowly, a pulling weight. The Prioress clasped it, gently pulling down. The lovely vulva closed. The smooth side of the pin rubbed very slowly up and down the labia. Love-juice extruded from the split, ran along the pin and dripped upon her ankles. When the side of the pin touched her clitoris, she whimpered in pleasure. The Prioress held

117

it there, moving it very slightly. 'And so – you are Tantalite, I hear?' she whispered. Iroise's mouth was already open; she gasped assent, then licked her parched lips. The pin continued to rub its wet, smooth, narrow edge of metal against the hard point of her bud.

'Nnnn . . . Annh!'

'Stay with it, Iroise.'

The Prioress felt a delicious coldness descend upon her as she drew the ring downwards, stretching the labia ever tighter while gently sliding the pin back and forth across the clitoris – trying to make it vibrate – until the depraved and beautiful creature moaned. Then she took the comb to the soft inner skin of the thighs and scratched more deeply, slowly upwards, raising fine welts on each thigh, then on her belly, then up her jellied, gathered breasts.

'Your nipples,' she whispered, 'so cherry red and neat. Shall we pin them?' She drew back the sweeping sleeve of her robe and smoothed the nipples down; they sprang again and thickened. 'Connal, dear, come here, please. Hold it – this one.' He took the warm, fleshy stump between his fingers and began rolling it. Then he held it lifted while the Prioress's fingers slipped down between the submissive's legs. 'I have a whip – a cat. I would like to use it on you while you are excited. Oh, yes. Did you see it move? Let Dariun see. She feels so hot between the legs. If only you could feel it. Connal, take her ring out, please. There. Oh, God. So naked now, let me squeeze.'

The whip was small, many-stranded. The strands, of waxed sisal, had tiny angular knots along their length and were linked together in a flexible band. The whip swung back. Iroise must have heard it; she sucked in her breath and stopped breathing. The Prioress's finger pushed up into the gap between her pubic lips. It stayed against her clitoris. 'Hold her by the nipples, Connal. Right up. Her breasts must be suspended – free to swing.'

The Prioress then whipped them. The knotted strands snapped against their naked skin; the shudders of submissive pleasure took them. The whip lashed fiercely. The fingers held her nipples pinched; then the whipping stopped. The Prioress wormed the tip of her finger gently against the clitoris. Iroise groaned; her thighs jerked open; the fingertip gently withdrew and began probing her clitoral hood. Again she stopped breathing.

The Prioress took the pin to the shiny knob, rubbing gently edgewise, upwards, while pulling the rubbery labia down. Of its own accord now, one leg arched, then lifted from the floor.

'Hold her leg, please. Lift it up.' Her labia opened. The Prioress dipped her fingertip inside, pressing down and back until she felt the ring-muscle open from inside. 'It feels as if she's coming – look.' When she pulled her finger out, the coming almost happened. The Prioress would have closed her eyes were it not for the compulsion to watch every sweetly sexual flicker of resistance to the beautiful agonising feelings she knew were there: the soft dull tingle, sucking at the clitoris outside and within, where it rooted in the body; the delicious pulling in the womb; the queasy aching want of pleasure before the first true contraction struck. But that culmination did not come: she was Tantalite and once the stimulation was removed, she was able to control it from within. But, oh, the struggle: her breasts and her belly moving as she fended off illicit consummation.

The Prioress stood back and watched until the tortured stilted stirrings of legs and belly had subsided. Then, she reinserted the metal ring through Iroise's flesh and hung a small chained weight to it, set it swinging, and again took the whip to her breasts, while Connal held them by the nipples, until Iroise again almost climaxed. With eyes almost closed, the Prioress watched the small weight, tugged by the beautiful contractions, imparting tiny jolts which drew the pubic lips and hood more clingingly about the clitoris.

'Fasten her legs open. Leave her blindfolded.' It was certain Connal would go inside her once they were left alone.

The Prioress went to Dariun, unbound him from the table leg and resecured his wrists behind him, then brought him to the blindfold Iroise. 'Kiss her – there between the legs.' She took the steel ring out so his mouth could get closer. 'I want to be able to taste her on your lips.' When her fingers slid surreptitiously beneath his gown, his young cock felt harder and hotter than it had last night, when she had spanked it with her bare hand, to the point of spillage.

The loving ache was still inside the Prioress when she returned with Dariun to the other room. The smell of boisterous semen ruffled the air. She looked across to the bed, and the ache deepened. The naked aides attending Saronam moved aside. Her breasts and cheeks and belly were wet. So was her hair. Their juice was on her arms, in the creases. Between her legs, the ring that had precluded proper penetration was smeared with clots of creamy spume.

Her head still overhung the bed. This posture would have made it easier as her lovers entered, allowing her to writhe and squeeze her thighs about the thick slippery metal ring. The Prioress pictured them thus, hunched forwards tightly – satyrs, thrusting for her throat, their hanging balls astride her nose, their claws around her sex-slicked nipples.

She thanked the men and their Captain. 'Take the ring out of her and leave it here. She will need to be taken down to the vaults along with Iroise,' she said, 'for whatever it is you boys need to do.'

When they were gone, she closed the door. 'Don't look so soulful, Dariun. I wanted rid of them. Now it is only Chloe and me and you.' She slid her arms about his neck. 'Quickly. Give me your mouth. I want the taste of your Tantalite lover.' She savoured it. 'Oh, Iroise,' she murmured as his penis hardened, 'I think she knew – even through her blindfold – that it was your lips sucking her lovely quim.'

She had to untie his wrists in order to remove his habit completely. She took his shirt off too, leaving him naked in front of the pregnant girl before retying him. His penis had not gone down. She slid her hand between his tethered wrists and under from behind. His sac felt deliciously velvety and heavy. Chloe was watching it move. The Prioress clothed her in Dariun's shirt but left it unfastened. The sleeves hung down too far yet, in her pregnant state, she was curiously attractive. The smell of male sweat was on the shirt. The Prioress held up one of the smaller torc-rings for Chloe to see. 'Lie back. Open yourself – both avenues of love. Now beg me to put it in you.' Poor Chloe could not utter the words. She crouched in the bowl of her chair with her legs wide apart, fingertips between them, her toes balanced precariously on the arms. The little ball-capped jaws of the clamp went only a tiny way inside her, at front and back, yet every twist of their tightening was delicious.

'Is she not pretty like that – so swollen and so carefree of her state,' the Prioress whispered in Dariun's ear. 'How are we to cope between us?'

The footgirl, bearing the porringer and receptacles containing the mistress's rings, quietly opened the bedroom door and slipped inside. Her eyes widened as she beheld the scene: she stood stock-still but gave no other indication of the turmoil she was feeling.

Her mistress was undressed though not naked; her eyes were closed. The pregnant girl was on the floor. She wore a shirt and, between her legs, a shiny ring like a bull-ring; another ring was clamping one nipple, which was exuding milk; the young kinsman lay completely naked between the mistress and the girl.

He was on his back, his head on a cushion in the seat of the chair. The mistress wore a red silk scarf which went around her neck and supported her breasts. She was mounting his mouth with her sex. Her breasts were trembling; the muscles of her thighs were shuddering above the tightness of her bright red stockings. She was clutching his head with one hand. In the other she held the crimson, ferruled cane against the root of his throbbing penis. The pregnant girl was trying to fit one end of a thick steel torc inside him.

The mistress's waist was narrow and her naked back was long and as pale as alabaster. Her breasts were small but her hips were generously rounded. The conjunction of narrow back and fuller hips made a deep shaded hollow at the base of her spine.

Before she even realised, the footgirl was beside her mistress, staring down at that naked back and perfect hollow, which was softly changing shape. Her fingertips hesitated, then lightly descended to trace the curve of spine and nestle gently into the warm smooth hollow.

Suddenly the mistress hunched forwards, eyes tight shut, breath held, her face red, her neck veins bulging and congested. The nestling fingertips continued to stroke lightly. Her forehead touched the back of the chair; the kinsman started groaning, his chest arching upwards in stabbing jerks as the mistress rode his mouth. His penis stood like a curving bone. The pregnant girl between his legs struggled to tighten the clamp that gripped inside his body and under his balls. The penis started to ejaculate when she tried to kiss it. Startled, she did not know how to deal with it properly, how deeply to take it, whether to suck it or just put a seal about it with her lips. Her pupils were dilated with excitement and fear. Her mouth was filling up. When the issue stopped, she pulled away tentatively and shut her eyes and swallowed.

The mistress's languid gaze turned upon the girl who had dared to touch her. 'For a callow footgirl with under three days' service, we find you presumptuous, Rhislin,' she whispered.

12

Into the Vaults

The drained and naked young kinsman lay on the floor with the pregnant girl still ministering to him with her tongue. But the Prioress ignored them and continued to stare at Rhislin. 'I confess, I am unsure what to make of you.'

'Ma'am?' Rhislin responded.

'I stop on the road and you appear out of the night. Then my Captain intercepts you, hanging around the carriages of girls and asking questions.'

'I was seeking work.'

'Are you on the run?'

'Not now, mistress.'

'You know that, for your effrontery just now, I could have you whipped?'

'Yes, mistress. I am very sorry. I don't know how it happened. But when I looked at you, I could not stop myself. You looked so –'

'Silence!' Yet even as she scolded, the pupils of her eyes were still dilated. Rhislin's gaze descended meekly, gliding past her mistress's belly – a lovely rounded alabaster whiteness with its tuft of glistening pale brown curly hair – then turned demurely to the side. Then she felt the Prioress's fingertips above her collar, stroking under her ear lobe, making shivers.

'Is Dom Enken still downstairs?' the Prioress whispered.

'There was no one there,' Rhislin replied. 'He took the girls with him.'

'I want you to find him and tell him he is needed in the vaults. And you are needed too.'

A gnawing pain came in Rhislin's belly as she stood in the clearing by the pool. The fish still basked in the shallows but the only signs of Iroise's presence were the charred remains of the fire, and the tethers still attached to the tree. She was in the Priory somewhere, perhaps hidden by the dissident kinsmen. But apart from Iroise herself, there was no one whom Rhislin could trust. She must bide her time, listen, and be cautious in enquiry.

When she turned round, a tall, stooped, grey-haired figure was watching her from across the clearing. When he approached and peered at her, Rhislin stood her ground.

'Fishing?' he asked, though there was patently no fishing line in her hands.

She shook her head guardedly. 'I was looking for Dom Enken. Do you know him?'

'Who does not?' He was staring at the remains of the fire. 'My name is Kin-Cague. You are with our new Prioress?' he frowned.

She nodded.

Suddenly he cocked his head on one side. 'Dogs – did you hear them?'

Rhislin started; her heartbeat quickened.

Kin-Cague listened, then sighed. 'Perhaps I was mistaken – it happens all too easily these days.'

Rhislin stared up at him with deepening suspicion.

'I'll be getting along, now. Good to meet you ... Mistress ... ?'

Rhislin, now far too wary to admit even her name, only nodded.

'By the way, your friend is in the dormitory.'

'What friend?' she asked in dismay.

'Why, your tutor friend, Dom Enken. Who else were you seeking?'

Rhislin was still smarting from this confrontation when she crept into the dormitory. It took a while for her to absorb fully what was happening, but when she did, her cheeks, already flushed, began burning. The novices had been put to bed though not to rest. The nuns had arrived. The torments that Rhislin had earlier glimpsed in the chapter house were continuing in variant form.

There were about a dozen occupied beds. Tall heavy curtains excluded most of the light of afternoon. Candles burned in a row down the centre of the dormitory. A nun of mature years sat at the far end with a girl who seemed more restive than the others. Like all the girls, she lay face down, her naked body covered from the midriff by a single sheet. The nun seemed to be tensioning the tethers at the girl's feet. Rhislin remained with her back against the door, her fingertips pressed against its wooden panels. Then a girl – the second from the right – began murmuring and moving.

'Help her.' The nun silently mouthed the words across the room.

Curiosity overcame foreboding and Rhislin moved cautiously to the bedside. The girl was lain with her cheek upon the pillow. She had short blonde hair. Leather thongs – tight as bowstrings – extended from under the lower edge of the sheet. Rhislin gently rolled it up. What she saw there made her shudder: the thongs weren't attached to the girl's ankles or legs; they went up her bottom and cunny. The urge to touch the lovely sensitive places where the taut strings went inside the girl was compelling.

Suddenly the door opened. A sharp-faced nun entered. 'What are you doing here?' she hissed.

Rhislin tried to explain.

'Dom Enken has been called away. He's with the Prioress in the vaults.'

'Can you direct me?'

'Find them yourself.'

'You're late,' the Prioress whispered. 'The soldiers have been dismissed. They took Saronam. But I wouldn't allow them this one.'

'Ma'am,' Rhislin said very softly, trying to contain her shock. Iroise – her first and only body-slave, whom she had lost – was there in front of her, staring back in wide-eyed disbelief. Rhislin, fighting down the turmoil, pretended to ignore her.

'You find her beautiful?' the Prioress whispered.

'Yes, ma'am.' Rhislin closed her eyes. But she could still see the scene: her girl in the flickering firelight of the crypt, and the naked men securing her precious body to the wheel.

'Dom Enken is here to ensure nothing goes awry. Connal is her nominated admirer.' The Prioress lowered her voice. 'Dariun is to be my own submissive, though he does not fully know it. He still thinks he is in love with Iroise.' She smiled. 'Yes look at him: I keep him tied so he can watch her. And Chloe is the very essence of profligate abandon.'

'And I?' Rhislin found herself murmuring.

'A pert little hoyden in breeches, just begging to be debagged.' The Prioress's eyes glittered. Rhislin tried to control her breathing. Her neck and cheeks were burning. Images flashed through her mind, of the men restraining her and stripping her trousers down for the mistress to examine her. She had never been examined by a woman or a man; such thoughts sent queasy shivers through her vitals. She pictured the nuns examining the dormitory girls' inner tethers – the female fingers delving from behind, opening out each cunny, then pouring buttermilk down the tether until the cunny overflowed.

'Come – get acquainted with Iroise,' the Prioress said, taking Rhislin by the hand.

The upright wheel was pivoted on a horizontal spindle projecting from a stout stone pillar. It was only as tall as a girl but was wide like a waterwheel. Iroise was being fastened to the outer curve of its circumference, which was clad in leather. Her body faced outwards and she was nude. There were tethering belts for forehead, limbs and waist. There were moveable counterweights along the spokes, so the wheel could be balanced. At present, Iroise's feet were still on the floor and she was leaning back against the wheel, her upper body already secure.

'Tighten her middle,' the mistress said to Rhislin.

Rhislin approached her secret slave, whose eyes were searching for a sign. 'You are beautiful, Iroise,' Rhislin said out loud. Bending forwards, she kissed her. Iroise's lips, soft and frightened, had reached in gentleness, sticking skin to skin. Then Rhislin's lips, displacing the silken blonde ringlets, nuzzled under her ear lobe. Iroise's finger-tips tried to grip her arm. Gently, Rhislin tightened the supple belt across that soft slim middle. She slipped the tip of her middle finger into the smooth pit crowning the belly and left it there, just resting in the warm repository, with the Prioress looking on – lips open, pupils dilated with desire – while the wheel was turned slowly back until Iroise gasped gently and her feet left the floor. As her legs sank down to either side, to be caught by the men, her lovely white outer cunny lips stretched and the pink-frilled inner lips protruded thinly.

'Kiss it,' the Prioress urged, 'while her legs are being fastened back.'

Hot frilly aromatic female velvet brushed back and forth across Rhislin's lips. The lovely weight of slave breast brushed Rhislin's raised arm; the nipple made a little stud. Rhislin shivered. The Prioress drew her away and breathed the scent of Iroise from her lips then kissed them. Gooseflesh swept up Rhislin's legs and belly, naked inside her trousers. When she could look again, Iroise lay splayed atop the balanced wheel, which was swaying gently back and forth.

'Go to it, men,' the Prioress declared. 'Young Dariun is waiting.'

The young kinsman was on his knees on the floor, his back to the couch. His wrists were fastened behind him and his gaze was fixed on Iroise. The pregnant girl, Chloe, was on the couch but at the opposite end. Rhislin, giddy with the taint of sadistic passion, crept quietly round the perimeter of the crypt, her trembling hands behind her, clinging first to the edge of the table, then to the door, then to the stone wall until Iroise's body was partly hidden by the thick stone pillar. She could see Dariun's quivering penis illuminated by the firelight, and his doe eyes fixed on Iroise.

Dom Enken began to turn the wheel until Iroise's body was upside down on the far side. The Prioress was whispering to her. Then Connal's naked belly moved closer. Rhislin closed her eyes. She heard only scraps of the whispered instructions: '. . . Throat . . .' 'Again . . . Let it in . . .' 'Try to swallow the shaft . . .', interspersed with wet, gasping pleadings. Rhislin looked through half-closed eyes at the ankles writhing in the air, at Dom Enken's double-fisted steady gripping of the spokes of the wheel, at Dariun's twitching penis. She wanted to hurt it. She clasped her arms behind her back, trying to imagine just how Iroise must feel – helpless, pinioned, unresisting. She edged further round the crypt, past whipping-posts and cradles, to the bottom corner of the canopied bed where girls were perhaps rested between sessions of sexual torment. A neat pile of crisp sheets stood ready. She could see the Prioress, now knelt beside Iroise, stroking her throat, directing the wet insertions. In the air, above Connal's hunched form, was Iroise's lovely naked cunny. A narrow glistening streamlet of her fluid had started snaking down her belly.

A terrible restless desire beset Rhislin. She looked at the girl who was pregnant, breasts weeping, one leg tucked up, cunny gaping, soft and pink – grotesquely beautiful and sexual. She had never felt inside a girl who was in that state, had never made a pregnant girl come.

Rhislin was already quaking when the Prioress came to her. 'Hold the bedpost. Wrap this arm around it. Put the other hand higher. Now hold on to this post as if your very life depended upon it.' Then the Prioress slid a slender hand down the front of Rhislin's trousers. Rhislin had never felt so deliciously sexually naked as she did inside those trousers. 'Sweet fuck, sweet perfect little silk-wet cunny.' Rhislin came in her mistress's hand, shuddering, moaning, trying to bite her mistress's ear lobe, staring out under heavy aching eyelids at the curving rod of penis coated with dense saliva coming out of Iroise's open throat.

Dariun was looking at Rhislin, as was Chloe. Rhislin felt deliciously warm inside. She let her mistress kiss her on the lips, and her lips were swollen with perverse wanting. 'Come, look at Iroise,' her mistress said, leading her by the hand.

Rhislin, on her knees in front of Iroise, looked up that beautiful, aroused slave-body. She kissed the fingertips that were so helpless; she kissed the nearer breast, its lovely studlike nipple, so pointed because the breast was dangling upside down. 'Kiss her throat,' the mistress whispered, and Rhislin planted a soft open-mouthed sucking kiss in the very centre. Iroise coughed gently. 'Draw her up, Dom Enken,' the mistress said. 'Slowly, gently.'

'Wait.' Rhislin, reaching, licked the oily sensual female drip from Iroise's naked belly. The mistress smiled assent. When Iroise was lifted, the mistress stood beside her supine body as it lay draped upon the wheel. Her fingertips delved between the thighs. 'Iroise is Tantalite,' the mistress explained. She clamped a waxed plaited leather thong to one of the labia. 'Open your mouth, Iroise,' she whispered. The hand pursued her shuddering, descending body as the wheel was slowly turned and the waxed thong slithered down her belly. Then the piercing that Rhislin had made with the fish-bone came into view: it had been widened.

Connal edged closer. 'Guide him,' the mistress told Rhislin. Her trembling fingers depressed the moistened tip of his glans; her other hand reached behind his sac. His flesh was already drenched in Iroise's saliva. The glans went in; the sac stroked wetness across her forehead. Her dangling ringlets tickled Rhislin's wrist. The Prioress knelt beside her. Her hand gently cupped the slender, curved column of Iroise's stretched throat. 'Go deeper, Connal. Oh, God. I can feel you in there. Rhislin, put your fingers here, just gently.' Rhislin touched and tested the girth of the swollen, dulled shape, then sucked the throat in that swollen place and Connal groaned and pulled out, soaked. Iroise gulped and shuddered. Curtains of saliva were dripping from her eyebrows. 'Take her further round, head down – just gently,' said the Prioress, catching hold of the slithering leather.

Rhislin sank back across the floor until she touched the couch. Her hand, reaching back, sought Chloe's knee.

Iroise hung with head down at the lowest point of the wheel; her pale body arched above it. The pink inner lips of her cunny protruded through the white; one was drawn out further by the weight of the dangling plait. The oily streamlet had renewed itself and dribbled further down her belly.

Rhislin's fingertips slid between Chloe's willing thighs at the precise moment that the Prioress started whipping the mouth of Iroise's cunny. Chloe felt soft, wet and tight inside despite the fact that she was gaping open.

Iroise's moisture made glistening splashes on the leather belt around her middle. 'Her mouth needs succour,' the Prioress said. Dom Enken turned the wheel back a quarter turn and in one slow movement, Connal's penis slid up Iroise's throat.

The Prioress then came to the couch. Kneeling beside Rhislin, she kissed her. 'How sweet her sound – the softness and the depth of suction, the gentle opening of her throat, which cannot stop it, nor can it swallow his flesh to completion, yet still her throat keeps making wet. She foams saliva like a starving beast. How sensual the sublimation of control. Look: her ribcage, so inflated with her overwrought breathing; her breasts, standing proud, the nipples so hard they must surely pierce his palms that try to pin her heaving torso to the wheel.' So saying she climbed on to the couch and urged Chloe's head back until the girl's shoulders balanced on the low backrest, with her back arched so tightly that her bottom lifted from the seat. 'Suck her, with your fingers still inside her.' The mistress's mouth descended, suffocating Chloe's moans as Rhislin's tongue tasted salty softness, and her shallow finger penetrations met a pulsing fleshy bulge of warmth.

Rhislin lay with her ear to Chloe's belly. The leakage from the girl's breasts was wetting the arm of the couch. The mistress was now with Dariun. Rhislin was imagining what it might feel like to put her naked toes between his thighs and squeeze his sac against the floor until the lumps inside them slipped and shifted. She knew it would hurt him but she wanted to do it till the spunk came out of his body. The mistress took him by the hair and made him kneel on the bed. Rhislin sat up to watch.

The mistress put something like a strap about his penis, near the end, below the cap, on the thickest part. She started tightening it. Then her hand disappeared behind him. He started gasping: she was whispering to him, mentioning Iroise. His gasps kept coming, his penis twitching, though every other part of his body was still, with a tightness so encompassing he might have been bound in invisible twine. There was sweat on his breasts and belly; his sac was lifting from the bed. The thick part of his stem was now thicker, so the strap bit into it and kept his penis rigid as a pole. The veins stood out. Nothing was touching it except the choking strap. The Prioress continued to whisper to him and to stroke his hair and Dariun continued gasping. His head suddenly arched back as if he needed her kiss; she continued to stroke his hair, with ever more gentle movements of her hand, always the same hand.

For the other was inside him, buried to the slim wristbone. The tendons on her arm were flexing: she was clawing inside him, feeling him, fingering, fisting, pulling. Then with a groan, he spilled his long-held pressure of desire for Iroise. It spouted as if a plunger had been pushed inside him, yielding one straight stream across the bed, with no after-pulse, no gulping, no trembling, no diminution of erection. Then another groan came, wrenchingly deep and more protracted than the first, but this time, no emission. The Prioress sighed. She kissed the sweat from Dariun's breast, then glanced at Rhislin, and her eyes flashed, shiny black, contented.

Rhislin went to the bed and stared at the emission. The mistress, having relinquished her inner grip on Dariun, dipped her fingers into the silvery trail. 'Take your pants down,' she told Rhislin. Rhislin shook her head. But her trembling fingers reached for the instrument that had given over the emission. It was hot and wet, still swollen yet distorted. Her fingertips kept sticking to it when she tried to free its little strap. The smell was of strong sea air. She imagined that sticky warm wetness, on the mistress's fingers, being painted between her legs, and an awful sinking sexual feeling came there, so arousing and unsafe. She almost knew why girls might risk the slip, without protection, under the lure of that feeling. The young kinsman's lumps retreated in his sac; the penis writhed; the strap came free. Rhislin was determined in what she would do.

Iroise's throat was being reopened; Rhislin could hear the hollow wet sounds. She acted very swiftly: in a second she knelt beside the gurgling Iroise. She slipped the strap round the base of the penis that violated that lovely throat; she tightened it mercilessly, not stopping. Connal cried out, withdrew and slapped her hard across the face. Gasping, he tried to free the strap but could not, for it had bedded deeply. Rhislin stood up, took her place by Iroise, who hung inverted: cheeks wet, eyes reddened, swimming in escaped saliva, ringlets dripping. Connal fell to his knees, his penis still swelling like a bloated, strangulated creature, jerking in helpless beautiful spasms.

Chloe stared open-mouthed; Dom Enken looked unsure; Dariun bit his lip. The mistress gave a tiny smile. 'Restrain her,' she whispered.

'Try it.'

The smile withered.

Dom Enken, half advancing, balked as Rhislin faced him. She did not hear the sound of the mistress rising from the bed, or of the ferruled red cane descending swiftly through the air. She did not even feel the blow.

When Rhislin woke, she was staring up at a very low wooden ceiling. A door opened near her feet, which were chained. The boards beneath her suddenly tilted. Kin-Cague stared down at her, his foot on the step of the carriage.

'Where are you sending me?' she whispered through dry cracked lips.

'Not I, nor any of the kinsmen,' he whispered with concern. He fed her water from a flask.

'Ask them at least to let me see her.'

He seemed torn by her entreaty. Then sounds came, of someone's approach.

'Then give her this –' Rhislin struggled to unbutton her collar '– as a sign, that I will not forsake her.' She pressed the gold chain and stolen Tormunite signet ring into his reluctant hand. He crept guiltily away as Dom Enken arrived at the carriage door.

'Well, my little hothead.' Dom Enken pursed his lips. 'It seems you may have played your hand too boldly – our little bird has flown.'

13

Shivering in the Rain

'What place is this?' Iroise whispered, peering at the dank, musty walls and crooked roof beams.

'A cottage of some sort. It should be safe. It seems deserted.'

She crept back to the door, her feet rustling across the straw-strewn floor. Out in the dusk was dense woodland and a barely trodden path. The horses were hitched in a tiny patch of mossy grazing. Streams of water ran from the reed roof. A pool lay across the doorstep. The sodden mendicant's habit clung to her like a heavy shroud, chilling her bones. The hood was her only protection.

'Come inside, you're shivering.' She did not move even when her rescuer stood beside her. 'The trees, the quiet,' Dariun whispered. 'It's like the place I first found you.'

Iroise stared silently at the ground then edged her bare foot into the little chill pool of rainwater. She heard his troubled sigh, then turned and looked at his anxious, frowning youthful face. 'I'll light a fire, then you'll feel better,' he said in a tremulous whisper.

She remained by the door. He found tinder and sparked it and there were dry sticks in the corner; at least he knew of this. He went outside and plucked herbs from the edge of the clearing. Soon a little pot was simmering on an iron bar above the hearth in the middle of the room. From the saddlebags he took bread and strips of meat and arranged them with the rest of the leaves on a small cloth by the fire.

'My lady, shall you grace my table?' He bowed exaggeratedly then seemed embarrassed. Iroise smiled wanly. She came across and crouched by the fire, drawing back her hood. He was staring at her with that same anxious expression. Her hair hung cold against her neck. The clinging, isolated raindrops began to scurry down her face; her hands were limp, soaked and weak.

He hooked the pot from the fire on to a flat stone. 'It has to cool.' He cut a chunk of bread and dressed it with some of the leaves and a strip of meat and then gave it to Iroise. 'Your hands are stone cold. We'll have to get you dry.'

While he rigged a frame on the far side of the fire to support the damp blanket, Iroise stared into the flames. She felt so tired; the flickering flames were mesmerising. The straw in front of her felt warm. Wisps of steam began rising from the blanket. She put the bread down.

'Eat your bread. You must eat something.'

She lifted the handle of the pot with her cuff and used a handful of straw to steady and tilt it, pouring some of the aromatic liquor into the tin cup. 'Here, take it,' she said.

'No, you,' he answered.

Resolutely, Iroise proffered the cup, forcing Dariun to accept it. He took a sip then a measure then gave it back. The warmth spread through her hands as she clasped it. It tasted like scented water. 'What is it?' she asked.

'Shallock and tine.'

'It's good,' she lied. But the warm water in her belly made her feel hungry. She put the cup down and started eating. The bread was good; the leaves were tasteless, felted with tiny soft white hairs. The meat was dry and crumbly, tasting more like fish. She drank again and continued eating. Soon the portion was finished.

'Some more?' he asked.

'I'm full. It was good. Are you not going to have some?'

'Later on.' He put more wood on the fire then turned the blanket round on the frame. 'It'll soon be dry.' She had to edge back from the flames but the warmth felt good against her face. 'You ought not to have gone into the water like that,' he said.

135

'I wanted to.' She had to bathe, to immerse her whole body in the cold pool fed by that pure spring water. After that, the rain had started and she had not warmed till now.

Dariun went out again then came back after a while with more wood. 'It's seasoned. It will not hold the wet.' Iroise was still staring into the fire, her eyelids desperately heavy. 'Here, it's dry.' He held out the blanket. 'Put it on and we'll dry your habit.'

Lethargically, she struggled to pull it over her head. Dariun gently helped her but did not attempt to touch her. For a few seconds she was naked in front of the fire, her body freezing cold and clammy on one side, heated on the other. He draped the warm, heavy blanket round her frail shoulders. She stood there, allowing the delicious radiant warmth to bathe her legs and breasts. He was arranging her habit on the drying frame, at intervals glancing at her almost shyly. She knew he found the hairlessness of her body attractive. The Prioress had known it too and had made him kiss it in that special female place after she had taken out the ring.

'You know much of herbs and wood – and drying,' she whispered.

He smiled.

'You are kind to me.' In some ways he was too kind and gentle for an Iroise that was so weak. 'Where are we going?'

He was startled by the question and suddenly less sure. He stood there like a hunted creature. 'Going?'

'Yes, where are we going? Where are you taking me?' The question that had been innocently posed suddenly seemed to carry great weight. Dariun struggled under its burden. Iroise's spirits sank.

'We had to get away. There's no future there – with her – for the kinsmen.' For the first time since the rescue, Iroise glimpsed some fervour in Dariun's gaze. She stopped herself from reminding him how the Prioress had picked him out from all the others, had found him special. And he was beautiful in body, none could deny it: she remembered that first night, when he had seemed gentle and strong.

'I'm tired now,' she whispered. She could hardly stand. The room slid sideways, the fire swung upwards and Dariun caught her. He laid her, with the blanket wrapped round her, on a bed of heaped, clean hay and she fell into a wearied sleep.

Then dreams came to haunt her – grotesque parodies of her rescue and escape – with Rhislin chained to the wheel and the Prioress, naked, urging a leather strap-on penis slowly down her throat, while Dariun cowered in a corner, his knees tucked up, his balls dangling down behind. And in this dream, Iroise had taken pity on his defenceless state and had abandoned Rhislin and taken Dariun.

Each time she woke, true recollection softened the ruthless selfishness of her dreams. For when Rhislin had been taken away by Connal and Dom Enken, the Prioress had entrusted Iroise to the young kinsman, ordering him, 'Put her to bed and stay with her. I will follow. Keep her mouth wide open – we are not finished in there.' Instead he carried her to the stables; Kin-Cague found victuals; Dariun went to get clothing. 'What of Rhislin?' Iroise had pleaded. 'I'll try,' Dariun had answered without force or conviction. He returned without her and within minutes they were gone.

No fault devolved upon the young kinsman – he was generous, attentive, selfless – so why did she feel this compulsion to hurt him?

She woke to crackling sounds. It was still night. Dariun was stoking the fire, and the air in the little room was very warm. It was still raining but the door had been made fast with a heavy branch and the dampness had receded. Three newly caught fish hung from one of the rafters. Dariun was drying his glistening-wet gown and he was naked. Iroise looked at him quietly from the shelter of her blanket. Her dreams had helped to lay some of the spectres in her mind. As long as he was unaware of being watched, he seemed confident, secure, almost as if this isolated ramshackle place was already his home. He was crouched on the opposite side of the fire, his body bronzed by the firelight, his sex unshaven, the belly hairs dark and shiny. She closed her eyes and listened to the hisses of the raindrops falling through the chimney-hole on to the glowing coals. When she looked again he was pouring hot drink from the pot. Then his gaze met hers and he was suddenly self-conscious. He tried to pull the wet gown from the frame.

'No, don't hide. I want to look at you,' Iroise whispered. 'Stand up.' He still clutched the cup with two hands, which was good because she wanted to look at his maleness. She propped herself up on her arm, the better to see him. Her breast became exposed; she sat up and the blanket fell away. She gathered it round her waist and looked at him while he was looking at her, and his penis started to come up as if her breasts enticed it. She felt warm in her belly. She wanted to lie against his nakedness and use him, wanted to feel that instrument that she had made erect, against her hairless cunny. She reclined with her naked breasts against the fragrant, heaped hay.

'What is this herb in here?' she asked, pointing minutely into the hay, compelling him to come closer. Shyness made him try to hide his arousal. His voice was quavering. 'Kids-ear,' he whispered.

'And this one?'

'Terris.' His breathing was uneven.

'You're shaking – cold. Come under the blanket.'

'Your gown is dry now. Let me bring it.'

'No.' She grasped his wrist and kissed it. 'Come, now.'

Her arousal mounted swiftly when she got him under the blanket. She lay with him, face to face, on her side and she led him. His skin was not salty: he must have bathed while she was sleeping. She kissed his chest and let her ringlets tickle. She was burning between her legs, where his penis nuzzled like a separate creature, warm, silky-skinned and naked. His shiny pubic hairs tickled under her hairless cunny. She pressed its lips against his shaft and made him murmur.

'I'm leaking,' Iroise whispered. 'I've wet your hairs. Feel it?'

Dariun nodded, trembling with excitement. She arched her belly against his swollen glans and felt her lips burst open round it. 'My breasts.' She shivered. 'Squeeze them.'

Her head went back; her mouth fell open; she breathed harder, deeper; her nipples came up deliciously tight. His hands were capable when he chose to use them. She wanted the feeling that her breasts would burst under the tightness of his fingers. She lay rigid, arched, immobile, wanting the lovely pressure of his glans against her cunny to go on and on. But he was nervous of her need and relaxed his grip upon her breasts and took her in his arms, allowing the beautiful pressure between her legs to ease. Perhaps he was too near to coming.

Iroise lay savouring the closeness of another naked creature. She kissed his nipples, finding that prolonged kissing and wetting there made his penis stand on end and feel like warm, skin-coated bone in her fingers. She pushed his head back gently and began to suck the hard small apple in his neck. She drew the blanket back and watched his penis trembling and then she sucked the apple even harder and made him cough. She told him she would straddle his mouth and that she wanted him tight in every muscle but unmoving.

She faced his feet so she could watch his penis; she put her hands on his chest and kept her arms rigid. She pressed her cunny down into his gaping mouth – harder, quicker, trying to thrust her belly down his throat. His chest rose and fell, his breathing through his nose came ever deeper, quicker, expelling cool tickles ever higher up her backbone, until she stopped, stock-still, and felt inside her belly a keen dull pleasure – not a climax – as if honey were being siphoned from her womb, and she felt sure that she was dripping down his throat. She leant forwards, hands pivoting on his chest and sucked just the very tip of his arching penis, stimulating deep trembles at the root. As she watched those trembles, the urge came to her again that she wanted to hurt him, to make the pressure of arousal build inside until it bruised him. She climbed gently off his mouth and kissed him with her hand clutched softly at his throat.

'The Prioress made it spill. I saw it while I was on the wheel. I could smell it. It looked so white upon the bedspread.'

'I want to make you come,' Dariun murmured.

Iroise drew back. 'It is forbidden. Sinful.'

'And good.'

'You would not try to make me sin?' Her fingertips clutched the hay.

'No.' But his gaze was wistful.

Iroise believed him. She smiled into his eyes. 'Lie with me again, Dariun. I want to feel you near.' She lay behind him in spoon fashion with her breasts against his back and she held his erect penis. 'How did the Prioress make you come?' she whispered. Iroise knew well but Dariun was too self-conscious to explain. Iroise wanted to speak of it.

'When I was being taken to the Abbey,' she told him, 'we were rested at a beautiful villa. There was a young male slave there whom my mistress forced me to have congress with. He was blond and handsome.'

'You enjoyed it?'

'The congress was not of normal kind.' She felt Dariun's penis swelling in her hand.

'What was it?' he murmured.

'They gave me a heavy ivory ball, smooth and shiny – it felt as though it had metal inside it. It was about the size of a large apple and so heavy that I could not easily lift it with my fingers. They told me to put it into him. They put us on the bed and watched. The mistress was interested in the male; the master wanted me. I could get the ball so far but the muscle would not yield and I did not want to hurt the slave, yet my mistress was adamant. After each failure she would whip him between the legs and I would get frightened in case she whipped me.'

Dariun turned round to face Iroise. 'But in the Priory you were put to a whipping. The Prior ordered it. I remember it.'

'But I was still frightened of the pain. That terror never goes away, Dariun, however many times it happens. The awful sinking.' She shivered. He kissed her nipples very gently and she held his head to her breast. As he lay there, nuzzling gently, she whispered, 'Put your legs together, like that. Let me hold your sac.' She drew his fleshy sac out in front. 'It feels like his did: fat and warm.' Her fingers cupped it; her thumb pressed from above. The balls inside divided. Her fingertips could feel a kind of hollow at the root of the sac, like the entrance that a girl possesses. The tip of his penis touched her belly. She continued her story.

'While the mistress was whipping him, the master was masturbating me very gently – prolonging it, making me sit up on the bed. He was good at playing with girls. I became softer and more open. Then he lay me down and kissed my mouth while my legs were in the air. He kept saying that if he could get my flesh soft enough then it would stay open.'

'Were you at that time a Tantalite?' Dariun murmured against her breasts.

'Yes. Both master and mistress knew it. When the mistress had done whipping I had to resume my task. I had never seen or kissed a penis that was quite so hard.'

'You kissed it?'

'She made me hold it in my mouth. Let me show you. Keep your legs together.' She wriggled down, sealed her lips tightly around the cap and poked her tongue-tip into the oily hole, sealing it, pressing till he moaned. Then she pulled back and looked at the penis. There was still a furrow round it at the fattest part where the leather strap had constricted it. She drew his balls forwards on the tips of her fingers and sucked their shiny skin. 'Turn on your belly.' She slid the folded blanket under his middle. 'Lie on it – like that with your legs tightly together.'

She sat above him, painting his naked back with her fingertips, stroking the shiny black hairs at the top of the crease. 'When I went to try again with the ivory ball, my poor victim was much tighter than before. The master said there was no hurry. He continued to play with me and I kept my thighs open for it like a little vixen. I started licking the place where the ball would go. My victim started moaning. The mistress made me stop and took again to whipping the mouth of his bottom. I was sitting up on the bed with my knees up to my breasts and my master was squeezing one flap of my cunny tightly between his fingers.'

Iroise gently spread the tight cheeks of the young kinsman. The hairs were shiny, soft and dark, whereas the slave had been shaved bald where her tongue had laved its spittle. She gently wetted the surface of Dariun's anus with her moistened fingers. 'When I tried again, his anus was so softened by the whipping that the ball went in. The mistress's thighs were round his neck; the master wanted to go into me. He turned me on to my back. Oh, Dariun, I was so willing by then, and being penetrated through my cunny felt so good.' She pillowed her head against his back and kept up the slow wet rubbing in the furrow – back and forth, swift, then slow, then stopping, repeatedly across that hot mouth just as if she were masturbating the clitoral sheath of a girl.

'The mistress wanted me to suck the slave while the weight of the ball was inside him. But when she made him straddle my face, the ball must have moved inside him – I could feel its weight under the root of his penis. The fluid spouted high above my lips and splattered on my breasts. The master smoothed it in. Then they made me retrieve the ball. My hand was inside him to the wrist.' Dariun was gasping, quaking. Iroise's fingers were still moving, rubbing slippery pleasure across that place.

'Lift up,' she urged him, wriggling under him, mouth to groin, her head on the folded blanket, her hands deliberately trapped beneath her. 'Push it all the way down my throat,' she begged, shuddering, breasts thrust out, nipples so erect they throbbed. As it slid in like a fat snake, she felt so sweetly defenceless, her head arched back, her mouth so wide her jaw was aching. He opened her limp, willing cunny with his fingers and started licking inside it. Her belly convulsed; her gulping throat struggled to accommodate the girth of arousal in his penis; his hot, soft ball-sac straddled her nose; his semen squirted pleasure so intensely it felt as if it were spraying the inner walls of her belly.

'Oh God,' he gasped, drawing out of her throat. His bobbing penile shaft was thick with her saliva. Semen still bubbled from the glans. She felt profound contentment, a deep warmth in her belly as if a wool-wrapped glowing coal were buried there. Her breasts were wet with saliva; how it had got there, she did not know. They made tight jellied mounds which Dariun's strong warm hands could not resist. Her tongue arched up eagerly to collect the runnel of bubbly fluid from the underside of his penis. And her cunny gaped softly open.

She made him turn round and lie with her, properly, his chest to her cheek. While she dozed she clasped his thigh between her legs, so her cunny stayed open, kissing his skin, and she played with his penis to prevent its sleeping.

The day was high when they finally woke with a start to a dreadful banging noise. Dariun jumped up, dragged his gown from the frame and grasped a branch for a weapon. Iroise hid in the blanket. The makeshift door prop collapsed and the broken door twisted open on its hinges.

Silhouetted in the doorway was a hooded figure. 'Well met, my kinsman,' the figure said softly, extending an arm.

'Kin-Cague?' Dariun gasped. 'Can it be? It is, too!' he cried, clasping the arm and shaking it vigorously. 'Are you alone?' he said, peering through the doorway.

'There is one other. Come. You, too, my little wood nymph. Come and see.'

Perched on the single horse was Chloe, wrapped in a fleece and blanket which barely covered her swelling.

'My God, Kin-Cague. How could you put her – in that condition – on a horse?'

'My dearest Dariun, her condition – of which you speak so captiously – is one of joy and bounteous beauty. And surely you would not have had me make her walk?'

14

Bridges

'How did you find us?' Dariun asked Kin-Cague as he offered the first drink to Chloe, who sat quietly in the hay.

'You said you planned to follow the river southwards.' Iroise – on her knees, preparing the fish for cooking – hung on every word the wise kinsman uttered. 'I guessed you would avoid the highway and hold to the forest. I suppose it was chance we stopped here, though there aren't that many shelters in these parts. I confess I expected you to be long gone by now.'

Iroise glanced away shyly. The fish began sizzling in the tin dish on the embers.

'We left not long after you, but had to go gently,' Kin-Cague added.

'You should have left me. I am a burden,' Chloe whispered.

Kin-Cague vehemently shook his head. 'No.' He went to her, kneeling beside her. For a while, he seemed unable to speak. His gentle eyes were almost moved to tears. He whispered something to her and Chloe put her arms around his neck and kissed him.

Iroise lifted the fish off the fire and placed it on the stone. She nodded to Dariun, who did not understand properly until she led him quietly out of the door. 'I want to look at the river,' she said to him, slipping her arm round his and leading him away from the hut. The sun was shining into the glade. Everywhere felt fresh after the rain. The warmth was still in her belly from the deep pleasure she had shared with the young kinsman. Yet the warmth was tempered with sadness.

They reached the river. 'So much water,' she murmured, pressing her cheek against his arm. It flowed so silently, high against the banks, and turbidly, bearing speeding clumps of weed and leaf-clad branches.

'It is from the rain last night. Its reach must surely go higher still: see how dark the sky is above the hills?'

Iroise turned, pressing her back against a tree, seeking strength from its sturdy frame.

'What is it?' Dariun asked.

'You know when you found me by the pool in the woods?'

'Yes,' he said, cagily.

'And my master had left me?'

He nodded.

'My master is a girl.'

He stared at her, sensing there was more.

'Her name is Rhislin.'

'Rhislin? The footgirl?'

'No – Rhislin, my master.'

For a few seconds, the anxious, uncertain kinsman stood revealed once more. Then Dariun suddenly rallied. 'I should have tried to save her. I did not know.'

'How could you, when I did not trust enough to tell?'

'Kin-Cague may know something.' He took her hand and turned back in the direction of the hut.

'Wait. Wait! Leave them be, for a little while.' She looked at him. 'Don't you understand what I've been saying to you?'

'You love Rhislin.'

She fell against his chest, tears of tortured emotion welling.

Chloe, propped up on one arm upon the sheepskin, shuddered in luscious ecstasy. Her heavy breasts rolled outwards. Her small hand clasped the base of Kin-Cague's penis – the part that would not reach inside her. Her moist, hot sex sucked the glans in beautiful, drawn-out spasms, which Kin-Cague counted out loud, making her smile.

145

'I want you to come – inside me,' Chloe murmured.

Kin-Cague shook his head. His vows would not permit it, albeit someone's seed-cast was already sprouted in that innocent womb. He drew out very gently. 'As it is, I fear I may have gone too deep. My flesh shall stay in wanting.'

'As punishment?' Chloe whispered keenly.

'Yes, my little treasure.' But how sweet a punishment – to have drunk from that beautiful female cup of longing.

'Then let me tie its collar.' Her eager fingers drew the small strap around the throat of his erect penis. 'It's gone bigger,' Chloe whispered. She hunkered down but could not reach it with her mouth, so she lay on her back and reached up, kissing the collar and simultaneously patting her finger directly down on to the mouth, sending strange sensations down the wick of his penis. The feelings were moving fleetly to the point of no control. He took Chloe gently by the wrist to restrain her. He wondered where she had found the small collar and where she had learnt these things.

When she stood up and put her arms around him while he was still kneeling, the desire swelled inside him so hard that his strangulated penis almost issued semen down her leg. Her soft full breasts muffled his ears and weighed upon his shoulders; the pressure made her nipples leak. She took the collar off his flesh and tied it round her wrist. She was still standing there proudly, brazenly beautiful when Dariun returned alone.

'Where's Iroise?' Kin-Cague said, reaching for some clothing.

'She wandered off.'

'Then get after her. There could be soldiers about.'

But Dariun came and sat by the remains of the fire. 'Kin-Cague, I need to ask you something.'

'What?'

'If a girl were in love with a girl, then why would she choose to lie with a man?'

'Iroise?' Kin-Cague pursed his lips. 'You did not coerce her?'

'No!'

'And did she say that she was in love with you?'

146

'No.'

'Then no covenant was broken. Did she say who the girl was?'

'Rhislin.'

'Ah.' Kin-Cague stared at Chloe.

'They took her away,' Chloe murmured.

'Yes – and you thought they would take you too.'

'But you saved me.' She threw her arms about him again.

'And now Iroise is very unhappy. What are we to do?'

Kin-Cague did not find Iroise until he thought to retrace his path upriver. She was sitting on a boulder, staring down into the swift flow and when he approached, she did not move or change her expression.

'You are considering returning to the Priory?' he said, quietly.

She nodded.

He took from his pocket the gold chain and the Tormunite signet ring that Rhislin had given him. 'Rhislin asked me to give you this.'

Iroise stared at it, then looked up at him.

'She is no longer held at the Priory,' he said, gently. 'The new incumbent could not suffer public defiance from a footgirl.'

As she took the ring on its chain, Iroise shivered, as though she had actually witnessed Rhislin's flogging. She stared at Kin-Cague. 'Where is she?'

'I know the place only by hearsay – a reformatory of some kind.' He stopped himself from saying more. The tears were already in her eyes.

She buried her head in her hands. 'Why do you bear me such woeful news?'

'Come with us, Iroise. For a little way, at least. Even in this land there are still outposts of kinship. We will find them.'

He offered his hand. Shaking her head – trying to shake away the tumult of tears – Iroise fastened Rhislin's chain about her neck. Then she took hold of Kin-Cague's fingertips and let him lead her back to the hut.

Chloe was beaming. Even Dariun was alert and unself-conscious.

'What?' Kin-Cague asked, looking from one to the other.

'We've decided what to do,' said Chloe.

'And what's that?'

'Go after Iroise's friend,' said Dariun. Iroise threw herself in tears upon him. Kin-Cague's heart swelled to witness the generosity of spirit of his young kinsman, breaking through the barrier of thwarted love, which might so easily have turned against Rhislin. And Chloe made him proud; she came to him and kissed him, spilling warmth and love.

'We'll need to make headway,' he declared. All eyes were upon him, relying on him to lead. 'Before the river veers west, we'll need to be on the other side.' From charts, he knew a little of the lie of the land but he wasn't sure how near a bridge might be, and he had never set foot on the terrain on the far side.

When he saw the height of the river, his heart sank. Every tributary swelled it further; there was blackness over the hills and there was the sound of boulders rolling on the river bed. He feared for the state of any bridges down-stream but dreaded the prospect of having to go back upriver in order to cross. So they rode on for some two hours, Chloe with Dariun at the rear, then Iroise's horse in the middle and Kin-Cague's horse leading. Chloe looked tired. Dariun looked increasingly anxious. Kin-Cague decided to turn back.

'We'll rest,' he shouted.

'Look!' Chloe suddenly cried, pointing vigorously ahead. 'The bridge!' Kin-Cague twisted round, squinting against the light and there it was, in the distance, standing solidly, majestically arching in three sections over the flood. The next second he was lying on his back on the ground, staring up, disorientated, but still holding the reins.

Dariun was swiftly on his knees beside him. 'What happened?'

'I . . . I don't know. I must have been off-balance when I twisted round. No broken bones, at any rate.' He pulled himself to his feet and dusted himself down. 'We'd better get across the bridge.'

'What bridge?' said Dariun.

Kin-Cague looked ahead: there was blank riverbank and some trees, nothing else. He looked to Chloe, who was staring at him strangely. Iroise jumped down from her horse and made him sit upon a rock and gave him water. She ran her fingers over the back of his head. Her expression was one of protective concern.

The more Kin-Cague thought about what had happened, the more he knew he must go on. Otherwise he would lose face and his companions would lose heart. 'Let me ride with you,' Iroise asked but he gently refused.

When they took up their journey, Kin-Cague found himself setting too swift a pace: his lead on the others kept increasing because he was so desperate to know what lay beyond each bend.

Then, at last, a bridge did appear. It was quite unlike the other, for it was a narrow, wooden trestle bridge partly overtaken by the flood – yet he was nervous lest this too might prove to be an apparition. He therefore waited for the others to catch up and said nothing, but studied each face, seeking corroboration.

'Can we get across, do you think?' Dariun asked.

Chloe was staring wide-eyed at Kin-Cague, prompting him to seek reassurance. 'You see it too, Chloe?'

She didn't answer, so he asked Iroise, who nodded, 'Yes.'

Then Chloe whispered in awe, 'You saw the bridge – in your mind.'

'Oh no, my darling.' He rode closer and touched her hand. 'I was tired and daydreaming. I have no powers to see beyond the natural compass of vision.' She did not look as though she believed him. And though he himself was sure of what he had told her, he was concerned: the fainting and the hallucination boded ill, suggesting some feebleness or vapours clouding his mind.

'Come on.' He set off, keen to make the crossing.

But as they neared their goal, it became obvious that there were problems. The bridge sagged in the middle. The

149

centre supports must have given way and the middle part, with water lapping over it, was being dragged out of alignment by the flow. Floating debris was piled against it.

'It's like a dam, ready to burst,' said Dariun.

Kin-Cague shook his head. 'It's too dangerous.'

Iroise looked devastated. Kin-Cague turned to Chloe.

'We have to try – for Iroise's sake,' she murmured.

'But what of you – your situation?'

'I want to go on.'

He looked at Dariun, who shrugged then nodded.

Kin-Cague dismounted and went to inspect. The bridge had been sited where the river widened and shallowed but the flow was still prodigious, with the current strengthening towards the middle. Forest flotsam – whole trees in places – was piled awesomely against it on the upstream side but he detected no sway underfoot: the first part seemed stable. And in the very centre – where the bridge was foundering and the deck pitched sideways, half immersed – was a pool of relative stillness, an eye of calm in the turbulent flow to either side. It gave him hope. He called for the others to join him.

Dariun and Iroise dismounted and cautiously led the horses to within a dozen paces of the disturbance in the decking.

'Can the horses cope with the tilt?' Dariun asked. 'And what of Chloe?' She was still on Dariun's horse.

'We can carry her.' Suddenly Kin-Cague glimpsed a large dark shape on the periphery of his vision. The floating tree hit the bridge at a point behind them. It shuddered and stood its ground. But the startled horses bolted forwards, into the submerging, tilted hollow in the decking, legs flying as they stumbled, sheets of spray shooting in the air, the deck rolling and Chloe clinging on for life. The trailing horse collapsed in the water then struggled back to its feet. Kin-Cague watched in horror as all three horses pounded across to the other side of the bridge and disappeared from view.

A dreadful string of creaking, snapping sounds issued from the tortured timbers below. 'Quickly!' cried Dariun. 'The bridge is breaking away!'

150

'Take my arm! Make a chain!'

Halfway across the dip, the decking groaned and began to founder. Kin-Cague slipped on the wet planking and hit his head. Stunned, he heard the others shouting as they tried to keep their footing. Kin-Cague was crushed underfoot; his body was enveloped in freezing water; his arm was being wrenched from its socket. A dark shape thudded into his chest and suddenly a cloak of blackness was draped upon him and all pain ceased.

15

The Winery

'No turning back now.' Dariun was staring across the water at the missing segment of the bridge. The horses were quietly grazing on the sunlit grassy bank where Kin-Cague was being tended by Chloe.

Iroise moved closer to the young kinsman. 'You were brave to risk yourself that way, to rescue Kin-Cague. I thought we would lose you both.'

He looked at her in that troubled way and though she ought not to have done it, Iroise kissed him.

'You're shivering,' he whispered, putting his arms around her.

'With this sun, I'll soon warm.' But she was not cold inside. With the bridge crossing – the fear, the excitement – her emotions burned strongly. She turned, keeping his arms about her. Ahead, the river swung round a low, craggy hill clothed in rows of dark green bushes which stopped abruptly at the foot of the hill. A small castle crowned the hill.

'What place is that?' Iroise asked.

Dariun shrugged. 'It's a pretty spot.'

'It looks as if the road goes that way,' Iroise said. In fact, it seemed to be the only route, for the ground rose very steeply from the riverbank behind her. In the afternoon sun, the pretty castle on its hillock looked idyllic. Iroise drew the young kinsman's arms against her belly and closed her eyes, imagining herself lain there, on the warm grass of the little hillside, in the dappled sunshine coming through the leafy bushes.

'Kin-Cague is recovered,' Dariun whispered. And it seemed that Chloe – like Iroise – was experiencing this same deep drive of emotion. But Chloe was more forward in expressing it.

'She makes him young,' Iroise said. Chloe had drawn her gown up to her neck and was feeding him her milk as he lay on the ground. Watching it was arousing Dariun. Iroise did not urge it nor dissuade it. She felt arousal too as she led Dariun back to the others.

Kin-Cague, sitting up, was back to his former, bright-eyed self. He too had observed the castle on the hillock. 'Do you not notice anything strange, Dariun?'

Dariun stared about him. 'Strange, kinsman? Where? I don't see anything.'

'You don't see any *people*,' Kin-Cague corrected. 'On the quiet tracks through the woods, one could understand it, but here – back on Tormunite ground, and where there's a river crossing and a castle – don't you find it odd?'

'I find it welcome. The last people I care to meet are the Tormunites.'

'Perhaps the castle is deserted,' Iroise said, 'and we can shelter there? The road goes past it. Chloe – just imagine it – a castle, all our own!'

Dariun shook his head but Iroise could see from the way he looked at the beautiful place that he was tempted. Kin-Cague was gripped by curiosity. A few minutes later, the little party was at the open gateway of the small estate.

'There are no gates,' Dariun said. 'There have never been any. See – no hinge-posts.'

'The road doesn't go past: it finishes here,' said Kin-Cague. 'But from the lie of the land – flat and grassy ahead – one would surely expect it to continue. Curious.'

'Let's go in,' Chloe begged him.

The driveway zigzagged steeply and stonily up the little hill. Now that they were getting closer, the building looked less like a castle and more like a house. The pebbles clinked under the horses' hooves; the afternoon was breezeless and a balmy heat billowed up to greet the travellers. The heavy mendicant's gown that Iroise wore was becoming oppressive. She stopped her horse and pulled the gown over her head: but for Rhislin's neck-chain and ring, she was naked. A soft pleasure enveloped her. She sat back in the saddle with her hands behind her, exposing her breasts to the warmth of the sun, conscious of the men's gaze upon her. She had never felt so free. Chloe too was disrobing. Kin-Cague had to hold her so she did not fall. Iroise smiled at the men in their modesty.

'I think the house is abandoned,' Kin-Cague ventured as they drew nearer.

At the next bend, Chloe cried, 'Look, grapes!' The bushes Iroise had seen were vines: they covered this side of the hillock in neatly manicured lines, bearing lush leaves and sun-soaked, plump, black bunches. She wanted to get down but the kinsmen dissuaded her.

'See how well-tended the vines are?' Dariun said. 'Someone surely lives here.' At the top of the hillock, the vista opened out. It was breathlessly beautiful in the sun. The tight curve of the powerful river surrounded the site on three sides; pure white sunlit streamlines slunk slowly along its opalescent green-grey surface. The valley broadened out on the far side of the river; beyond were mountains that scraped the clouds.

Kin-Cague was frowning. 'Dariun – look – the river makes a loop that's almost closed. That's why the path goes no further: with that crag across the narrow neck of land from one side to the other, there's nowhere to go.'

'But the bridge is down.'

'It seems this little jewel of seclusion is flawed,' Kin-Cague sighed.

'I thought you knew where you were going.'

'We must have missed a crossing somewhere upstream.'

'But it's nice here,' Chloe whispered.

Iroise had dismounted. She tied her horse and, still naked, began to walk to the house. She felt no fear of any kind. She was inquisitive and, at every step, felt even more certain that it was indeed deserted. The great latch lifted easily and the heavy door swung freely. She expected it to be dark inside but generous light filtered through the tall

154

windows, illuminating an entrance hall floored with a beautiful mosaic of a sylvan scene. A polished wooden staircase lay directly ahead and branched left and right. A very thin film of dust overlaid everything; as she advanced, she could feel it underfoot. Then she realised that the mosaic included a representation of this very place – the house and vineyard on the hill beside the sweeping river. Cattle grazed the flatter foreground; there were more trees than at present, and by the gateway of the estate, two young figures – a male and a female – stood arm in arm. She reached the foot of the stairs.

'Go carefully, Iroise,' came Kin-Cague's warning. The others crept in behind him.

'There are no footprints but Iroise's,' Dariun said. 'The place is empty.'

'But why?' Kin-Cague replied. 'Where has everyone gone?' He followed Iroise, who was already halfway up the stairs. She turned to the right and looked up: the two branches of the staircase joined a common landing; this part of the house was laid out like a square. Mosaic panels covering the walls of the staircase showed scenes of woodland, hill and river, agriculture and animal husbandry. Each image was framed within a depiction of vines, some bearing fruit, some leafy, others bare.

'It's the seasons of the year in picture,' Kin-Cague said.

At the top of the stairs, Iroise halted before a door. On the adjacent wall was a mosaic panel of a beautiful girl: hair as black as charcoal, skin pale, eyes rich brown. She was dressed like a country girl but there was elegance in her poise. 'Who is she?' Iroise whispered.

'Probably they once lived here.' Kin-Cague had moved along the landing and was staring at a matching panel of a handsome young man: black-haired and blue-eyed and dressed like a woodsman. 'They look like siblings.'

Iroise opened the door; inside was indeed a girl's boudoir – welcoming, neat, light and airy, not dusty or faded. The curtains were open. The bed was made. 'It's lovely. Can I sleep here tonight?' Iroise asked, then she saw the kinsman's worried expression. 'What is it?'

He shook his head as though something was amiss. He suddenly seemed concerned that she was nude.

'Kin-Cague! Iroise! Come down here,' Dariun shouted.

Iroise followed the hurrying kinsman downstairs and along a corridor into a large, spotless kitchen, where Chloe was seated nude in a wooden armchair and Dariun was investigating the cupboards.

'You've lit a fire?' Kin-Cague said to him accusingly.

'No, I haven't.'

Kin-Cague stared next at Chloe. She shook her head. 'No.'

'Then until we find whoever did, we should stay together.' He proceeded to lead the little group through the house – dining room, drawing room, still room – and then down to the cellars. Candles already burned there. As Iroise watched the warm light playing across the rows of dust-laden flagons, she realised that Kin-Cague saw only moving shadows. She did not feel his fear, nor did Chloe. And even Dariun was becoming intrigued. To Iroise, it was as if this house had feelings and, bereft of company, it was now laying out a welcome for the road-weary travellers.

There were two glasses and a flagon sitting on the narrow table. Iroise unstoppered the flagon and sniffed its contents, which was rich, fragrant wine. She poured a little into each of the two glasses. Neither kinsman would drink so it was left to Iroise and Chloe to savour that liquid delight. Kin-Cague looked on anxiously as if expecting the women to slump unconscious on the floor. The warmth slipped down Iroise's throat and evaporated in her belly, sending delicious feelings of languor through her limbs, dissolving the chill of the previous day's wetness that had seeped into her bones. Chloe's cheeks darkened warmly in the candlelight. When nothing worse happened, Kin-Cague wanted to continue the troubled search of house and grounds. But outside it was now the warmest part of the afternoon and Iroise did not want to waste it. She convinced the men to allow them to bathe in the sunshine. It was what she had wanted from the first time she had seen this place.

Iroise and Chloe lay in the sun until evening, when Kin-Cague came to fetch them. Dariun had found vegetables and had prepared a pot of food. Iroise was not hungry. She was tired. Kin-Cague upbraided her. 'But you slept all afternoon.' When she told him where she intended to sleep, he tried to dissuade her, whispering, 'Chloe will want to follow.'

'Why shouldn't she? There are two big rooms. Come with us.'

He shook his head.

'Why are you so afraid?'

'Dariun and I will share a watch.'

Chloe took the bedroom of the young male; Iroise the girl's. The two images in the mosaics would guard them in the night: that was how Iroise saw it. She felt no fear; she took to the beautiful room just as if it were her own. She slid between the crisp clean sheets and, as she drifted into delicious sleep, she was thinking of the girl.

She woke late. The sun was streaming through the window. Kin-Cague appeared at the bedroom door looking far less anxious.

'There's breakfast in the kitchen – rabbit. Dariun caught one.'

Iroise smiled.

'We're going to reconnoitre the area to try and find a route. Do you want to come with us?'

'No. You go. I'll stay with Chloe.'

When he had disappeared she saw beside the bed a little silver goblet. It hadn't been there the previous night. Iroise peered at it. It contained wine. She looked around the room. Then she picked up the goblet and drank. The same delicious warmth that she had experienced from the wine in the cellar again moved through her being. It was only a tiny measure yet she felt pleasurably woozy. She did not feel at all hungry. She collected Chloe and went into the grounds.

The sun shone from a blue sky. They found a place overlooking the river from on high, where the lines of bushes channelled the sunshine on to the ground. Iroise cast aside the mendicant's habit she had thought to use as a mat and lay nude on the sunlit grass. Chloe did likewise a little way away, in the next grove. Iroise leisurely closed her eyes. Warmth spread through her body; her sun-starved skin consumed every living morsel of radiant light that fell upon it; the grass caressed her wriggling toes. She spread out her arms and her thighs in sweet abandon; the sunlight breathed its gentle warmth upon her naked cunny like the close breath of a lover. She daydreamed softly, images of gentle sensuality kissing her mind. She thought again of Chloe's breasts dripping milk into Kin-Cague's mouth; she thought of the soft black line down Chloe's belly, the visible mark of her transgression. She thought of her own mark inside her cunny: the bright red fruit that, however beautifully fashioned, still symbolised that she was a chattel of love. Eyes closed, she opened herself and felt the pure sunshine inside her body, bathing the place that had suffered such ill use. She lay like that a long, lovely while. Intermittent cooling trickles of breeze rolled downslope over her naked skin; then the sun's warmth re-enveloped her. There was no sound except the lightest rustling of the vine leaves.

She opened her eyes and thought she was dreaming: kneeling on the grass near her feet, toying with the stems and lost in thought, was a pale-skinned girl in a mendi-cant's habit – Iroise's habit; the girl had taken it. Iroise immediately looked around for Chloe but could not see her through the dense leafage.

The girl looked at Iroise and said, 'You looked so peaceful there, I did not want to wake you.' She drew back her hood. Her hair, though very short, was as black as soot. Her face was beautiful. Iroise shivered.

'You're the girl in the picture,' Iroise whispered in awe.

'Ah. In the house? Oh, no. You see, that picture is very old. And as you see, I am young. But she is a distant relative, or so I am told. And I am flattered that you discern a likeness, for I have always admired her.' She glanced down at the habit. 'I hope you don't mind. I took the liberty of trying it.'

Iroise shook her head and the girl smiled engagingly. She was beautiful – a little like Rhislin but much darker of hair and more finely featured, and the black hair made her complexion look like alabaster. 'My name is Eloise,' she said, and Iroise was taken aback by this name, so similar to her own, that the girl had to prompt Iroise to return the compliment. 'Iroise – a lovely name,' she then murmured, without any comment about the similarity. 'Have you eaten?'

Iroise shook her head.

'Good.'

'But we tasted your wine.'

'I know.' Eloise stretched out alongside her. Her skin was gently fragrant, like primrose. 'You have beautiful eyes, Iroise. Let me study them.' Eloise stared into them without blinking; her irises were rich, dark brown, the pupils black. Delicious gooseflesh covered Iroise's skin. She drew back to take in the rest of that beautiful face. The nose was delicate, the mouth small, its lips pale pink, the ear lobes tiny. Iroise wanted to touch that black, black hair. 'Close your eyes,' Eloise whispered and Iroise found herself obeying every instruction she was given. She liked to be near girls, especially this girl. Eloise touched her as she lay on her side with her breasts heaped one upon the other: soft, lithe finger strokes caressed her from belly to nipples, then toyed with the ring on her neck chain. The girl-touch was so gentle, the fingertips so small and light and so inquisitive.

'Let me touch the hairless place,' Eloise murmured.

Iroise lay with eyes still closed. She parted her thighs then shuddered. Eloise was touching her like a blind girl would, swiftly at first and very lightly, taking in her essential shape, then checking in detail: the outer lips then the inner, reporting what her fingers had discovered. 'You've gone silky in the sun.' Then the clitoral hood, pushing it up gently, feeling beneath, eviscerating her clitoris – Iroise knew she was studying it; then searching out the seam of flesh beneath her cunny, finding and repeatedly testing the piercing. She made her lie on her back. Iroise shuddered again as the girl opened out the lips of her cunny. She felt the tip of a finger stroking the surface of her tattooed inner skin then she felt the hood being pushed back and held.

'Open your eyes,' the girl whispered. She was holding a single black grape, covered in velvet bloom, which she lowered until it barely touched the pointed tip of Iroise's aroused clitoris. She started rubbing it against the tip very slowly. A precise circle was being inscribed by the tip of Iroise's clitoris into the purple bloom. 'This is how we make a wine glass sing,' Eloise whispered, holding back the hood. The film of oil at the tip of Iroise's clitoris was being gently rubbed away by the steady friction. Strange and beautiful sensations were being transmitted up inside her. Utter commitment to the task was written on Eloise's lovely face. Iroise wanted to see her naked, wanted to part that black, black bush that she was sure lay between those lithe pale thighs and –

'Ohhh!' She tried to sit up. Her shoulders lifted from the grass. Her breasts heaved; the muscles of her belly went rigid. Tiny jewels of perspiration split the sunlight on her skin.

Eloise's dark eyes glittered. 'And if we continue, we make fire.' Iroise lay back defencelessly as the ravishing clitoral torture continued. The pressure was there all the time, the fingertips pushing back her hood until it felt that all her sexuality was being squeezed out on to the surface of that pointy blister. A delicious tightness gripped her womb. Her head twisted back and to the side – and there, through a gap in the leaves she saw Chloe on her back, sucking the glans of a huge fat penis which would not fit into her mouth.

'My brother,' Eloise declared proudly. At that moment, Iroise's rubbing clitoris pierced the skin of the grape: the juice spurted over her cunny as her clitoris wormed into the fruit like a greedy maggot. Eloise tried to slide the thinned hood around the impaled berry but it would not stay in place unassisted. She held it while Iroise lay with her clitoris buried, feeding on the sweet pulpy sensations. On the other side of the bushes, the semen from the disembodied swollen penis gushed into Chloe's mouth.

Luscious warmth spread through Iroise's womb, where the tightness had been; she felt as if her clitoris was drinking desire like a drug from the swollen berry. 'Kiss me,' she begged. Eloise bent over her face and opened her small mouth to Iroise's probing tongue and kept the berry pressed against her cunny. And the kiss, her tongue inside the mouth, with the pressure round her clitoris, was beautiful.

When she looked again she glimpsed the brother, lithe, black-haired and beautiful like his sister, but naked as a baby and with a penis that would hurt. He was lifting Chloe from the grass. 'Where's he taking her?' Iroise asked.

'To the winery – the same place I am taking you.' She tied a ribbon round Iroise's waist and between her thighs to bind the shiny berry in place. The ribbon was already streaked purple: she must have used it before in this fashion. Iroise experienced deep arousal, being used sexually by a girl. The ribbon split her cunny lips; its presence as her only clothing made her feel more naked yet. Eloise kept stopping her and testing its seating. It felt as if the berry was part of her; walking with it bound so tightly up against her made her thighs shake. Eloise led her round the shallow parapet fringing the top of the knoll. She said she wanted to display her but there was no one to witness it. The movement engendered peculiar feelings, as if the berry were a poultice that was drawing on her knob. When she reached the far extremity of the parapet, Eloise made her halt.

'Stand open,' Eloise ordered. Her face was level with Iroise's knees. The slender fingers came between Iroise's legs to test the seating of the berry. 'Firm and good,' she whispered, clutching it and squeezing. 'It's taking.'

Iroise moaned: it felt as if her clitoris were a tube and the squeezing was pumping desire through this tube, directly into her womb.

'Turn round. It needs the sun upon it.' It felt tight against her ribbon, as if it were growing. Eloise's thumb rubbed the ribbon deeper into the crease of Iroise's buttocks. When she pushed it up her bottom, the pressure at the front made Iroise tremble on tiptoes, on the verge of coming. When the thumb came out, the ribbon stayed in. Eloise made her walk on to complete the greater part of the circuit. Then she helped her down and took her into a stone and wooden building behind the house.

One wall was hidden behind six huge oval, tapped casks. The floor at one end was covered with baskets of grapes. There were wooden presses. Three enormous shallow wooden tubs on plinths were arranged down the middle. Two were empty. One was full of pulp and purple juice and Chloe. The nude young man was bathing her. He was slim, muscular and pale. Chloe was lying back against the side of the tub nursing his large erection.

'Let Brammen see what I've done to you,' Eloise coaxed. She led Iroise to a narrow trestle bench. 'Sit astride; close your eyes.'

Iroise felt Brammen supporting her gently and tilting her back. 'Open your mouth,' he whispered. A glass was put to her lips; she tasted sweet, aromatic wine. 'Drink it. It will help you. There.' She felt light-headed.

'The graft is taking,' Eloise whispered. 'No – don't be frightened.'

'Let me look,' Brammen whispered.

Iroise, shivering, felt the ribbon being loosened.

'Careful,' Eloise warned.

Through half-closed eyes Iroise watched Brammen's fingers draw the end of her ribbon down. The grape protruded like a shiny ball from the top of her cunny. Her hood was now clinging to its surface. Her belly was trembling. 'Don't detach it,' Eloise warned him. His penis was hard and his breathing strained.

'Lie down, little beauty.' Iroise's hands were trapped under her. Her legs were draped to either side of the narrow bench. He withdrew the ribbon gently from her anus. Eloise smothered her moans. Brammen's finger went inside her liquid cunny. The fat grape swayed like a leech upon her knob. She wanted to come. 'Can we leave her ribbon off?' Brammen asked.

They lifted her open-thighed into the tub. Her buttocks settled into the pulp. Bubbles drifted towards her across the surface. Cool purple juice issued up her cunny and made a tickling line around her belly. She lay with arms outstretched along the side of the tub.

Eloise disrobed herself of the mendicant's habit and laid it on the bench. Her breasts were beautiful and her bush was black and shiny. She had shiny black hairs under her arms. With rising desire, Iroise watched her approaching. Her scent was strong and female, her skin smooth and salty; Iroise kissed it – velvet breast-skin, moist underarms, cool neck and warm mouth – as the girl craned over her.

Brammen was already in the tub. Gentle waves of juice washed over Iroise as he crouched between Chloe's legs and laved her breasts with juice.

'See how wide she spreads?' Eloise whispered. 'Though he is big, she wants him in there.' Chloe's toes were poking like islets out of the liquor. Her thighs were submerged. Her nipples lay balanced on the surface and Brammen kept fondling them, drawing dense streams of milk through the purple. Spreading out from her black paps were two slicks of purplish pink. The round mound of her belly made an island over which his broad penis slipped as it tried and failed to penetrate her. But Chloe was excited by the slippery friction.

Eloise's fingers slid down Iroise's belly into the liquor, found the submerged split and opened it completely. 'Let it soak inside. Let all resistance drown.' Bubbles rose between Iroise's legs. Her cunny felt pregnant with heavy liquor. Then Eloise began patting her berry.

Brammen, sitting on his heels, had lifted Chloe astride his lap. His tongue sought the pink runnels streaming down her belly. She stood up and fed her dripping sex into his mouth and grasped his bulging penis poking from the liquor.

Eloise asked Iroise if she wanted it inside her. But Chloe was determined to be first: when she could not get it in at the front, she turned round and gently impaled herself to the vitals.

'Soon you too may be obliged to take it that way,' Eloise whispered. 'Your grape is swelling.' The drawing feeling between Iroise's legs was stronger. With every undulation of the liquor, the berry tugged the apex of her cunny. Eloise slid her arm under Iroise's back and lifted her. Her berry broke surface like a bobbing ball and it was frightening to behold its size yet the feeling turned exquisite when Eloise kissed her and squeezed it. She saw Brammen's eyes flash with desire. He began touching Chloe's cunny while her bottom was still impaled upon his penis. When she started to come, he stood up with his penis still up her bottom. Her toes, jerking down in spasms, burst the broad red bubbles on the surface of the liquor, and her breasts hung outwards dribbling milk.

'She needs to go to bed,' he called to Eloise.

'They both do. We all do,' Eloise answered.

Brammen carried the two dripping girls, one on each arm, across the courtyard, into the house and up the stairs, with Eloise leading the way to his room and generous bed, where she drew the covers back while he laid the girls down on the pure white sheets. Everywhere their skin touched turned purple-red. Iroise sat huddled, afraid to sully the pristine surface, afraid to open her legs and yet unable to close them properly on account of the swelling blister between them. Brammen rolled Chloe over and over, on her belly and on her back. Cloud shapes, bulbously feminine, were imprinted indelibly on the sheets. Juice was escaping from Iroise's cunny. Eloise sucked her juice-slicked nipples. 'Open. Show him.' She propped her against a pillow and pushed her ankles back until her heels were pressed against her buttocks. Brammen lay on the far side of Chloe and she was sucking the base of his penis.

'Look, Brammen, how swiftly her grape has taken hold.'

'Detach it.'

Iroise shuddered at the words.

'She is frightened. There is nothing to fear, my darling. Hold her.'

They made her drink from a silver cup. The room softened and swooned; her eyelids felt heavy yet her skin felt more sensitive than ever to touching. She sat with her head back against Brammen's shoulder as Eloise's lips placed slow kisses all the way down her centre line from her neck to the top of her cunny. Brammen pinned her arms behind her with one hand. The other held her nipple pinched. When Eloise's tongue-tip touched the join between berry-ball and the stretched skin hood adhering to its shiny surface, Iroise shuddered again. When she pulled it with her fingers, Iroise moaned.

'It's like an acorn, tight in its cup,' Eloise whispered. But Iroise saw it was far bigger. 'It needs to come away without breaking.'

'Twist it,' said Brammen. 'Feed her more mesmeric, first.' The little silver cup of fluid was readministered. 'Look – her breasts – so tight,' he whispered. He sucked one. Her thighs jerked open. And suddenly, she felt as if she were being lifted up and turned, and in her mind she was floating, staring down at a naked girl on her back now, her belly arched over the pillow under her middle. Between her legs, a grotesque and beautiful purple-red blister the size of an egg pushed the lips of her cunny out of shape. Brammen was at her head, pinning her blonde locks with his knees, pinning her breasts with his hands, his curved erection poking out above her face. Eloise was pinning her knees open and Chloe was looking on with detached equanimity. Eloise's open mouth descended between those frightened thighs.

'Get it cleanly,' Brammen warned.

'Nnnnhh!' Suddenly Iroise was back inside her body, moaning, gasping. Pinned, she could not move, could only reach up with her lips to suck upon those heavy dangling balls as cruelly as the pleasure pulled between her legs. It felt as if a hundred tiny needles were being drawn from the inside skin of her hood. It felt as if a tiny collar around her clitoris was being tightened to make it burst. Then a feeling came that was frightening and sexually deep, as if an oily knotted thread were somehow being drawn out through her clitoris and was rooted in her womb. The berry-ball came free. The cool air touched the newly exposed flesh.

Brammen climbed off her hair and Iroise stared down between her thighs to see the plucked fruit burst between Eloise's teeth. The girl's head went back, that her mouth might lose no spillage. She sighed and swallowed. A dense blood-red trickle issued from the corner of her mouth. Brammen reached for her and licked the dribbles. Then the girl bent forwards swiftly, sucking between Iroise's thighs, pushing the thinned hood far back, sucking the tortured newly aired clitoris, making the feeling come that a fine canal now existed between clitoris and womb. Then she put her sex against Iroise's interleaving lips, so the inner surfaces of the two right lips touched each other. 'I want to taste your mark inside me,' Eloise murmured. She lay flesh to flesh against Iroise, black curls tickling Iroise's naked skin, while Brammen lay with Chloe. As he curled around her, limbs intertwined with Chloe's bulbous breasts and belly, he milked her nipples with his mouth and Chloe milked his penis.

Eloise fell asleep in Iroise's arms and Iroise experienced languorous pleasure, holding this beautiful female creature so intimately close, caressing her curves, feeling those breasts against her, and brushing her lips across the lovely eyebrows and up to the shiny black aromatic hair.

Iroise could not recall drifting into sleep. When she woke, candles burned around the room. The kinsmen had not returned. It was as well for she was certain they would never understand – Kin-Cague especially. Iroise had not eaten but the only hunger she felt was for the girl, who stood naked at the foot of the bed, watching Brammen administering the silver cup of liquor to Chloe. A throbbing yearning lay between Iroise's legs. When she looked she saw a new berry was in place there.

'Don't touch it,' Eloise warned her. She came to Iroise. 'If you watch, you can see it swelling.' She stared into her eyes. 'Drawing all your goodness out for me.' Iroise shivered and spread her thighs wider to speed the sexual swelling.

When a girl puts her fingers into you at the front, the feeling of possession is keen and special: the fingers are delicate, not coarse like a man's, and the pressures are subtle and knowing.

Brammen was rubbing liquor from the silver cup into Chloe's leaking nipples. Her breasts looked fuller than ever. Her belly looked tight, less smooth, as if the flesh itself were thinned. Her cheeks looked hollow, her skin pale. Like Iroise, Chloe had not eaten these two days. All nourishment in her body was being channelled to her womb and breasts. She was kneeling up. Brammen lay on his back, his head between her legs and he started licking. Chloe held her cunny open.

'Is she not ravishing, so close to dropping?' Eloise whispered. 'Brammen told me he can get his tongue against her womb.' Eloise's fingers were still inside Iroise, lifting now, causing the swollen ball to move. 'Put your legs together.' The ball squeezed upwards, ruby red. It remained balanced there when Eloise gently removed her fingers. Chloe hunched forwards; pleasure pulses surging through her body, her nipples dripping milk upon Brammen's erect penis. Eloise stretched across the bed and rubbed the milk into his flesh.

'Are you jealous of my touching him?' She stared up at Chloe. 'Then come here – this end. Give me your fingers. Wet them well with your milk. Now push them up here. Oooh. Good girl.' Brammen writhed in pleasure. 'Inside the male is a gland – like Iroise's blister but within the body, behind the penis. Feel it? Press it. Try to lift him on the points of your fingers.' She came back to Iroise and ordered her to spread. Then she settled down with her head pillowed on Iroise's inner thigh and made love with lips and tongue to the swelling blister, keeping it moving all the while. The prolonged unstinting pleasuring between her legs made something happen in Iroise's body: it felt as if velvet waves of languor emanated from her womb. She clung gently to Eloise's head, caressed it softly, while its bright-red lips pressed their luscious sucking torture upon her cunny. She drifted in and out of slumber. Her body felt limp and deliciously weak. When she lifted her leaden eyelids, she saw between her pallid thighs Eloise on her back, her skin pink and warm, her red lips suckerlike about the ruby blister. It felt as if the invisible, knotted, oily thread was being sucked continuously through her clitoris from her womb. She did not want so lovely a feeling to desist. Across the way, she saw Brammen's shiny semen-wet limbs curling round Chloe's body like a snake, sucking liquid pleasure from her nipples. Chloe was in climax. Her fingers barely touched it, yet his penis leaked continuously over them as if he were a sucking insect overfilled. Iroise looked again at the beautiful girl between her thighs. Had Iroise had the strength, she would have lain upon that beautiful body and kissed every inch. The legs lay casually open, the black-fringed cunny agape. And she saw inside and thought she was dreaming – the right lip, the one that had lain so close and lovingly against her own, bore a pattern, an image, a vivid and unmistakable reflection of her own tattoo.

16

River Deep

'My God, Kin-Cague, you were right! This is the entrance! We've gone full circle round the walls.'

'And spent half the night doing it.'

Dariun stared up in awe. 'But how can it be? This morning there wasn't even a gate here. And now these vines, as high as the wall itself, like a thicket. And look, bunches of fruit, already ripe.'

'Don't touch it!'

'Why?'

'Take the horses back – over there – and hitch them well. I'll get brushwood.'

'Why?'

The thicket burnt like tinder. Even so, it took many anguished minutes before the two kinsmen, using heavy branches as clubs, could break through the smouldering tangle.

'You run on, Dariun. You're quicker by far. Just find them!'

Kin-Cague had hoped that the commotion and the fire would have brought the girls out but there was no sign of life. Dariun disappeared ahead. In the dawn light, an eerie calm surrounded the house. Kin-Cague was breathing heavily as he reached the top of the hill. The door was open: inside, once his eyes had adjusted to the dim light, everything seemed as they had left it. He made straight for the stairs. At the top he heard a clatter. Dariun emerged breathless from the first bedroom.

'No one there,' he gasped. 'I'll search downstairs.'

'Wait! Look. The other room.' Kin-Cague pointed. Leafy tendrils issued from under the door. The kinsmen burst it open. Early sunlight filtered through the curtainless window. Some of the leaded panes were missing and vines had grown through the gaps. Candles, distributed about the room, still burnt; one began to gutter, sending a dense wisp of whiteness to the ceiling.

The two girls were strewn naked on the bed as though cast there in drugged abandon. They lay still but they were breathing.

'They look so pale, Kin-Cague. What is it?'

Everywhere underfoot were the vines. They had climbed the bedposts and were draped across the counterpane. Dark, frightening patches stained the sheets and pillows. The kinsmen stared down at the comatose girls.

'Dear God!' Dariun cried.

'Don't try to pull it out! Get a knife from the kitchen – quickly!' The vine draped across Iroise's thigh had entered her body. Its leaves were shaded purple. Tendrils like fine bootlaces encircled Chloe's nipples, choking them, seeming to pulse with her breathing. Milk ran continuously from her nipples, down her sides and soaked into the grim, dark stains on the sheet. Kin-Cague tried to rouse the girls from their deathly slumber. Only when Dariun had returned and the creeping strands were severed did they show signs of waking.

'We'll have to carry them. Take Chloe. Take care with her. No, don't try to remove the stems of vine yet. Get her downstairs. We'll need to see if the other horse is still in the stable. But wait for me. Don't leave her unattended.'

Kin-Cague watched his colleague lift Chloe. Her head hung back almost lifelessly. He waited until she was safely clear of the room then he lifted Iroise. She was murmuring incoherently but was alive enough to cling to his neck. Her arms were freezing cold.

The horse was where they had left it. They found the girls' clothing in the dust of the disused winery. Hurriedly, they dressed them and balanced them on the horse's back.

Iroise began hallucinating, pointing towards the grassy mounds at the crown of the hill and mumbling a name. 'There's no one there,' Kin-Cague reassured her gently. He turned to Dariun and whispered, 'I want to make quite sure. Lead on slowly. Don't stop until you're outside the walls.'

Kin-Cague ascended to the highest point and stared all around. But there was nothing save the last grey smoulderings of the charred vines around the entrance, and the clink of the horse's hooves on the loose stones. In the distance were the beautiful broad valley and the soaring mountains beyond. This was indeed a commanding scene.

As he turned to go, his gaze fell again upon the twin grassy mounds beside him, verdant in the early light. Perhaps Iroise, in her dazed state, had mistaken their little crosses for distant figures. A sadness touched him as he dwelt upon the fragility of human life.

Beyond the walls, they made camp in a copse beside the river. Dariun made a broth of dried fish and mushrooms and fleshy roots that he dug from round about. Both girls consumed it hungrily, for which Kin-Cague was mightily grateful. They spoke little, for they were weary, as if every drop of strength had been sapped from their bodies. But he asked them if they wished to bathe. 'It may help detach the tendrils from your skin.' There was a shallow pool floored by sand on the sunny side of the copse. Its water was warm. Iroise was the more frightened but Kin-Cague hid his own anxiety when she asked him to accompany her. He knew she would want him to try to take the tendril out of her. With Chloe it would be simpler, for the attachments were external, but even there, there seemed to be a partial fusion of tendril and skin. Dariun had said that a true fusion between flesh and plant could not happen and that the tendrils must simply be bedded through tightness. Kin-Cague was not so sure.

'It feels strange inside me,' Iroise whispered, anxiously. She was sitting in the pool and Kin-Cague was gently bathing her. The purple-tinged vine frond wafted between

171

her thighs. 'It feels as if I am swollen in there at the front.' She clasped his arm.

'Let the water inside you. It will help.' But he was not sure that it would.

Dariun was bathing Chloe's breasts, from which the snags of severed, milk-soaked vine hung by their tightly coiled tendrils.

A feeling of hopelessness welled from the pit of Kin-Cague's belly. Anything they attempted might only worsen the situation. Already the fronds between Iroise's thighs looked brighter than before.

'Kin-Cague, it's coming off her!' Chloe sat with gritted teeth as Dariun unwound it like string from its bedding round her nipple.

Kin-Cague heaved a heartfelt sigh then recovered composure. 'Don't lose it. Put it on the fire.' He waited while the second tendril was removed.

'Now me,' Iroise whispered.

'I'll get Dariun. His hand is steadier.'

She shook her head. 'You.' She closed her eyes and leant back, waiting for him to do it.

Kin-Cague knelt between her precious thighs. He knew he must cloak his fears with calm precision. He took firm hold of the protruding stem with his right hand. The water had made the stem more flexible: perhaps it would not snap inside her. Gently, he pulled. She murmured. He relented. 'No, go on. You must,' she begged. He clenched his teeth and gradually strengthened his grip. The stem tautened. Her knees tightened; her belly moved towards him in the water; her knees locked. She bit her lip and moaned. A clinging frond detached from her inside her labium. Then the stem started moving, very slowly, a long, long strand with little nodules mounted upon it, ever thinning, ever brightening from purple to red. Little billows of redness clouded the water. The strand came out as a single piece. Kin-Cague breathed again.

'Stay there. Everything's all right.' The frond appeared to have absorbed some of the stain from Iroise's tattoo. He left the pool and cast the complete stem into the fire then went back to Iroise. 'Let me look. All perfect.' He noticed that her clitoris was engorged and a minute lump was present under the hood. Very gently he drew it back.

'What is it?' Iroise asked.

'A seed – a pip – tucked under.' Carefully, he removed it. 'There. All fine.'

Iroise was shivering. He gathered her in his arms and laid her on a blanket by the fire. He cast the pip into the fire then began to dry her with his gown. There was no blood between her thighs but he had noticed something else.

'Your tattoo. It's gone,' he whispered. Contact with the vine leaf had somehow expunged it completely. He expected her to look. She remained still for a moment or two, then nodded.

'She took it,' she replied knowingly.

As the day progressed, Iroise found her strength returning little by little. For much of the time, Chloe had slept in Kin-Cague's arms. He said he could detect no ill effects in the girls, beyond exhaustion and paleness, which he blamed on lack of food and drink. Dariun attended to the cure and Iroise was content to be pampered. Though the two kinsmen seemed less anxious, it was plain that they wanted to leave this place before nightfall. By late afternoon, Kin-Cague had broached his plan.

Chloe was on his lap, Iroise was on her blanket and Dariun looked on. Kin-Cague took a stick and drew a tight nooselike curve in the dried silt by the fire.

'The bend in the river,' he said. 'At this end, the broken bridge – at least we have gotten over it. But across the neck of land is a crag of solid rock. And we are here.' He stabbed the point of the stick into the loop he had drawn. 'The crag is passable on foot: Dariun found the start of the trail yesterday. It's overgrown and very steep: a horse can make it but cannot be ridden.'

Iroise glanced at Chloe.

'I can walk,' Chloe said.

Kin-Cague shook his head. 'It's too harsh and high, my brave one,' he said gently.

'I can carry her,' Dariun said.

Again Kin-Cague shook his head.

'Then what?' Iroise asked him.

He pursed his lips. 'There's a boat: we found it in the early hours while we were floundering round the wall. It's beached high on the bank above a ruined boathouse.'

'Kin-Cague, I told you I wasn't happy about splitting up,' Dariun said.

'Splitting up?' Iroise repeated.

'Only for a while. Look.' Kin-Cague traced the routes in the silt. 'I'll lead the horses over the ridge. Chloe and you go round it in the boat with Dariun.'

'Kin-Cague, the girls will be safer with you in the boat. I don't even know where I'm going.'

'You have youth, strength and quickness. The flood is ebbing. As for direction – you cannot go wrong. Remain with this bank and follow it downriver. Stay on course until you have rounded the ridge – Iroise will navigate – then beach and wait for me. Whatever happens, I will find you.'

Kin-Cague helped them drag the boat down the bank. At this point, below the wrecked bridge, the river was wide even though the water level had dropped considerably. They used a little inlet by the boathouse to launch the small craft. Two of the panniers from the horses were loaded into it together with some blankets and nearly all of the food. Chloe was lifted in at the front, Iroise took charge of the tiller and Dariun took the oars. Chloe kissed Kin-Cague.

'Wait,' Iroise said. She took the chained ring from round her neck and placed it round Kin-Cague's.

'But it's yours,' he said.

'Wear it for luck,' she whispered.

He squinted at the Tormunite cross on the signet. 'I used to fear this icon, little guessing it to be a harbinger of luck.' He sighed and shook his head. And Iroise kissed him.

All three watched Kin-Cague's figure receding with the horses.

Though the flow was sluggish, the scene seemed to change quite swiftly as the boat moved out from the bank towards the middle of the broad river. The scale of everything appeared different from this distance; the hill with its vineyard soon looked tiny against the towering ridge of land behind, that Kin-Cague had to cross alone. Dariun stopped rowing and peered at it. He said he could see the path where it crossed the summit of the ridge. To Iroise it looked like a hairline scratch on the crag tops in the hazy distance.

'How long will it take him?' she asked.

'Three or four hours, I guess.'

'Surely longer?'

'Perhaps. But then we just do what he said – bed down for the night and wait.'

Wait where, she wondered. The landscape was vast. 'That path, Dariun – if it is a path – seems to be going in the opposite direction.'

'But the river will swing round,' he said.

'Into the ridge?'

'Well, yes,' he frowned. 'It's true it looks a greater obstacle than we reckoned.' Then he brightened. 'But the river must cut through it and come out on the other side.'

Gradually, as Dariun rowed on and the boat neared the bend, the scene beyond was revealed. The river had narrowed and deepened, beautiful tree-laden steep banks encroached from each side as it swung in slow twists to left and right. Dariun rested and the boat continued to glide through this lovely scene. Iroise steered a perfect curve down the middle. There were no waves; the water was glass-clear all the way to the rocky bottom. The afternoon sun funnelled warmth upon the travellers. They began gently to roast under the heavy garb of the habits. Chloe was first to divest. She spread her gown beneath her then relaxed upon it, draping the tips of her fingers in the water.

Iroise sat for some minutes getting uncomfortably hotter before she finally followed Chloe's example, trying to appear nonchalant about it in the confines of the little boat, with the young kinsman facing her and trying too hard to appear unconcerned.

'If you want to sleep,' Dariun offered, 'just pin the tiller in place with that dowel.'

Iroise accepted. She made a pillow of her gown and lay upon it, under the tiller, facing back, curled across the seat. The sun warmed her. She drifted into sleep, listening to the intermittent steadying swish of the oars and wondering what Dariun might be thinking. When she came out of the first deep slumber and turned over, he was sitting in the same position but he too was now naked. Iroise watched him rowing: the way the muscles tightened across his belly as he leant back upon the oars, and the way his burden of male flesh swayed. It looked silken in the sun. She submerged again into a deep sleep and then a dreaming sleep beset by feelings in her belly, flutterings which – in the dream – she reported to Dariun and he examined. He kept touching the place where her tattoo had been, rubbing the tips of his fingers across the unblemished inner skin while she lay on the edge of coming. He rubbed unknowingly in this way until oil spilled from her body, making him recoil when it wetted his fingers.

When she woke again, the bobbing boat was empty but for herself, and the light was fading. She jumped up, naked, in a panic, banging her side against the tiller. The boat had been tied against a rocky ledge projecting from the bank of the river. Dariun and Chloe were on a blanket on the shingle. They were immersed in mutual petting. Dariun, seeing Iroise, came to help her from the boat. He did not seem shy of nakedness or of bearing an erection and Chloe looked blissfully happy. Iroise allowed him to carry her across the shingle.

'I can feel your heartbeat,' he whispered to her.

'I thought the two of you had left me.'

'We didn't want to wake you.' Then he said, 'Your thighs are wet – what happened?' Iroise was mortified. 'Let me look. May I?' He set her down on the blanket.

'What is it?' Chloe wanted to know.

Dariun started to touch Iroise, almost in the way that had happened in the dream. Iroise did not stop him.

'She's making "nice",' Chloe sniggered.

Iroise expected Dariun to blanch and falter. He did not. He sat between the two girls, one hand softly examining

176

Iroise between the legs, the other gently coaxing milk from Chloe's nipples. His erection was swollen larger than Iroise had seen it. She curled round, closed her eyes and kissed its head and tasted on its skin the 'nice' from Chloe's cunny.

Suddenly Chloe shouted, 'Look – the boat!'

But it was too late: it was already out at the edge of the ledge, trailing its mooring rope.

Dariun flew across the shingle. Iroise followed. He started wading out, lunging for the end of the rope.

'No!' Iroise cried. 'Leave it. It's going out too far.' He caught hold of the end. Then, suddenly, he was out of his depth, and it was plain he could not swim. 'Hold on!' Helplessly, Iroise watched him being sucked along in the slow current. She ran along the bank, gradually falling behind as the current picked up speed. He kept disappearing, struggling, pulling on the rope. The boat slewed round, crossing the centre line of the river. Then she saw the rapids. She wanted to hide her eyes. The boat crashed over tier upon tier of white water, then tilted on its side and wedged between two massive boulders. Dariun hauled himself out of the water, dragging Iroise's sodden gown. But he was on the opposite bank.

'I'm all right,' he shouted, wringing out the gown. 'Look after Chloe. Stay there until I find a way back.'

Iroise picked her way back along the bank, her heart sinking as she wondered how Dariun could ever hope to get across. She rounded the ledge of rock where the boat had been moored, then stood transfixed: the shingle bank was empty. There was no sign that anyone had ever been there.

17

Loggers

Iroise stared in disbelief: Chloe had gone; so had the two panniers, along with Dariun's clothes and the blankets. The light was failing quickly. She called out but there was no sign of life on the river or across it. Behind the shingle a natural bowl was cut into the valley side; its steep side was covered in trees and underbrush. Iroise followed the shingle bank upriver across the mouth of the bowl, calling out repeatedly. No answer came. Then she saw a flickering glow reflected from under the tree tops high on the edge of the bowl. Quickly, she retraced her steps to the place where she had left Chloe. She walked across to the brush-clad slope, looking for signs of an upward path: Chloe could never have gotten up there unassisted. She went back to where the boat had been tied: there were scuff marks in the gravel and broken branchlets in an irregular line ascending the ridge from the rocky ledge. Straining her ears she could discern, above the sound of the river, a crackling noise from the direction of the glowing light; she thought she heard voices. Warily, Iroise picked her way upwards through the bushes. Even for her, the route was steep and tricky; if Chloe had been taken this way then she must have been carried, and there must have been several abductors. It had happened so swiftly – the runaway boat, and the abduction without audible cries for help. Whoever had done it must have lain in wait, witnessing what had happened on the blankets and coveting Chloe as a plaything in her defenceless state.

The flickering light above grew stronger, the voices more distinct: they sounded like men's voices. Iroise, all too conscious of her own nakedness, was grateful for the encroaching darkness. Suddenly, it occurred to her that these men – if they had been watching – must surely know she was abroad. Gripped by fear, she stopped in her tracks and tortuously slowly peered around. When nothing moved, she crept slowly into the darker undergrowth, away from the obvious route. But now she was conscious of every little rustling sound stirred by her movement through the bushes. As she tried to hold her breath against the rising fear, her breathing came ever more strained and noisier. Eventually, she reached the top of the bank and crouched to look. The bushes thinned and the ground sloped away before her.

She was on the edge of a clearing advancing in a wide swathe through the woods. Newly felled trees lay haphazardly nearby, with piles of trimmed logs lower down. A little below the middle of the clearing, a large bonfire crackled fiercely with silhouetted figures grouped around it. There were makeshift huts and a small corral of carthorses. She heard voices and glimpsed naked flesh reflecting the firelight; from their gait the naked ones appeared to be girls. To get nearer, she had to creep round the edge of clearing, at one point having to race across a wide, rutted track, praying that no one would see her in the open. Even in the darkness, her pale skin would show like a beacon. She made a wide circle through the woodland on the lower side before risking an approach. She must have been twenty or thirty paces from the edge of the clearing when she came across the young man.

Her heart nearly burst through her breast from shock. She was almost close enough to have touched him but he couldn't see her, for he was blindfold. Iroise stood before him, completely confounded. Clearly he could hear her breathing – his neck craned towards her – yet he did not speak: he was too frightened. His wrists were tied up under the horizontal branch of a tree and he was naked but for his tunic top, unbuttoned and drawn open by his upraised arms. His sex had been shaved and was semi-erect. On the ground beside him lay a tilted wooden flagon. Iroise quietly backed away.

She reached the edge of the clearing – this time, just above the corral and much closer to the fire – and could see everything. There were men – one or two – but the voices she had thought were men's were girls'. The men lay silently submissive to the girls' whims. Several of the girls wore nothing but a halter round their ample breasts. They were carousing, drinking from wooden mugs that they recharged from a foaming bucket propped against a tree that had a spiral knife wound down its stem. In their midst was Chloe, sitting cross-legged and being made to drink. She looked dazed. Iroise knew she had to try to save her friend but did not know how to.

Then she thought of the tethered male: perhaps he would help if she were to free him? She turned to retrace her steps and immediately found herself staring at a girl, whose arms were folded under her haltered breasts. She was carrying a thin rope. Iroise turned to run. Quick as lightening, the girl lunged, grasping her by the ankle, making her tumble forwards on to a heap of leaves. Iroise twisted round but the girl had her ankle in an iron grasp.

'Weak struggles,' the girl mocked. 'A sure sign of a Tormunite-tarnished slut.' The girl was slight of figure yet muscular. Her hair was brown and short like a man's. Her breasts were disproportionately large. The girl stared at her with narrowed eyes: she was younger than Iroise but Iroise was afraid of her.

Expertly swiftly, she looped the end of the rope round Iroise's ankle. 'Get up.' Iroise flinched when that hand extended towards her cheek. The fingers furrowed under her matted silken ringlets, combing them close to the roots, then withdrew. The girl breathed Iroise's scent from her fingers. 'Turn round.' She continued to stroke her curls. Iroise could feel the frank gaze searing into her back. The rope suddenly snapped against her bottom. 'Turn round!' The girl glanced in the direction of the clearing. 'Kneel down,' she whispered. She was naked from her halter down. A rich bush of hair sprouted from between her thighs. She grasped Iroise's head with both hands and suddenly the strong scent of girl filled Iroise's nostrils; the soft moist cunny lips engulfed her mouth; the thighs closed tightly round her ears. The girl tried to climb upon her face. Iroise could not breathe, yet the girl still forced her head back. Iroise's kneeling body was bent back like a bow. Her breasts protruded, nipples tight. A waft of cool air between her legs softly chilled the naked lips of her cunny. Her face was soaked with scorching girl-flesh and stifled by humid redolent hairs. She went giddy and limp, slumping backwards. A stinging slap burst across her face.

Then a shout came from the clearing – a name. 'Kerun!'

'Get up, Tormunite slut!' the girl ordered. 'Start walking.'

Iroise stumbled into the clearing, tears running down her face, dissolving into the film of wetness that the girl had put there. Chloe gasped to see her friend dishevelled, with the rope round her ankle. Great interest was stirred amongst the woods-girls. They gathered round the new captive, then cleared a way for their leader, who was older and wore a shirt and trousers. Her hands were large; her skin was weatherworn and marred by little scars.

'What have we here? Stand still, girl.' She grasped the back of Iroise's hair and drew her head back, exposing her throat. 'Good work, Kerun.'

'Trivenn, she was spying on us,' Kerun declared.

'Was she now?'

Iroise tried to speak. The woman clamped her mouth shut and dragged her by the hair to her knees.

A girl beside her said, 'Trivenn, the patrol is back.' Two girls, clad like Kerun in halters, approached from the direction of the path.

'This one got past you,' Trivenn said to them.

The girls glared at Iroise. Then one said, 'The male escaped across the river, more's the pity. But we wrecked their boat.'

'The little one still denies they are Tormunites,' Trivenn said, simply.

'But we found monks' clothing beside her,' the second girl said.

Trivenn shook her head. 'Monks don't get girls pregnant. Or if they do they cover their tracks better.'

'But this one is a Tormunite,' Kerun interrupted peevishly, pointing at Iroise. 'And I caught her spying.'

Trivenn shrugged.

'Ask her,' Kerun insisted.

'You ask her.' Trivenn released her grip on Iroise and stood back, folding her arms.

'Tell them,' Kerun pushed Iroise who began to cry as she stared fearfully from one harsh face to the other.

'I c . . . came to help my friend,' she whispered feebly. 'I thought she was in danger.'

'She is, if you don't tell the truth,' said Trivenn. 'Are you a Tantalite?'

Iroise swallowed. She stared at the ground then bit her lip. 'Yes,' she muttered. 'But –'

'See!' cried Kerun.

Trivenn frowned. 'I doubt she's a spy. A collaborator or a harlot, more likely.'

'But a collaborator is still a mortal danger to our group,' the second girl said.

'Then cultivate the harlot in her. Whip her. Use her as you would the male prisoners. Give Kerun first crack at the cherry.'

They tied a short piece of log to the rope round her ankle to hobble her and prevent her running away. Everywhere she went, she had to drag the log. They forced her to drink the foaming sap drained from the tree; when she tried to refuse any more they slapped her face until her ears and cheeks burnt and her eyelids were swollen with tears. They would not let her use her hands; one girl – the second and crueller of the patrol-girls, whose name was Lindren – pinned her arms behind her while Kerun fed her the drink. If Iroise spilt any, Kerun slapped her breasts. This was done in front of the captive males by the fire and Kerun did not stint. The males, though frightened, were aroused by witnessing Iroise's domination by the haltered girls whose swollen breasts jostled with every slap.

One of the males was being shaved. A beautiful girl knelt bared-thighed astride his belly and worked the razor down his oiled erection. When the stem was bare and near to spilling she fitted it with a pig's-bladder sheath and continued shaving his sac.

Some of the women were roasting meat on a wire griddle over a smaller fire. Others sat in groups talking and laughing, sometimes watching, as if sexual punishment was an everyday event and participation could await their choosing.

A little cluster had formed about Chloe; there was laughter as her milk sprayed in the air. One of the naked males was dragged across and lain beside her, head to toe. Then the cluster swelled, with some of the women standing to secure a clearer view.

The drink made Iroise's nipples and clitoris swell. The girls laid her on her back and took turns astride her face. They tied her ankles together and used a finger against her knob. They discovered that her arousal came keener with her hands pinned beneath her and her mouth gently hushed by a cunny. 'It's like a hard little ball rolling under my finger,' Lindren whispered. 'It makes me want to push her little ball inside her.' Iroise's thighs went rigid; she gurgled into Kerun's cunny.

Kerun, climbing off, stretched out alongside Iroise. 'Lie still,' she demanded. Then she pinched and stretched her nipples cruelly. 'Lie still.' When she kissed her, she bit her lip. Lindren's agile fingers worked all the while between Iroise's thighs, developing her erection only to keep pushing it up into her body. Iroise's belly was slowly melting. 'Poke your tongue out,' Kerun ordered, then she held it fast between her teeth and continued torturing Iroise's nipples. When Kerun finally pulled away, Iroise's tongue felt numb and swollen. 'Did I tell you to put it back?' Kerun slapped her face. 'Now poke it out, like the slut you are.'

One of the older women had stopped to watch.

'Now call me "Mistress",' Kerun was saying. Tears issued down Iroise's face as she tried to lisp her reply around her poking tongue and Kerun slapped her again. Iroise's tear-wet face turned for succour to the watching woman, who knelt beside her face, murmuring, 'She's beautiful, Kerun, truly beautiful. Such silky blonde curls, so cool to the touch.' She stroked the flaccid ringlets that framed Iroise's face and were spread in disarray against the grass. 'Keep your tongue out, sweetly lewd, as your young mistress has demanded. May I kiss her?' The woman's mouth descended gently; the lips took expert suck upon the underside of Iroise's tongue and the lip-touch there was so arousing that Iroise shuddered on the brink of pleasure. The woman knew, and drew away. She kissed each fatted nipple lightly and Iroise felt as if her belly were being opened with an invisible knife. 'Lindren, spread her knees, let me kiss between her legs.'

'Oh, no . . . Oh, please . . .' Iroise begged.

'But you are ready, so ready. I can tell.'

Tears welled from deep inside her: what the woman said was so keenly true. Iroise shook her head. 'Please . . . No,' she begged again.

'No, don't hit her,' the woman said. 'There is more to this than obstinacy. There is true anxiety, deeply rooted.' She turned to Kerun and Lindren. 'The Tantalites often train their girls to believe that female ejaculation is wrong – sinful, as they put it.'

Kerun stared askance at Iroise.

Then the woman said, 'I need you girls to help me retrain her.'

The woman's name was Suidin. She was second in command in the camp and the younger women seemed to look to her for counsel. Kerun, concerned that Iroise might escape corporal punishment, said cruelly, 'Trivenn ordered a whipping and told us to use her like the males.'

'She has no need of shaving for she seems to grow no pubic hair,' Suidin observed. Her fingertips roved gently over Iroise's naked belly. Then she whispered to Iroise, 'Is it something that the Tormunites did to you?'

'I don't know. They used to shave me and put lotion there; then after a while there were only individual hairs. Once these were plucked they did not regrow.'

'Then they did well: it is pretty.' She turned to the two girls. 'Loosen the rope round her ankles. Open her knees properly. There.' Her voice fell again to a whisper directed at Iroise. 'Can you not understand why I want to kiss it to completion?'

Iroise closed her eyes. Suidin gently kissed her mouth and cupped her naked cunny and luscious arousal welled inside Iroise.

'Take her into the trees and whip her soundly then bring her back to me.' The hand delved further underneath, between her legs, trying to take all of her sex and bottom and squeeze them lovingly, and Iroise's cunny split like an overripe fruit about the thumb and its liquid middle trickled.

'Is she ejaculating?' Kerun asked.

'Oh, no, not yet,' Suidin whispered, squeezing until her thumb glistened with oily weepage.

It was deep night before they brought her back to Suidin's tent. The fireglow illuminated Iroise's naked, punished skin. 'Put her on the blanket.' Iroise shrank away from her tormentors. Suidin instructed them to come back later. She gently untethered the wooden hobble from Iroise's ankle, where the rope had made a reddened ring. Iroise, her eyelids swollen by burning tears, watched the older woman ministering to her.

'I can make them leave the hobble off you if you promise not to try to escape,' Suidin whispered, looking up at her as she sat rubbing the ankle.

Iroise had nowhere to escape to. 'Make them leave me alone, and I will promise,' Iroise murmured. They were cruel and hurtful, especially Kerun.

'You cannot set preconditions, not here. Amongst our group you are lowlier than the lowest woods-girl.'

Though the chastisement was gentle, Iroise was already fighting back fresh tears; she wanted so desperately to throw herself upon this woman's mercy.

'Please, do not put me to them again,' Iroise begged anew.

'I must, but not through malice. Their needs must be considered too.' She looked at Iroise with a calm strength that brooked no resistance. 'So, shall I leave the hobble off you?'

Iroise nodded slowly.

'You will not seek escape?'

She shook her head.

'Even should I put you to the girls and make them whip you very hard – which I shall certainly do?'

Emotion surged in Iroise's breast; tears brimmed in her eyes; tightness and nausea clutched her belly. 'Even . . . then . . .' she blubbered, casting herself into the flood tide of submission, offering herself up in unconditional love. Suidin, eyes bright in the semi-darkness, took her limp, lithe body in her arms and kissed her tear-wet lips and neck and nipples and held her. And all the harshness of the whipping was worth it – for the warmth of these generous womanly arms and the intimate butterfly caresses of these gentle lips.

'Tell me what they did to you,' Suidin said.

'Can you not see the . . . the marks?'

'I want you to tell.' She reached down and planted a perfect kiss upon the lip of Iroise's umbilicus, taking the upper edge of its shivering rim softly between her lips and pulling. Iroise's fingers touched the woman's hair, which was short, wavy, wiry, and strokable. She glimpsed bare, freckled shoulders down the back of the open-necked shirt. As the lip-pull came again upon the rim of her umbilicus, she was thinking of the woman's threat to kiss her between the legs and she shuddered and could not disguise it.

Suidin put a dense bedroll at one end of the blanket and laid Iroise against it. 'Don't hide this pretty belly,' Suidin said, for Iroise had kept her knees together from fear that Suidin would see the symptoms of desire there. Suidin waited till the knees were separated. 'Now tell me,' she repeated.

'They put me over a log,' Iroise whispered.

'Who did?'

'Lindren held my arms. Kerun whipped. She used a birch stem.'

'Sit up.' Suidin propped the bedroll against her back. 'Your knees,' she murmured, 'straighten them.' Then she lifted her ankles apart. 'Sit up straight now, bottom pushed back.' She firmed the bedroll against the small of Iroise's back. 'Which way did they lay you? Astride the log? Across?'

'Across.'

Suidin's hand slid down to rest between Iroise's thighs on the blanket, her fingers tantalisingly near. Iroise stared anxiously at her toes, which could not keep still. She could feel the fire's warmth on the soles of her feet.

'How did they make you lie for your whipping: belly-up or belly-down?'

'Belly-down.'

'Then this was incorrect. Lie down – just as you are – across the bedroll. Don't move your legs at all. Just drape across it, belly-up, high. Beautiful.' She glimpsed harsh determination, gritted teeth. Then the thin, stripped sapling switch thrashed down three times, swiftly. It felt as if her naked belly had been sliced open with a burning razor. Then Suidin's hand was there, cupping her erect labia while her tongue descended to lick the umbilical rim. 'Sit up again.' Suidin kissed her nipples and left them wet. She held her wrists behind her with one hand. The other was between her legs, pressing gently with the rhythm of riding. Iroise's toes were straining as if she were suspended by a sling under her crotch with her feet trying to touch the ground.

'Tell me what it felt like when they whipped your bottom.'

'It made me shiver,' Iroise gasped. 'They would not stop whipping and I could not stop shivering; my bottom hurt so much.' The fingers closed about the lips of her cunny, which stood like proud flesh, the blood pumping into them because of the way she was sitting. Suddenly gooseflesh swept upwards, enveloping her breasts and cheeks. It was like the shivers that came when the girls were whipping her bottom. 'And then the feeling came inside my throat,' she murmured.

'While they were still whipping?'

'Yes.'

'What feeling?'

'A tickling, but deeper, keener, as if a cord inside my throat was stretching tighter.' It was there now: it felt as if the cord was stretched all the way from throat to belly to cunny and every heartbeat made it quiver.

'What happened after they whipped your bottom?'

'They pushed something up my cunny. It kept it open while they made me walk.' Though it had since been removed, still she felt stretched inside. Suidin insisted on looking and feeling. Iroise sank back, the firm bedroll pushing into the base of her spine and raising her flesh for examination. The fingers went inside and lingered while she continued her story. 'They took me to the place where the male was tethered blindfold and they made me watch. A girl was winding a thong round his genitals and Chloe was trying to fit him with a sheath. She couldn't do it properly because he was so distended.'

'Would that I had been there,' Suidin whispered, 'to kiss her swollen belly.' Iroise shuddered. 'Squeeze my fingers,' Suidin urged. 'Hold them tightly inside you.' The tips of the fingers bunched against the entrance to her womb. 'Did they make her ride him?'

In her mind's eye, Iroise relived the scene: she was standing with the heavy fetter round her ankle, the skin of her bottom flayed and hot, Lindren's coolly inquisitive hand against it, exploring between its cheeks; Kerun crouched before her, her cruel young fingers thrusting the round wooden device ever deeper into her cunny.

'Chloe tried to climb him,' Iroise whispered, 'but she was too short to reach and the ill-fitting sheath kept pulling off.' His chest and belly were smeared with her milk. 'When Chloe tried for the third time, his fluid came out.'

'The girl should have known the thong was too tight,' Suidin said. 'You can force ejaculation just by binding.'

Iroise nodded. Chloe had clung to his torso as if this might stem the spillage but her tight, pregnant belly pushing up against his penis seemed to burst it. Still Chloe had clung there, his trickles running down her leg.

'And would you have liked to have been the one to fit him with the sheath or would you have preferred to do the binding?'

'The binding,' Iroise whispered.

'Sit up. I love you. Come here – close. You're leaking. Show your breasts off. Lay them over my knees.' Suidin tipped Iroise forwards, pinioned her hands behind her back and masturbated her keenly, too keenly.

'Oh, please,' Iroise begged. Then she felt a cloth gag being slipped between her lips and tightened, trapping her tongue, gently impeding her breathing. She felt her wrists being tied behind her. Then she was laid with breasts and belly in the coolness of the grass. She felt loops being fitted to her ankles then stakes being driven into the ground. Suidin knelt beside Iroise. 'Chin up.' As one hand slipped around her throat, the other slipped from behind, between her legs. The slow masturbation recommenced.

Women drifted past the open entrance to the tent; Chloe was being carried. Iroise could not close her thighs, could not support herself, could not speak; the hand at her throat applied a gentle lift to keep her body arched. Her nipples grazed the grass tips. She made wet between her legs until it seemed the hand that squeezed and stroked and teased was soaked in female syrup. The gag became humid and stifling; saliva came too copiously for her to swallow; her nostrils flared; Suidin's fingertips were clawing the slippery flesh between her legs. Then Suidin's lips laid butterfly kisses gently over the back of her naked shoulders while her sex was being played with and her throat was being held. This contact – so gently, lovingly and cruelly put – was decisive. Suddenly her legs cramped and she cried through the gag, for there was no escape from the dreadful, searing, beautiful pleasure that burst inside her body; she felt as if her flesh was being slit from anus to umbilicus and her burning womb had been eviscerated and laid, still

189

beating, on the cool indifferent grass. Suidin supported her until the renting throes of climax ebbed.

Then she covered Iroise with a blanket and let her sleep restrained. Whenever Iroise woke, she saw the woman watching her. Sometimes, Suidin would lie close and kiss her gagged mouth and cradle her head gently until she went back to sleep.

In the morning, she unfastened her, fed and watered her and allowed her to attend to her toilet in the trees then to bathe in a little stream. Most of the women had dispersed in groups, going about their tasks of felling trees. The captive males were kept tethered in wooden cages. Only Chloe and Iroise were allowed the privilege of being unshackled. Chloe was set to helping the camp-girl, who also had charge of the males. Iroise was put to grooming and watering the heavy horses. They were beautiful, gentle giants. Iroise pulled fresh succulent sheaves of grass with which to reward them. She longed to be allowed to ride them when they were pulling the logs.

She was bringing buckets of water from the stream when she noticed a commotion by the corral. When she got back, Suidin was already there with Trivenn. Iroise dropped the buckets. Fear gripped her: the patrol had returned with three horses she knew well – the ones that Kin-Cague had been shepherding over the mountain.

'Where did you get them?' Suidin was asking the patrol-leader.

'We came across a monk,' the girl answered. Iroise started trembling.

'Then where is he?'

'He was too old. And he was asking about her –' she pointed to Iroise '– and the other slut. So we gave him a hiding and sent him packing.'

'Corral the horses with the others.'

Suidin came to Iroise and lifted her chin. 'The girls prefer the young ones; we all do.' Silent tears were rolling down Iroise's cheeks. 'Trivenn has been asking about you. She wants to book your favours for tonight.'

* * *

After dark the two women – the leaders of the pack of girls – took her to the makeshift hut. Iroise had never been made to perform for the simple amusement of mature women. She did not know what they would want to do to her. Even though it was too large, Trivenn made her don the monk's habit that had belonged to Dariun. Then she made her take it off and stand nude by the fire. They tied her wrists up to one of the supporting poles of the roof and intimately examined her hairless cunny. One woman stood in front of her, the other behind. This examination was so prolonged and her sex was so opened and her clitoris so tortured and laid bare that she came to pleasure between these women's fingers. Wetness was running down her leg.

'She favours the right side,' Suidin whispered, clasping her soaked inner thigh. Trivenn took her shirt off. Iroise felt her strong arms sliding under her armpits from behind and clasping her suspended wrists. Then the hot, naked, womanly breasts pressed into her back, forcing her own breasts round the pole. Suidin was still playing with the slippery flesh between her legs.

'I can smell her cunt juice,' Trivenn murmured. The scent was rising with her warmth. Suidin began spreading the juice up Iroise's hairless belly. Trivenn toed her ankles apart; her sex gaped open. 'Make her fuck the pole.' From the front, Suidin grasped her ankles and lifted. Iroise's belly collapsed against the pole, which was smooth and shiny in that place. Iroise was suspended by her wrists and trapped by the pressure of Trivenn's breasts pinning her from behind. Then Trivenn's thick thumb went up Iroise's bottom, urging her clitoris up the slippery pole until a new climax came more strongly than the last.

'She likes being handled,' Trivenn said.

'She needs more drink to keep her juice flowing.' They kept her fastened with her thighs around the pole and fed her the fermented tree sap. Her seepage, working gradually up the pole, reached her breasts. The women decided to free her wrists and to tie her up by the ankles. Her head and arms swung down; her bottom pressed against the pole. Suidin found the necessary rhythm to stimulate the sexual flow, then she maintained the steady milking masturbation. With no hairs to impede it, the fluid ran in swift trickles down Iroise's skin. It ran round her breasts and under her arms and chin. Trivenn's hand, seeking to trap the flow, closed moistly round her throat. Iroise cried out: a third climax had burst inside her belly.

'The girls will have heard you,' Trivenn murmured. She was still stroking Iroise's throat when Kerun and Lindren arrived with Chloe, whose flesh was liberally flecked with semen. The women lowered Iroise gently to the floor, then gagged her and tied her wrists. 'Take her outside and whip her. Leave the little one here.'

Once outside, the girls fed a thick rope between Iroise's tethered wrists and over the branch of a tree, winding it round repeatedly until it supported her weight and left them free to do what they wanted. They kept her open-legged in the moonlight and the light of a single lamp which they used to examine her. One girl whipped her bottom, the other sucked and played with her cunny. They changed places. When her toes left the ground for the second time, her cunny muscles spasmed and she came in Lindren's mouth. Her legs closed automatically, with Lindren's warm, unhaltered, bulbous breasts slipping between her shaking, soaked thighs. The warmth of breast so near her open sex made her belly queasy.

Kerun unwound the rope from the tree and Iroise collapsed to her knees. The muscles of her shoulders were so numbed by the stretching that she couldn't lift her arms. Lindren pulled her gag down and kissed her while Kerun tied a tight double knot in the end of the thick rope. 'Hold her,' she whispered, cruelly. The rope was dry and harsh.

Iroise whimpered in Lindren's arms, her face buried between Lindren's breasts. Lindren held her head and made as if to breastfeed her. Iroise's lips groped the soft, jellied, rounded weights and sought the nipple. Her bottom did not want to open so wide. Kerun spread the cheeks and whipped its mouth until Iroise slumped against Lindren's belly.

'Enough,' said Lindren.

'She has to learn.'

'Then do it now, before it gets too swollen.'

Iroise shuddered at the stretching; Kerun was a strong girl. Lindren crouched and kissed their victim's neck then clasped her cunny, which was being pushed forwards by the pressure of the dry, double knot that Kerun was forcing up her bottom.

'Oh, you feel so hot,' Lindren murmured into her ear. Iroise shuddered again as the rough knot stretched the fleshy ring and the muscle trembled in thwarted closure. The rope was captive inside her body, the knot distending her bowel, the rough frayed strands tickling inside her, the protruding length precluding closure.

'Look, she has a tail!' Kerun cried gleefully.

They retied her wrists behind her back then made her walk through the woods dragging her heavy rope tail. The knot kept pulling the muscle from inside. Lindren grew more aroused with every pace she watched her take. She kept stopping her, kissing her and fondling her rope as if it were indeed an extra part of her body. They reached a pool in a clearing.

'No, don't touch her,' Lindren said excitedly. She turned to Iroise: 'Drink.' Lindren's breathing was as unsteady as Iroise's halting attempts to execute this command with hands tied behind her. When first she managed to kneel she was too far from the edge of the pool to reach it with her lips. At the second attempt, her knees were in the water. Still she had to splay her legs to be able to drink. She heard Lindren's gasp as her lips touched the water and her hair fell forwards. Then something inside Iroise's belly melted and she just knelt there, shivering, her nipples dangling, her ringlets softly drowning in the water.

They picked her up and laid her on her back on the grass, her tail drawn out between her legs, and took turns to mount her mouth, suffocating her gently, in the way girls do, while her cunny was weeping on to the rope. Then they took her back to the hut.

Suidin and Trivenn had been using Chloe's body to extract semen from a captive male. Now that he had spent, the women handed him over to the girls who took him into the trees. Chloe was still trembling with excitement, her swollen cunny splashed with his ejaculate. Trivenn began working it into Chloe's body.

'Come here,' Suidin told Iroise. 'Come across my knee.' She brought her to climax with her wrists tied behind her and her rope still inside her.

'Try soaking it,' Trivenn said. 'It will make it swell tighter.' Suidin brought warm water then looped the rope up between Iroise's tethered wrists. Over the next hour, Iroise shuddered helplessly as Suidin kept resoaking the rope and playing with her, and the rope kept expanding.

Lindren appeared at the entrance to the hut, shouting, 'Trivenn, the horses are gone!'

'The new ones?'

'All of them – the corral is empty!'

Iroise froze with guilt: had she left it open? 'Get up!' Suidin threatened to drag her by her tail. She scrambled outside after Suidin and Trivenn. And the gate was indeed open.

Trivenn examined its fastening then peered into the darkness. Suidin and the girls had disappeared in pursuit down the length of the clearing. Word had spread; other girls gathered round the corral. Iroise stood there, trailing her coils of rope, waiting for the accusation to fall.

'What was that?' cried Trivenn. 'Behind the hut – something moving.'

'Where?'

A girl was despatched to investigate. She came back. 'There's no one there: the hut's empty.'

'Where's Chloe?' Iroise whispered in alarm.

'Quick!' Trivenn shouted, pointing at the terrified Iroise. 'Get hold of that one – now!' Iroise meekly offered herself up to the nearest girl. 'Don't let her out of your sight!'

'But why?' the girl asked.

'Because the old monk that you waylaid is obviously back to reclaim his chattels!'

18

Plans

'If only she had stayed in the hut, Kin-Cague, I might have rescued her.'

'And if only I had kept a better hold on their horses, Dariun, we would have something with which to barter for her.' Kin-Cague shook his head. Then he crouched, staring again at Chloe, taking her hands as if reassuring himself. 'But you brought our little one, safe and well.' His voice, normally steady and measured, faltered, and he turned his face to the shadow.

Dariun, after being stranded across the river, had taken a half day to trek down to the first bridge. On his way back upriver he had met the dazed and distraught kinsman. Kin-Cague had soon recovered enough to hatch a plan. And he had remained stolid up to the point where he had first heard Chloe's voice asking after him as he lay in wait with the horses.

Dariun stripped off the small mendicant's habit and donned the gown – his own – that he had retrieved from in front of the fire in the hut, where Iroise must have placed it. He could smell her scent within its folds.

'I'm going back for her,' he announced. 'I'll take two horses. You take Chloe on to the meeting-point that we agreed.'

Like a nest of ants, once disturbed, the camp was seething with activity. Dariun took a wide precautionary sweep around it before risking an approach from the upriver side.

The horses – so necessary for swift escape – were a liability when trying to move in silence through the woods. He tethered them at a safe distance at a place he was sure he would be able to find, then advanced on foot. He took a knife.

At the edge of the clearing, he took up his station, crouching in the darkness and watching. Groups of women were gathered in the vicinity of the great bonfire and the corral. One of the heavy horses had already been re-covered. Dariun's fear was that, as the search expanded, either he or his own horses might be unearthed. Any movement on his part could only attract attention so he propped himself against a tree and settled down for a long wait. Having had no proper sleep for two days, he struggled against tiredness but succumbed several times. In time, the second heavy horse was brought back into the corral and within a further hour the camp had quietened. It was time to make his move.

There had been no sign of Iroise out of doors; he guessed she was back in the hut. He crept round the edge of the clearing, past the fire and reached a point opposite the hut. All was quiet; no guard was posted. He could discern firelight through the makeshift screen of pine-fronds cover-ing the window. Silently – knife at the ready – he crossed the gap. There was no movement from any direction. He waited until he was quite certain and his breathing had steadied. Then, cautiously, he pressed himself against the wall and peered through the lower corner of the window. The vision pierced him like an icy spike driven up his spine.

Iroise was there. She lay naked on the floor between two men. One seemed to be pulling on a rope between her thighs while she had hold of the other's erection. An older woman was looking on. Dariun watched benumbed until he wrenched himself away.

He stood amongst the trees, shaking, staring across at the hut before creeping off without looking back until he came to the horses.

It was dawn by the time he arrived at the meeting-point – the top of a small conical hill commanding a view over the river – and began searching for his friends. He found their camp under a rocky overhang below the summit. Kin-Cague emerged from the trees and Chloe woke up. Dariun tied the horses then crouched by the fire. An unseasonable coldness overwhelmed him.

'Did you see her?' Kin-Cague asked.

Dariun nodded, disconsolately.

'And?'

'There are men in the camp.'

'Soldiers?'

'I couldn't tell. They were naked.' He stared into the fire.

Kin-Cague fell silent.

Then Chloe said, 'They're prisoners.'

'Prisoners – the men?'

'Suidin keeps them caged and makes them do things.'

Dariun thought again about what he had seen: the vision, revisited over and over again in his mind, now had three victims instead of one. Yet his torment remained, for Iroise had been experiencing pleasure with the flesh of other men.

Long after dawn, he was still sitting by the smouldering remains of the fire. He was picking at one of the carcasses of roasted dove when Kin-Cague beckoned from the top of the crag. 'Dariun, quick!'

When Dariun reached him, Kin-Cague was shading his eyes and pointing. 'The river – below the rapids, where it spills on to the flatter ground, in that broad bend – see?'

'Logs in the water.'

'That's how they must move them – by rafting them downriver. And look there, back towards the camp. Your eyes are keener.'

'Get the horses.' Dariun began scrambling down the bank.

'No, don't rush it. We need a plan.'

Dariun carefully drew aside the branchlets just enough to be able to see. Behind him, the river emerged from a short gorge: there were no fears of being surprised from that direction. It then swung round into a wide shallow embayment almost ahead, where the logs were floated into the water. There were two cabins on the bank. He hadn't seen them when making his way downriver on the other side because he had bypassed the gorge and rejoined the river lower down. So far, he had observed only two women stationed in the vicinity. But more women and girls were now approaching with the heavy horses that were dragging the logs slowly down the furrowed grassy slope. Perched on the leading horse's bare back was Iroise: unmistakable, even from the earlier viewpoint on the hill, her beautiful blonde locks shining in the morning sunlight, her poise graceful. She wore the same halter top as the girls. Her body was otherwise naked apart from a thick rope wound around her middle. The loose end of the rope bore a fist-sized knot.

The picture formed again in Dariun's mind of what he had witnessed last night – the men and Iroise, and the rope between her legs and no knot visible: resentfulness surged within him, against the way they had used her.

As the convoy drew nearer, he could see the apprehension in her lovely face. The women were speaking harshly to her. She became frightened as the leading horse moved into the water: she clung to his mane, looking anxiously behind her as the women shouted instructions from the bank. Then, as the horse advanced too far, a girl splashed after him and restrained him. While the logs were being released, Iroise was scolded by the girl. Then the horse was brought round on to the bank.

Iroise was pulled from the horse and slapped until she cried. Dariun felt the mettle rising inside him. Then two of the girls dragged her to her feet and led her towards the very bushes where he was hiding. He had to act swiftly while he had the edge.

He burst out from the bushes directly in front of them. None was more shocked than Iroise. Dariun grabbed her round her waist and at the touch – the nearness and warmth of her body – the torrent of emotion left him shaking. He felt dizzy even as he threatened the girls with his knife. Though they backed away, it was plain they were not truly alarmed. One picked up a heavy stick. Already the element of surprise was lost: he was in the open amid the hostile group. Some of the women in the background had axes at the ready. The two girls nearby separated so as to block his escape. He prayed Kin-Cague had seen his plight and would come crashing through with the horses. But nothing happened and the women were closing in.

Iroise, who had not uttered a word, sank limply to the ground. Dariun felt sick. He sheathed his knife. One of the women laughed. He just stood there. Then, slowly, he bent down. Slowly and sturdily, he gathered Iroise in his arms – then he ran.

'Oh, no!' she cried. 'No, Dariun, they'll hurt you! Stop!'

He did not make it to the cabins; he was trapped on the water's edge with Iroise in his arms, and with no hope of getting past the line of armed women. He couldn't swim; he couldn't leave her. Desperation drove him on. Iroise, clinging to his neck, gasped when she realised what he meant to do.

He bolted along a heavy log that projected into the water, then jumped on to the next, then on to a loose raft of logs – tripping, almost overbalancing with her, dodging across the subsiding gangplanks into ever deeper water. Two or three of the girls began pursuit. Dariun reached the outermost log and lowered Iroise on to it. 'Sit astride. Hold on tight.' She was terrified of letting go of him. As soon as she did, he crouched behind her and launched the log by bracing his feet against the rafted pack. The log swung sideways, pivoting about its downstream end that was jammed against the log in front. Still arcing round, it finally broke free and slid diagonally before slowly aligning with the current. But they were facing backwards. Iroise was trembling, prostrating herself against the gently rocking log; Dariun, exhausted, tried to comfort her as he watched the group of girls receding.

There was no sign of attempted pursuit on land. He scanned the bank, looking for Kin-Cague and the horses, for the kinsman must surely have seen the confrontation and escape. The current, though sturdy, was slower than the walking pace of a horse, so Kin-Cague would easily catch them up. Dariun wanted to keep a good distance between themselves and the woodland women.

He kept glancing behind him, towards the direction of travel, to make sure the way was clear but without risking levering himself round and perhaps precipitating a disastrous spill. Gradually, as he realised that the current funnelled its flotsam safely round the sweeping curves of the river, he was able to relax a little. There was no sound from the river. Iroise still clung like a limpet to the trunk of the log. She hadn't spoken since her outburst on the riverbank.

'Iroise, are you all right?' Dariun asked, gently.

'Yes.' Though her cheek was pillowed against the log, her eyes were open and she was watching the bank sliding past. 'What about Kin-Cague? Is he hurt?' She held her breath.

'No, he's fine. Chloe too. We'll see them very soon.'

She sighed deeply and closed her eyes. He laid his palm softly against the small of her back and shivered privately at her warmth. He stroked there gently. The rope was still wrapped round her middle.

'Do you want to sit up? You'll see better.'

'No.'

'Perhaps unwrap the rope and we can loop it round the log and you can hold on to it?'

'No!'

He did not mention it again. In any case, he doubted he would have been able to feed the rope underwater around the wide girth of the log: the drag of the current would have prevented it. But he wanted the rope off her: if she were to fall into the water with it on, it might tangle and put her in yet graver danger. And the rope might come in useful to effect a safe landing. He sighed and sat back.

'Please, don't take your hand away, Dariun,' she whispered. 'Hold me.'

The surge of emotion swept through his body. He pictured again that first time, when he had found her beautiful body staked out so sexually in the grounds of the

Priory, and he pictured the time when he had carried her naked from the little boat and placed her with Chloe on the blanket, and Iroise had allowed him to examine her and he had found her already wet. But that beautiful pleasure of touching her nakedness had been interrupted and the next time he saw her, she was lain between two men.

Dariun shivered as he laid his fingertips against the dimples in her perfect back. He clasped her hips gently then, bending forwards, kissed the warm flat place near the base of her spine. He ran his fingers softly down her trembling body, from her shoulders, over the cord of her halter, over her rope, over her buttocks to her thighs. When her hands reached back to caress his fingers, he took her firmly by the arms and drew her upright. She gasped then swooned unsteadily against him, her arms trapped gently between their bodies, his hands about her lovely belly and haltered breasts, holding her so she could not fall, her cool smooth locks against his neck.

'Let me take the rope off you,' he whispered.

'No.' Her thighs trembled in compression as they gripped the log. But she let him tighten the last coil of rope safely about her belly and tuck in the loose end. While he was doing it, her fingertips, sliding down, grazed his erection through his gown. He shuddered and she felt his shudder: her fingertips responded provocatively.

'Hold me,' Iroise said again, stretching up so his hands slid down and came to rest in that beautiful female place which in Iroise was exquisite. And she was so perfectly positioned for touching: thighs open, gripping, trembling, yet completely unable to close.

He balanced the tip of the little finger of each hand in the smooth hollows at the tops of her thighs. Then he pulled the inner lips gently out of her body and left them standing while he stroked their outermost edges. Warmth and firmness combined with silkiness, passivity with arousal. When he split the inner lips apart, they stayed open as a gently cloying cup for the tips of three fingers. He ran his other hand up her belly, under her halter, lifting

201

it and finding the nipples firm. 'Lie back,' he whispered. When she pressed against him he sank back, still clutching her naked breasts, still delving in her cloying cup – then finding her clitoris, milking it, teasing – and her knees came up and even her toes lost contact with the log and she was balanced on his body, so aroused now, yet so terrified of moving. It seemed deliverance came to her; her clitoris retracted in little tugs even as her nipples came up harder and her chest expanded and all he could hear was pulsatile breathing coming through her nose. Still in the throes, she levered herself backwards up his body and freed his penis, which sprang up between the lips of her sex, where her fingers kept it pressed against her. Her burning insides seared its flesh; her fingers compressed the frenum until the boiling wetness stored inside him burst all over her naked belly.

She kept pressing until no more jerkings could be induced. Then she linked her hand with his, interlacing their fingers. She closed her thighs round his erection and squeezed. She dipped their conjoined hands into the liquid semen he had sprayed all over her belly. And he could feel her clitoris like a burning blister poking into his stem.

The underside of a bridge swept across his line of vision. He new it must be the same bridge he had crossed yesterday. The distance had been covered swiftly. It was time to make a landing. But he lay with Iroise a while longer.

When at last he lifted her up, she made no move to wash herself. Carefully, yet determinedly, she turned herself round to face him. He took her in his arms and embraced her frail, beautiful body and did not want to let go.

'Let me wash you,' he eventually said.

'No. I want it on me. None has gone inside. I like it on my skin.'

Her words triggered a fresh tremor of jealousy as he thought of her with those men. But as she put her arms around him again and hugged his chest this tremor was deliciously quelled.

'What's that, ahead?' Iroise asked.

Dariun twisted round and saw, in the distance, buildings on the riverbank. 'It looks like a village.' Then he realised the buildings were too large. 'Warehouses, perhaps?'

As they drifted closer, the current slackened. The bank receded into a bay in front of the buildings and the log drifted in towards a raft of stationary logs. Dariun could see distant figures in front of the buildings. He swung both feet into the water on the same side as the bank and the log turned before it reached the pack and instead headed slowly for the shore. Still the impact with the silted shelf was jarring, propelling him feet first into the shallows. After floundering, he found his footing, lifted Iroise down and carried her to dry land.

'We need to be near the road,' he said, 'ready to intercept Kin-Cague.'

'There's someone coming,' Iroise whispered.

Two men – one short, one tall – were hurrying down the slope towards them. Dariun swung round and placed himself protectively in front of Iroise.

The men stopped at ten paces, suddenly checked by what they saw. They stared at Dariun and tried to peer round him at Iroise.

'What do you want?' He tried not to sound unnerved as he weighed them up. They were clad in well-worn shirts and breeches.

'Sir, we meant no harm,' the short one drawled. 'We saw you on the river.'

'On a log,' the other added.

'And Trask said, "That's a monk-lord with a woods-girl." He sent us down to see what's going on.'

'We were waylaid,' said Dariun, 'cast adrift with only what we stand in. My colleague fared better. He escaped with our horses and should be on the road. We hope to meet him here.'

'At the sawmill?' the short one asked.

'At the first settlement,' Dariun said.

'The last, some would call it.'

Dariun caught the brief exchange of glances between the two men.

19

An Unmasking

'Dariun, why would they want to give us food and board, like this, with nothing in return?'

Iroise stood by the window looking down into the courtyard with its mill buildings on three sides, piles of split logs in the middle and the river beyond. Evening was approaching.

'They think I'm a Tormunite and they're afraid of what the Tormunites will do if they step out of line. That's why they're so anxious to please. Their livelihood probably depends on Tormunite gold.'

'But the women in the woods aren't afraid of anyone.' Iroise looked out again: the workers had left the yard yet one man remained. He was propped against the wall. 'He's guarding us,' she whispered.

Dariun sighed. He got up from the table, walked across and stood behind her. 'Watching you, more likely.'

'Hold me,' she said, defiantly. He slid his arm around her, under her haltered breasts and Iroise closed her eyes.

She could have moved away from the window or denied Dariun that familiarity yet she did neither. She stood there, clad only in her woods-girl's halter and the rope that she had refused to remove from her waist, even when she had bathed. It was still damp and made strange contact with her skin. The window was tall and its sill was low and the man in the yard would surely see her naked cunny and her rope-bound belly and would desire her, as the captives in the hut had desired her to bursting point before she had made them spill.

She turned round and kissed Dariun, putting her arms about his neck and standing on tiptoes, bare-bottomed in the window, tonguing his mouth until his erection burgeoned under his gown.

When she looked again the watcher was still there, eyes uplifted, hungry.

'This room, Dariun. You know it is the place where the Tormunite masters bring their girls – to use them?'

'Perhaps.'

Gently releasing him from her embrace, Iroise withdrew across the room and brought out some of the things she had discovered while he was bathing. She did not tell him she had already sampled the precious dust. 'Sit in the chair, master,' Iroise whispered teasingly. 'Let me light the lamp.' Unsated lust lingered deep inside her, fired by the death throes of her Tantalite training. Her vows were now in tatters; each orgasm came more deliciously than the last. Before dealing with Dariun she went again to the window, where the light was better. The man was still there. She waited until she was sure he was looking directly up – 'up', so sweet and sensual a word – and she rubbed a fingertipful of powder slowly round the edges of the open inner lips of her cunny until she needed to close her eyes. But she kept them open, controlling him. But she could not control her murmurs as the potent resin seeped into her body through the edges of her lips.

'What is it?' Dariun's voice was shrouded in concern. When Iroise turned to show him what she was doing to herself, his breathing snagged and his cheeks reddened. But she could see his cock was set on hard.

'Stay there. In time I shall come to you,' she whispered. She placed her bare bottom on the broad sill of the window, raised her feet on to it too then draped her body along it as if it were a bed. And on this bed, on public view between her subject kinsman and the watcher in the yard, Iroise masturbated her aroused nude cunny, slowly, deliciously, single-handedly with the other hand under her halter, teasing her nipples, exposing their tips for the men to see. Her gaze stayed fixed upon her toes which were creeping ever further up the opposite upright of the frame, displaying legs ever longer and more lithe. Her orgasm came, so wrenchingly strong that she cried out. Her roped belly heaved. It felt as if a leather bucket full of heated water was being poured from a height into her open cunny. The pressure waves of heat melted the insides of her womb.

When she looked again, there were three men watching from the yard. She closed her eyes and twisted round, on to her side, her knees tucked against her belly, her bared breasts against the cool glass. She called to Dariun. She heard his chair move, then heard his footfalls across the floor.

'Stroke my back,' she whispered.

'They're watching,' he murmured, hoarsely. 'They can see everything.'

Iroise parted her knees against the window. 'Stroke me,' she repeated. The drying rope was growing tighter round her belly, its twists impressing themselves deep into her skin. Its strong embrace made her giddy.

Dariun knelt on the floor: probably from fear that the men would see his state. Iroise felt his hand at the base of her spine, rubbing gently. His hand was nicely warm. She tucked her knees up tighter, so her feet pressed against the cool glass panes. With the rhythmic pressure at the base of her spine, arousal came. She thought again of the captive men in the hut and the ejaculations her cunny had stimulated, under the guidance of the older women and against the deep pressure of the knotted rope thrust up her bottom. Dariun's hand kept pressing warmly; her thighs rubbed against her rope-girdle as her belly thrust out between them; and the lips of her cunny, coated with the powder, kissed the cold glass and infolded.

Dariun lifted her bundled body and carried it to the table, laying it down amongst the array of Tormunite sheaths that Iroise had spread there. Her halter was rucked up to her armpits. Her knees were up and her anus was exposed – he would see the marks of cordage there – and her cunny lips were still infolded.

He started to unwind the rope from her belly. She arched her back to assist. When he got to the part that was impressed into her skin, he went gently. The peeling sensation, as the damp buried rope began to be separated from her skin, triggered shivers inside her. He paused to finger-test the moulded furrows and to open out the infolded lips between her aroused thighs. The knotted rope straggled across the table, its last loops still encircling her belly.

Then the door burst open. Three men walked in. Two were mill men. The third was a tall monk but he wore a broad-brimmed hat instead of a hood. He had the harsh air of a warden or magistrate.

'Restrain him,' the monk said. As the mill men set upon Dariun, wrestling him to the floor, the monk's gaze turned on Iroise. She was frozen with terror. He marched across to the table and stared down despisingly at her prostrate body.

'Don't hurt her!' Dariun cried, his voice muffled and half-choked.

The monk took a step towards him, then took his hat off. Iroise heard the heels of his boots click together then a split second later heard a sickening thud and Dariun was silent.

'Get the impostor out of here.'

'What shall we do with him?' the men asked.

'Just get him out of my room.' Dariun was dragged like a sack through the doorway. The door banged shut.

The monk came back to Iroise's shaking form. He cast his hat on the table. His hair was greying and shaved close to the scalp, though his features were unlined. 'He told you he was a Tormunite master?' He grasped her face in his gauntleted hand. 'And doubtless you thought yourself a privileged whore?'

Iroise shook her head. 'No,' she muttered limply, but he took no notice.

'Well – road-weary though I am – I shall now take the time to instruct you in the precepts of legitimate Tormunite rule.'

The door opened again and one of the men crept back in. 'Dom Qevrinn,' he muttered.

'What now?' the monk snapped.

'The prisoner . . . Trask says he needs to know what you want doing with him. Shall you be taking him with you?'

'Has your foreman no initiative beyond putting this way station in the hands of every tomfool itinerant who garbs himself in a habit? Are we Tormunites fated to be dogged by simpletons wherever we set foot? Get out and never interrupt again when I'm conducting a lesson.'

The lesson that Dom Qevrinn taught was one that Iroise would not forget.

'They let him drink our wine and plunder our sheaths. Lie still, girl.' He stood between her lifted knees, examining her by lamplight with gauntleted hands. Cold, supple leather thumbed her open with meticulous skill. 'Ah, Resin of Carne,' he whispered, rubbing his fingers together. The tip of his tongue tested the powder he had brushed from the lips of her cunny. He looked about the table, found the container, opened it and thrust his gloved middle finger deep into the golden dust. Then he opened Iroise and pushed the coated finger to the hilt inside her cunny. Her hands clutched the edge of the table; her toes writhed. He nudged her feet over the corner edges, so her legs dropped down and the lips of her cunny tightened helplessly round his finger. The powder melted to ice and warmth. He thrust her halter to her throat and milked her nipples till they stood on stalks. He put his arm under her shoulders and started to pick her up with the only other support being the single gloved finger thrust inside her at the front.

'Oh no, master,' Iroise begged him. 'Please?'

'Then put your arms round your master's neck.' He carried her across the room like that, with legs dangling, rope trailing and the single purchase of the finger pushed inside her at the front. He stood her on the window sill. 'The moon is up. Up.' She was forced on tiptoes. The rope had wrapped round her leg. She glimpsed the men in the moonlit yard. 'The dogs at bay,' he whispered, 'awaiting the scraps from their master's table. Hold your halter high – against your throat. Expose yourself.' She started coming even before he had got her fully round to face them. The halter swathed her throat. Her naked breasts and belly were bathed in moonlight. She trembled on her toes. The gauntleted hand was between her legs, the finger deep inside her, urging the climax to completion for the men. The feeling came that she was wetting herself. Her cunny stayed in spasm while he unsleeved his fingers and left the glove dangling between her legs with its middle finger still inside her.

Then he showed her a phial. 'It contains aris – you know of it?'

Iroise shook her head.

'Good, the effect will be more potent. It is the purest form of Resin of Carne, so finely milled it moves like vapour.' Shaking the phial, he dragged a chair across and placed it facing the window. Then he brought the lamp, saying, 'Through their gawking, they may yet learn. Tell me your name.'

'Iroise, master.'

'Iroise, are you willing to teach them?'

She bit her lip.

'Hesitation is a failing. Hold your halter high – higher – pull it off. Give it here – better without it.' Her breasts were trembling. 'Now kneel on the chair. Don't worry about your rope. Let it go where it will. But face your audience – let them see. A girl must always show. Arms behind, over the back – right over. Head back. Belly out. Knees open.'

Then he flailed her bare breasts and belly with the halter until its cords had twisted like twine, and the gauntlet clutched inside her was expelled. While she gasped for breath, he clamped his hand across her mouth and administered the vapourlike dust directly through her nose.

In the yard, erections burgeoned as the cries of girl-pleasure issued through the glass, and the lamplight cast its mellow glow upon those heaving swollen-teated breasts and that moist-lipped naked split that seemed to gape in spasms as if an invisible egg were being delivered.

'There's not a man down there who wouldn't sell his soul for one free shy at this.' With bare hands, Dom Qevrinn slapped her cunny open.

Then he unwound the last coils of rope from her belly, exposing deep damp furrows in her skin. He lifted her up and licked her furrows. She lay belly-up across his arms. The wet tongue-tip made her shiver; nausea and tickles melded; she reached up imploringly and touched his short-cropped hair. All her senses were heightened; the wool of his gown prickled like nettles; she could smell the scent of mare upon it; she could see every pore in the skin of his cheek; she caught words from the yard that were only murmured. The belly-licking felt as if a smooth cold silver gobbet on a stick was being twirled inside her womb.

Dom Qevrinn took her naked downstairs, saying it was to be a little journey of discovery. He collected a bundle of sheaths for her protection and he made her carry her coiled, knotted rope.

At the foot of the stairs he stopped her in a small storage room before taking her outside. 'They need time to wonder,' he said, nodding in the direction of the voices. He lifted her on to the top of a sturdy barrel near the solitary lamp, then spread her legs and with surgical deftness opened her cunny. 'It needs to breathe,' he said, propping its walls ajar with the naked middle finger of each hand. 'I can feel your pulse inside you.' She could feel the blunt-nosed tips of fingers sliding deeper along the walls, inducing feelings that made her want to close. Cool air was sucked inside her. The fingertips curled outwards until it felt as if they pressed against the tops of her legs from inside. Then a pressure came that made her catch her breath, a dull visceral ache of pleasure like the jaws of a clamp being slowly tightened round her womb. 'Sit forwards – closer.' Her moving heightened the penetration. 'Rest your head on my shoulder.' The deep inner explorations continued; her nipples rubbed against the rough wool of his gown. She murmured, hunched – still clutching her coils of rope – and moaned. Her lips closed sensually about the side of his neck. She could feel his pulse thumping as she tongued the skin. A hot, hard helmet of male flesh slipped out from his gown and touched the top of her open cunny, depositing sticky liquor all around her protruding knob. He pulled away and took his fingers out and Iroise was still aching – pleasure-stretched – and her knob was sticking out. He spread her haunches wider across the flat top of the barrel. Then he found the little hole that pierced her ridge of flesh connecting her bottom and cunny.

'Lift up.' She leant forwards on her hands. Moving round, he squeezed her piercing from the back, flattening the flesh until the numbness caused a peculiar pleasure. 'Who put it here?' he said as she trembled.

'The Prior,' she answered.

'That vagabond you were with?'

'No. The Prior is leader of the kinsmen.'

'He aligned it incorrectly – a lengthwise piercing is much better here. Lean back. Keep your legs out, wide.' Her shoulders slumped against him, her belly protruded. He slid his hand under from the front. His fingers searched the length of the velvet ridge of skin. 'We call this part the "Thong of Venus". Not all girls have it.' He felt his way along it to where it disappeared into the closed mouth of her bottom. Then he gently tugged it. She closed her eyes. He pulled again more firmly. She shuddered as she felt her velvet skin-thong being pulled out a tiny way through her tightening rim. 'Lie back – all the way – you're flexible.' He supported her under her waist to prevent her toppling backwards. Her calves gripped the top of the barrel; her head and arms draped down behind, with the coils of rope heaped on the floor. Her body was almost doubled back; her belly bulged; the lips of her cunny pouted. He started playing with her: drawing out the lips in alternate fashion, pushing her erection back up inside her and waiting for it to come out again, which it did each time he put her velvet thong into renewed traction.

While he played with her he asked what objects the Prior had put through her piercing. 'Did he make you sit with them in place?' he asked. She answered all his questions truthfully. 'Did he use you through your bottom?' She shuddered then, for he was pulling her velvet thong as if it were an extraneous insert up her bottom, yet it was attached. 'It's forming a little nodule – a tag – just in front

211

of the entrance,' he whispered, squeezing it. Then he pushed her knob inside her body again and held his fingertip pressed there and she had the overpowering urge to sit up. 'Remain still,' he ordered. The finger-pressure eased and the pulling came again on her tagged skin-thong where it fed through the mouth of her bottom.

He sat her up with her legs still wide apart and she felt so dizzy that he had to hold her by her wrists above her head. He kept her sitting forwards on her open cunny while he took hold of the little nodule he had formed and he prised her skin-thong ever further out of her bottom from behind. He said that when he got her to the monastery they would do her piercing properly. The rough wood of the barrel lid itched against her open cunny.

When he lifted her down, her legs were weak from the stretching and there were marks inside her thighs from the edge of the barrel. Then he explained to her how he wanted her to walk when she went into the yard to meet the men. 'I want you to look enticing, for they have been waiting with such patient expectation.'

The cooler air of the yard made her nipples stiff. Her breasts shook with every step because her feet were arched and she was walking on her toes with her back kept deeply hollowed. 'Your pouch must be visible from behind.' He would not allow her to close her thighs. With this strictured gait she tottered out into the group of inquisitive men.

Dom Qevrinn watched her drowning in a sea of seeking hands, rough hair-clad forearms tickling her naked furrows. 'Feel how smooth her belly.' The master told them of her skin-thong. Two separate hands kept her body open at the front. All the while she had to stand with thighs wide. Her breasts were cupped, her nipples were worked as if in milking. Her thong of flesh was being drawn out of her to make its wrinkled nodule. A finger wormed up the tight tube of her bottom. 'She's boiling inside.' The finger curved down. Iroise collapsed forwards into the palm of a hand. She could feel the fingertip stabbing like a tongue from inside her and the hand trying to grasp it as though it were an erectile part of her cunny.

'Stand back men – give the girl space,' Dom Qevrinn said, advancing behind her. 'Every one of you will get his way. But we need to keep a girl willing.' He stretched her arms out behind her, then raised her wrists. She hunched forwards. 'No, stand straight. On your toes. Head up. Eyes open. Now, I need a volunteer. Right, you know where a girl's knob is? Good. Then put a little dab of this on it with your fingers.'

The man crouched between her legs. He found the place immediately. All the arousal gravitated to this one sweet slippy focus. At the moment before deliverance, Iroise felt as if the very skin of her knob was being peeled back, exposing the inner core of nerves to the rubbing of the finger. Dom Qevrinn had to hold her up. Her nipples hurt, though no one was touching them.

'Keep rubbing it,' he whispered. She groaned. Her thigh muscles quivered like plucked bowstrings.

'Oh, sweet fuck!' the volunteer cried. 'It's running down my finger.'

She was still shuddering when he held it glistening to the moonlight.

'Here –' Dom Qevrinn cast coins on the cobblestones '– get yourselves a drink. Build your stamina for later.'

Her master walked her through a gap in the buildings to the edge of the river. He stripped a branchlet from a bush. 'Stay on your toes. Legs open. I want to be able to see it from behind. Hollow. Hollow deeper. Fold your arms behind.' He stood beside her, balancing his spread finger-tips against her pushed-out belly. Holding the instrument vertically, he started whipping into the crease of her bottom while she tried to stand on her toes and keep her cheeks open for it. She kept overbalancing and he was dissatisfied. He walked her along the bank, on her toes, with her arms still folded behind her and the mouth of her bottom stinging cruelly, until he found what he was looking for. It was a tree with a strong, horizontal, breast-high branch. He made her rest her breasts upon it with her arms still folded behind her and her legs spread while he whipped more keenly into her crease.

Then he fingered the narrow zone of flesh he had whipped. Her thong of skin had swelled grotesquely. He started pulling it. The manipulation of the swelling excited him; she could hear his laboured breathing. Reaching round to the front with one hand, he held her labia closed and continued pulling. She could feel the knob of her clitoris sliding between the lips of her cunny like a bead of gristle. Steadily, he tried to pull her swollen thong of skin out through the tumid mouth of her bottom. She moaned: she felt the sexual pulling all the way up inside to her throat. Her breasts slipped on the mossy coating of the branch. He was trying to make her come by this pulling. His fingers found her piercing, which had almost closed. He told her he would reopen it when he found something to put through it.

'Stand up.' He still had hold of her swollen skin-thong, trying to squeeze it flat, while he frogmarched her along the bank and into the little tavern.

The small crew of mill men filled the single-room tavern with animated ale talk that belied the gnawing craving that dwelt in every belly. Crouched half-forgotten in the corner was the bruised impostor, Dariun, tethered and broken, the butt of a petty raillery inspired by a jealousy that had now lapsed into indifference. All the waiting, the watching and the brief tantalising touching of the girl had distilled itself into this lustful craving. Then, just as they were starting to believe that the Tormunite envoy had betrayed them, he delivered her into their hungry midst.

She was naked, radiant in her fear and longing. The monk was carrying her and she was clinging to his neck – her face half-hidden in those shy blonde curls – and he was bestowing reassuring monkish kisses upon her frightened lips, before offering her up to these worldly men. Her knees were tucked over his arm, almost touching her lovely nipples, and he was holding her so that all between her legs was showing: every hairless detail of her pretty quim, and her rose-hole, now red and swollen, spawning questions in the watchers' minds, since it made so stark a blotch of lurid colour in the paleness of her skin. He wanted everyone to see what he'd done. And yet she was returning his kisses with tongue-sucks of love. It was this unsettling mix of shyness and promiscuity that marked these Tantalite girls as special.

She hid her face completely when she saw her former lover huddled in the corner. Her new master had to coax when he lowered her to the table and she realised she was being given over totally to this group of new men. At the point where contact with her protector was broken, her posture was beautiful and moving.

Iroise was balanced on the toes of her arched feet and the fingertips of one hand. Her haunches weren't touching the table. Her other hand hung in the air, reaching in vain for her master's retreating figure. She looked like a hunted creature primed to spring into escape. But with a room full of avid men, there would be no escape. Yet they remained gentle at the start.

Two took an ankle each, another her wrist that hung in the air. One slid a hand under her bottom to steady her as she was lowered the rest of the way on to the table of love. Belts were unbuckled, trousers kicked off, revealing bellies of every kind – fat, thin, smooth, hairy, muscular, solid – with every cock fervidly erect.

Because there was no time limit set, they proceeded slowly. The master stipulated only that sheaths be used whenever she was penetrated – he spread the collection on the table – and that her suitors pay attention to her pleasure; and that, should she at any stage fail to cooperate, then the impostor should be punished. He promised her, 'If your performance pleases me and you give of yourself completely, I shall let him go unharmed. You understand me?' She nodded selflessly, though her lovely eyes were frightened. Dom Qevrinn searched between her open knees and touched that perfect flesh, bestowing there a fingertip blessing. When she shuddered, he kissed her bottom lip. 'Again,' he said. 'But this time look at him – show him that you truly care.' He turned her head and forced her gaze on Dariun. Her knees remained wide open and when the fingertips went between them again they exposed a sexual nodule that was firmer than before. And, when the master drew aside her silken curls and kissed her ear lobe – that her line of vision might stay uninterrupted – her small nodule moved and he heard her catch of breath and felt her shudder come again. He kissed her throat and had the urge to put his own flesh deep inside her. But he relinquished control and pleasure to the men.

He poured a beaker of ale and watched from the next table. There was no stampede. There were fingers putting questions to her flesh: seeking answers in the smooth creases at the tops of her legs, the backs of her thighs, the jellied arousal of breast, the moist pleasure of female armpit, the squeezable bald ridges of the outer lips, the paper thinness of the inner, the tiny belly-hole, ankles that could be encircled with the fingers, the cusps of flesh – velvet nipples and shiny exposed clit – her gentle face, full lips, small nose and perfect eyebrows and the cool, silk ringlets that slip between your fingers – all these places that spoke of girl, even before she was turned over.

The ale quaffed, Dom Qevrinn left the tavern and sought the mill-master to check the inventories and confirm the requirements for supply of timber for the next quarter. He shared with him a late repast of ham and pickled grain but refused wine, which made the head befuddled. He made his excuses and did not care that the mill-master watched him retracing his steps to the tavern. He entered quietly.

Her former lover was crouched in the corner, unable to avert his gaze. Trask's heavy body was knelt on the table and Iroise was impaled astride him, facing him, her belly too high for frontal penetration, his arms under her knees, her feet over his shoulder, her gaping buttocks thrust into the recess of his lap. She was clinging round his neck and whimpering. There was scarcely movement – save the gentle bouncing of her cantilevered feet – for the cock had gone so deep. The two of them were locked in this perfect embrace. Every man in the room was silent, listening for her gentle whimpering to change tone. The foreman was steadfast, clasping her tightly bundled slim body so it could not move. Her quim would be wetting his belly. She started to writhe upon the impalement and, at the same time, to reach up to kiss his face and to murmur as if he were doing something beautiful to her, as if the decorated head of the sheath had hit a pleasure centre deep inside. Her whimpers turned to moans then deep, open-mouthed gasps, then four powerful shudders slammed through her body.

'She's bit his cheek!'

'And drawn blood, by fuck! The hussy.'

Her stalwart lover displayed her mark with pride as, still impaled, Iroise was lowered to the table. Her body was as limp as if she had fainted. Yet desire still yearned within her: her arms stretched out across the pools of semen on the table, her wrists overhung the edges, her fingers writhed until they secured warm leverage. Trask nudged her body forwards until her head overhung. When the new cock slid into her throat, her body arched off the table. Her chest inflated. Her ribs, straining against her skin, were capped by these curiously soft mounds of breast with rigidly standing nipples.

Dom Qevrinn surged forwards, thrusting his bared arm through the arch beneath that slim body now being penetrated at each end. He simultaneously touched her open quim, so beautifully warm and red, its lips so limp and weakened by arousal. Very gently he gathered her Thong of Venus in his fingers and pulled, and pulled, against the keen resistance of Trask's cock inside her bottom. And her belly arched higher, so splendidly tight. She was coming to orgasm again. He curled his bare arm around her slim waist from beneath and fingered that belly-tightness, and her lips clamped tighter about the cock thrust down her throat. He blew a steady stream of cold air over her exposed clitoris until the contractions came in earnest. Then he finger-spanked it rapidly and the orgasm was sustained, inducing lavish ejaculation of the sheathed cock up her bottom and the bare cock down her throat. Watery semen was running down her wrists from the two erections that her fists were wringing.

The night shift carried her into the mill. She was passed around. Protection was incomplete – naked penetration happened even up her quim. it was electrifying to watch her take it. She came to climax standing. They made her bestride a log being milled. She climaxed on the deep vibrations transmitted through the wood.

She was beautiful – unique – in loving. Dom Qevrinn now knew it. He would not fail her. He collected pine-bark sawdust and fist-sized lumps of amber resin, for use in separate places. Some irritancy would ensue but would not stem the precious pulse of pleasure. In the morning, he would set her in the saddle, blondely naked but for his grey broad-brimmed hat, and he would keep wresting gratification from her beautiful body on their journey to the monastery.

20

Liann

At daybreak, Kin-Cague's overnight camp was beset by female bandits. They pinned him to the ground, clamouring, 'We've caught ourselves a monk!' Chloe was screaming.

A brown-haired girl stepped forwards, staring at Chloe then at Kin-Cague. 'Let him go,' she whispered.

'Why?'

'I know him.' She extended her hand to help him up. 'He's a kinsman.'

Kin-Cague, bemused, frowned at the proffered hand then squinted at the girl against the light.

'You don't remember me?' she said softly.

He pursed his lips.

'I'm the one you spoke up for – against the Prioress.'

Suddenly he realised. 'Rhislin?' He shook his head. 'But I thought she had you carted away?'

'She did. What happened to Iroise – is she safe?'

Kin-Cague levered himself up to a sitting position and Chloe wriggled across into his arms. He held her very gently, one hand slung protectively under her bursting belly, the other supporting her weighted breasts. As Chloe stared wide-eyed from one girl to the next and they stared inquisitively back, Kin-Cague outlined all that had happened since that fateful parting, up to the time when he saw Iroise and Dariun floating away down the river.

'You mean she came looking for me?' Rhislin asked.

219

'She is still looking for you.' He showed her the chain and the signet ring then began to take it off to give to her.

'No, you keep it safe for her,' she whispered.

He noticed that a sandy-haired girl in the group was watching Rhislin and hanging on her every word. Rhislin seemed to have grown markedly in confidence and strength of purpose since he had last seen her.

'And you and Dariun agreed to come with her?'

'It was no sacrifice: we were already dispossessed by Tormunites. And we could not leave this precious little one in their hands.' Chloe reached up to kiss him. 'And she is nearer by the day.'

'We know of a safe place for her confinement.' Rhislin glanced at one of the girls, who nodded agreement.

Chloe pressed closer to Kin-Cague. He said, 'The two of us have been following the path of the river but our progress has been slow and we have seen no sign of the others.'

One of the girls said, 'They may have reached the settlement.'

Rhislin nodded then turned to Kin-Cague. 'The people there are like this with the Tormunites.' She hooked her two forefingers together. 'They are not to be trusted.'

'Spineless,' said the girl.

'Then I must make haste,' Kin-Cague said, anxiously.

Rhislin glanced round the group before saying, 'We'll go with you.'

'No,' the sandy-haired one whispered worriedly.

Rhislin looked at her with compassion. 'Come here, Liann.' She took her by the shoulders. 'In adversity we must be strong. Remember what I told you in the compound? We must never be seen to falter. Now show the kinsman what they did to you.' The girl started to sob.

'Please,' Kin-Cague interceded, 'don't compel her.'

On the approach to the settlement, the group of riders came upon the bedraggled figure of Dariun in the road. He was disoriented and badly bruised. He gave no indication of having recognised Rhislin but fell to his knees before Kin-Cague.

'They've taken her,' he cried wretchedly, clutching Kin-Cague's gown. Chloe's warm and rosy cheeks turned ashen. Kin-Cague fed his battered colleague water.

Rhislin looked grim. 'His injuries need attention. We need to get him off the road and under cover. Liann, see to it. Asha, come with me.' The two rode off at the gallop in the direction from which Dariun had come. Kin-Cague helped his young friend on to one of the spare horses. Then Chloe and the kinsmen were led away from the road and river and into the hills.

They reached a mossy cave where they set up camp. The girl Liann followed her mistress's instructions diligently, attending to Dariun, who seemed utterly exhausted. Kin-Cague could not settle without word of the pursuit. It was several hours before the two girls returned.

'Their lead is too great. We were told they were gone by dawn. The chances of catching them before they reached the monastery were always slight but it was worth a try. Now we need to rethink.'

'Kin-Dariun is getting worse,' Kin-Cague said.

'Can he be moved?'

'But where?'

'The homestead isn't far.'

The overgrown trail climbed steadily through the trees, crossing small streams and passing sunlit glades. The party moved slowly, more on account of Dariun's state than Chloe's: she coped bravely with the uneven ride. It was nearing dusk when they reached a clearing high on the gently sloping southern flank of the hillside. There were three or four small fields overlooked by a single-storey dwelling and a group of outbuildings. The field closest to the house was planted with vegetables and fruit and there were goats in a pen at the back.

Two women of middle years came out to greet the party. They looked like sisters. They marvelled on seeing Chloe was pregnant; when they saw Dariun they were filled with concern. 'Get the boy inside – help him. There. Through to the back, now.' There were two neat small bedrooms. 'We're used to Asha's invalids.'

Dariun was put into one room, Chloe into the other. Liann immediately staked her personal claim on Dariun's care and supervision. The sisters smiled their approval at her. One whispered to Kin-Cague, 'She's a good girl, that one – such a warm and generous heart, yet so mistreated by those villains.' She looked askance at Kin-Cague's attire.

'Despite our garb, mistress, we are not Tormunites: those creatures defile the cloth.'

'Why, clothes don't make a man, sir – else scarecrows would be roaming free!' she replied, charitably.

That evening they dined upon a hearty meal of goat meat with herbs and freshly baked bread. The bathing was in a natural rock pool fed by a spring. The girls bedded down on the open porch and in the kitchen.

Chloe wanted Kin-Cague close. She was propped against an upended pillow at the head of the bed, and Kin-Cague was caressing her belly. She drew pleasure from the contact, as he did. He stroked the black centre-line that ran down from her protrusive umbilicus.

'You're gentle with me,' Chloe whispered.

He smiled and bowed his head, took between his lips the pink protrusive knot crowning her belly and kissed it, licked it. He felt her small warm fingers stroking his hair.

'It feels strange,' she murmured. 'It makes me want to pull away. No, don't stop.'

Her sexuality was increasing as her pregnancy burgeoned. The more she swelled the more beautiful she became, in his eyes. Her breasts were deliciously pear-shaped. The surrounds of her nipples made wide, black, velvet discs. She kept wanting him to lick her leakage, even to milk her. And though she still desired penetrative conjunction of the flesh she always sought to precipitate his climax with her mouth, that she might swallow his issue. This craving seemed to stem from her sojourn with the woods-girls and their captive males. The time that Kin-Cague had spent alone with her on the road had been soaked in pleasure. She liked to lie on her back, her lips clamped about the head of his penis, her bulging pear-shaped breasts swaying, and she would be grunting, her throat rippling as it drew from deep inside him every last drop of his issue. Afterwards, he would collapse by the camp fire and take her in his arms and want to sleep but Chloe would try to stimulate new issue. Exhaustion never came so sweetly to any kinsman.

'I want to check on Dariun,' he told Chloe. He levelled her pillow and she settled down.

There was no call for concern: Dariun was in good hands. Kin-Cague stood quietly at the open door and watched Liann. This beautiful, sandy-haired girl who only this morning had seemed so timid, was now in control. She seemed to have knowledge of herbs: he had earlier seen her collecting them from the rocks around the spring and now the selection was arranged neatly on her table. She had borrowed a pestle and mortar from the kitchen and was feeding the young kinsman the infusion she had created. Intent upon her task, she did not notice Kin-Cague. He returned to Chloe.

Finding her asleep, he settled down in quiet contemplation in the wooden armchair. He weighed the options: Dariun was unlikely to recover his strength for some days; Chloe was ever nearer to delivering, but at least she would be safe here. And what of Iroise? Kin-Cague, unlike Rhislin, knew neither the lie of the land nor anything concrete about the place where Iroise had been taken; beyond being a willing pair of hands, he was superfluous. He was sure Rhislin had a plan but she hadn't chosen to discuss it with him. He wondered what the morrow would bring. When he looked up, Liann was watching him from the doorway.

Kin-Cague smiled yet her face wore a curious determination as she entered the little room.

'How is he?' Kin-Cague asked softly, so as not to wake Chloe.

'Sleeping.' Liann nodded. The determination was still there. She stepped in front of him. 'When Rhislin said I must show you, I was shy. I am shy of men. I want to be braver.' She started to unfasten her taut trousers, which buttoned down the side.

'No, there is no need. Your steadfastness shines, through the way you treat Dariun. I watched you . . .' His voice trailed weakly away. Liann was not listening. She had embarked upon a task she meant to complete. Her fingers were delicate, the buttons broad, the loops stiff. The hairs on the back of Kin-Cague's neck began to prickle. The door was open, others might see, Chloe might wake. Liann had fine sandy eyebrows, a high forehead and hair trimmed short, its strands light as gossamer. She appeared mesmerised, as though re-enacting a scene in which she had been well grounded. The last button came free. She peeled the trousers down to her knees. She wore nothing underneath.

Her short heavy overshirt terminated just above her belly, leaving her naked to her knees. She remained still as if awaiting instruction or inspection. Her belly-skin was white; the hairs were so fine and pale as to be almost invisible. There were strange, ill-defined dark lines across it that resembled faded writing. There was no reddening except in a single place: a swelling or something unnatural at the top of her sex, above her clitoris. He wanted to investigate but was afraid to move. The trousers dropped to the floor, the slim feet pulled out, trampling the cloth beneath them. Liann came to him.

The self-control he believed he had long ago mastered when dealing with nubile girls was swept away by the innocent sexuality of her pose. He tried to conceal his arousal. Liann was plainly aware of what it signified but made no direct response. He pictured her performing the same enactment for the monks that had held her captive. He pictured a chamber in a gothic hall, two monks or more and this beautiful nubile creature being slowly stripped naked.

Her stiff shirt stood out from her belly. He could smell the delicate girlish scent of her skin. His gaze was drawn to the scrawls resembling writing, and more keenly to the place of swelling: coarse gold twine had been pushed through a piercing from beneath her clitoral hood and was knotted snugly on each side. The fatter of the knots was bedded under the hood; it made it look like a fleshy weighted swelling; the coarseness of the glistening twine irritated the skin to ruby redness against the whiteness of her pubic skin.

'The monks put it in me,' Liann whispered.

'We can take it out – cut it free. It won't hurt.'

'Oh, no. I cannot break the penance.'

'Penance for what?'

'They said I was fair of face and figure.'

'How can that merit penance?'

'Because it made me a temptation to men. Look –' she pointed to the faded writing on her belly '– they scribed it on me. You can still see: "Temptrix".' Kin-Cague was aghast that monks had done so spiteful a thing.

'But your beauty is a grace, not a bane,' Kin-Cague said, gently. 'It was wicked of them to try to assuage their guilt by heaping it on you.' Then he realised he was touching her fingertips.

'But the first night, after they had put the cord into me, my demon woke.'

'Demon?'

'The monks tied me open on a bed and left me in the dark with my penance itching between my legs. I fell asleep like that, then, suddenly, in the depths of night, I was awake again and gasping for breath as if I had been running a long, long way. And between my legs it was as if I was being stabbed but the stabbing did not hurt. It was nice. Yet afterwards I was afraid. I knew something dreadful had happened. The monks told me what it was.'

'What did they tell you?'

'It was the demon – raised inside me, through my badness fighting the penance. I could feel it in my belly. Every night the monks would try to drive it out but it's still inside me.'

'Have you not spoken of this to Rhislin and the women?'

'Don't tell them,' Liann said. She put her arms about his neck. A second later she was on his lap. His heart was bursting through his breast. She was naked from belly down. Even as he tried to explain to her, he felt his integrity as a kinsman slipping away.

'Liann, every woman – every man – is possessed in this way. You call it raising a demon, but it is not an evil thing. It is but a temporary sublimation of control to a pleasure that elevates the spirit – your own spirit, not a spirit from without that has wheedled itself into you. You must cast aside this sad encumbrance. The only badness stems from those monks who ill-treated you.'

'But you are a monk?'

'A kinsman.'

'Raise my demon,' she murmured, taking his hand, directing it.

The simple touching of her weighted swelling made the desire burn inside him. While he toyed, she made a halting confession about further practices to which the monks had introduced her and other girls, under the guise of sexual penance. It made him more anxious than ever about Iroise, who must by now be deep in their clutches.

Liann's demon came twice, rearing its beautiful, lustful, trembling head below her faded lettering and between her soft white thighs. Then a sound came from the next room and she hurried away trouserless to attend to Dariun, leaving Kin-Cague guiltily erect.

When he turned to check on Chloe, she was wide awake. Her jealousy fuelled her arousal. Her demon fired swiftly, for he used his mouth. Then he caressed her until she slid again into slumber.

He saw Rhislin entering Dariun's room. A few minutes later, she came out and retrieved Liann's trousers. He could not recall having fallen asleep but in the morning he recalled the dreams, vivid exorcisms of beautiful clitoral demons. He wanted to look upon Liann's face again in the early light. He crept to the door and peeped into the next room. Dariun was sleeping soundly. Liann was slumped in the chair, her trousers tied like a belt round her middle and thrust up under her breasts. She lay peacefully beautiful, as if all her demons had been expelled. Then Kin-Cague realised he was not alone at the door. Rhislin was behind him. He remained still until he heard her whisper, 'We will use her as bait. And, kinsman, we need that signet ring, and you too, if the plan is to work.'

21

Fornicatrix

'Her name?' The monk stood with pen poised as he peered over the lectern.

'Iroise,' Dom Qevrinn answered coolly. Her nude feet shuffled on the stone-tiled floor of the antechamber. Her nude body trembled.

'Charge?' The monk cocked his head.

Iroise shied away from his penetrating gaze.

'Don't look so shifty, girl!' he snapped. 'This is a house of correction, to which I am Registrar. We are well used to dealing with sneaky girls whom the normal avenues of rectitude have failed. You wheedled yourself into your master's cell where you languish like a whore these past two nights.'

'I am grateful that your minions found her,' Dom Qevrinn sighed.

The Registrar primed his pen again. 'So, Dom Qevrinn, the charge?'

'Promiscuity: engaging the flesh with a tavernful of men.'

The Registrar stared cruelly at Iroise. 'A fornicatrix? Deny it?'

Her heartbeat quickened; she stared at the floor and suddenly knew that too was wrong. She looked back in dread. He was already writing. 'I record the charge as cited . . . The absence of denial . . .' He stared at Iroise again. 'Mitigation?'

She froze.

'None. And so, the verdict . . . Guilty!' His gaze carried cruel satisfaction. 'Come round here, girl, quickly, now.

Don't squander my time.' She stepped clumsily on to the dais. He glanced at Dom Qevrinn. 'A short, sharp castigation?'

'Open-ended.'

The Registrar smiled insidiously then inscribed the page. 'Sign.' He held out the pen to Iroise.

'I cannot write,' she whispered.

He shook his head in grave annoyance. 'Yet you can fornicate and will happily put aside time to practice that?' She saw hateful desire in his gaze. He turned to Dom Qevrinn. 'Brother, help me with the fornicatrix. She must make her mark.'

Dom Qevrinn pinned her arms behind her and made her open. The Registrar crouched.

'Tut, tut. She is red here.'

'A little.'

'And there is wood dust and tiny splinters.'

Dom Qevrinn shrugged.

Iroise shuddered when the quillful of ink flooded under the hood of her clitoris, stinging her abraded flesh. 'Lift her, quickly. High.' She shivered above the lectern, with the ink prickling down her left labium. 'Now, put her to the page. Don't smudge it.' Tumbling feelings came in her belly as she was lowered. The vellum sucked the ink from her clinging flesh. 'Good.' Imprinted on the page was a small black button crowned by a cap with a wavy vertical smudge on one side. They stood her down. Dom Qevrinn countersigned the judgement.

The Registrar then pointed out to her master that the simple act of her signing the judgement had stimulated genital response. He held her from behind. 'The lips are bloating; the clitoris protrudes.' Then, he said, 'I must ask that you leave her in our charge now, that her immurement may begin.'

'Then I shall not have access?'

'It is a condition. The emotions must be free to soar, else the baring of the soul is impeded. And, unfortunately, the exercises in the public areas have had to be curtailed: there was an abscondment.'

'You recaptured her?'

'There were two. The ringleader caught her instructors off-guard by pretending compliance; she took another girl with her. It has never happened before. The Abbot has set a bounty for her recapture.'

'You will not be troubled that way by Iroise.'

'I shall make certain.' The Registrar made her face him. 'Well may you look, girl. Heed me.' She started to shake.

Her master kissed her lips, touched her nipples and clitoris one last time then left the antechamber. As she stood there nude, afraid, the Registrar unlocked an iron gate on the far side of the room. He dragged her through – 'Get up the stairs' – slapping her with his bare hands when she stumbled. She tried to cover her breasts. 'Get those hands behind you!' He slapped her breasts too.

They came out on to a stone-flagged landing of small cells overlooking a cloister. There were naked girls outside several of these; some were staked against the wall, others were being made to stand to attention by the monks supervising them. Noises – gurgles and subdued cries – issued from some of the cells. She glimpsed the beds: their headboards and footboards were fashioned like punishment stocks, with holes for the neck, hands and feet. The Registrar drove Iroise onwards, then suddenly stopped her by grasping her hair. He thrust her through the doorway of an empty cell. Then, he gagged her with a bandage. Terrified, she watched him remove his broad leather belt.

'Face the wall – your wall. Get to know it. Spread yourself against it. Tight.' He lashed her legs and bottom till the pain was so intense and so heaped in layers that she wet herself. Through her trying to prevent its expulsion, the wet coated her flesh and ran down her legs. And it made the punished skin burn as if a branding iron had been laid against the backs of her thighs. She heard him rebuckle his belt. 'Turn round.'

A nude girl was standing in the doorway with a tray of writing things. She was small but very swollen-breasted. One nipple – the left one – was grossly enlarged by a thick, gold, rope tag forced under it through a piercing. Her breathing was unsteady; she was aroused by Iroise's whipping.

'Becca, put your tray down,' the Registrar said, gently. 'Come here.' As she snuggled against him, he fondled her distorted nipple. 'Iroise can neither read nor write,' he whispered, menacingly. 'You must show her.'

Becca eagerly picked up the quill. 'Sharpen it,' he told her. He went to Iroise, who began trembling violently, stood behind her and held her. Becca, eyes glittering, approached with the needle-sharp quill and the ink. Iroise could not contain her sobs of abject terror. 'Shh. Keep still, girl. We must mark you up, so your instructors know. Push your teats out nicely. There.' He told Becca what to write. Symbol by symbol the quill tip scratched female cruelty into the skin of Iroise's breasts. 'Keep still, I said!' Her tears flooded, wetting the gag. Becca kept recharging the quill. He reached under Iroise's arms and held her breasts up. 'There, now. Plain for all who care to use you: "Fornicatrix".'

Then he made Becca scratch more symbols across Iroise's naked belly. The callous abuse after the whipping was more hurtful than the burning pain. Her legs were still wet and her conscience was seared by the shame of what had happened. When they had done with their dire inscriptions she was dragged to a mirror on the back of the door. Even through the welling tears, even to anyone who could not cipher, the dense knots and links of blackness marching across the whiteness of her skin were besmirchments, permissible because she was deemed worthless. 'Now read out this one, Becca.' He touched Iroise's belly.

'It says "Urinatrix",' Becca announced proudly.

'Good. Now make her get a cloth and pail and clean the floor.' Iroise wanted the floor to open up and swallow her.

Sobbing through her gag, she crept out after Becca, dropping down some stone steps into a wide corridor that eventually led to a stone-flagged pump room. Becca was fondling her gold-tagged nipple and watching Iroise with a fixed expression. Iroise managed to get the pump yielding water and she found a cloth. 'They'll tag your body; they always do,' Becca said. Then she crudely fingered Iroise's bottom and cunny while she was still kneeling. She would not let her go until her fingers glistened. Then, Iroise had to set off with her bucket, haltingly and fearfully, back to her cell.

When she entered, there were two monks speaking with the Registrar. Becca was dismissed. The monks were younger than most here. One was dark; the other had copper-red hair. Iroise crept nervously across to the damp patch she had made on the pale plastered wall, and the shiny pools of wetness on the floor tiles. As she set to work on hands and knees, she felt the men's gaze upon her even as her cheeks burned with embarrassment. Yet the steady working with water and cloth gradually softened the edge of her fear. She stole a glance at the men, who no longer seemed to be taking notice of her. The water soaking into the tepid plaster walls made a reassuring earthy scent; there was no smell of pee. She flooded the tiles with the water-soaked cloth then carefully wrung it out and dried the area all around. When she sat back on her heels the two monks were behind her, one on each side, and the Registrar was leaving.

The red-haired one took the cloth from her fingers and dropped it into the bucket. 'Iroise,' he said softly. She felt his fingers at the back of her head, freeing her gag. 'I am Tiriun; my colleague is Benedict. We have been assigned to your training.' He dropped the gag into the bucket then, supporting her under the arms, raised her to her feet. Benedict turned her around so her front was exposed. Automatically, she hunched her shoulders and half crossed her arms.

'Put your arms back,' Tiriun whispered, sternly. 'Concealment is a trespass. That is your first lesson.' He lifted her chin. 'Is your first lesson understood?'

She nodded. Her heart was racing.

'Then say, "Yes, master".'

'Yes, master.' Her tongue clung to the roof of her mouth.

'Stand back against the wall. There is still a trespass.'

231

Gooseflesh spread across her as she opened her legs for her masters.

'And your eyelids – never hide behind them. We need to judge your progress. See, brother, already there is dilation there.'

The dark-haired one, Benedict, now stood in front of her. 'You cannot read?' he asked.

'No, master.'

'But you have been told what your writing says? Then tell me.'

'Fornicatrix, master.'

'Meaning?'

'A badness of the flesh.'

'It means a girl with a compulsive desire to engage in copulation, a trait that weaker men admire. It is a badness, brought about through demons that have inveigled themselves deeply and must be excised. Hence.' He indicated the bed with its stocks for restraining her limbs. 'And the other word?'

'Ur . . . urin . . .'

'Urinatrix: a girl deriving sexual pleasure from urination – peeing.' He examined that place. Waves of prickles issued across it. 'There is inflammation: the usage has been harsh.' Then he discovered the minute pinewood splinters. 'Lift her on to the bed.' They put her feet through the stocks to keep her open. They swabbed her cunny with warm water to soften the flesh. Tiriun drew the splinters. Her clitoris became exposed during the drawing. Benedict touched it as if it were a precious jewel. They made her tell how the splinters had got there and she spoke too about the lumps of amber resin that Dom Qevrinn had put inside her before setting her, bare-bottomed, into the saddle. 'It made me swollen at the front,' she whispered. She felt swollen now. Tiriun was holding her cunny open and Benedict was gently swabbing her knob. Her ankles were restrained; at any second, clitoral pleasure might come, through swabbing. 'Each time the horses were rested, he made me stand up straight while he rubbed the pine dust up my cunny.' She shivered at the remembrance. Then, a fat drop of warm water from the soaked, dabbing swab, splashed against her pee-hole, and the pleasure came.

'Her demon enkindles!' Benedict cried out. Instantly, Tiriun hauled her upright, shuddering and gasping, legs still fastened, with Benedict's fingertips still moistly swabbing her pulsing cunny. Tiriun put his arms about her naked body and kissed her. He whispered eagerly, 'You will be fitted with a braid. It will help you. Dom Qevrinn has specified where.' He put his hand between her legs, searching expertly under her trembling cunny and finding the cord of raised flesh connecting to her anus. Her legs turned to jelly.

When two men are touching you and kissing you, and you are belly-naked – fastened open – the arousal is so suffocatingly sweet, you cannot breathe; you feel you are drowning, yet you want this honeyed suffocation to go on.

'There are demons, still,' Tiriun murmured. Benedict nodded. Her ankles were released and she was lifted from the bed and taken from her cell. 'No, leave your bucket,' Benedict said, quietly. Each master held an arm as she was led past cells where deep training was in session. In one a girl, spreadeagled across the window, cast a cross-shaped shadow on the floor. In another, a girl was crouched naked on the tiles, with her head and hands arched back, immobilised in the stocks at the foot of her bed. Her trainer was putting an instrument inside her.

Iroise was then diverted through a door leading away from the cloister, through a dark corridor so narrow that her masters had to turn her sideways to be able to proceed while still restraining her arms. Her nipples grazed the wall. Beyond the corridor was an even darker, small, six-sided room which had a short horizontal slot in each wall. Shafts of lamplight cut through each slot. Benedict put a finger over her lips. Then, she was led by the arms to one of the slots. It was a spyhole: her masters raised her on tiptoes. Iroise watched in silent complicity, afraid to breathe.

A beautiful, bronzed girl was perched with one thigh over a padded kneeling desk and one foot on the floor. A blonde girl with long straight hair was kneeling at the desk. She was clasping the bronzed girl around the narrow waist

233

and sucking her between the legs. Both girls were naked. A powerfully built monk was directing them. The bronzed girl was so near to coming that her distended breasts were already trembling.

The blonde girl was touching herself between the legs and her mouth was so clamped against the girl's belly that the veins on her neck stood out. Then, suddenly, she coughed and slowly drew away and Iroise shivered with delicious excitement and wonder, gazing up and down between the lovely, bronzed, trembling, swollen breasts and the long, erect, saliva-coated penis being unendingly shed from the blonde girl's mouth. The girl sat back, her mouth still gaping, her throat rippling as she endeavoured to swallow the excess saliva without closing her mouth. She looked to the monk for further instruction.

Iroise shivered again as she tried to come to terms with the scene of the beautiful girl with the penis and breasts and swollen ball-sac. She pictured herself as the kneeling girl; she wondered what the penis smelt of – man or girl – and she imagined it in her throat and wondered what those breasts would feel like, kneaded in her fingers. The teats looked like dark brown velvet.

At that moment, Tiriun touched Iroise between the legs, his fingertips grazing the weighted lips of her cunny, while her arms were still restrained and she was watching what was happening in the cubicle. She wanted to press her cunny against the plaster wall and come while her dominators held her against it.

Inside the cubicle, the monk was standing by the kneeling blonde girl, lifting her long, straight hank of hair. Scrawled across her back were ciphers. He ran his wrinkled hand across them then slid it down until the middle finger found the puncture in the crack. She shuddered as it wormed inside. He took the other girl's erect bronzed penis by the base and urged it into the blonde girl's mouth, until her slim body was spitted between finger and penis, and her lips were sealed against the heavy brown sac.

Tiriun was still touching Iroise. He whispered that he was raising demons. The tip of his finger found the sticky entrance to her pee-hole, pressed and pulled away and pressed again, and Iroise wanted to crouch and let him bring her to completion.

The masters dragged her away from the spyhole and took her to another, across the six-sided room. All the while, her arms were restrained. They felt numb and would have dropped like leaden weights had the monks released their grip.

In this cubicle, a girl in a black vest and socks was bundled in a chair with her knees pushed up to her ears. A monk in a grey cassock was playing with her cunny. A second girl, with her naked bottom leant against a table, was oiling her fingers. She kept glancing at an hourglass beside her, trickling sand.

'See the one in the chair?' Tiriun whispered beside her. 'A masturbatrix. Their duty is to work her continuously – to try to bring her on, each time before the sand expires.' He edged Iroise's feet apart, and she felt as if a delicious weight was sinking in her womb. He fingered her gently from the front. Benedict's cool hand ascended the back of her leg, found her Thong of Venus and nipped it as she looked through the secret slot.

The girl's knees were trembling. Her monk's fingers rubbed swiftly across the top of her cunny. The second girl came across to kiss her and to tongue her mouth. The monk's hand became a blur of movement. The climax was precipitated: the girl's knees jerked as if she were astride a horse and were spurring him to the gallop. The monk withdrew and the girl's oiled hand took over the duties. The monk turned the hourglass before the sand had expired.

Iroise was still being held by the arms and – between the legs – by her Thong of Venus and the swollen lips of her cunny. Her knob was aching to be sucked or rubbed. When her masters moved her to the next spyhole, she could hardly walk. They pushed her breasts against the plaster wall and continued playing with her.

Inside this cubicle, a girl wore a thin gold chain about her waist. To this was fastened a second thin chain threaded through a ring dangling between her legs. When she was turned it could be seen that the ring was attached to a plug distending her bottom. Her trainer was carefully inserting a very fine flexible tube between the lips of her cunny.

Iroise groaned in pleasure; her legs were giving way. 'The demon,' Tiriun whispered in awe. He was gently pushing the tip of his finger against the mouth of her pee-hole while Benedict was pulling her thong of flesh. Her belly sank against the cool smooth plaster. Her mouth caressed it; the fresh earthy scent filled her nostrils. 'Let it come,' Tiriun whispered. 'Piss it out against the wall.' He spread her labia against its powdery surface. She was shivering on the edge of delivery of pee or pleasure but neither would come. The masters turned her in the darkness. A hand was clapped over her mouth. 'Keep silent,' Benedict hissed, for she must have been gasping out loud, 'the demon must not be frightened back inside.' They lowered her on to her knees in the darkness. It was like being immersed in a pool of blackness. Above her head, the illuminated slots threw weak yellow beams across the secret room. She felt as if her sex and bottom were plunged into a sea of groping hands. The pleasure came – and a little urination – while she was kneeling: Tiriun nuzzled her neck and Benedict nuzzled her nipples and she shed her little sprays over their hands. Tiriun whispered that the demon had cloven inside her, that excision was incomplete. She tried to grope him under his gown and though he stopped her, she was able to tell that he was burningly erect, and it was good that they were desirous men. She wanted to prostrate herself on the floor in the blackness and let them finger her up again and come inside her mouth. And she would surely swallow all their semen as a salve against the sweet cruelty of this cloven demon. She tried to collapse backwards but they pulled her up. Tiriun kissed her, swiftly, on the lips.

They took her out of the secret room on the opposite side from where they had entered. After some turns and steps down, they emerged near a corner of the leafy cloister where a blindfold girl was being sexually punished on a horizontal pole. It was less wide than her wrist and she was straddling it, with hands behind her head and her feet off the ground. Her masters steadied her by her breasts and shoulders. Her nipples were erect. She kept trying to tighten the cheeks of her bottom but they kept prising them open.

Benedict brought Iroise near to the girl. His hand silenced Iroise's trembling lips as he led her nervous fingers up to her. The touch – the lovely soft warmth of female arousal – electrified Iroise. She felt as if the girl would hear her heart pounding through her breast. The girl's masters watched Iroise with deep attention; they edged the girl back with her buttocks spread and watched the roaming fingers trigger murmurs. Iroise held the lovely cunny lips gently closed and rubbed them round that little knob; she wanted the girl to know she was being played with by a girl. She would have kissed the trembling breast-points had her mouth not been sealed by Benedict's hand. The little shiny girl-knob came out; she touched its firmness with her finger, tapped it repeatedly. The girl grunted gutturally then Benedict drew the stymied Iroise away.

They let her watch as one of the masters lowered the girl's aroused body gently backwards until her belly protruded then the other master beheaded a flower and inserted it by its stem into her pee-hole. 'The demon may be drawn into the living flower tissue,' Benedict whispered. Iroise squirmed and Tiriun put his hand under her bottom and cupped her cunny, pressing the tip of his finger into that selfsame place. He lifted her up like that and carried her with legs dangling, then sat her on the shiny cold stone balustrade of the cloister. Frightened of toppling backwards she tried to use her hands to steady herself but Benedict told her, 'No!'

Tiriun prised her legs open. The arousal of her two masters was palpable. Iroise had never experienced such feelings since being under the Sisters of Servulan. But the monks at Servulan had always been more secretive in their usage of the girls for pleasure. Here there were no sisters to direct the monks or to stop them pushing flowers into such places. Her legs were now wide open: her cunny was showing. Benedict disappeared behind her into one of the rooms adjoining the cloister. The girl had been taken off her pole with her flower still lodged as if its bloom had seeded from within her. They made her walk with its stem inside her. Tiriun said they would keep it up her until it wilted and that this might take a long time, for if the stem probed sufficiently deeply, her moisture might make it grow.

Again he put his fingers between Iroise's legs to peel back the lips of her cunny. He was intent on touching the place where she peed from. The feelings he induced there made her back hollow and her belly bulge down until it touched his wrist. Her bottom moved back in an effort to escape these feelings but the probing tip of his finger followed. She heard a bucket being placed on the flagstones behind her. She glimpsed glistening tubular metal being put into its milky contents, then she heard the clyster being filled.

'Oh!' she gasped. 'Oh!' Her bottom was not ready for this acceptance. Tiriun held her head cradled to his chest while he chanted soothing utterances in an unfamiliar language. He kept his finger pressing against the tiny hole inside her front. The clyster had a bulbous shiny teatlike vent; it burst her protruding rosebud and slipped up her bottom. She shuddered when the weighted, cold fluid began to fill her. It kept coming and she kept shivering and Tiriun chanted ever louder.

They put a second clysterful inside her. Her thighs were trembling and she was sweating under the arms, which remained exposed because her masters made her keep her hands behind her head. Sweat trickled down her sides. Tiriun said it was the demon drowning inside her. He anointed her clitoris with the trickles while he kissed her lips and she moaned into his mouth and the muscle of her bottom sucked milky fluid from the shiny teat of the clyster.

The bucket was half-empty. They told her they must keep filling her until her demon was stilled. They lifted her down from the balustrade and on to her feet. 'Don't tense – acquiesce,' Tiriun whispered. 'Let your belly distend. The catharsis shall come keener.' He slapped her belly gently with a cupped hand.

They made her walk the perimeter of the cloister while they watched her. 'Slowly, gracefully. Head up. Hands behind your neck.' When she reached the three-quarters point a door opened beside her. She was suddenly staring at a frightened girl. Propelling the girl forwards was the Registrar; she looked helpless and afraid. Benedict sprang across the cloister, as if he meant to challenge this interruption to Iroise's training. Then he recognised the girl and his expression was surprised and pleased. 'Liann,' he whispered, taking her by the slender shoulders.

'She's come back to seek expiation of her trespass,' the Registrar smiled, cruelly. 'Her penance shall be long.' Liann hid her face.

'She'd be better with us,' Benedict offered.

The Registrar refused. 'Had she been properly supervised, she would never have been away.' He lifted her chin and forced her to kiss him. His hand went between her legs and grasped a bulblike fleshy swelling at the top of her cunny. The touching made her squirm. 'Stand aside, please, the Abbot wants to see her.'

Benedict watched Liann being led away then he turned to Iroise. 'Shall you run away too?' Iroise shook her head. She felt warmth for her tormentors. When Tiriun arrived at their corner of the cloister, Iroise was kissing and being kissed. Tiriun touched her from behind while she kept kissing. The two monks then lifted her on to the stone balustrade. She stood unsteadily open, with one hand on the pillar and the other against the canopy. They spoke of what had been done to Liann to instigate the swelling and of what would be done to Iroise. 'We'll put a thick gold braid through here,' they said, pinching the skin-thong connecting her bottom to her cunny, 'as a pinion for exorcising demons.' Then they brought the bucket and clyster. 'Turn round. Hold the pillar tightly.' The restricted width of the balustrade meant she could not get her feet far enough apart for easy entry by the clyster. 'She's beautiful,' Tiriun murmured, stroking her shaking buttock cheeks as Benedict pushed the silver teat into her. Iroise clung to the pillar and moaned. Her bowels filled to bursting. Her naked breasts rubbed against the stone. Tiriun opened her cunny and slid his finger up the oily back wall. Her legs began shaking. 'One more,' he said, his finger still in place.

'Oh, no, please,' she shuddered. They made her take it, then lifted her down and carried her, moaning, out of the cloister, through the yard, out of the walled enclosure of the grounds and into the shady woodland. Still carrying her they pushed the soles of her feet against a mossy tree trunk and masturbated her deeply, without hurry, taking turns. On the crest of climax, she expelled. They flushed her bottom twice with chilling water from a woodland stream. She stood there, a shivering white nude figure set against the darkening green. Tiriun enveloped her in his arms. She hid her face in the coarse woollen cloth of his gown.

'It's still excited, down here,' he whispered to his colleague. Iroise gasped softly as he drew the hood of flesh back and stroked her naked clitoris anew. He kept the hood drawn fully back and held her close to him, so her clitoris was plunged against the tickling strands of coarse wool. 'Flush her frontal pouch – the demon spirit may reside there too.' He held her shivering body very gently as the nose of the instrument opened her burning cunny like a cool, smooth penis coming from behind. She climaxed when the freezing water gushed inside, with Tiriun gently clutching her buttocks and lifting her from the ground. He told her afterwards that he could feel her knob poking like an exposed bone against the muscle of his thigh. She had wet his gown. He made her stand while he opened her with his thumbs. The water, warmed by her body, surged out spasmodically while Benedict milked her teats. After that, she started to shiver acutely so they picked her up and took her back inside.

They drew criticism from the other monks for having taken her out of the compound. 'She might abscond –

don't smile, brother. You know it has happened these few days gone. The Abbot has set a curfew.'

'Dom Lenk fears that, should you escape, he will not get to fit you with your braid,' Tiriun said gently.

That night, Tiriun allowed two of the other female inmates to whip and to play with Iroise. He saw how her demon came better with girls. They scrawled ink across her lovely shivering breasts and dripped wax from a burning candle into her body. And the girls themselves became deeply aroused by all the punishment and kissing. They made her lie the wrong way round on the bed, but face-up, with her head and hands through the footboard stocks. Her head hung down, her throat was exposed. Tiriun stroked it. He had the urge to plunge his flesh deep inside it, but he left her pleasuring to the girls. Becca released her little caged mouse on to Iroise's naked body. The lanky girl accompanying Becca had smeared honey over Iroise's clitoris and under its hood. The tiny nibbling sucks between her legs caused gurgles in her throat.

When Tiriun carried Becca back to her cell, he could feel her arousal. When he went inside her naked body, pinned to the wall, and her swollen, braid-implanted nipple pressed against him, liquid demons of lust spawned from her soft gloving cunt; her warm clear body-paste ran down his balls. He carried her to her bed, still impaled – her feet locked round him, her body still racked by splintered demons, and her mouse dancing in the tiny cage clutched tightly in her fingers. Then he went back to Iroise and shared her with the lanky girl. They tried to stay inside her body all night, keeping her skin-thong tightly stretched between them – lanky hand and monkish penis, soaked in Becca's paste, lending comfort in their deep, tireless, coexistent penetration.

22

Goading the Demons

'Sit her on the table.' It was morning and Iroise had been taken by her instructors to Dom Lenk for her fitting.

'Might she be better standing?' Tiriun asked.

'Whatever she chooses. I have harnesses if she needs them.'

'Iroise is brave. She shall not need restraint.'

Tiriun stood her on the massive marble table where it abutted against the frescoed wall. Dom Lenk went to get his implements. Benedict sat patiently on the end of the table.

Iroise stood naked, high above the men, her fingertips resting against the garden scene frescoed on the wall, her toes cold on the marble table. Deep inside, her bottom throbbed from the distension of last night; the lips of her cunny were bloated. Tiriun reached up – she thought to seek them – but he wanted to test her fleshy string. She shivered with legs bowed open for him.

Dom Lenk returned with the gold insert that was to be put through her flesh to goad the demon. It was as thick as Iroise's little finger but shorter and was braided like a rope, crowned at each end by a solid stud fashioned into a perfect knot. He unscrewed one stud and placed the goad between her ankles on the table. She glimpsed a fat steel needle and suddenly the room slid sideways.

'Support her, brother. She'd be better kneeling.' Benedict climbed on to the table to hold her under the arms.

The feeling – of being made to give herself like this, to be punctured and threaded on to a golden tag – caused a faintness both dreadful and delicious. Her fingertips and toes were tingling. Waves of submission splashed up her belly as she hung from Benedict's arms. It felt as if the flesh between her legs was being coaxed into an icy saddle. Tiriun sucked her goosefleshed nipples. His warm fingers held the cold lips of her cunny up and open. The needle made a dull pressure underneath, focusing ever more keenly. She felt the puncture then freezing metal reaming out her fleshy string. The needle resurfaced – she felt its exit – then the gold rope goad followed tortuously slowly in the same direction.

'It's a thick one – tight.'

'Try playing with her.' They persisted through her moans and Tiriun's gentle smacking down of her protruding clitoris. She was lowered backwards on to the freezing table and into Benedict's arms.

'It's done,' Dom Lenk declared, screwing the studs tight.

'You can see the pattern of the braiding through her skin,' Tiriun said, touching the stretched tightness, stirring feelings like the dull sweet aching that comes there near the point of climax.

Dom Lenk traced the ink-lines across her belly. 'A urinatrix? May I?' He spread her swollen lips and touched her frightened pee-hole. 'Have you administered drink? Then we must attend to that directly. Keep touching here.' He left her with the others. She lay prostrate on her back on Benedict's lap. She could feel his rigid penis pressing through his gown. Each time her cunny constricted as Tiriun probed her pee-hole, the braided goad reared up. It felt like a weighted sucking creature bedded into her flesh. Tiriun said it would draw demons. The knotted cap kept taunting the mouth of her bottom. Tiriun put his finger into her cunny and pressed down, keeping the goad moving. 'See how swollen her knob is become,' he whispered, excitedly. Benedict reached down her belly to touch it. With the pressing finger still inside her cunny and this new caressing of her knob, she was helpless on the brink of coming.

Dom Lenk came back with a pitcher of scented water and a cup. They sat her up to make her drink. Dom Lenk tenderly fondled her nipples. Tiriun gently urged her knees to her shoulders, the clearer to expose her cunny, and kissed her toes. Benedict prised the empty cup from her fingers, kissed her lips then refilled the cup. 'Drink swiftly.' The water was weakly perfumed with gentian; it nurtured her thirst. They spoke of water demons and kept her drinking. When Dom Lenk put a hooked finger up her cunny, the focused pressure made her moan. 'Sit her on the edge.' Her drew her clitoral hood right back and reapplied the upwards pressure from inside her until the moan came deeper. 'The demon resists expulsion.' Tiriun kissed her nipples anew and Benedict kissed her mouth and Dom Lenk masturbated her trembling cunny, projecting over the edge. 'I feel a goad is needed here, to aid convergence. Stand her on the floor. Let her hold it open.'

Her fingers trembling, Iroise watched the instrument being introduced between her legs. It was a chain of gold beads with a little tee-shaped bar at one end to arrest complete ingestion. When the first bead touched, so cold and so invasive of that sensitive narrow tube, her legs almost buckled. 'Stay still and open. Lovely. Feel them going in? Look at her.' She shuddered. 'Steady. Don't spray me! One more little push. Good.' He wiped her thighs.

The feeling was of being opened by a tiny beaded icicle, a deeply intimate and precise penetration of the sexual heart from where she would pee. Dom Lenk, standing up, touched the little gold bar that dangled from its mouth. Benedict fondled her goaded skin-thong from beneath and slid a thumb inside her bottom. Tiriun kissed her. They lifted her astride an iron drying bar in front of the cold fireplace, directing her goad and cunny to one side of the bar. Benedict masturbated the closed lips of her cunny against the iron while Tiriun made her drink. She could not stop herself moistening the iron with little trickles. Dom Lenk was already dealing with a new girl. When she was first placed on the table, her cunny-lips were fully sheathed and her belly was completely smooth, with a barely visible slit. When they were finished with her, the inner lips were so stimulated and stretched that they could not fit inside. A fine tube was being put inside her pee-hole.

Iroise was brought over to watch. Benedict gently stirred the chain that dangled from her dripping pee-hole. He said she felt pregnant because of the bloating; he smacked gently upwards between her legs, saying he was smacking her water demons. When her climax came, the monks had to hold her. Dom Lenk then explained that her purging would now continue under the tutelage of the Abbot. Her instructors had to carry her. She was clutching to her breast a fresh flagon of scented water.

There were already three girls in the Abbot's quarters. Iroise recognised them all. She had watched two of them – the long-haired blonde girl and the man-girl – through the spyhole in the darkened room: they now lay together on the bed. The third girl was frightened Liann; she was sitting in the Abbot's capacious lap in his armchair. His dark blue dressing gown was open at the front and Liann was partly inside it. He had dense white bushy eyebrows and warm pink skin. His eyes seemed gentle, his voice soft. 'I shan't get up,' he sighed. 'I see the girl has legs. Put her down and let her use them.'

Then he saw her plight. When the monks had gone he said, 'Come hither, Iroise.' He extended his left hand, which bore a thick gold ring crowned by a sparkling blue jewel. Iroise sank uncertainly to her knees and kissed it. His fingers, though thickened by age, were soft. Their scent was yeasty. The nails were ridged and misshapen but scrupulously clean. 'Put down your flagon. Stand. Show your lovely belly – let us read the infractions written there. Ah.' he sighed. 'Water demons.' He put his fingers there and made her shiver. 'What think you of Liann – is she a good girl?'

'I cannot tell, my lord,' Iroise whispered, trembling on her chain. He continued touching her while he drew his gown aside.

She shuddered gently to see that thick-stemmed pink penis bedded so tightly in Liann's beautiful cunny. 'Liann was led astray,' he murmured. 'Though she is getting back

245

on course.' He put his lips to hers and Liann strove to accept the oral contact without shrinking away. 'Open, Liann.' Her head slumped against his shoulder. A little of the penile length emerged from her body. Her bloated clitoral hood stood prominently and a drop of her expressed oil was creeping slowly down his stem. Then he said to Iroise, 'Come up, here. Sit upon the arm of my chair. And bring your flagon.' He guided her with fingertip hold of the chain inside her pee-hole.

'Don't dally. Sit properly.' She was fearful of putting pressure on the goad under her cunny. She shivered as it touched the leather. 'There, now.' She was facing inwards, perched above the interlocked couple. When she opened her thighs fully, the chain slipped inside her, a tiny pee-hole pulling fraction that made her moan. The Abbot handed her flagon to Liann. 'Administer this in doses to Iroise.' And to Iroise he said, 'No, my dearest. Keep your legs open – we need to study each loving convulsion.' Then as Liann fed her drink, the Abbot stimulated the goads in Iroise's quaking cunny – 'Sit forwards, nicely . . .' – stirring the captive braid embedded through her thong of skin, and pressing the gold beads gently deeper into her pee-hole. Her belly squirmed, for she was bursting; gooseflesh spread across her front; her nipples hurt. When the flagon was empty he took her naked toes and pressed them softly between Liann's thighs until Liann murmured and her body slackened. 'Her demon is quite near,' the Abbot whispered, relieving her limp hand of the flagon and putting it on the floor. Her grossly swollen clitoral hood slipped like a warm shiny ball under Iroise's gently pulsing toes. The toes moved down to touch the penile shaft, dipping into the clear, warm droplets of Liann's lubricant. When Iroise dug her toes into the soft underbelly of the shaft, Liann's cunny expanded with the swelling. The Abbot, gasping, drew Liann's body carefully off him: he seemed scrupulous in avoiding expulsion inside her.

Iroise leant forwards and kissed his temple; he seemed confounded about what the kiss meant. His pulsing erection bobbed to the side. Iroise almost wanted to circle

246

his wet penis with her finger and thumb and bring his fluid out. At this thought, her own wetness suddenly sprayed, shocking her with its force and fineness. The Abbot murmured, 'Beautiful.' It had lasted only a second before she tightened and stopped it. It had radiated sideways, on account of the chain. It had wet her thighs but because she was twisted round, kissing the Abbot, it had sprayed both him and Liann. Liann's eyes were wide with curiosity. The Abbot made wet lines from the droplets that had showered Liann's belly. Iroise's fingers nervously collared his penis near the top. She squeezed it and a little blob of whiteness issued. The Abbot encouraged Liann's head down. As her lips sank so submissively round the head of the penis, something melted inside Iroise. She heard the spray – her spray – and was afraid to look but felt warmth and wetness over her thighs and a feeling low down at the front, pressured and delicious. Liann's hair was now wet. The Abbot was already smoothing it down. 'Gentian,' he murmured, breathing the scent that Iroise's cunny had put there. Liann lay back against him, eyes half-closed, lips shiny, belly thrust out, and her bottom gently opening to the coercion of his penis.

'Judi, bring Sulime, if she's ready,' the Abbot said with laboured breathing. 'Shh,' he reassured Liann. The blonde girl helped the strange man-girl from the bed. Iroise watched in fascination as the girls kissed and Judi's fingertips kept stroking the generous length of Sulime's penis. Sulime's skin was bronzed, her breasts were full, her legs were slender. A swollen ball-sac filled the gap at the top of her thighs.

'Would you like to explore Sulime?' the Abbot invited, stroking Iroise between the legs, brushing the backs of his fingers across her chain. These words aroused her. She watched the heavy ball-sac being lifted in Judi's hands. Iroise looked down and saw that the backs of the Abbot's fingers were slickened with her oil. He let Liann kiss it away. Iroise's heart was in her throat as Judi brought Sulime closer. Liann was slumped against the Abbot with his penis stretching her bottom wide.

Dutifully and sexually, Liann held her cunny open, shuddering when the bloated glans of Sulime's penis touched it. She gasped as it tried to nose inside her. Judi wetted it with her spittle; the Abbot added Iroise's oil. The bloated glans started to slide into Liann, who grunted with pleasure when her nipples touched Sulime's. She came to climax through the double distension. The Abbot declared there were still demons within her. Judi, smiling wantonly at Iroise, crouched on the far side of Sulime's body, clutching her heavy sac tightly, making Sulime writhe and Liann shudder anew. She reached over and took Iroise's wrist.

'Ride postillion with your fingers,' Judi said. Iroise did not understand. Judi coated them with slippery saliva then pushed them into Sulime's bottom. 'Push down, as if to push your fingers up her penis from behind.' Sulime then began to ejaculate – Iroise could feel the pulsing through the tips of her fingers. Sulime's penis, stuck fast in Liann's small cunny, could not withdraw far enough in time. Thick semen bubbled over the lips then Sulime continued squirting, under her own breasts and Liann's. Judi spread the fluid between them. When Liann reached up to kiss Sulime, the skin of their breasts adhered. When they drew apart, fluid continued to be expelled from Liann with each contraction of her cunny. Judi smeared it round the lips and forced it under the swollen hood. 'She shall need a douche, my lord,' Judi whispered. It was administered to make her safe: the Abbot then undertook the search for deeper demons in Liann. Judi led Iroise back to her cell with Sulime.

Judi stood at the door of Iroise's cell, making fast the restraints. She watched the two girls on the bed. Throughout, she had remained mistress, directing Sulime and Iroise, but she felt drawn to Iroise's lovely body. Iroise liked girls; Sulime preferred to be reamed by men. Iroise had revealed to Judi during secret kissing that she had had a female master called Rhislin. Judi had encouraged Iroise to tell all – for the telling moved that lovely body to delicious, tractable passion. Iroise turned weepy: this slave-love was deeply ingrained. Judi pretended she knew nothing of Rhislin and she intimated nothing of Rhislin's link with Liann. But she steered Iroise into confessing desire for Liann. She asked her which parts of Liann she would like to kiss. Then she kissed those parts on Iroise.

She would not allow Iroise to relieve herself and she kept her drinking while Sulime watched. The loss of control aroused Iroise. Her bottom became wet. Her neck burned with sweet shame. Judi put her open-thighed on a pillow, with her ankles through the stocks. Then she spanked her, bare-handed, one hand thrust into the pillowcase under Iroise's belly, clawing her knob and chain, the other spanking her bottom, and Iroise started peeing and coming at the same time. Her buttocks convulsed as if she was fucking the pillow. And her squirts of boiling pee sprayed through the cloth on to Judi's clawing fingers.

Judi led Sulime by her erection to the place near the door. She tied her wrists up to the restraints then put a tiny stool in front of her. She went back to the bed and freed Iroise's ankles. 'Sit up.' Her breasts were wet. The scented nipples came stiff when Judi kissed them. She led the lovely girl to the tiny stool in front of Sulime and forced her into oral congress with Sulime's penis.

Judi gently held the swollen tagged place below Iroise's cunny and forced the shuddering girl to drink. Controlling a passive girl is a beautiful pleasure. Judi kept her open-cunnied on the stool, her chain pushed up to its little bar inside her pee-hole, her arms drawn back, wrested tight. Her throat stayed dutifully submissive to the intromissions of hot penile flesh and cooling water from the recharged flagon. Her stool silently overflowed; her warm liquor spread across the floor, flooding the gaps between Sulime's trembling toes, tripping Sulime's climax in noisy surges into Iroise's obedient throat.

When Sulime seemed exhausted and her glans would not come properly erect, Iroise asked about tubing. She said she had seen it done to a girl. Judi found some. While Iroise was worming it in, Sulime's penis shrank until it looked as if a thick bone filled its girth within an inch of the base. The tip remained soft yet arousal was still with it and Iroise manipulated it until ejaculation came again – more tortuously this time. Iroise and Judi shared the fluid coming through the tube.

They left Sulime with the tube partly inside her body and went for girl-play on the bed. Judi lay between Iroise's naked thighs. She asked if Rhislin used to do this, and the words and the genital contact brought Iroise to shuddering pleasure. Then Judi sat toying with her, where her braid was fitted, and taunting her with sexual tales of punishing Liann. Iroise wanted to go back to Sulime to torment her. She would not rest until the tube was fully worked down Sulime's penis and the wet erupted uncontrollably. 'Leave her with it in,' Judi whispered, taking Iroise back to bed.

Judi smacked Iroise between the legs, forcing another wet climax, and drawing the chain out to make the climax stronger. Then she pushed it all the way in, closing the lips about the bar. Then Iroise slumbered in Judi's arms. But in the night she woke, hungry to taunt Sulime.

Judi strapped the dildo round Iroise's waist then played with her, feigning rubbing her dildo to stiffer erection. Then she watched her: her lovely face intent, her breathing strained, her fingers reaching round gently to hold the half-erect, entubed penis as the dildo entered Sulime's body. She pumped till the semen issued, thin as milk, from the bobbing tip of the flexible tube.

Iroise said afterwards that when she had felt this milk coming out of Sulime's body, trembling up her entubed penis, a shock of pleasure had jolted Iroise's body, from where the dildo pressed her pee-hole, then through her bottom, up her backbone to her throat. Judi finger-probed each of these places, retracing the line of pleasure. Then she let Iroise sleep in Sulime's arms, her face nuzzled in Sulime's breasts, Sulime's penis against her belly, alongside her dildo, seeping milky semen through the night.

In the morning, Iroise was called to breakfast with the Abbot. He waited to see how she would sit. She could not prevent a shudder when her chain touched the chair and her gold implant pressed into the swollen bridge of flesh below her cunny. He studied her with quiet affection. Then he said, 'I must return you to Dom Qevrinn.'

Suddenly, her eyes were hunted. She bit her lip. He stared without any indication of what he wanted her to say.

Then the door opened behind her. The Registrar entered, went round the table and began a whispered conversation with the Abbot. Consternation spread across the Abbot's face. 'Here? Now?'

Suddenly, a voice boomed out behind Iroise. 'Yes, my lord, I am here. And I want action – now!'

Iroise turned. Her mouth fell open. Looming in the doorway was a familiar profile, but the countenance was transfigured by trenchant resolve.

23

Zephyr

The slap descended so hard across Iroise's face, that she was knocked from her chair. Tears of reproach flooded silently as she knelt on the floor, dazed and frightened.

'I shall wipe the smug insolence from your face, girl. Have her sent to my quarters.'

'Dom Cague,' the Registrar apologised, 'we were not expecting you. Your accommodation is not yet arranged.'

Iroise looked up at the man so changed she scarcely recognised him. When he glanced at her again, she cringed.

'Deputy Abbot . . .' Dom Cague began.

'I am Abbot, sir,' the reply came coldly.

'I am here to collect a girl named Rhislin. As I explained to your man, here, I have documentation from the Barony of Servulan – whence it appears she decamped – and the counterseal.' He banged the papers down on the table.

'Tormunil,' the Abbot whispered, staring at the seal.

'We believe the girl to be a troublemaker. We understand she was taken in by the Priory and then sent here. Such action – though dutifully meant – was outwith the authority of the Prioress. The girl ought to have been returned to the Baron. I am here to claim her on his behalf.'

The Abbot paled. He looked to the Registrar, who winced then croaked, 'Dom Cague, there is a problem. She is not here.'

'Not here?'

'She has run away.'

'What!'

'But – please, calm yourself – we have someone who may know of her whereabouts, a girl who was with her but has since been recaptured.'

'Then where is she? Get her here, now! Time is short. I had not anticipated delay; it will not report well.' He glared at the Abbot. 'You have a garrison?'

'A small one.'

'I shall need the loan of your three best men.'

'At once.'

'Wait. I'll pick them myself.'

He grasped Iroise by the hair. 'And I shall need a bull-whip.'

Kin-Cague carefully selected the most shiftless troop. He kept the girls bound in the saddle and drove the party south, into the lowlands until nightfall, when he declared a camp in dense woodland.

An hour after dusk, female voices were heard and a light was seen in the distance. The soldiers went in hot pursuit. When the trail went cold they returned to find the camping place empty.

The shadows of afternoon cast diagonal lines across the veranda of the homestead.

'Chloe's time is near,' Iroise said.

Kin-Cague nodded and continued to stare across the treetops into the hazy distance. 'You spoke to Dariun?' he asked softly.

'I wanted to thank him. He is a good man, kind and generous of spirit. Liann is still with him.'

Iroise's fingernails plucked nervously at the bark-encrusted veranda posts. 'Why did you hit me?' she whispered.

Kin-Cague turned to face her. 'I had to do it. I needed some pretext for securing you, but without risking any indication of our acquaintance. Liann was to try to make contact and apprise you of our plan.'

'Liann said nothing to me.'

Kin-Cague's brow furrowed. 'Then you saw her? I didn't know.'

Iroise was fighting back the tears. Kin-Cague took her hands, which now hung limply by her sides. 'Don't look at me,' she whispered, biting her lip. He took her in his arms and held her head to his breast.

He spoke gently. 'But the tears are not about Liann's jealousy?' Iroise shook her head. 'And not because I hit you?'

'I know you could not help it. You were doing what was best.'

'Then what?'

'Liann has Dariun. You have Chloe.'

'I am too old for Chloe.'

'But you love her very deeply?'

'Oh yes,' he sighed.

'Then you understand what I am feeling.'

'Rhislin? Then you must go to her.'

'She ignores me,' Iroise sobbed.

'Rhislin is leader: duty weaves a cloak to the emotions. Be braver – ask to meet with her. Be guided by your heart.'

Iroise emerged from the broken woodland on to the crown of the hill behind the homestead. There was no breeze; the air was balmy; all the branches of the trees and every blade of grass were still and silent. Inside, she was in turmoil. She picked her way across the rocky summit in the direction of the setting sun. But the hilltop was deserted.

Just beyond the highest point the ground fell away precipitately. Balanced on the edge was a solitary tree – little more than a single stem, its roots clinging to the dry naked rock, its wispy branches frail and graceful. It bore no leaves, only tiny, pure white starlike flowers bursting from the bare wood. Iroise approached it. Even before she reached the edge, she was enveloped in its beautiful perfume – more luscious and intoxicating than any she had known. All the sadness she was feeling turned to sweet exhilaration. The warm surge of emotion was giddying.

In the far distance, way out beyond the trees, she could see a vast expanse of water stretching to the horizon. She closed her eyes and raised her arms and breathed the heady flower perfume, and the airy spaciousness surrounding her made her feel like a zephyrine spirit. Only her toes kept her chained to the Earth. Her heart surged again and the chain was broken.

For a timeless beautiful moment, she floated. She heard a distant cry then felt the cool rush of breeze against her face. Then a velvet wall of soundless blackness struck her.

'My God!' It was Kin-Cague's voice, but Rhislin's face, ashen against the darkening sky. This vision rotated slowly above Iroise. Still glimmering high above were the pure white flower-clad branches of the little tree. 'My God –' again, Kin-Cague's voice, but faltering with emotion '– she went over the edge and she lives!'

Rhislin could not speak. There were lines of wetness down her cheeks. Iroise tried to reach to kiss them but she could not move her arm. Her leg lay twisted beneath her on a bed of broken bushes. Yet the sweet exhilaration was still with her. When those lines of precious wetness descended to caress her trembling lips, her heart soared and the beautiful faintness almost overwhelmed her.

'All that way, you followed me,' Rhislin whispered, tenderly. 'You had two good men. I can fend for myself. What need was there to put yourself in jeopardy for me?'

'Because you were my master – my one and true,' Iroise murmured.

Rhislin could not gainsay it: her tears spoke a truth more telling than words. She tried to bundle Iroise into her arms.

'Don't move her,' Kin-Cague said. He tested each limb very gently then pronounced, 'A broken arm and perhaps the wrist . . . Lacerations . . . Severe sprains to the knee and ankle . . . Yet a miracle, I'd say. But we need to get help to manage her round the slope.'

'I'm not leaving her.'

Rhislin remained true to her word. Chloe delivered not one but two fine and beautiful babies – a girl and a boy, both with jet-black hair and eyes of a knowingness evocative of those portraits at the haunted winery. Kin-Cague was moved to tears. And the bond between Liann and Dariun survived his convalescence and bloomed: a new clearing was begun in the woods. Rhislin relinquished command of the women to Asha. And when Iroise was mended, their journey was begun, westwards towards that great expanse of sea.

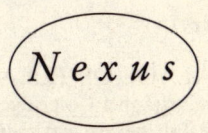

NEXUS NEW BOOKS

To be published in March

STRAPPING SUZETTE
Yolanda Celbridge

The fetid heat of French Guyana affords manifold possibilities for the perverted. Suze, a famous English model thinking to get away from it all, finds herself prey to the locals and their arcane, mysterious SM rituals. But the gifted employees of the French space programme have sexual foibles eclipsed in bizarreness only by their own intellects, and make the locals look like rank amateurs in the ways of corporal punishment and kinky sex. Against the forbidding background of the old penal institution that is Devil's Island, Suze realises that if she wanted to find freedom, this is the last place she should have come . . .

£6.99   ISBN 0 352 33783 4

COMPANY OF SLAVES
Christina Shelly

Michael is twenty-one, and a recent graduate looking for a career. Winsome, slightly feminine and sexually unsure, he's recruited by Lovelace Fashion and Design, purveyors of classy women's fashion and lingerie. Armed with a letter of introduction from his stentorian aunt and friend of Emily Lovelace, the imperious MD, he is appointed in no time. Michael does not at first realise the compromises he must make for the sake of his career, however, nor quite how much he will learn to enjoy them. Feminised, sissified and constantly aroused by the application of strict discipline, Michael completes his transformation into the perfect embodiment of LFD's ideals.

£6.99   ISBN 0 352 33784 2

TAKING PAINS TO PLEASE
Arabella Knight

It can be a punishing experience for willing young women striving to please and obey exacting employers. On the job, they quickly come to learn that giving complete satisfaction demands their strict devotion to duty. Maid, nanny or nurse – each must submit to the discipline of the daily grind. In their capable hands, the urgent needs and dark desires of their paymasters are always fulfilled: for these working girls find pleasure in taking pains to please.

£6.99   ISBN 0 352 33785 0

To be published in April

THE PALACE OF PLEASURES
Christobel Coleridge

The city-state of Estra is a thriving port and trading centre, ruled over by a Sultan who finds relief from the pressures of power amidst a selected bevy of intimate Companions. Carria, a mysterious and striking young woman arrives one night aboard a trading ship and rapidly finds herself offered the opportunity of joining the Companions. However, before she can she has to pass the schooling and selection, run by the Sultan's mistress Jnie. The training is, of course, very rigorous, and discipline is maintained with a firm hand. There are many different uniforms and articles to wear, and there are many strange and elaborate punishments for failure, including both humiliation and pain. Carria, however, has her own agenda. When it comes to fruition, nothing in Estra will be quite the same again.

£6.99   ISBN 0 352 33801 6

PEACH
Penny Birch

Penny Birch is currently the filthiest little minx on the Nexus list, with 15 titles already published by Nexus. All are equally full of messy, kinky fun and, frankly, no other erotic writer has ever captured the internal thrills afforded by the perverse shamings and humiliations her characters undergo! In *Peach*, Penny's friend Natasha comes unstuck – stickily. The peach in question is of course Natasha's bottom, as ripe as ever for a spanking, and everyone wants a piece. The pert but mischievous Natasha is bound to get her just desserts.

£6.99   ISBN 0 352 33790 7

MISS RATTAN'S LESSON
Yolanda Celbridge

Thomas Peake joins an Oxford set of female devotees of discipline: dominant Edwina Cheshunt; voluptuous mulatto dancer Lucinda Lalage; and Miss Mann, whose disciplinary academy painfully recreates a Lady's schooldays. Thomas's London delights with his group of enthusiastic submissives are interrupted by a summons to claim his Caribbean inheritance. Ransomed after enslavement by the fierce Queen Orchid, he makes his plantation a ladies' holiday resort with a difference – always governed by Miss Rattan's rules.

£6.99   ISBN 0 352 33791 5

If you would like more information about Nexus titles, please visit our website at www.nexus-books.co.uk, or send a stamped addressed envelope to:
  Nexus, Thames Wharf Studios,
  Rainville Road, London W6 9HA

NEXUS BACKLIST

This information is correct at time of printing. For up-to-date information, please visit our website at www.nexus-books.co.uk

All books are priced at £5.99 unless another price is given.

Nexus books with a contemporary setting

ACCIDENTS WILL HAPPEN	Lucy Golden ISBN 0 352 33596 3	☐
ANGEL	Lindsay Gordon ISBN 0 352 33590 4	☐
BARE BEHIND £6.99	Penny Birch ISBN 0 352 33721 4	☐
BEAST	Wendy Swanscombe ISBN 0 352 33649 8	☐
THE BLACK FLAME	Lisette Ashton ISBN 0 352 33668 4	☐
BROUGHT TO HEEL	Arabella Knight ISBN 0 352 33508 4	☐
CAGED!	Yolanda Celbridge ISBN 0 352 33650 1	☐
CANDY IN CAPTIVITY	Arabella Knight ISBN 0 352 33495 9	☐
CAPTIVES OF THE PRIVATE HOUSE	Esme Ombreux ISBN 0 352 33619 6	☐
CHERI CHASTISED £6.99	Yolanda Celbridge ISBN 0 352 33707 9	☐
DANCE OF SUBMISSION	Lisette Ashton ISBN 0 352 33450 9	☐
DIRTY LAUNDRY £6.99	Penny Birch ISBN 0 352 33680 3	☐
DISCIPLINED SKIN	Wendy Swanscombe ISBN 0 352 33541 6	☐

THE TORTURE CHAMBER	Lisette Ashton	☐
	ISBN 0 352 33530 0	
UNIFORM DOLL	Penny Birch	☐
£6.99	ISBN 0 352 33698 6	
WHIP HAND	G. C. Scott	☐
£6.99	ISBN 0 352 33694 3	
THE YOUNG WIFE	Stephanie Calvin	☐
	ISBN 0 352 33502 5	

Nexus books with Ancient and Fantasy settings

CAPTIVE	Aishling Morgan	☐
	ISBN 0 352 33585 8	
DEEP BLUE	Aishling Morgan	☐
	ISBN 0 352 33600 5	
DUNGEONS OF LIDIR	Aran Ashe	☐
	ISBN 0 352 33506 8	
INNOCENT	Aishling Morgan	☐
£6.99	ISBN 0 352 33699 4	
MAIDEN	Aishling Morgan	☐
	ISBN 0 352 33466 5	
NYMPHS OF DIONYSUS	Susan Tinoff	☐
£4.99	ISBN 0 352 33150 X	
PLEASURE TOY	Aishling Morgan	☐
	ISBN 0 352 33634 X	
SLAVE MINES OF TORMUNIL	Aran Ashe	☐
£6.99	ISBN 0 352 33695 1	
THE SLAVE OF LIDIR	Aran Ashe	☐
	ISBN 0 352 33504 1	
TIGER, TIGER	Aishling Morgan	☐
	ISBN 0 352 33455 X	

Period

CONFESSION OF AN ENGLISH SLAVE	Yolanda Celbridge	☐
	ISBN 0 352 33433 9	
THE MASTER OF CASTLELEIGH	Jacqueline Bellevois	☐
	ISBN 0 352 32644 7	
PURITY	Aishling Morgan	☐
	ISBN 0 352 33510 6	
VELVET SKIN	Aishling Morgan	☐
	ISBN 0 352 33660 9	

Samplers and collections

NEW EROTICA 5	Various ISBN 0 352 33540 8	☐
EROTICON 1	Various ISBN 0 352 33593 9	☐
EROTICON 2	Various ISBN 0 352 33594 7	☐
EROTICON 3	Various ISBN 0 352 33597 1	☐
EROTICON 4	Various ISBN 0 352 33602 1	☐
THE NEXUS LETTERS	Various ISBN 0 352 33621 8	☐
SATURNALIA £7.99	ed. Paul Scott ISBN 0 352 33717 6	☐
MY SECRET GARDEN SHED £7.99	ed. Paul Scott ISBN 0 352 33725 7	☐

Nexus Classics
A new imprint dedicated to putting the finest works of erotic fiction back in print.

AMANDA IN THE PRIVATE HOUSE £6.99	Esme Ombreux ISBN 0 352 33705 2	☐
BAD PENNY	Penny Birch ISBN 0 352 33661 7	☐
BRAT £6.99	Penny Birch ISBN 0 352 33674 9	☐
DARK DELIGHTS £6.99	Maria del Rey ISBN 0 352 33667 6	☐
DARK DESIRES	Maria del Rey ISBN 0 352 33648 X	☐
DISPLAYS OF INNOCENTS £6.99	Lucy Golden ISBN 0 352 33679 X	☐
DISCIPLINE OF THE PRIVATE HOUSE £6.99	Esme Ombreux ISBN 0 352 33459 2	☐
EDEN UNVEILED	Maria del Rey ISBN 0 352 33542 4	☐

------ ✂ --------------------------

Please send me the books I have ticked above.

Name   ....

Address ....

....

....

.... Post code....................

Send to: Cash Sales, Nexus Books, Thames Wharf Studios, Rainville Road, London W6 9HA

US customers: for prices and details of how to order books for delivery by mail, call 1-800-343-4499.

Please enclose a cheque or postal order, made payable to **Nexus Books Ltd**, to the value of the books you have ordered plus postage and packing costs as follows:

UK and BFPO – £1.00 for the first book, 50p for each subsequent book.

Overseas (including Republic of Ireland) – £2.00 for the first book, £1.00 for each subsequent book.

If you would prefer to pay by VISA, ACCESS/MASTERCARD, AMEX, DINERS CLUB or SWITCH, please write your card number and expiry date here:

....

Please allow up to 28 days for delivery.

Signature ....

Our privacy policy.

We will not disclose information you supply us to any other parties. We will not disclose any information which identifies you personally to any person without your express consent.

From time to time we may send out information about Nexus books and special offers. Please tick here if you do *not* wish to receive Nexus information.   ☐

------ ✂ --------------------------